B. TAYLOR LEWIS

A Vessel of Mercy

First edition

Editing by Julie Frederick
Cover art by Lynn Andreozzi

This book was professionally typeset on Reedsy.
Find out more at reedsy.com

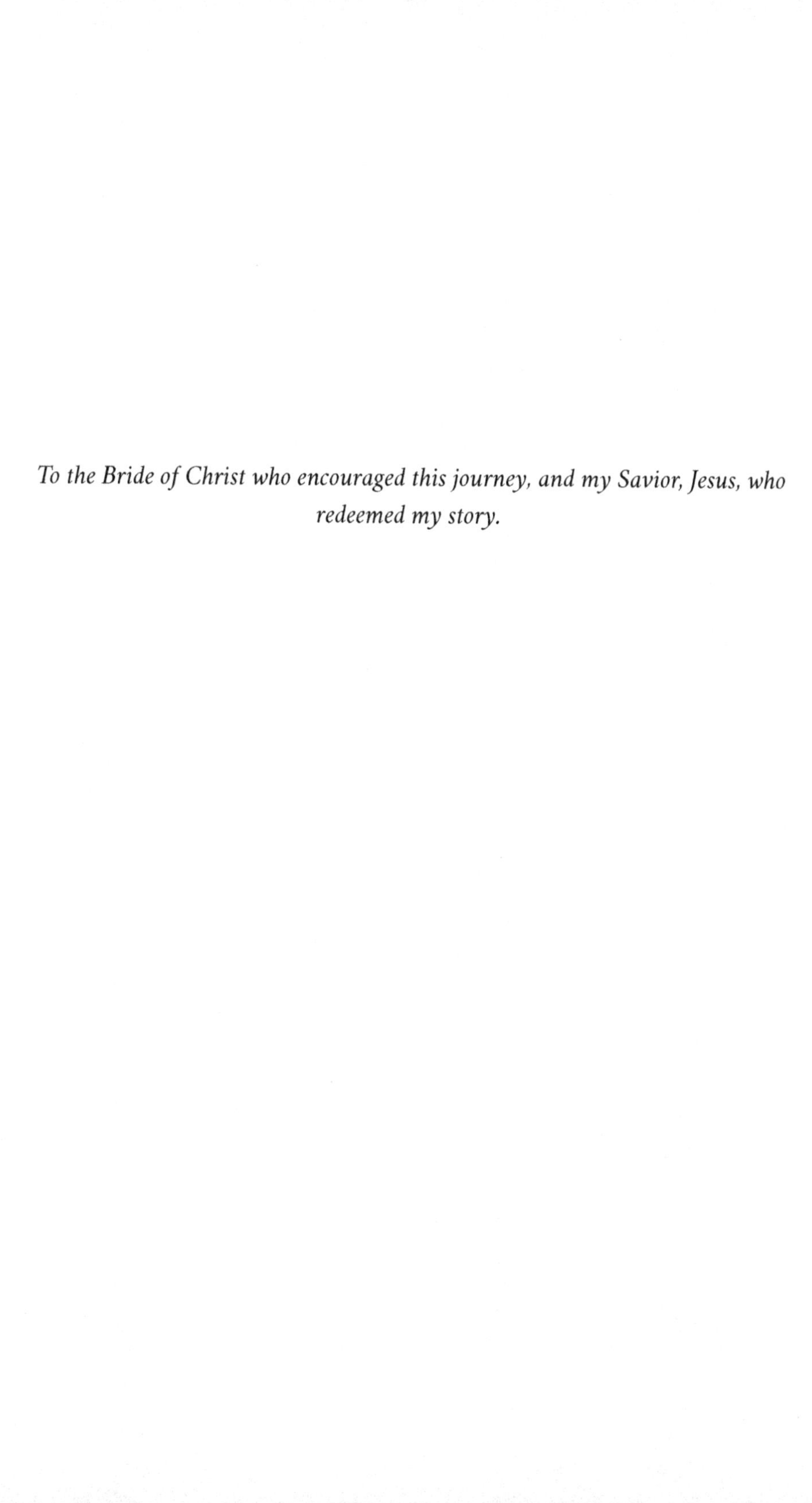

To the Bride of Christ who encouraged this journey, and my Savior, Jesus, who redeemed my story.

Preface

Charlotte Bronte, author of my favorite work of fiction, *Jane Eyre,* often addresses her audience as 'Dear reader,' and that is what you are. You are dear. I wrote this with you in mind; not to just entertain, but to challenge you to consider the depths of God's grace, just as I have.

When I started this writing adventure, I began with a question, albeit, a difficult one. "How far does your forgiveness extend? And if a person can really be forgiven by God and man, can they ever forgive themselves?"

For my first novel, I suppose I took on a difficult theme. But, one of our main characters, Abby, seemed to take me by the hand and sing, "Come with me, let me show you a redemption story." For seven years I journeyed with her and Charles Henderson.

Hers is a difficult story to tell, just as many women's are. During this process, I did not know that the #Metoo movement would take flight. I did not know that sexual assault and crimes against women would stand center stage in our culture.

With those things in mind, I want to caution you that this work of fiction does deal with sexual assault, but I have tried to steer away from anything graphic. Trust me, if I take you on a journey through darkness, we will end up in the light. **The point of this work of fiction is not to prescribe what should happen in any situation, but rather to speak to God's power in it. God is a God of justice and mercy. In that truth, there is this beautiful tension that must be explored and reckoned with.** How do we balance those two things? While this story is surely imperfect, God himself has demonstrated that balance PERFECTLY through Jesus in the greatest story ever told from Genesis to Revelation, the Gospel. There, His sovereign hand reveals His character and His relentless pursuit of His children.

My hope for you, dear reader, is that you would hear God's heart for man through this work of fiction. Forgiveness and healing are REAL through the Gospel though we are not excluded from the pain of the process, a process that will ultimately be finished on the other side of Heaven. My prayer is that you would see that no matter what the offense, the Lord has the power to redeem.

For more information about how to find healing as a victim of sexual assault, there is a helpful book, *Rid of My Disgrace: Hope and Healing for Victims of Sexual Assault by Justin S. Holcomb and Lindsey A. Holcomb.*

To receive the FREE prequel novella, Her Mother's Daughter, jump on my website!

https://www.btaylorlewis.com/

I

Part One

"Trust the past to God's mercy, the present to God's love and the future to God's providence."
—Saint Augustine

Chapter 1

1838, New York

The *Shenandoah*'s hull skipped across the waves, pulsing up and down. Abby leaned forward over the railing, her face misted with sea spray, her eyes fixed on the horizon. A flutter of jubilee rose in her chest as the ship steamed ahead, so that she thought nothing could taint her happiness.

She put a steadying hand on her bonnet that threatened to join the gulls squawking overhead and send Miss Robins, her graying maid, into an uproar. For once, just this once, Abby allowed herself the liberty to smile. And smile she did, for tucked safely inside her cloak was a letter addressed specifically to her. It was the reason she stood, beaming, ready to embrace a new country. Her fingers found their way back into her pocket tracing the edges of the broken wax seal. The dimples in her cheeks deepened. *Finally I will be able to commit him to memory*, she thought.

She often tried imagining his face, but it was a slippery thing, the colors never fitting, nor the shape of his eyes nor the bridge of his nose. All her memory managed to conjure of him was the outline of his silhouette, the back of his head, and his signature silk hat.

His pen, however, Abby knew by heart. She alone carried this great family name scrawled on the front of the letter. Her fingers held the privilege of breaking the seal, and her eyes the honor of divulging whatever information he wrote of to Miss Robins. This annual letter had inspired her to learn her letters and their sounds, her favorite part being its closing:

Your Father,

Sir Rathburn Wyndham

After seven years of waiting, this year's post had brought with it a promise for the future. He requested she pack her things, leave London behind, and join him in America. She gleamed, staring out at the capping waves, her heart galloping with each dip as the vessel bobbed over the sea. Then, her smile dropped, and she stared into the churning waters below. She felt Miss Robins' eyes studying her, for her maid could read between the lines of Abby's countenance just as easily as she uttered the Lord's prayer.

"What's got you in a stew?" asked Miss Robins.

Abby shrugged, wanting to disregard the rising alarm in her chest.

Miss Robins would not be deterred. "Out with it, dear. What's amiss?"

"What if he does not recognize me?" asked Abby, fighting the tremble of her chin. Miss Robins leaned over, cupping Abby's face. She repositioned Abby's bonnet so that it showed her dark ringlets.

"There'll be no mistaking you, my dear. You're the perfect picture of your mother," said Miss Robins as the wrinkles at the corners of her eyes gave way to a smile.

Abby assumed this was a good thing, for she had only the fondest memories of her mother, whose face shone like eternal sunshine in the back of her mind. Abby feared losing her memory, but one look in the mirror and her mother's face flickered back like a firefly on a summer's night.

The vessel pressed towards the shoreline, littered with pluming chimneys and bloated sails rising and falling with the swells of the sea. Throngs of people were gathered at the docks to greet the passengers arriving at port. Hats danced through the air in sweeping waves, joining whistles and shouts of laughter, all in the expectation of joy-filled reunions.

Miss Robins caught Abby with a squeeze around her shoulders. "My dear, there he is."

Abby took in a sharp breath, bouncing on her toes. "Where?"

"There, towards the back of the dock."

CHAPTER 1

Abby squinted against the glare of the sun. Hiding in the shadows of a docked ship stood a tall man, his vest buttons in the straightest of lines, his pocket boasting a golden timepiece. The silk hat shadowed the top half of his face, revealing only the bottom of his chin. Miss Robins held her hand to her heart, patting it in a flurry. Then she lifted her bonnet, waving it to and fro.

"Are you certain that is Father?" asked Abby.

Miss Robins' eyes narrowed. "I'd say so, my dear. I've worked for his house my whole life."

As the *Shenandoah* glided closer, the planes of his face became more visible. From the curve of his cheeks to the shrewd purse of his lips, he was as foreign as the shoreline. His frame stood tall, the unmistakable air of propriety creating a pocket of distance between him and the crowd.

Miss Robins' waving ceased. "He's much changed," she said.

Abby bit her lip, still studying this man who was her father, willing that elusive face to become familiar. He nodded at Miss Robins, and then his gray eyes fell on Abby. She held her breath as the slap of the waves clapped the side of the boat in rhythm with her heart. The ground beneath her feet swayed, and she gripped tighter on the railing. Then, his brow lifted, revealing a glint of recognition. Abby smiled, her chest swelling as she lifted her hand. "Father!" she cried out, her rosy cheeks still carrying the roundness of childhood, her curls bouncing around her shoulders as her eyes lit up expectantly. But, he stood like a tombstone, his arms stiff beside him, his feet planted solidly on the ground.

The ship turned about-face nearing the dock, and Abby stilled, letting her arm drop to her side. Her head tilted as worry muddled her brow. The lines of his face twisted into a grimace. He looked away, then back at her again. Panic rising, she offered another smile, but her warmth never seemed to reach him. Color drained from his cheeks, giving them an ashen hue.

Abby swallowed. "Is he ill?"

Miss Robins looked down at Abby, chewing her lip. "I imagine he is surprised to see you so grown up. That's all, my dear," she said, her voice wavering.

Abby nodded. "I suppose I should wave again, to let him know I am glad to be here." Miss Robins shook her head. "That's enough waving for today."

Abby's bottom lip poked out, and the threat of tears pricked her eyes.

"Oh, I suppose one more won't hurt," said Miss Robins hopefully.

Abby lit up and spun back around. Standing tall, she lifted her right hand and waved—not as a child would but as a noble lady—searching her father's eyes for that gleam of approval. He stood unmoving, expressionless until dread lodged itself into Abby's stomach like a fist. Then he turned his back, walking towards the carriage in the distance. *No!* Abby thought. *It is just like before...* A memory resurfaced from that terrible day, seven years ago, when her head had reached no higher than her father's waist. The last time she had seen him.

* * *

Servants had lined the front of the estate, ready for their formal farewell. Her father stood ready to leave, towering over her. She kept her eyes on his freshly polished boots, their scent like a robust cologne. The tips of her fingers felt numb against the late autumn chill. She wished for her mother's warm hand to squeeze. At the thought of her mother, a hollowness opened up inside her chest, exposing the gaping hole where loss lived.

"I expect a good report while I am away," he said with a light pat on her head.

He stepped backwards, and she caught his hand, trapping it between her fingers. He sighed.

"You must not cause a scene. It is not the Wyndham way."

Then, he pried her fingers from his. His boots crushed the gravel with his heels as he walked away.

"Don't leave!" she cried out, the ache in her chest expanding.

"Miss Robins, take her inside," he ordered.

Miss Robins' hands pressed on Abby's shoulders, willing her to remain composed. She held cries captive in her throat. *Wyndham ladies do not cry aloud,* she chastised herself over and over. She let the tears fall quietly as her father stepped into the carriage and pulled away. The horses trotted around the drive, their hooves building rhythm past the lily pad pond. Then they charged ahead, the coachman whipping their backs as they galloped toward the gates at Devonsfield.

Abby broke free of Robins' hands, chasing after the carriage, but her father did not look back. Just before the gates opened, the horses reared to a halt beside the East Garden. The door of the carriage swung forward, its window catching the glare of the sun.

Abby nearly cried out with joy, wiping her tears on her sleeve as she ran to catch up. Sir Rathburn's bare head leaned out.

"Papa," she cried. But he was silent.

His gaze remained fixed on the garden where the last of her mother's roses clung to their stems, losing their petals with each fresh breath of wind. There her mother's body lay blanketed by earth's rich soil next to the tiny mound of dirt, so insignificant it would scarcely have been visible without its small headstone.

Abby's heart rose to her throat. Father would not leave. Not without her.

"Papa!" cried Abby again, gaining speed on the gravel drive. Her eyes watched anxiously, willing the door to open further and for her father to step out. *Wyndham ladies do not run*. The thought flitted through her mind, then she lifted her skirts anyway. Beneath her slippers, the balls of her feet screamed against sharp stones. She careened forward, then her toe caught the ground. With a thud, she found her palms stinging, her face covered in a cloud of dust.

The coachman shouted at his steeds, the wheels groaned, and the carriage lurched forward.

* * *

Now, as she prepared to disembark the *Shenandoah*, she again saw not her father's face but his back. Abby shook her head, dizzied by the memory. She suddenly felt her childhood trailing behind her like the wake of the vessel she stood on.

The steamer's whistle bellowed through the air, announcing her arrival, and the crowd below clapped and cheered. Abby's knees felt weak, and a haze clouded her vision before she realized she had been holding her breath. She dropped her hand. The back of her glove caught the straying tears, but Miss Robins reached after her with a gentle squeeze as they turned from the railing. Abby kept her eyes on the worn planks of the deck, trying to hide her face.

"Wear them, my dear," said Miss Robins gently.

Abby's lashes fluttered, fighting their threat. "Wyndham ladies do not cry in public," she said.

"They ought when the occasion fits."

"A lot of good it will do."

Miss Robins bent down, picking up Abby's parcel, and ushered her ahead.

"The shame is not yours. Holding back your tears will only turn you sour."

Abby looked up, her chin quivering, "I was so foolish to think—"

Robins squeezed her shoulders, insistent. "No. Not foolish. Hope's not foolish."

Abby took in another ragged breath, begging the emotion to subside so no more tears would follow.

"I did not recognize him," she said.

Miss Robins nodded. "I don't think your memories would do much good anyhow—it's been so long. But if there's one thing I do remember, Sir Rathburn Wyndham's not a man to be kept wait'n."

Abby nodded and they made their way to the boat ramp.

In the eyes of any passerby, what followed would be seen as nothing less than a joyous reunion between father and daughter, made all the more alluring by their obvious high status. A small throng of people lingered, their curious eyes falling on the budding young noble girl as she stepped forward into her statuesque father's long shadow.

Abby was glad Robins had taken such care that morning dressing her and taming her hair, for she felt her father's probing eyes assessing every stitch and curl. She strained, keeping her back straight just as she had been taught. She dipped into a low curtsy and heard gentle applause from the crowd surrounding them. Her eyes searched for her father's, but he would not return her stare. Still, he gave a dutiful bow. Abby offered her hand, looking into the cool planes of his face where neither smile nor warmth met her. The tendons in her neck constricted as she swallowed back her doubt. Had she done something wrong? Had she overstepped some unknown rule of propriety to deserve this coolness?

When Sir Rathburn climbed into the carriage and the coachman closed the door, it was as though another stranger had crawled in beside all three souls, and his name was Silence. Abby thought her father must enjoy his company, for he did not appear bothered by it. This loathsome friend bothered Abby a great deal, for she had thoughts and questions bubbling at the tip of her tongue but had not the courage to ask them. Her father's chin pointed out the window, signaling his disinterest. Even uttering a word felt like breaking a rule, so that Abby bit her tongue to quell her rising panic.

Miss Robins, dear Miss Robins, with age that allowed for social cues to go unnoticed, filled the space with her quick tongue. Her jaw wagged on, inquiring of the health of her employer. Then, pressing further about his feelings towards this new country. His nods and "yes" or "no" replies seemed to go entirely unnoticed as she babbled, offering not a few details about the life they had left behind.

"Miss Abby has proved to be quite the musician. I do hope you have a piano tuned and ready for her dainty fingers," she said, beaming. Sir Rathburn nodded mechanically. Abby's fingers tingled at the thought of the cool keys beneath her fingers, and she wished she had practiced more often.

"And her governess remarked just before we left about how she had ne'er taught so fine a pupil."

Sir Rathburn's eyes moved from the window to Abby. His whole body seemed to tense as though he were bracing himself before a violent gale. She smiled, trying to hide a blush. When Miss Robins had exhausted her long list of praises, Sir Rathburn lifted his brow, his eyes cool, calculated, unfeeling.

Finally, he spoke. "No doubt her skills will need improvement to ensure she is useful when her time comes."

Miss Robins leaned forward. "When might that time be, Sir Rathburn?"

"When else is a girl of any use?" he asked, lifting his chin.

Miss Robins wrung her fingers in her lap, the apple of her cheeks twitching against her submissive smile. Abby's eyes grew wide looking at Miss Robins, who shrugged.

"I am at a loss," said Miss Robins.

Sir Rathburn's gaze returned to the window. "When she is of age and can be married off at some benefit."

Abby's lips parted, her chest burning. She took a deep breath and looked away from her father, locking her eyes on the red padding of the carriage.

"Is that all Mother was good for?" she blurted, then, realizing her impropriety, put a muffling hand over her mouth.

Sir Rathburn's icy glare bore through her in a moment, so swift she felt as though it were clamping around her throat.

"I see you have neglected to teach her a lady's sole duty"—his gaze turned back to the window with a dramatic pause—"to hold her tongue."

Miss Robins shook her head ever so slightly at Abby. Heat flushed Abby's cheeks and she lowered her face. The carriage jolted along down the path, yawning at each turn. Birds swooped past, squawking, as they teemed in circles like swirls of moving clouds. Abby's eyes followed them as they swarmed up toward the pitches of the rooftops, and suddenly she wished she could be back in England listening to the birds chirping from outside her window.

Reaching into her pocket, she again traced the wax seal of her father's letter. The jagged ridges of the seal were still fixed to the envelope though split in half from when she had first torn it open, so eager to read its contents. The parchment had lost its crispness, feeling less like paper and more like cloth due to her constant handling of it. She sucked in another breath. Her nails slid across the letter until her hand clenched it. Muscles in her fingers tensed, threatening to crumple the helpless folds as she fought bitter tears. But she wouldn't, she decided, releasing her grip of the letter. For better or worse, she had arrived in America, her father the only family she had. She snuck a sideways glance at Sir Rathburn, who leaned against the side of the carriage, his thin lips pursed sternly, and composed herself.

So would be the pattern of Abigail Juliet Wyndham's existence in her new life in America. But despite her father's coolness, an unassailable wind triumphed in Abby's heart, bringing her feet to foreign shores. Though abandoned by her earthly family, she knew a deeper love; it was this that would give her the strength to triumph despite her circumstances. As she stared out the carriage window at this strange new world, she felt her heart quicken with an intuitive knowledge of what lay ahead. Scandal already thrummed inside her—and scandal, she knew, was what Sir Rathburn most despised.

Chapter 2

1842, New York

For Charles Henderson, the Astor Ball held one purpose—to make his existence known to the nobleman from England, Sir Rathburn Wyndham. Rumor had it that, in addition to his vast wealth, Sir Rathburn had another attractive asset: a daughter.

The warm spring night whispered promise, for, at the ripe age of seventeen, it was the young woman's first season of society. Notable families like the Astors, Fitzgeralds, and Rockefellers had daughters, but they were either too young to wed or already promised. This left Sir Rathburn's daughter of pertinent interest to every bachelor from New York to the Carolinas.

Charles waited at a watchful distance on the balcony overlooking the ballroom floor where crowds of ladies batted their lashes behind flapping fans, buzzing with excited chatter. He stood taller, straightening his bow tie.

"Mr. Henderson, is that you?" came a voice from behind.

Charles turned to see the greasy smile of Dirk Allen, sending his eyes rolling. Over the top of his shoulder, he spotted Dirk's thick frame wading through the gathered guests headed right towards him, his generous gut bouncing beneath his too-snug vest while his wiry mustache twitched as he laughed. He already nursed a glass of brandy and walked with a notable swagger. Charles cringed knowing that brandy made Dirk even more uncouth. His eyes scanned around to see who might be watching.

"It *is* you," said Dirk, clapping his fleshy hand against Charles' arm.

"Who else would it be?" said Charles, unamused.

"I don't know, son. I thought I was see'n the ghost of your father. It's not been that long since his funeral," said Dirk, draping his arm around Charles' shoulders.

Charles cocked his head, making no move to reply. Dirk sucked in brandy from the rim of the glass and lowered his voice.

"Your tie's all crooked."

"This from you? I imagine you're already seeing the room sideways and it's only seven o'clock," replied Charles with a nod towards Dirk's glass.

Dirk leaned over, attempting to whisper in Charles' ear. His breath oozed a sickly sour smell mixed with a fresh whiff of brandy. Charles recoiled, turning so that his shoulder put space between them.

"How did things go with Lucille at the pub?" asked Dirk with a grin, revealing a front tooth protruding at an odd angle. Charles recalled the hazy pub brawl of a few nights before that had resulted in his fist landing squarely in Dirk's jaw. Based on Dirk's overfamiliarity with him now, Charles could only surmise he had been too drunk to remember it.

"Not now. Not here," Charles hissed.

Dirk let out a wheezy chuckle and attempted to lower his voice. "You can afford the pretty ones now," he said. The patter of fans thrummed behind them. Charles felt as though the whole room was privy to their conversation. He turned to see a group of gray-haired women, their ears drooping in their jewels, watching him with interest.

Charles reached for Dirk's arm, squeezing it so hard as to turn him sober.

"Another word about me here, and you'll regret it," said Charles, looking over the balcony railing with a cool, collected smile.

"Ah, I see. You're here wanting to make the likes of the finer ladies. Who's got your eye tonight?"

"You see, Dirk," Charles said, changing tack, "the thing I like best about you is that you need me. I have vessels, you have goods waiting to be shipped. I am ever so happy to service this need. I do think it works rather well, don't you?"

Dirk's forehead wrinkled. "Sure does."

"It would be a pity to ruin this relationship while your drunken mouth disgraces us both," said Charles, leaning over the railing.

Dirk laughed again, oblivious to Charles' threat.

Down below, women graced the floor like delicate budding flowers. A particular set of eyes beckoned Charles' attention behind a fluttering fan. Eliza Pennington's golden spun hair spiraled in two ringlets beside her ears, bouncing as she feigned a blush. Tonight she donned a costly pink lace-trimmed gown that matched the tinge of her lips. Charles nodded, and she smiled and then shot a narrow glance at Dirk, still crowding his space.

Just then a hum of hushes silenced the room. Fans stilled, all eyes fixed on the front entryway. Charles inched further away from Dirk.

The caller's breast swelled. "Sir Rathburn Wyndham of London escorting his daughter, Miss Abigail Juliet Wyndham."

Sir Rathburn stood tall, his gray hair meticulously combed to one side. His appearance was nothing new to Charles, who had seen the Englishman from a distance over the last few years since he was a youth, but it was his daughter that held the stares of the entire room.

Her gloved hand hardly brushed Sir Rathburn's arm as he escorted her down the stairs to the ballroom floor. Her dark hair was gathered in a mass of ringlets piled up on the crown of her head, curls sweeping over her shoulders. Her gown, a mirage of a blue starless night sky, hugged her slender figure. Whispers drifted through the air drawing a deep blush from her cheeks. Charles' lips parted, enraptured by her emerald eyes, which flitted nervously across the crowd, her bosom showing her quickening breath. He wondered if she would fumble this dawning of her first season with tears or clumsy footing, but she remained collected.

Charles watched as the old women leaned in to peer at the young maiden between the shoulders of crowding men, whispering their devilish praises and jealousies to their flocks as they preened their dresses, suddenly nostalgic for their prime. A few beats later, the room resumed its baseline.

With seeming disinterest, Sir Rathburn dipped down to mutter into Abby's ear. She lifted her head higher and stiffened; her eyes stilled and then she nodded. Sir Rathburn handed her off to the arm of the first man to his left. The young man's glee was nearly palpable, his face the color of a ripened tomato. She stared after her father, forlorn in the hands of a stranger, while he made his way to the corners of the room where his own collection of acquaintances waited.

What a fool, thought Charles.

Dirk's thick elbow belted his ribs, "Ah, so you have an appetite for the English fare, eh?" he said with another chuckle. Charles simmered, thinking that if Dirk were closer to the edge of the balcony he might have sent him over the railing to his certain death. Truth be told, English or not, Miss Wyndham's beauty was compelling, despite Charles' preference for blonde hair. Her elegance came as a pleasant surprise, for he had already determined to pursue her.

Dirk slapped his back. "You aim too high. That's a genteel family. They've got their own connections and high tea—and manners," he said, reeling.

Charles brushed his sleeve off with the back of his hand and readjusted his jacket, intent on deserting the crass creature who seemed bent to jeopardize all of his plans. A smile hid in the corner of his mouth.

"Oh Dirk, look. Isn't that your wife?" he said, nodding in the direction of the far end of the room.

Dirk's eyes grew wide in astonishment, "She said she was stay'n home," he gasped.

Charles nodded casually to the fictional Mrs. Allen.

"You might need to sober up; she's coming this way," said Charles between gritted teeth. He brushed past Dirk, a sly grin escaping from the corner of his mouth.

By the time Charles made it downstairs, Miss Wyndham graced the arms of another gentleman intent on winning her favor. Charles studied her, noticing her timid smile as the young man whispered into her ear. Sir Rathburn was elsewhere, however, and instinct told Charles that he was the target.

Charles spotted him under the overhang of the balcony, leaning against the wall in the shadows beneath plumes of smoke. Among him were men that Charles recognized—Chancy Fitzgerald and Clebold Rockefeller, mumbling in between slow inhales of their cigars. This was an older crowd, past their prime but with deep pockets and connections spanning generations. Charles' eyes narrowed slightly, as he considered how profitable those men's pedigrees could be for Henderson Gold Line. If he could get in with this crowd, he would have no need for men like Dirk Allen ever again. Charles positioned himself closer so that he was within earshot, pretending to watch the dancing.

Clyde Garrison, a wealthy client of Charles' late father, joined the circle of men. Charles decided to seize the opportunity. As Charles walked towards them, Mr. Garrison's eye squinted behind his monocle.

"Well well, Mr. Henderson, it is right good to see you out and about again," said Mr. Garrison as he greeted Charles with a warm smile.

"I couldn't stay away longer than necessary," said Charles. Mr. Garrison gestured to the gentlemen who nodded, mumbling hellos, but it was Sir Rathburn who spoke up first.

"I've not had the pleasure," he said. His voice brimmed with indifference, his eyes leveling Charles.

"Charles Henderson the third, son of the late Charles Henderson." Charles matched Rathburn's gaze, thinking that the nobleman looked significantly smaller than he had a few moments before.

Mr. Garrison's head bowed, his tone somber. "Your father was a very good man. I am sorry for your loss."

Sir Rathburn's eyes softened ever so slightly. "My sympathies, Mr. Henderson," he said. Charles noted Rathburn's posture, how his frame stooped forward, betraying his age. But the man's eyes shifted, alight behind the glow of the cigar, constantly calculating. "I do recall meeting him. He seemed a proper gentleman," Rathburn continued.

"That he was," replied Charles, remembering his father's dramatic account of the exchange; how he'd said that he had "entertained nobility." The thought made him smile to himself, for his father's simpleton ways rarely attracted notice. Henderson Gold Line—his father's shipping company—had a meager twenty clients whose goods had been delivered regularly for the past thirty years. Charles had tried to push his father to expand into new ventures but to no avail. Then, while poring over manifests in his office early one morning, his father died, leaving his only son to inherit his company. As tragic and untimely as his father's death was, Charles did not waste time, soon exploring less palatable means of enterprise—"changes," Charles reasoned, that would secure not only his, but also his mother's, welfare. This proved true, as, in only two months, he had doubled the company's profits.

"Your father was quite fond of a small estate in Upper Manhattan," said Sir Rathburn, lifting his gaze to meet Charles'.

Charles nodded. "He mentioned it before. What's the allure?"

Sir Rathburn paused, his gray eyes polling. "Should not a young man like you be leading a lady in the *La valse à trios temps?*"

Charles smiled, a genuine smile. He looked over Sir Rathburn's shoulder where his daughter held the palm of another gentleman. "Dancing can only carry a man so far."

A smirk slipped from the corner of Sir Rathburn's mouth. "I wonder if my mother would have taken such an excuse?" He chuckled. Then answered himself, "I would think not. The English variety have no sense of humor when it comes to dancing."

Charles humored him with his own laughter as Sir Rathburn motioned to the servant toting a tray of drinks.

"My father hoped to buy the property you mentioned. How would you describe the place?"

Sir Rathburn cleared his throat. "It was suitable, Mr. Henderson."

"Suitable?"

Sir Rathburn nodded, his chest expanding with the puff of his cigar. "Yes. For a man of his means."

Charles shook his head in reply, feeling the subtle sting. His family had no crest, no history beyond the business his father had built up through hard work and grit. True, his father had collected a small fortune over the course of his life, but he had been so tight with money that he squeaked when he walked. As such, he was considered respectable by most, but as for power and influence, he was as good as a pauper.

"If you might be so inclined, I was wondering if you might have something more to my taste," said Charles. Sir Rathburn cocked his head, as though he had missed something before.

"You are in the market to buy?"

Now I am, thought Charles, nodding. He took a deep breath, and his collar seemed to have shrunken in the course of the conversation.

"City or country?"

Didn't Sir Rathburn live at a lavish estate just out of the city?

"Country."

"Cottage or villa?"

"Neither."

Sir Rathburn's eyes gleamed behind another slow pull of his cigar. A few embers escaped, floating into the air. He waved for another servant holding an ashtray. The end of the cigar butt sizzled against the chill of the tray.

"An estate then?" he said.

"Do you have anything in mind?" asked Charles.

"Perhaps. It might be a stretch. And with your business in the city, you would have to hire a driver. And run a house of staff."

Ignoring the bile rising in his throat, Charles grinned, eyes flashing. "I'd like to see it." He could almost sense the ghost of his father staring in horror as he gambled for a shot at a woman with a name—a real name. Not to mention his dear mother, still deep in mourning. He dare not think what she would make of his aspirations.

Sir Rathburn let a smile pass over his face. "I would have thought a man to grieve." There was no mistaking his sarcasm, but Charles held to the truth of the statement.

"I'm only continuing a conversation he started," said Charles, revealing a slight smirk.

Sir Rathburn leaned forward, his eyes tilted towards Charles.

"I knew I liked you." He gave Charles a rough pat on the shoulder, then continued. "Business calls me to the road, but I will send for you in a fortnight. No need to inquire yourself; I know where to find you," he said, dismissing Charles with a nod.

Charles' chest swelled with pride. He had passed through some unspoken test of nobility and was sure that he was closer to the dowry and prestige of Miss Wyndham than any of the sheepish boys standing hand-in-hand with her on the ballroom floor.

* * *

They met early one Thursday morning when the sun hailed in the cloudless sky, giving Charles' eyes a shock. His head throbbed with the residual effects of the previous night. He could not remember much, but what he did, he sought to forget. It did him no good to recall any woman aside from the one he had yet to meet. Miss Wyndham was the ultimate prize. Purchasing this estate was merely a means to obtain her hand, to prove himself worthy of Rathburn's pedigree.

Charles arrived at the estate before Sir Rathburn, eager to get a full measure of the property in case its grandeur caught him off-guard. He did not want to be seen gawking.

The Hollows Estate towered above the country landscape, a beacon on a hillside overlooking a creek that carved itself out from the Hudson. Broad maple trees surrounded the north lawn, guarding the house against the prying eyes of passersby on the dirt road. Lush untamed shrubs dotted the roadway until they halted at the foot of a stone wall delineating the boundaries of the property. A stable stood behind the house, whispering hints of Gothic inspiration, and appeared large enough to house over a dozen horses. Charles only had two.

The house itself boasted a style that was decidedly American. It was two or three times larger than the one Charles had been accustomed to in the heart of the city. The lowest floor was the most noteworthy, its elongated front portico towering over the hillside on handsome stone columns. Charles swallowed, taking it all in. There was no doubt a large bounty on this estate, but that price could be the only way into Rathburn's graces. A risky purchase indeed. He sighed.

He reasoned he had enough cash flow to impress Rathburn with a solid buy, but that would tie up all of his money, restricting his investments. Charles' mind raced. Within a few seconds, he was exploring avenues of enterprise. He spun through the results before coming to the conclusion that he could use his connections for a few more voyages from Virginia to New Orleans and to Galveston. He had already done it once—and not without risk, particularly that of public scorn. Hauling slaves did not sit well with everyone's palate, but there was a growing demand from the South, meaning even higher profits. A few months of those routes, and he would be worry free.

"She is glorious, is she not?" came Sir Rathburn's voice from down the hill. His dark waistcoat blew behind him in the breeze as he walked towards Charles. He appeared all business with lips tight in a tell-tale frown at the corners. As he neared, Charles detected uncertainty in his face, as though bothered by something. Charles' stomach turned. Surely he was not the culprit.

Charles dismissed these thoughts, intending to call on all of his charms. "I'm not sure how this compares to the motherland, but here in America she is definitely something."

Rathburn scanned the roofline. "Indeed. I rather prefer it. It has a newness, a freshness, but with all refinement. It would be fitting."

Charles looked sideways at Rathburn. "For whom?"

Rathburn paused, his eyes working. "Whoever can pay the price, or holds his cards just right."

"So you personally own this property?"

"Indeed. I stumbled upon it when the last owner was in, shall I say, a *difficult* position."

"How difficult?" asked Charles.

"The kind of difficult that only few have the power to rescue others from."

"How honorable of you," replied Charles.

Sir Rathburn turned, but not before Charles caught the edge of his grin, then he motioned for Charles to follow, and they walked around the fence line as the sun peeked through the shade trees. When they reached the top of the hill, Sir Rathburn traced the boundaries of the estate, looking down on stretches of green vegetation and the winking trickle of the stream. He then led Charles up the steps of the back of the house through the servants' quarters. The two wandered through the halls of the estate, opening heavy doors of vacant rooms where Charles' imagination filled each space with luxurious furniture, carpets, and laughter over a popping fire. But his conscience nagged him about such musings, saying the whole of it was much too grand, as he had only been managing Henderson Gold Line for two months. This sounded too much like his father's voice; he did not heed its warnings, all sensibility lost as he watched *the* Sir Rathburn Wyndham stroll through the halls so that Charles could no longer separate want from reason.

"What are you selling her for?" he asked, noting the intricate engravings in the cabinetry.

"Perhaps you should get to know her first, at least before we reveal all of her secrets," chuckled Sir Rathburn as he headed back out into the hall. Charles tilted his head, following him. They walked to the north wing of the house where the dining room's high walls framed bare waxed floors, above which a crystal chandelier dangled. She seemed to whisper hints of future parties, hands of poker, and business deals with all of the right kinds of people. Then, Sir Rathburn led him to the staircase.

Charles paused at the bottom of the stairs, his eyes scanning upward. He placed his palm on the mahogany railing, running his hand over its smooth finish as he climbed up the crimson steps one by one, their flights unfolding before him until he had reached the heights of the third floor. Sir Rathburn stood observing from below, a queer smile gracing his face. Minutes later, when Charles made his way back to the main level, his mind was made up.

"Still interested?" said Sir Rathburn.

"Very."

His face betrayed no surprise. "I must admit, young man, my curiosity is piqued. What sort of shipping business do you have?" asked Sir Rathburn with narrowing eyes.

"The profitable kind," replied Charles.

Sir Rathburn grinned inscrutably, raising his brow. "So I see."

"We haven't discussed your price."

"Ah," said Sir Rathburn, now in visibly fair humor. "Shall we not dance around in pleasantries first? Do you have plans for tomorrow evening?"

"I can move things around," said Charles, a trill of excitement thrumming in his bones.

"Have you met my daughter?" asked Sir Rathburn, eyes flickering.

"From a distance."

The gentleman smiled. "I would be pleased if you would dine with us. We can discuss business after we have sufficiently stuffed ourselves."

"I look forward to it."

"As do I."

Charles tipped his hat to him, the Sir of England, the father of the most prized possession in all of New York. But a shadow marred his reverie as if his father's squeaky shoes were walking behind him. He pushed the thought aside. Still, one nagging unavoidable question lingered at the tip of his tongue: how much would this investment cost?

Chapter 3

Abby's lungs filled with crisp morning air as she gathered speed down the hillside along the gravel path, feeling the thud on the balls of her feet course through her body. Wild wisps of curls swirled around her face with each stride. In her hand she held a simple bouquet of wildflowers, white and yellow bursting forth their spring pride. She giggled as she neared the bottom of the hill, red flushing her cheeks and perspiration beading on her brow, for she rarely enjoyed the simple pleasure of running. For a few moments, she existed—free and uninhibited by titles, troubles, or the sinking feeling of rejection.

Two weeks had passed since the Astor Ball, and Abby had not received a card from any suitor though all had promised. She felt silly and foolish to think that a man might find her interesting or appealing. And even worse, that her heart had surged in the hope of it—a hope as fleeting as the dappled orange and black flash of a monarch butterfly unfurled, for a split second, before taking off in flight.

These realities once again weighed on her, her steps slowing on the gravel path dotted with patches of dandelions. Sweet honeysuckle tickled her fingers as she ran them through the vine. She had ventured far from home, swept away by the spring life budding on every new hillside. The blossoms reminded her of pleasant afternoons long forgotten back in England when her mother was alive. She reveled in the nostalgia, musing that it seemed as though God had ordained each season for the sake of recognizing something more. This thought alone bolstered her hope, for it was more than any man could dare offer her.

The drum of hooves roused her attention, and a panic set in. *Could Father be returning from Baltimore so soon?* She patted her head, feeling the tendrils of hair blowing about. It had long since lost its neat order. Straining to see, she found it was indeed her father's carriage careening her way. She looked around and, thinking of no other options, stepped off the path and hid herself in the thick of the sweet vines.

With any luck, perhaps Langley will not see me. Oh, Father would surely curse me for looking such a disheveled mess!

The trotting neared, the horses' breath so close she could almost feel its warmth behind her until the wheels rolled past. She gritted her teeth, waiting a moment longer until the rear of the carriage was in full view.

Relieved, she untangled herself from the vines, pulling twigs from her hair. But she had hardly taken a step when the wheels slowed and the horses whinnied. Langley stood in the driver's chair, squinting against the glare of the sun. The dust settled, and there stood Abby, flushed and rumpled, in broad sight.

"Miss Wyndham, is that you? And so far from home?" he yelled after her.

Abby's face glowed red and she offered a sheepish curtsy.

The carriage door thrust open and Sir Rathburn leaned his head out, grumbling, "What is the bloody meaning of this?"

Abby saw Langley wince and ran forward, pleading, "Forgive me, Father. Langley only spotted me on a walk."

"Inside. Now," Sir Rathburn commanded.

Abby exhaled, her pulse pounding between her ears. She stepped up into the carriage, abandoning the spring sunshine.

"Do you always go gallivanting around in the wilderness when I am away?" asked Rathburn beneath his furrowed brow. Abby swallowed, begging for peace to calm her anxious spirit. She had come to learn that her father's sternness rarely softened.

"How was Baltimore?" said Abby, as calm and cool as she could manage.

"I am no fool. You are changing the subject."

Abby's voice lowered along with her head. "I only wondered about your travels."

"Next time you see fit to wander it will be with Miss Robins by your side."

"She could scarcely keep up."

"My point exactly," said Sir Rathburn.

"I am no hound in need of a leash, Father. I meant only to get fresh air and stretch my legs."

"A daughter is of little worth if someone sees her frolicking among milkweeds like a wild goat."

Abby diverted her attention from her father's glare to the ceiling of the padded carriage and then back down again to the cushion beside her father, where sketches of an estate lay open. She felt the heat in her chest rising, and if she did not know better, she might have screamed. But his eyes still bore into her, waiting for a response.

"I do not think anyone of importance would be offended by my appearance here unless you have sought out dukes and duchesses to visit us from abroad."

"It should be enough that *I* am offended by the sight of you."

She bit the inside of her cheek, feeling the threat of stinging tears. *Mend this, or it will only get worse, Abby,* she told herself.

"If my presentation has offended you so, then I'll not 'wander' again."

Sir Rathburn's vein pulsed on the right side of his neck, his jaw clenched tight. His cold eyes held his daughter's until he was satisfied she bowed in submission. Then he took a breath and his face returned to its normal pale hue.

Langley shouted at the horses outside, willing them to pull harder. They galloped on in a frantic rhythm, sending the papers beside her father to the floor. Sir Rathburn swore.

"What is the hurry?"

"Things far beyond your comprehension, I assure you. And besides, I was so rudely interrupted, as I had to fetch my daughter from the wilderness," he said.

"Are we expecting company?" It was customary for her father to return from a trip and then entertain a few guests for dinner. Typically, her father would drink, play cards and smoke cigars well into the evening hours. Abby was never permitted to attend these occasions.

"A certain Mr. Henderson is to dine with us."

Abby sunk back into the cushion, her mind reeling. She had never met any Mr. Henderson. Yet her father had said "us," meaning she would be in attendance. Was this what Miss Robins had meant when she told Abby that things would change after the Astor Ball? Suddenly she felt keenly aware of her billowing hair, the dirt stains on the hem of her skirts, and the perspiration beading on her forehead.

"Do not look so disappointed," said Rathburn.

"I'm not meaning to be, but I haven't had one gentleman request to see me since the ball."

"There were many ladies aside from yourself in attendance. Are you so vain to think *you* would get every note?"

Abby's cheeks gave way to the shame of her rejection. "I have not received even one."

Sir Rathburn kept his gaze out of the window.

"And why would you expect to?" he said.

Taking great care to not raise her voice, Abby replied, "Every girl of seventeen expects to, especially in her first season."

"*You* should not."

Abby took in a sharp breath. Although she had grown used to her father's disparaging comments, his words still stung. Perhaps he was right. Perhaps she lacked the grace and poise that required men to come calling. Yet how could she have so misread the glint in their eyes, the warmth in their smiles, as they bowed before her, asking whether they might have the pleasure of seeing her again? Then a thought clouded her perception as she looked at her father's pale face staring blankly out the window. *Could Father have received the notes and neglected to give them to me?*

But this made little sense to her, for she knew a daughter's purpose in the Wyndham family was to be married, securing connections and status. Wasn't that the reason her father had allowed her to go to the ball?

"If I am to receive no callers here in the states, may I expect some when Robins and I go for the London season?" she asked rather boldly.

"You are not to go to London," said Rathburn, denying her even the decency of looking at her.

"I beg your pardon?"

It was Sir Rathburn's turn to change the subject. As he began talking, his face contorted into a smile. "The gentleman we are receiving this evening is of pertinent interest to me. His enterprises are new and profitable."

Abby's jaw dropped. *New and profitable?* she thought, her anger simmering. She fought to regain the ladylike composure that had been drilled into her since birth. "But you promised to send me to London with Miss Robins. She is expecting to visit what is left of her family. Father, please allow us to go," she said.

He glanced at her, then avoided her eyes.

"And you will be sourly disappointed to not be flaunted in London, I know. But it is a mere triviality. I had planned to send you away, but now it suits me more to keep you here. I do not see why you think you are too good for the American fare. Lord knows, most Englishmen are up to their waistcoats in debt. Besides, *you* would be scoffed at in any real society. I would not chance your queer manners tainting my name by frolicking abroad like you do here, now would I?"

Her hands balled into fists hidden in the folds of her skirts.

"I only want to visit home," she said.

"In that case, we are nearly there," he said, nodding towards the road ahead.

"I meant England."

"England has not been your residence for the last four years. You are as much American as our Irish neighbors down the lane."

"Father, you don't even have to come. Just allow me to go with Robins."

"You are staying here. And so is your maid, for without her you would look like steerage."

"What must keep me here?" she exclaimed.

Sir Rathburn's lip twitched, a tell-tale sign Abby had come to understand as a warning.

"Like I mentioned before, we are receiving a guest tonight," he said through gritted teeth.

Abby sat up straighter, taking in shallow breaths, her mind spinning. Why would this guest be so important when she had only heard of him three minutes before?

"So this Mr. Henderson—some profitable business-minded monkey monger, seeking to gain his own advantage from your wealth just as much as you seek to gain his—is coming to dinner, and *that* is why I am unable to go?"

"So, quick-witted, aren't you? Now, get England out of your little head. There is nothing for us there."

"What of your title, Father? You cannot run from it your entire life. You haven't even visited Mother's grave since you left. Just let me go home for a visit, never mind the London season. I will stay only at Devonsfield."

"I said to never mention your mother!" he roared. "I said it and I meant it!" The shadow of his hand loomed over Abby's face like a cobra waiting to strike, but the blow never came. Though she trembled with fright, she knew he resisted only for the sake of appearances. It would do him no good to have her cheek discolored.

She bowed her head low, wanting to dam back her tears, but failed to do so. When they arrived at Bristol Estate, Miss Robins waited, wringing her fingers just outside the door, her gray hair bound back in a bun. Abby tried to smile.

"Child, where've you been?" she whispered.

Abby kept her head tucked low, feeling her father's glare on her back.

As he stepped out of the carriage, his upper lip lifted in disgust. "I did not know I kept livestock here. Do I not pay you to ensure she not get so sullied?"

Miss Robins nodded, taking an awkward curtsy. "Pardon me, Sir Rathburn."

"We have company arriving in less than two hours. Have her dressed and ready for dining. Coach her in manners, and do not let her get away from you again or neither of you will be allowed to Sunday services until next year."

Miss Robins' eyes grew wide. "I'll have her ready to make you proud."

Sir Rathburn regarded his daughter. "Doubtful," he spat. Abby flinched, feeling the sting. He continued, "Be advised to keep your mouth shut this evening lest it get you into more trouble."

Miss Robins' lips pressed together, worry marking her forehead. Abby lifted the hem of her skirts, escaping to the stairs with Robins following just behind.

* * *

In the course of an hour, Robins successfully rinsed the spring breeze from Abby's hair and stilled her tears enough to apply powder to her face. The room held a hush except for the soothing hum of Robins' voice while she pinned Abby's hair in place. She could not find it in her heart to tell her maid they would not be traveling to London. Miss Robins had sacrificed so much by remaining Abby's maid, and for what? Her master's constant reprimands, and now, his refusal to allow her to do what she wanted most—see her family.

The knock from downstairs jolted Abby's mind to attention. The guest must have arrived a few minutes early.

"Have you heard anything about this Mr. Henderson?" asked Abby.

"Just that his father passed a few months hence. T'was said he left him with a shipping business, and now this Mr. Henderson is making the company known and turn'n a profit mighty well," said Robins. "Of which, I just overheard from downstairs gossip. Who knows how true 'tis."

"I suppose Father is bored of selling property," said Abby.

"Yes, I think you're quite right." Robins' skilled fingers repositioned the emerald comb that mirrored the hues of Abby's gown.

"This color does suit your complexion so well. You'll be sure to look the part of a fine young lady ready for the most exquisite of ev'nings," said Miss Robins with a smile.

Abby's brow wrinkled. "It's not like I am going to another ball." She laughed. "Perhaps I should change into something less formal."

"Oh no. Your father said your best gown. Aside from your ball gown, this is it, my dear. Besides, we have no more time."

"Why is Father making such a fuss? I have never heard of this gentleman."

Miss Robins' eyes grew wide. "Oh my dear—I thought you understood?"

Abby shook her head, "Understood what?"

Miss Robins lowered her stare. "This gentleman is quite the bachelor."

Abby reached for Robins' arm. "But I do not know him! Surely Father does not expect anything in that regard. He mentioned nothing about it on the ride here, except in being adamant that I shouldn't expect any callers from the ball."

Robins bit her lip, her hands shaking ever so slightly.

"What is the matter?"

Her light eyes looked across at the young woman who had been her charge for these last eleven years. She turned to Abby, lightly pressing on her shoulders so that she might sit back down. "I do believe other gentlemen have inquired about you, but your father turned them all away."

Abby gasped, her cheeks paling. "He would not dare!" But even as she said it, she knew it to be true.

"So he will accept no gentleman on my behalf then?"

Robins tilted Abby's chin up, tears welling in her own eyes. "My dear, he has accepted this one."

Abby's breath caught in her chest. "You mean, this stranger whom I've never met?"

"I do."

"But Father said this man has come for business," she said, recalling fragments of conversation in the carriage only hours ago.

"Indeed. But you see, Mr. Henderson is a bachelor with wealth and a shrewd eye for business. He knows of you, dear, whether or not you know of him."

Abby's chin trembled, tumultuous thoughts whirling through her mind. She longed to be on a walk again, all by herself, in charge of the path set before her. But alas, her choices were made for her, and she must endure them in the same way her mother had—and, no doubt, her mother before her.

"Dear, dear, don't get so misty-eyed. Your tears are wont to keep running on your face once they start, and the dinner bell is expected too soon to dry them up."

"Mother would have never wanted this."

Robins shook her head in understanding. "I know, but the tea has already been poured, bitter though it is, and there's no spooning it back in the pot."

"This is the only gentleman that Father will receive?"

Robins sighed, a deep heavy sigh of the soul. "If there is one thing I've learned about your father 'tis that he is a very decisive man, and what'ere his motive, his intentions are clear."

"It is business. It is always business."

Miss Robins stepped back, a satisfied smile taking over her tired face. "Stunning. Simply stunning."

"So this is it."

Adorned in her best evening gown, with hair laboriously tamed, and the weight of her mother's jewels heavy on her neck, Abby waited, nerves gnawing at her insides.

"It feels as though your mother is stood right in front of me. If it weren't for the aching of my knees, I would think I were living twenty years ago," Robins said, marveling at the young woman before her.

"I feel ill all of a sudden. Must I go?" said Abby.

Miss Robins took Abby's hands in hers. She nodded and gave a gentle squeeze of encouragement, then silently left the room.

Numbness coursed through Abby's veins as she steeled herself to face the reality that awaited her. Suddenly, the gong of the dinner bell reverberated through the house, as though unwittingly signaling Abby's metamorphosis from child to woman. She remembered her mother—specifically her mother's love, and the countless prayers she'd spoken over Abby. Now, Abby too prayed.

Lord, give me the strength to accept what I must.

Her palm held the doorknob, cool and polished to a sheen. *Who has Father chosen for me?* She pulled it open and willed herself to assume the cold countenance of a statue, to guard the wild beat of her heart. Her eyes traced the carpeted path toward the staircase.

She shut her eyes, taking in a deep breath, then exhaled slowly and stepped towards the railing. Her eyes wandered beyond the curved steps until they stopped at the bottom of the stairs. A dark-haired man stood chatting with her father, one hand resting in his pocket. His strong build towered over Sir Rathburn's, whose shoulders appeared more stooped than Abby had remembered. Sir Rathburn paused, looking up, and the man's eyes followed until they settled on her.

Abby took in a ragged breath as the man's lusterless eyes captured hers. His lips curved upward against his strong jawline, and she felt him peruse her figure. Color flushed Abby's cheeks, but he boldly held her gaze. Only when she cast her eyes to the ground could she lose his stare. Her heart caught in her throat, and for a moment she wondered if she might faint.

One, two, three, four, she counted. Each step brought Abby closer to her fate and further away from her childhood. *Eleven, twelve, thirteen.* She looked up and Mr. Henderson's dark figure waited for her. She gripped the railing tighter, desperately willing herself to remain composed. It was not thrill that beckoned her, but fear.

She feared the lure of his cold, handsome face; the unknown depths of his eyes. Just before she reached the last step, she turned slightly, Mr. Henderson's eyes boring into her, and resumed the facade. Her ivory face held itself still, smooth, and inscrutable, like the visages captured in paintings of all the great Wyndham ladies of old.

Chapter 4

Four months later, on a sunny morning, Charles strolled down Shermerhorn Row with the bonny-faced Miss Wyndham at his side. They weaved through throngs of people at the foot of tall red-brick buildings that housed the many businesses of the bustling port. Cool coastal winds brought welcome relief from the humid summer air. Charles looked down at Abby, now his fiancée, pride welling in his chest. Even in the mounting heat of the sun, she glistened. Aside from the Astor Ball, Abby had seen very little of the city, and Charles thought this a severe discredit to himself. With a new business venture to attend to, he saw it as the perfect chance to flaunt his secured connection with Sir Rathburn.

"Just a half block more," said Charles, positioning Abby's hand on his arm so that the sunlight caught the cuts of the diamond perched on her finger just so.

She nodded and smiled between flushed cheeks, her eyes taking in the bustle of the morning. Just before they reached the entrance of the hotel where their meeting was to take place, a familiar voice caught his attention. It was Mr. Shermerhorn. Charles hid his pleasure, as Mr. Shermerhorn's eyes lit anew at the sight of Abby.

"Am I seeing a vision?" said Mr. Shermerhorn warmly, his tall frame bowed low. Abby returned a polite smile and dipped into a low curtsy. "Ah, it is her, Miss Wyndham, like the sun herself." Charles heard nothing of this exchange except the jingle of gold filling his pockets.

"You are most kind, Mr. Shermerhorn," said Abby.

The old man shook his head, amusement playing on his features. He turned to Charles. "All the rumors are true then? How is it that you won the hand of such a fine creature?"

Abby offered another polite smile as a tinge of pink warmed her cheeks.

"But surely you cannot have thought so little of me?" Charles jested.

Mr. Shermerhorn winked at Abby. "Did he woo you with flowers and poetry in so short a time?"

Abby's dark lashes lifted. She stole a glance at Charles, and then returned her gaze to Mr. Shermerhorn. "I suppose Charles is not one for poetry," she remarked. Charles was rather taken aback by her assumption. He did not hate poetry, though he could think of no practical use for it. At any rate, he'd had no need to resort to such trivialities; Abby had been promised to him.

Mr. Shermerhorn leaned in closer to Charles. "You've a lifetime to mend that offense; you could steal a few lines from Shakespeare."

Abby looked up, a little more boldly than before, with a grin hiding in the corner of her cheek. "Is courting not between a man and a woman's father?"

Mr. Shermerhorn let out a laugh. "Perhaps in the motherland." Charles couldn't mask his surprise; he did not think the woman next to him capable of such a quick-witted response.

She continued, "But you see, Father has become very fond of Charles. He is like the son he never had," and as she said this Charles' pride was placated, and Mr. Shermerhorn nodded in full approval.

A farmer shouted at his mule pulling a wagon laden with an assortment of fresh vegetables. Charles could make out the bundles of fat carrots and bright green heads of cabbage, as the wagon trundled towards the market. *Perhaps the tobacco crop will be prime shipping this year*, he thought.

"Have you set the day?" asked Mr. Shermerhorn

The sound of splintering wood called Charles' attention over to the road where the wagon full of produce jolted to a stop as stray vegetables tumbled onto the road. The bushy-browed farmer spat out strings of curses between his cavernous teeth.

"Oh my," said Abby, then she looked up at Charles and Mr. Shermerhorn, whose attention had returned to their previous conversation.

"Early December," said Charles.

Mr. Shermerhorn's eyes glimmered. "I do hope you will remember this poor old man when you send out the invitations. In the meantime, don't let her get away from you," he said, winking.

Charles grinned, shaking his head. "I think she is quite content at my side," he said, only to find his arm bare of Abby's hand, and her nowhere in sight.

"What did I tell you? Women can be slippery things," he jested.

Charles turned around towards the hotel entrance but did not see her.

Mr. Shermerhorn set a firm hand against Charles' shoulder and spun him around. "Over there," he pointed. There, on the road, chaos had broken out around the wagon. A few brats wearing little more than rags scuffled in front of the lame cart, wrestling over a bunch of carrots. One burly youth's arm secured the other gangly child's head in a hold so that the child's arms and legs flailed about as he screamed and wailed, tears spouting from his eyes. Amid the commotion came a voice—clear, calm, commanding utmost authority: "STOP!"

Charles took in a sharp breath, his brow arched in alarm. *Surely that is not Abby?* The tenor of the voice sounded familiar, but Charles had never heard her use such a sharp tone before. Much to his surprise, as the dust settled, Abby's tall, graceful figure came into view.

"You will excuse me, Mr. Shermerhorn," whispered Charles before leaving the old man behind.

The children stilled, looking up at Abby. A crowd had gathered around the wagon, watching the whole scene unfold. The boys stood up straight, each trying to smooth their crumpled shirts and ruffled hair as their chests still heaved from their skirmish.

"Now, are these carrots rightfully yours?" she asked.

The boys shook their heads, which now hung low as they looked down at Abby's boots.

"Then why do you fight over something that belongs to neither one?"

The younger of the two looked up to Abby, his chin quivering. "We's hungry."

Charles strained to hear above the murmurs around him. The flow of traffic had slowed to a crawl, and people milled around the scene at the wagon.

Abby paused, holding the carrots aloft. Her mouth fell open, but she was silent. Charles began elbowing his way forward to extricate Abby from the scene. He had not thought it proper to find his English lady sullying herself amid the scuffle of orphans.

He stepped past the huddle of onlookers, taking his place at Abby's side, but she did not acknowledge him. Her eyes were misted over, a delicate crease impressed between her brow. Charles took her free hand. "Let's go; you shouldn't trouble yourself with this sort," he hissed.

Her eyes were quick, looking on Charles as though wounded. "But Charles, they are hungry."

Charles leaned into her ear and whispered, "If you feed them today they'll only be strong enough to choke at each other's throats tomorrow." He squeezed a little tighter on her arm, pulling her along to make their leave. But she willed herself in a different direction, breaking free of his hold. Charles pinched his lips shut as she stepped closer to the children, kneeling down so that her eyes reached the height of theirs. She dug into her coin purse, the hem of her skirts grazing the muddy street.

"I believe you two would be far less hungry if you worked together—you know as friends do. They look out for one another. I saw there is a bakery around the corner that just pulled fresh loaves from the oven." Extending her soft, ivory hand to the younger boy, she placed a one-cent piece in his palm. "Now, you take this and go together as friends. There is no need to turn on each other, for nothing is accomplished that way." She closed his hand around the coin and smiled, doing the same with the older child.

They looked into her eyes with awe and then at each other. In a moment, they scurried off, leaving the circle of people behind. Abby returned the carrots to the farmer who had finally reloaded his wagon.

Charles took her arm again, rather firmly this time, whisking her away from the crowd back towards the entrance of the hotel. Mr. Shermerhorn still stood where Charles had left him, his mouth agape.

"Good day to you, Mr. Shermerhorn. We've business to attend," said Charles brusquely, eager to draw his attention away from the scene that had just unfolded. As he ushered Abby towards the doorway, she stopped.

"What now?"

She lowered her eyes. "Have I upset you?"

Charles regarded her. "I didn't realize you enjoyed causing such a . . . *scene*."

"I didn't realize you were so—" she began to say and then bit her tongue.

Charles did not give her the chance to finish her thought.

"You embarrassed me in front of an entire crowd with your brazen philanthropy. You made me out to be a fool. Not to mention, you are now covered in the same dirt as those children when we are due for my meeting with men of such influence they hold the power to secure my—*our*—future."

Abby sighed, but Charles continued. "Now when I come back here, do you know what those rascals will expect from me? Bread money," he spat.

"I see," she said.

"What do you see exactly?"

The luster of her eyes died down replaced by quiet calm. "Only that Father would say the same thing."

Charles' eyes narrowed. It was no secret to him that Sir Rathburn held little affection for his daughter, but he was unsure of what sounding like him meant to her.

"Then we have come to an understanding?"

Charles thought she looked paler than before. She glanced over his shoulder. "If you will excuse me, I will go to the lavatory and make myself presentable."

Charles nodded, and she walked off.

* * *

A few days later, Sir Rathburn invited Charles to spend the afternoon at Bristol Estate. Specifically, Sir Rathburn had requested they discuss the "business side" of marriage, and Charles was eager to oblige. He arrived earlier than anticipated and decided to look for Abby instead of waiting in the Great Hall. With servants seeing to other matters, Charles went to find her.

She was tucked away in a quaint nook just off the Great Hall. A large window dominated the room, offering sweeping views of immaculate front gardens. Two stuffed chairs sat near the window at an intimate distance. Abby sat in one, her day dress undulating around her, her eyes closed. As Charles moved closer, he noticed that her head was slightly bowed, and she held a book open on her lap. Charles studied her for a moment, wondering what he had stumbled upon. Then, he leaned on the adjacent chair and sighed audibly.

Her eyes shot open and she jumped, letting out a yelp. "My word! How long have you been there?"

Charles grinned and looked around the room, scanning for more information. Finding none, he said, "I didn't mean to wake you."

She shook her head. "You did not wake me."

"What were you doing then?"

"You could have knocked," she said.

"I know, but I didn't."

She looked at him, indignant.

"You are a strange creature," he said.

"*Strange* is wandering around someone's home and barging in unannounced. I was only praying."

Charles let out a laugh, fully amused. "In the middle of the day?"

"Just as I find the need," she said.

He made himself comfortable in the chair next to her, slouching back in the cushions. She glanced towards the door, which had been pulled nearly shut.

"What would a woman like you have to pray about?"

Abby shut the book in her lap and rose from her chair, creating more distance between them. "A woman like *me*?"

Charles grinned. It was the first time he had been completely alone in her company, and it was proving more than entertaining. "Yes, like *you*. You have everything a person could possibly want."

Her cheeks flushed as she paced the floor. "How would you know what I want?"

Charles arched his brow. *She has a point,* he thought. What did it matter what she wanted after all? "Enlighten me then."

Like a frightened doe, she looked around the room, biting the corner of her mouth. "Father would hardly approve of that wayward topic."

Charles rose, and in a single stride he had closed the gap between them. She stepped backward, sinking into the chair. "Do you always obey your father?"

"No," she said, her eyes narrowing.

"Well, maybe I could help you get want you want," said Charles, grinning.

It was her turn to laugh. "Whatever you think I want is far from what I was going to say."

"You are so naive."

"What do you mean?"

"Someone with more *experience* would understand all this world has to offer—its delights, all of its distractions and pleasures. No prayers necessary. Especially for you."

"You mock me," she said coldly.

Charles could not contain his smirk. Abby squeezed past him, standing freely.

"I may lack your 'experience,'" she began, "but in saying that you negate my own. Who is the author of pleasure? That is to whom I pray; that is what I need more than anything. I dare say no good can come by abandoning all conviction." As she said these things her face reddened, and Charles noted the unmistakable feeling behind her words. It unnerved him. Who did she think she was? A saint?

Charles snorted. Abby seemed to be making a habit of speaking her mind. In their previous meetings, Sir Rathburn had always spoken for her, and now he understood why. What had at first seemed amusing changed course, like the sudden surge of an ocean current. He shook his head, puzzled with this peculiar woman's way of seeing the world. To him, it smelled of bigotry.

Though he did think that such high morals went nicely with her perfectly English accent.

"Perhaps you should be sent off to the convent," he said.

A light flickered in her eyes. "If it were more beneficial for Father to have me in a convent, that is where I would be. But I fear you would be quite put off by it," she said. Then she offered a brief curtsy, and without another word made her leave.

The thought occurred to Charles that Abby might prefer a convent to marrying him, and as much as he tried to console his pride, it wound its way around his gut, gnawing at his resolve.

* * *

At dinner that evening, Abby sat at Charles' right across from Sir Rathburn. Charles' eyes followed her as she placed her water glass back on the table, and he noticed the absence of a wine glass. All that was offered to her was water and tea. His mind reeled, and he thought back to dinners and even the few balls they had attended together. She always waved away the beverage tray. He gritted his teeth, spying out more bigotry, which he assumed displayed the influence Miss Robins held over her. Charles had become aware of the pattern. Every Sunday the old woman brought Abby to Reverend Truitt's church. Charles did not know much about the Reverend, except that he was known to oppose hard drink. No doubt all of those years Abby had been apart from Sir Rathburn had molded the child's mind to her maid's foolish regard for piety.

Charles pondered these thoughts a moment more as he spun the brandy around in his glass and sipped down the last bit. He finally came to the conclusion that if such piety were molded, it could also be undone with time, attention, and persistence.

"Timothy, serve my darling something more appropriate for the occasion—some sherry perhaps?" The servant's brow furrowed. He hesitated in the corner of the room, looking to Abby.

"No, thank you," Abby said firmly. The servant nodded and stepped back into the corner. Before Charles could insist, Abby, with admirable dexterity, changed the subject. "After all of this time, Charles, I have not quite understood what your industry is about. Do tell how despite such grievous times you have managed to turn Henderson Gold Line into such a profitable enterprise?"

Sir Rathburn's eyes narrowed on his daughter as he sipped the amber liquid from his glass. "I fear the topic would bore you," he said.

Abby's soft lips pursed together, but she insisted. "I do not think Charles' accomplishments could bore me, Father."

Charles smiled, amused at her wiles. He glanced at her, his reply decidedly short, for there was no reason to actually bore her when it came to his accomplishments.

"I decided to venture into cargo that my late father had refused. Opportunity knocked, and I opened the door." He reached to her side, covering her hand proprietorially with his own.

"What sort of cargo?" she asked.

Sir Rathburn's eyes darted to Charles', flashing a quick warning.

"The usual, my dear," replied Charles softly.

Abby looked down at her lap and moved her hand to take another drink of water.

"Tell me about your meeting at the hotel. Was it as beneficial as you hoped?" asked Rathburn.

Charles chuckled, remembering the encounter with Mr. Shermerhorn. Much to his relief, when Abby had returned from the lavatory she assumed her usual quiet disposition, observing all the rules of propriety in keeping with her status. She had hardly spoken a word, except when directly addressed.

"I think it went on rather well. I am certain more will come of it. Timothy, more brandy," said Charles.

"But what is *the usual*?" asked Abby.

"I beg your pardon?" replied Charles.

Abby's eyes turned to Charles. He noticed how her dark curls danced on her neck, and her cheeks still held the color from his touch.

"What cargo does your company transport? Why would your father refuse such a lucrative opportunity?" she asked.

Charles let out a light laugh. "Oh, only the usual goods: coffee, tea, tobacco . . . slaves. There are a great many things the South needs desperately, and we now can ship them quickly, efficiently. And then we do it all in reverse; whatever the North needs, we bring from the South on the way back. There's money in our pockets, and plenty more to spare."

As Charles talked, the color drained from Abby's face, and her hand covered her mouth.

"Are you all right?" asked Charles.

She looked down at her dish of sweet fruits, pushing them around with the tip of her fork. "*Slaves?*"

Sir Rathburn laughed. "Abby is quite principled, Charles."

Charles put his hand on her shoulder and felt her muscles tense. "It's only business, my dear. There's no need to worry your mind with the particulars. The thing to note is that in the last few months we have quadrupled profits, and the year is not yet done. Now, how about a celebratory glass of champagne to mark the occasion?"

"No, thank you," she said just above a whisper.

"It'll bring back your color," he said.

She took a deep breath, taking it in as though pained. "You know I do not drink, Charles."

Charles shook his head. "You aren't a child, Abby."

Sir Rathburn interjected, a smirk forming around his lips as he spoke. "You just noticed this? She might have offended her own mother with this preference."

At the mention of her mother, Abby lifted her gaze to her father. Her jaw hardened into a delicate line.

"Ah, a house divided. What's your cause?" Charles said.

She swallowed. "Perhaps another time," she answered. This time her face remained void of the polite smile that was her signature. She folded her hands in her lap, glancing up at her father, then back down at the untouched fruit on her plate.

As satisfying as it was to see her keep her opinions to herself, Charles would prefer that she had no opinions apart from the ones he shared. "Have you ever tried it?" he pressed.

She shook her head, biting her bottom lip.

Sir Rathburn huffed out a grunt of disgust. "I offered, but she made quite the scene of it. Thankfully, no one else was there to witness it. One thing is clear: she listens more to her reverend than her father."

"So, you form judgments over something which you've never experienced?" asked Charles, his voice smooth. In his mind he was equally amused and unnerved at the woman who sat beside him. Though she appeared a sensuous image of flesh and blood, she was showing herself to be quite the foreigner, even in her own home.

She was silent beneath her father's palpable glare for a few moments and then she spoke. "It is true. I have never chosen to partake, but Reverend Truitt leans towards temperance because of his own experience of addiction. He even works with addicts on the street who beg for liquor instead of a warm meal. And besides, I happen to agree with the Reverend."

"On what account?" said Charles.

"I need not explore that topic," she said, with a quick blink towards her father.

Charles pressed further. "Oh do entertain us, go on. Explain this 'experience' that has so shaped your seventeen-year-old mind."

She breathed in deeply before responding. "I have observed that it changes one's demeanor, inhibitions, and actions. That is something I feel more comfortable refraining from at this point in my life."

A dark laugh filled the room. Sir Rathburn shook his head and took another bold swallow.

Charles pressed again. "You think my thoughts are inhibited? And your father's?"

"Perhaps at times. I do not know. Really, can we not discuss something else?" she said, her voice wavering.

"Oh, but we are merely having a friendly conversation," said Sir Rathburn with a sly smile.

"So, according to your thinking, my judgments are questionable because I have had a glass or two?" Charles' blood pumped through him, and even as he said it he knew he was thoroughly enjoying Abby's discomfort. "Though I would dare say many a good business deal has been sealed over a glass of brandy. Am I right?" Sir Rathburn nodded, grinning behind the rim of his glass. Charles continued, "There's room for honesty at this table. Do you think me 'wrong'?

"Not necessarily," she stuttered.

"Ah . . . there's nuance? But I imagine you think yourself better for abstaining?" he questioned with a knowing grin.

"I never said that," she replied, her voice strained.

"But your reverend deemed it wrong. So, it follows that us heathens who do wet their lips with a drop must be doomed to damnation."

"It is not wrong in and of itself. The matter is really more complicated than—"

Charles interjected, leaning in close. "—Let me pose this to you, my dear. Do you not think your own temperance gives you another vice to cling to?"

Abby chewed the inside of her cheek, her breath quickening.

"What might that be?"

Charles smirked. "Pride. Self-righteousness, tainting your innocent soul."

She lifted her chin and glared angrily at him, but for the moment she was speechless.

"How strong are you that you refuse the world, Abby? How honorable that you choose to walk the higher road?" Charles smiled, noting her gasp. "Did not even Jesus despise those Pharisaical practices more than the drunkards themselves?"

Charles' comment hung in the air. He watched as her lips parted as though she were about to speak, but no words came. Then she fixed her stare on the empty table, while Timothy came to take away the last course and administered the liquor glasses to Sir Rathburn and Charles.

Charles lifted the glass to his lips and took a long sip, sucking the last of it through his teeth. He let out a deep-bellied laugh, his eyes still on Abby as she shifted in her chair.

"Sir Rathburn, please reveal more of your daughter's peculiarities," drolled Charles.

The old gent laughed harder, the liquor easing his gray mood. "Well, to start off, as I said before, she is very sensitive," to which both Charles and Sir Rathburn howled in apparent amusement.

Abby's cheeks now burned red. Although she kept her eyes low, Charles could see the tell-tale flutter that betrayed the onset of tears. Her sensibilities appeared too weak to combat their dark humor.

As the laughter died down, she took a breath and again replied, "You may be right, for I can find no honest rebuttal."

Charles smiled, unable to resist the urge to carry on with this game of taunting. "So, now you pretend to be humble?"

He noticed a flicker in her eyes, a spark that he supposed he could fan into flame.

"No, pray you. Yet you stab at me with your own judgments," she said, the fine distinction of her collarbone becoming more defined as she tensed.

"Prove it," said Charles.

"Prove what?" Her eyes were fiery now.

"That you are not as proud as you appear."

"I have already admitted my own pride—what else do you want? Who am I to change it?" she said.

Sir Rathburn roared, "Abigail—for God's sake, have some wine to ease our guest's misgivings! I am not ready for a civil war just yet."

"He is hardly a *guest*. He should at least pretend to understand why I would choose to abstain after seeing the state of you every evening."

Sir Rathburn glared, his eyes wide. She took in a sharp breath and clasped a hand over her wayward mouth. She stood abruptly, her hands trembling along with her voice. "I think it time I excuse myself."

Charles reached for her before she could step away from the table and clasped her wrist firmly. "No, you should sit." The brandy had long since dulled his sensibilities, and he willingly succumbed to its whims.

Abby caught her breath as he guided her back to her cushion. She looked over at her father, who let out a dark laugh before saying, "Actually, I must excuse myself momentarily; it appears you are in good hands at present."

She started to speak, but a full word had yet to escape her lips before her father rose and stumbled towards the door, quite obviously to relieve himself in the privy down the hall.

As soon as Sir Rathburn had left, Charles took advantage of the moment. "Timothy, leave us," he ordered.

The servant nodded warily and left the room.

Charles leaned back in his chair, taking another deep breath between sips. "You shouldn't be so stiff, my dear," he said, idly swirling the pungent liquid around the crystal glass. It felt cool against his fingers, and as he regarded his soon-to-be bride, he allowed himself the pleasure of imagining the feeling of the glass on Abby's virgin lips.

He leaned forward so that the front legs of his chair jolted on the ground. Abby flinched.

"Have this, just to appease me. Then you can go. Don't think I can't be as stubborn as you," he said, revealing his most winsome grin.

She sat up straighter, her arms stiff to her side, her fingers gripping around the edge of the chair like a child refusing dinner.

"No, thank you."

"Are you so afraid of yourself, Abby? Come on, take a drink."

He lifted the glass to her lips. She turned her chin away. Charles seethed, gripping the glass tighter until he slammed it onto the table with a loud *clank*. Abby jumped, yelping like a wounded animal. A ringlet escaped the crown of her head, falling in front of her eyes.

"If that's not the banner of a bigot, I don't know what is!" he thundered.

She lifted her eyes boldly to his, but in the tremble of her chin he saw her resolve shaken.

"It is not myself that I fear."

A burn crept its way up from Charles' belly, potent anger. The pulse of his neck beat against his collar.

Abby's eyes fell in a panic, and she reached for the crystal glass. With the slightest of tremors, she put the rim to her lips and downed the entire draft, wincing after the swallow.

Charles relaxed, an approving smile forming across his face. *She can follow orders,* he thought. Then, what was anger morphed into desire; heat pulsed through his veins. Before she could take a breath, Charles grabbed the back of her head and pulled her towards him, pressing his lips to hers and tasting the remnants of brandy, his fingers tangling themselves in her silken locks. He held her, moving his lips lower to the nape of her neck. Then she shoved him away, her genteel hand striking his cheek with a loud *smack*. She sprang from her seat, backing away.

Charles froze, his pride stinging more than the welt forming on his face. Abby stood over him, her chest heaving.

"How dare you!" she said, a fire glowing in her eyes.

"It is my right."

The soft hand that had stung him moved to wipe her gaping lips. Her hair had unwound, billowing around her face, her eyes wild and frightened.

"I thought you at least a gentleman," she hissed.

"*At least?* I am more than that," he spat between clenched teeth.

Abby steadied herself on the edge of the table, swaying ever so slightly. Then, she smoothed her gown and swept her fingers through her hair, as if to regain her composure.

"I'll not drink that again."

"I didn't force you."

She glowered, holding her wrist in her hand. "Of course not—you just ushered me into the holds of the ship with a smile on your face and whip in hand."

The door opened at that moment and Sir Rathburn sauntered back into the room.

"Leaving already?" asked Sir Rathburn.

She nodded and, turning on her heel, spun towards the doorway. Charles stared after her as she fled into the hall, the edge of her petticoat peeking out from the hem of her skirts as she climbed the stairs towards her room. His cheek stung afresh.

"Welcome to the family," Sir Rathburn chuckled. "At least she has a substantial dowry attached to her."

Chapter 5

Abby's head spun from the liquor so that she could hardly make it to her room, but once behind her closed door, she allowed herself a moment to think. She had never seen Charles so angry. The hatred of his eyes rivaled even her father's. If it weren't for self-preservation, she would never have drunk it. But fear had grabbed hold of her, and she hoped to appease the god in him demanding her sacrifice. *I was foolish,* she thought, for the result of her actions had only fed his lust.

A strange warmth spread through her limbs, bringing a false sense of calm like a sweet elixir, temporarily dampening her fear, yet her hand still stung from the force of the blow. Her eyes welled with tears. *What good did that do?* she thought.

A knock stalled her thoughts, and she looked up with trepidation. Miss Robins poked her head in. "Shall I get you to bed?"

"Straight away," said Abby.

"You seem unwell. What's amiss?"

Abby turned around so that Robins could untie her stays. "They're intolerable together."

Robins pulled loose the strings until Abby was free. She did not wait for her maid to brush her hair but fell into bed. "There there," Robins soothed. "It couldn't have been so bad?"

"How am I to marry such a despicable man?"

Robins pulled the covers up over her.

"Your cheeks are flushed," she said with a worried look. Her hand felt cool against Abby's face.

"He hates me. I am sure of it. He hates me as much as Father does."

Robins covered Abby's mouth. "Hush. You shouldn't say such things."

"He only wants my dowry, and I dare say my flesh"—Robins' eyes opened wide—"And Father only wants a son. Am I to pretend I want nothing?" said Abby tearfully.

Robins fanned herself and shook her head. "Well, what is it that you want?"

Abby sat straight up. "To see the good in him, but I find none. He is wholly awful, and because of him I can scarcely see the good in me." Abby could hear the thump of her own heart beating in her head, and the room seemed to spin around her.

Miss Robins grew very grave. "My dear, we are surely all awful in some way. Myself included."

"Not you, Robins."

"Pish posh! I can't say a word for him, but I can say that we're all in the same pot of soup, simmer'n in our wrongs. Some just show theirs more than others, and we're all in terrible need of grace."

"Do you think I am prideful, Robins?"

She pressed her lips together, studying Abby's worried face. "I reckon there's a measure of it."

"Oh, what a horrible thought."

Miss Robins stifled a laugh. "My dear, we are all in need. That's where pride dies. Now, I believe I will stay with you tonight."

Abby lay back down and shook her head. "No, no. Your back will ache tomorrow morning if you sleep on that lumpy chaise."

"Child, I can survive one night there."

Abby smiled. "And see, I am no longer a child. I insist—I am fine."

Robins offered a wary look, and finally gave in. She bent down, kissing Abby on the forehead and whispered a prayer over her.

* * *

Charles' mind raced in a loop, recalling Abby's fiery eyes and her outrage.

Once she had left, he and Sir Rathburn moved their conversation to the dim lights of the study. Sir Rathburn's voice droned on, detailing his grand plans for their future, but Charles hardly heard him.

Defiance. It was as though Charles had cracked her porcelain veneer, in an instant shattering any notion he had of her placid compliance. She would be a hard one to tame, he thought. An unusual strength revealed itself within her, and he knew that no amount of pure breeding, or well-practiced feminine graces could conceal it. She bowed in humility, while standing in self-righteousness. Regardless of what she said, Charles believed Abby imagined herself better than he. These thoughts assaulted his unfettered mind.

What would set her so far above me? he thought. Was it because she actually enjoyed listening to the deathly drone of a clergyman's voice, and he despised it? Or, perhaps she thought that denying herself earthly pleasures would ensure her place in whatever afterlife she envisioned? Whatever it was, Charles reasoned, Abby knew nothing of how the world functioned—in business or in pleasure; nothing of what it demanded. And, Charles surmised, the world had asked nothing of her—yet.

"Charles?" asked Sir Rathburn.

Charles jerked his head to attention. "Sir?"

"Do not mind her little tantrum. You are giving her the upper hand by allowing her to consume your thoughts," said Sir Rathburn, now settled and relaxed in his chair.

But Charles did mind, and his snort of disgust made that very clear.

"Get used to it. She is a woman after all. I will set her straight tomorrow, and she will certainly be at your mercy. Shall we get back to business?" asked Sir Rathburn, sipping the last drop of liquor from his glass.

"Of course."

Business was a needed distraction. The servant topped up their drinks, and Charles and Sir Rathburn lit their second round of cigars while they laid out the logistics of merging and expanding. It seemed that between Sir Rathburn's landholdings and connections, and Charles' shipping ventures, they could become an unstoppable enterprise. They exhausted the subjects of vessels, both steam and sail, before moving on to the profitable market of shipping slaves south. Sir Rathburn's eyes glowed greedily, his cheeks growing ruddy the more he drank.

"There's a short window for this particular market," said Charles.

Sir Rathburn nodded. "How long?"

"I'm not sure, but I do know we can capitalize on it while it lasts. Then duck out before politics get in our way. Hands unscathed."

"Indeed," Rathburn agreed. "We don't want to land on the wrong side and make enemies of the right people."

"Who are the 'right people'?"

"Whoever lines our pockets," said Sir Rathburn with a grin.

The clock chimed at the top of the midnight hour, but they paid it no heed, drinking and dreaming. Sir Rathburn finally dismissed the servant, who poured late into the night until his weariness made him waver. While the burn of their strong drink relaxed Charles' body, it served only to stoke the fire within his mind. After writing out a plan for the merging of their resources, Sir Rathburn sank back onto his couch and into unconsciousness. As unseemly as the sight was, Charles rather admired him for his ability to slip into sleep so easily. Charles downed the last swallow from his cup, biting his lips with his teeth. Then, he rose and stumbled towards the door.

The halls were dark except for the light of the moon casting long shadows on the tiled floor. At this late hour, even the servants had finished their duties and retired to their quarters, at the south end of the estate near the kitchen, far off from the main rooms. Silence had settled over the house.

As Charles approached the stairs he paused, leaning on the railing. His mind wandered back to earlier—the sting of his cheek, the gentle curve of Abby's ankle peeking out from her skirts while she rushed up the stairs. A fire blazed in the pit of his stomach, hungry for sustenance, thirsting for an object to which he could transfer its heat.

A chuckle escaped Charles' throat, a mad sort of sound, at the thought of Abby sleeping peacefully in her bed. Desire stirred within, stoked by a disjointed stream of images.

The curve of her mouth over the edge of her glass.

The flutter of her dark lashes blinking in defiance.

The tickle of her long ebony locks.

The taste of brandy on her lips.

His sudden arousal mixed like a toxin with his rage. The very shadows that surrounded him seemed to whisper that she was beyond him not only in class but in morality. Yet, in five long months, Abby would be his. His to have, his to hold. His to break, his to control. But could he stifle her piety? Could he erase what seemed to be so innately part of her?

She needed to be humbled, brought down from her high horse, to his level. And what was morality to a woman but her virtue? This he could control; this he could have. There was a way to supplant that as long as her shame remained his secret.

He climbed to the top of the stairs on a sure path to Abby's quarters, where he had spied her looking out of her window over the months of their courtship. The doorknob was cool in his hands. For a moment he held it, then gently turned it and heard a click as it yielded.

Moonlight trickled in through the drapes, bathing Abby's face in a soft glow. Charles paused in the doorway, watching her breath.

Chapter 6

A fitful sleep tinged with sinister specters and taunting smiles plagued Abby as she lay in her bed. Then, the course of her thoughts changed, and the bed felt like a sea of churning water, her pillow a remnant of a shipwreck, her mind mired in murk. Dreams tormented her.

Sea spray stung her eyes as she clung to what was left of a vessel. Fire danced on the surface among the wreckage; the smell of burning singed the air. Black waters raged, seizing her, casting her adrift in the inky darkness. Ominous clouds swirled overhead, teasing the soupy cauldron with gusts of wind until the waves swelled high. She sank in the depths of the ocean, the undertow pulling her down.

Her body jolted, and Abby sat straight up in her bed, gasping for air. Her head swam in a blur. *It was only a dream,* she thought. She clutched her pillow tighter, waiting for the fringes of the dream to pass, when the sound of shuffling alerted her to reality.

Her tongue stuck like dry paper against the back of her throat as she tried to open her mouth to speak.

"Who's there?"

A figure emerged from the corner of the room, swaying unsteadily. The door clicked shut.

The figure neared, its silhouette taking on a familiar shape.

Blue glows of light flickered over its form as it crept toward Abby like a creature from the deep. She squeezed her eyes shut, willing her dream to cease.

When she opened them again, she saw him distinctly—there, just in the middle of her room, illuminated by moonlight, broad-shouldered and towering; he peered at her menacingly. Charles. He moved to the edge of her bed, leaning on the post.

Terror gripped her throat like the choking of seawater. She slowly leaned over to grab the string that would ring the bell for Miss Robins at the other end of the house. It was far out of reach.

"Don't," came a voice that she knew too well. She swallowed.

Her arm fell back to the bed.

"Hello wife," he said, slurring on the last syllable.

The air seemed thin, and Abby's breathing quickened. "I am not your wife yet, Charles. What do you want, coming into my room at this hour?"

"To see you, of course." The hatred in his voice pricked her like shards of ice, sending shivers down her spine. Charles had drunk himself into a rage. Thinking quickly, Abby reached for logic to assuage him.

"Father is downstairs," she said, struggling to keep her tone measured. "He would not permit you being here."

He chuckled, "Yessss, sleeping."

"It is late, Charles. Clearly you've had too much to drink. Please go home," said Abby, sitting up straighter. Then her own head was spinning. She inched back against the headboard, pulling the covers up to her chin.

God, help me! she thought.

"Drunk? You think this is drunk?" said Charles, gurgling a low laugh. "Is this what you're so afraid of?"

"Mr. Henderson, leave this instant."

"No," he said, "I'll stay right here, and so will you." The absoluteness of his statement sent Abby into a panic, constricting her throat. She could scarcely breathe.

If only Robins had stayed, or the servant quarters were closer, or Father had never brought him here . . . she thought. As Charles came nearer, he crept onto the mattress until he hovered over her. The stench of tobacco and brandy soaked the air making her gag. He loosened the belt around his waist.

"No, please. No."

She tried to shout, but no sound came out. She was powerless, trapped in her own fear as he closed in on her, pinning her beneath his weight. His hand covered her mouth, and her screams went unheard in the East Wing of Bristol Estate, for no soul slept there but her.

His rough hands held her fast, pressing down so that she felt she would break. Then, piercing pain. And Charles was a hurricane of desire and rage; a beast's fury had awakened, while Abby became the victim of its wrath.

Then the storm stilled. As he rose to leave, his eyes lifted from the bed to hers, and for a moment his demeanor shifted so that she thought she could read a note of disbelief, even shame, on his face.

"What . . ." was all she could say against the chattering of her teeth. Her thoughts raced, her mind unable to articulate the way she felt, bile now gnawing at the bottom of her throat. Abby did not know exactly what had happened. No one spoke of these things, especially to a girl of seventeen; she had no mother to turn to.

Charles leaned over her, his face pale and clammy.

"What have I done?" he said. She shook her head.

He stood up, swaying, so that he had to steady himself on the bedpost. He reached over for her blankets and threw them on top of her.

"You can't say a word," he hissed, suddenly more sober than before.

Abby's eyes widened in alarm. She trembled but said nothing.

"I mean it. Not a word, Abby. One word and you are ruined."

"Ruined?" she gasped.

That word began to draw back the curtain. *Ruined*—the formidable unspoken word only maids whispered of.

Charles nodded, the look of terror in his eyes even more evident than before. "Understand?"

She looked past him, her eyes welling with tears.

"Abby," he said low.

She did not understand. How did that word now apply to her? She sobbed, unable to hold back the tears. The sound made Charles cringe.

"Hush," he warned, "or someone might hear you."

She nodded and placed a hand over her mouth. She understood.

Charles stumbled away, catching his foot on the leg of her vanity chair and sending it toppling to the floor. The door closed behind him with a final click.

Abby reached for her pillow to muffle her sobs, but she felt the traces of filth sullying the sheets and scrambled off of them. She crossed the room, her bare feet padding down the hallway to the lavatory. Her legs carried her there, but a weary numbness filled them so that they felt like sacks of flour. Every movement hurt. She grimaced, trying to turn the spigot to fill the bucket with warm water. The tub waited all the way down the hall in the dressing room adjoining her bedchamber. After three laborious buckets were filled, her arms were past use. They strained against her, shaking violently with her efforts. The fourth bucket sloshed across the floor, leaving a trail of steaming puddles in its wake. She gave up and, peeling away her soiled garments, resigned herself to a shallow bath.

In the dim light of the dawn Abby detected red bruises marring her neck and collarbone. She squeezed the sponge, filling it again with water, and scrubbed until her skin was pink. But there are some things, she now knew, that cannot be washed away. Her hair fell around her like a heavy curtain of shame. She trembled in the tub, her tears mingling with the water which turned as cold as her soul felt. She prayed then, to the God of her mother, the one to whom she had entrusted her very soul and who now seemed so far removed from her lament.

I am ruined.

You are mine.

What am I to do now? Who am I now that . . .

You are mine.

She wept. For shame, for powerlessness, for all that she could not prevent or control.

A few minutes later, she heard the rustling of skirts shuffling down the hall. Abby lifted her head to see the rays of the rising sun through the window. She could not think of tomorrow; tomorrow that was now today. So, when Miss Robins rushed in, all she could do was tremble.

"My word! What's wrong child?" Miss Robins exclaimed, rushing to

Abby's side. Abby lifted her head and looked at her faithful friend.

"I did not want to wake you. It is only my monthly time."

"So soon? But you've been crying? And the mess in the hall. 'Twas why I came a run'n," Miss Robins questioned further, the wrinkles of her eyes deep with concern.

Abby took a pained breath closing her eyes. "I was—" Her chin trembled as flashes of the horror began to replay in her mind. She remembered Charles' warning, and fear gripped her heart. "—I was in pain, and then so sad thinking of Mother. I wish she were here." A genuine look of sympathy crossed Robins' brow, and Abby felt a stab into her heart, the deceit bitter on her tongue. *This is what being ruined is,* she thought, *lying to those I love.*

"Can you send breakfast up here?" she asked.

"Of course, dear."

When Miss Robins left on this errand, Abby rushed to dry and dress herself so that the marks on her skin would remain hidden.

Miss Robins returned and made a place on the chaise while the servants changed the bedsheets. The chair still lay on its side, calling suspicion its way. Robins eyed it, her face pinched, while she fret some unknown thought when Abby walked in from dressing.

"I've been so clumsy this morning," she said.

The second lie came easier than the first.

* * *

The rest of the day wilted away in silence. Miss Robins concocted a tea remedy that helped with pain and made Abby sleep, but even while sleeping, she was tormented.

Sir Rathburn remained absent from the house until late that evening, returning just before dinner. Miss Robins sent word that Abby was ill and again had her meal sent to her room, where the plate sat untouched on its tray. When Miss Robins came to prepare her charge for bed and bid her goodnight, Abby was already dressed in her nightclothes and sitting with a book.

"Shall I have Sir Rathburn call for the doctor?" she asked.

Abby shook her head.

Robins lingered in the room, humming softly as she busied herself with petty tasks that could wait until tomorrow. She laid out a dress, straightened up a few drawers, and even set out jewelry for the next day. Abby pretended to read, but Miss Robins was far too perceptive. After failing to turn the page for some time, Robins came closer. She peered over at Abby, biting the edge of her lip. Abby kept her gaze focused on the page of her book, her mind teeming with questions far beyond the printed letters in front of her nose. The whys turned into silent accusations, an unbidden voice hissing in her ear. *It is all your fault. You should have kept your mouth shut like your father told you.* Abby shivered.

Miss Robins cleared her throat, and Abby set it down.

"I have something for you, my lady."

Abby shifted her attention to Miss Robins' wary eye. Robins rarely applied the formal term "my lady" when addressing Abby unless in the company of her father or guests.

"Forgive me," said Miss Robins.

"Why would that be necessary?" said Abby, fighting to keep her composure.

"I should've brought this earlier," said Miss Robins, withdrawing a small card from her apron pocket. "Your Mr. Henderson sent it early this morning. I'm terribly sorry, my dear."

"For what?" said Abby more curtly than intended, her nerves ragged.

"I thought it odd when he dropped it off himself. I had such a strange feeling in the night. Perhaps it was a noise I heard . . . really, I can't understand it myself. Then, this morning I found you in such a state—" Miss Robins' face twisted into a pitiful look of remorse, and tears blotted her cheeks.

Miss Robins handed over the letter. Charles' seal was broken. Abby's eyes grew wide, dread crawling up her spine. Her face hardened, fighting to remain composed as she unfolded the letter.

Robins took in a ragged breath as Abby read:

> *Dearest Abigail,*
> *I trust you slept well, and I hope you remember our discussion for I have not forgotten it. We must keep to our plans, or else all else would unravel at your expense.*
> *Yours ever faithfully,*
> *Charles*

Bile rose up in the back of Abby's throat, and she fought the urge to crumple the paper in her hands while Robins looked on.

"You're as white as a sheet," said Miss Robins, and Abby wondered how she could be so keenly perceptive at such an old age.

She returned her gaze to her maid, the woman who knew her better than anyone. She opened her mouth to speak but quickly caught herself. Not even she could know.

This fact, this damning secret, set itself to work so that in the span of a few blinks, Abby's very heart stood barricaded behind walls of stone so thick and high that none could scale.

She looked back at Miss Robins. "You read this?" Abby's voice poured out cool and collected.

Miss Robins nodded.

"And?" said Abby, sitting up straighter in her bed.

"Well, what does it mean? What has happened?"

"Nothing. I do not know why you thought it such an affair. It was only a small disagreement between Charles and me," said Abby, the words slipping out effortlessly this time. Even as she spoke, her mind began darkening with visions of the previous night, collecting like lingering cobwebs.

Miss Robins folded her arms, studying Abby. Abby saw that her answer had hardly satisfied Robins' fretful mind.

"Leave me. I am tired," said Abby.

Miss Robins started for the door then hesitated.

"Shall I wake you for church in the morning?"

"No," said Abby before she could stop herself. Miss Robins nodded again like a timid dog submitting to its master. This, Abby could not bear.

"As you wish," said Miss Robins and then she turned away without another word. Abby's heart dropped—she could not endure any more pain, especially pain evoked by her own actions.

"Robins," she called out softly. Miss Robins stepped back across the threshold.

"I am not upset with you," said Abby.

Robins nodded again and left the room. Abby longed to chase after her and cling to her skirts like she had as a child, confessing all of the horrors that had befallen.

With the night came floods of tears to stain her pillow. The initial shock had worn off, leaving her defenseless. She thought of Charles, wrestling with questions beyond this world. He had sought her out to hurt her in the vilest way possible. This she could not understand in her pain, and she despised him for it. For his control over her, for his ruthlessness, for heaping shame upon her that she did not deserve, and for dooming her to loneliness and isolation from those she loved dearly. The glowing coal hardened, cooling into a hatred she had once thought herself immune from. She held it like a stone in her hand, ready to hurl it at Charles given the opportunity.

An hour before dawn, three simple words came to her mind: *If Father knew* . . . She trembled. "Wyndham" and "scandal" did not coincide. The consequences of her father knowing equaled disownment. The streets would forever be her pillow, loneliness her only friend.

There was nowhere to bury this horror except inside herself—and Charles. She was trapped in the sickening thought. She must marry Charles Henderson, for he alone could hide the disgrace he had heaped upon her.

She looked to the window, drawn shut by a simple latch. One turn and it would open to the chill. One step up and her bare toes would teeter on the ledge and the wind would swirl her shift around her ankles. One step out and . . . the sweetness of relief. The end.

No.

She sobbed, thinking herself too weak to submit her life to purposeful death. Yet, even in her despair, there was a resolve that no scandal—and no man—could dampen. She sensed it, taking some small comfort in the One to whom she could tell all, the One who already knew her heart. The One who, she knew, would redeem her.

Chapter 7

The carriage offered little comfort against the chill. While Abby waited, she could see the early traces of fall etched across the landscape. The large oak tree already bled rich reddish hues at the tips of its leaves. When the wind let out its breath and whipped through the gaps in the carriage door, the tree shook with fury.

Abby shivered, closing her wool coat tighter around her. Sitting opposite her, Robins studied her pale face, a look of concern marking her brow. The sun rose above the hanging clouds, every second ascending higher into the sky.

Langley tapped his foot on the stone steps, "Where is he?" he said, seemingly unaware that the wind carried his mutterings straight to Abby's ears.

Robins pursed her lips in worry and leaned over to Abby. "Your father came in late last night from his visit with Mr. Henderson; I heard him fumbling in the servants' quarters downstairs again."

"You mean the wine closet?" asked Abby.

"Yes. I supposed Mr. Henderson liked to send him home sober."

Abby winced at the mention of Charles. Had he confessed to Father? Perhaps that is why her father had sought solace in drink last night.

Just then, Timothy came rushing down the steps of the front door.

"My lady, Sir Rathburn asked for you to tell Reverend Truitt he's ill."

Abby nodded.

"But he did say he will be ready to dine at noon," he added.

Abby sighed. "Very well, then."

On Sundays Charles had taken up the habit of dining with her and her father. Perhaps today he would find an excuse to stay away. The carriage jolted forward down the gravel pathway toward the church. Abby's stomach had been knotted with worry, but now she breathed a small sigh of relief, thinking that she at least did not have to endure the presence of her father and his mockery of the "Institution of Modern Christendom." Nor did she have to deal with his judgmental stare.

The country road rocked the carriage, making Abby aware of each ache in her body. She bit the inside of her cheek, staring out of the window.

They arrived just five minutes before nine o'clock, in time to be greeted by Reverend Truitt and his wife, with their endearing warm southern drawl. The Reverend's full cheeks showcased the sincerity of his smile as he welcomed each of the parishioners inside. To all women he offered a gentle kiss on their hand. Normally Abby thought nothing of this simple gesture, but today panic seized her at the thought of receiving it.

Her turn came before she had convinced herself how she should respond. "Miss Wyndham, always such a joy to see you," said Reverend Truitt, reaching for her hand. She mustered a weak smile but kept her hands clasped in front of her. "Father sends his regrets, Reverend. He was feeling out of sorts this morning," she said, avoiding his gaze. She felt the heat rising in her cheeks.

"I'm sorry to hear he is ill," he said. Abby nodded and quickly slipped away, offering a polite smile to Mrs. Truitt.

Miss Robins left her side for the company of an old friend. Robins rarely spent any time apart from Abby, and to deny her maid this rare pleasure was quite out of the question despite Abby's sense of isolation on this particular day.

The scene felt surreal to Abby, when only a short week before she had glided through those same aisles freely, catching the smiles of a few rowdy children. Now shame clawed at her conscience. Even with her frock's collar rising clear up to her chin, she felt exposed. All because of Charles. Hate smoldered in the recesses of her mind. Remembering where she was, she kept her attention focused on the empty pew in front of her.

Eliza Pennington rose from the end of the pew to greet Abby, her blonde ringlets bouncing on her shoulders. With Sir Rathburn's urging, Eliza had become a close acquaintance since Abby's arrival to the states. She was two years Abby's senior. The Penningtons had secured their wealth from a host of whaling ships off the coast—a fact that suited Sir Rathburn, for their wealth and connections cast his net wider.

Every stitch adorning Eliza's curvy figure bespoke affluence. She moved like a feline around men, as though she were stalking her prey with undulating exaggerated movements and deep dimpled grins, until they were securely trapped in her talons. It worked in her favor, for she never wont for a gentleman's hand at any ball.

Though Abby herself had never experienced the lash of Eliza's tongue, she feared it. Once, Eliza unleashed a stream of whispers about Beth Donnaway, saying that the young girl had been spotted kissing her beau. Before the day's end, nearly everyone knew of the "incident," and Miss Donnaway was shipped off to Virginia on the early morning train to stay with her aunt.

As Eliza neared, a crease formed on her brow as though she were trying to weave together clues as to why Abby looked so out of sorts.

"Well, don't you look chipper this morn," she said. Abby offered a thin smile in return.

"And that dress. It so suits you," she said, tilting her head so that her curls bounced with her perusing eyes. Abby looked down over her plain cotton printed dress picked out specifically to draw the least amount of attention.

"Thank you, Eliza," said Abby, looking past Eliza's shoulder to see if another spot was vacant next to Robins, but Robins was already nestled between a couple of older widows, deep in conversation.

Eliza inched closer so that Abby could smell her sweet breath. "Do tell me what your wedding gown looks like. I hear that your father sent a merchant all the way to Paris after it."

Abby's heart sank. The thought of wedding Charles in any gown felt like shackles pulling her down . . . down . . . down.

"Abby?"

Abby's attention returned to Eliza. "Sorry . . . what were you saying?"

"Is it true you got satin and lace from Europe?"

"Father ordered some, but I refused it," said Abby.

"What would possess you to do that? All we have here are boring old washes that every other girl will be wearing this season," said Eliza.

"My mother," said Abby.

Eliza knit her brow together, then blurted out, "I can't see why that matters. Didn't she die ages ago?"

Abby's mouth fell open.

Eliza continued, "It just seems like your mother would rather you get what you want, right?"

Stunned by the callousness of Eliza's remark, Abby countered, "I'll be wearing her wedding gown. That is entirely what I want, and the closest thing I can get to her being present herself." It was true. When she and Miss Robins had pulled the gown from the old trunk, Abby knew it was what she wanted for her wedding day. Her father abhorred the idea, insisting a Wyndham would only wear the finest for such an occasion. But it was indeed in mint condition, intricately styled, and when Sir Rathburn saw it laid out before him, he uttered no retort; instead, he turned and rushed from the room without another word.

Eliza sat quietly for a moment, then let out a light laugh. "What a pity. It's probably moth-eaten by now. Well, if it were *my* wedding, I would choose something simply splendid. White satin maybe? Oh, yes, just like Queen Victoria. Pastels are so blasé nowadays, and I would be certain to make a statement in front of all of those people," she said, gesturing to the congregation that had gathered with a dimpled grin. Eliza returned her attention to Abby and patted her arm. "But don't worry. I'm sure that old gown will suit you perfectly. White would probably just wash you out. Especially today. You do look so pale."

Abby sat, silent for a moment, and then decidedly replied, "If it would suit you, when your day comes, I will bid my father to fetch you your very own white satin bolts from Paris."

It was Eliza's turn for her mouth to drop. *There's one way to dam her tongue,* thought Abby, offering a polite smile. When she moved her attention to the pulpit, Eliza still sat, dumbfounded.

Reverend Truitt rose and called the congregation to prayer. The crowd hushed against the solemn tone of their reverend, and Abby sat down next to Eliza with a healthy buffer of space between them.

Sore in mind and body, Abby did not sing along to the lively hymns the Reverend's wife pounded on the organ. Eliza's high soprano voice scrambled all wholesome thoughts trying to edge their way into Abby's mind, so that she could not even mouth the words. The chord of her soul seemed to play in a minor key, incongruous with the melody around her.

Then Mrs. Truitt's fingers slowed, working their way down the scale. The Reverend opened his mouth and began to sing a tune that Eliza did not know. Abby closed her eyes and listened. His smooth tenor voice fell on her ears, as though a soothing balm to her soul.

> *Though the angry surges roll*
> *On my tempest-driven soul,*
> *I am peaceful, for I know,*
> *Wildly though the winds may blow,*
> *I've an anchor safe and sure,*
> *That can evermore endure.*
> *And it holds, my anchor holds:*
> *Blow your wildest, then, O gale,*
> *On my bark so small and frail;*
> *By His grace I shall not fail,*
> *For my anchor holds, my anchor holds...*
>
> *Griefs like billows o'er me roll;*
> *Tempters seek to lure astray;*
> *Storms obscure the light of day:*
> *But in Christ I can be bold,*
> *I've an anchor that shall hold.*

By the hymn's end, stray tears were rolling down Abby's face—a full public confession of her turmoil.

At the waning of the Reverend's voice, Abby opened her eyes to find none standing beside her. Heat filled her cheeks as she felt the stares of the entire room bore into her back. As discreetly as possible, she lowered her head and wiped the last of the tears from her face. Eliza grinned broadly at the person sitting on the other side of the aisle. When Abby turned to her, Eliza's brows arched high, with an air of smugness akin to a peacock ruffling its feathers at a quail. Abby tried to find her seat, but as she squeezed into the crowded pew, she bumped into a solid frame next to her.

"I'm so sorry," she whispered as she looked to see who had ventured so near to her seat. "No need to apologize," said Charles, his dark eyes making her stomach lurch.

Her breath caught in her throat. A guttural instinct to scream out or hit and claw at him threatened to overtake her. When he settled his hand on top of hers she fought to hide her mounting fear, for all eyes were keenly aware of the prominent couple in the third pew. Eliza turned to Abby as Abby subtly withdrew her hand from Charles' touch.

For the remainder of the service, Eliza's head bobbed from Charles to Abby and back to the pulpit. Every now and then, she would catch Charles' eyes and sneak a coy smile. All the while, Abby battled every muscle in her body by remaining still in the blur of rising panic. *Leave,* she thought. *But then all the townspeople will wonder why . . .* She felt his every breath, as the Grendel of all of her terrors sat poised beside her like a man with a clear conscience. It appeared Charles Henderson feared no one, not even God.

At the closing benediction, the congregation was dismissed. Abby turned from Charles only to be confronted by Eliza's inquiries.

"You're awfully pale; are you sick?" she asked, and in the same breath she looked past Abby to Charles. "She didn't look quite so dreadful just before you arrived."

Abby gripped the back of the pew in front of them because now she did feel ill, and Eliza's internal glee at her discomfort was written across her face.

"You should get some fresh air," said Eliza, stepping aside so that Abby could pass. Abby shuffled by without a backwards glance, exiting the nave and making her way toward the crowded foyer. Before Abby could make her way into the throng, Miss Robins caught her with a tap on the shoulder. "Won't you ask Mr. Henderson to ride in our carriage back to the house? He walked all the way this morning. Your father said he would be dining with us this afternoon." She paused, looking past Abby to Eliza's blushing cheeks and trilling laughter. Robins' voice lowered to a horrified whisper. "And by the looks of it, Miss Pennington might eat him for lunch. She's quite the church-belle today. The way she carries on with him—an engaged man—and I haven't seen such a disgraceful Sunday dress in my entire time on God's good earth."

Suspended in a fit of laughter, Eliza's shrill voice rose above the crowd. Abby looked over her shoulder. Eliza's hand rested on the top of Charles' arm, while her plunging bustline revealed entirely too much of her well-endowed bosom. *You can have him,* she thought. Still, desperate to get outside, she continued towards the exit.

"Quickly now, or else the room will be buzzing," called Robins after her.

"Let it buzz," said Abby.

The church doors were too small for all of the people pouring through them, but Abby could wait no longer, so she waded her way through the sea of smartly dressed men and women and restless children, pressing for the open air. She kept her head down so as not to invite any further quizzical stares. Reverend Truitt waited in his usual place holding the door open. Abby slipped by as a young couple grappled with their two toddling children.

Behind the church a makeshift garden butted up against its back wall. The area held only a few shade trees and purple wisteria vines. Abby retreated there, leaning with her shoulder against the wall, and wept.

"Miss Wyndham, is that you?" came a voice, pulling the reins on her thoughts. The scuff of footsteps drew closer. Abby turned, squinting in the glare of the sun, to find Reverend Truitt approaching. She hurriedly pat her face on the back of her gloves. He reached out, offering his hand. She ignored it and continued using the wall as a support instead. The Reverend studied her with a sideways glance, worry clouding his smile.

"You all right?"

Abby shrugged.

"I know a troubled soul when I see one. Is there anything I can do to help?"

Abby did not trust herself to answer. She fixed her gaze on the leaves rustling in the distance. They wriggled and writhed against the branches, but their green stems held them fast. In a few more days they would wither and die, but at least they would fly free. Abby's eyes stung with the threat of fresh tears. *Is it so wrong to wish I were dead?* she thought.

Miss Robins' voice echoed through the garden.

"Sounds like they're waiting on you, Miss Wyndham. Shall I walk you?"

Abby looked into the Reverend's eyes, finding a gentleness that struck her as incongruous for a man. It grieved her.

"I suppose that would be okay, Reverend. Thank you," said Abby, finally taking the Reverend's arm.

As they circled towards the front of the church, Charles waited beside the horses, glowering at her, before climbing into the carriage. The Reverend tilted his head towards hers and spoke quietly. "If you find yourself in a difficult situation, know that you always have a friend in my wife and me." Abby looked at him, suddenly nervous that he had somehow seen the truth.

"What would make you say that?" she whispered back.

He nodded towards the carriage where Charles hunkered in the shadows. "Like I said before, I know a troubled soul when I see one." He gently squeezed her arm and managed a grim smile.

"Thank you, Reverend. You are so kind to walk me," she answered so that Charles could hear. The Reverend offered her up into the carriage, whispering again into her ear, "Take courage, dear Abigail."

Chapter 8

One question gnawed at Charles as he reclined in the far side of the carriage. Across from him, Miss Robins had already begun her prattling and Abby sat beside her maid, intent on ignoring Charles' presence. *Whom has she told?* he wondered.

The carriage bounded along toward Bristol Estate. He glanced at Abby, but she refused to acknowledge him, her blotchy cheeks still puffy, dark circles shadowing her eyes. Charles swallowed and looked away. Robins felt the thick of the tension, he was sure of it. She wrung her fingers and bit her lip so that it appeared to Charles the old woman no longer had any teeth at all.

Charles flexed the muscles in his jaw, seething. All of his plans now hinged on the composure of the weak, wounded, feeble mind of a young girl who had already raised suspicion with her careless antics at church. He could not understand why she would come to church only to make a pathetic spectacle of herself. Yet, he could not fully silence the nagging truth that clamored for his attention when he took in the sight of her. In spite of himself it stabbed him, for although Abby suffered, she was still wholly devoted. She was still good in a way that he would never be.

When Miss Robins leaned over to get a clearer look at Abby, Charles rolled his eyes.

"Are you all right dear?" she asked.

Abby nodded weakly, but Miss Robins hesitated before sitting back in her seat.

Charles sat in silence until his anger quelled. But Robins nattered on foolishly to no one in particular, remarking on the exceptional weather for this early fall day, and her preference for the weather here compared with London's. As she continued, Charles hatched a plan to douse his fears. And when they crossed the bridge, he was ready for action.

"It is beautiful this afternoon, Miss Robins. I don't know if I would have seen it without you pointing it out. Look Abby, see how the leaves are beginning to change color?"

"Indeed," she said, keeping her head down.

Charles tilted his head towards the window, making a concerted effort to peer out at the sunlight.

"And here we are wasting the day away in this stuffy carriage." He pushed the door open, leaning his head out. "Stop, driver!" he exclaimed.

"You'll give Langley a stroke, leaning out so far while going this fast," cried Robins.

Langley pulled the reins and the horses trotted to a stop, a cloud of dust collecting around the carriage.

Charles leaned towards Abby. "We're only a mile away. I know how you love a good walk."

Abby sat up straight, her eyes glossy. "I am not feeling well," she said.

"The sunshine will do you a world of good," Charles insisted.

Miss Robins nodded. "You do love a good walk about, and at least Charles can keep up."

Charles noted this comment, and felt momentary relief thinking that the old maid at least must be unaware.

Langley opened the door and Charles stepped out. He ducked his head back inside and held out his hand towards Abby.

She sat straight and stiff, her fear almost palpable as she glanced at Charles and then again towards Robins, who for once was clearly oblivious.

"Come on now, Abby. If it proves too much for you, I will carry you," he said with his most charming smile. She did not move. Charles let out a laugh to dispel any hint of suspicion.

"Come on, before I snatch you out of there myself," he said playfully.

Her visage transformed from fear to resignation. "It seems I have no choice," she said icily. When he took her hand, her whole body tensed. Her fingers felt cold and clammy in his palm.

Miss Robins let out a nervous laugh. "If any trolls come, I trust you'll keep her safe."

"No doubt," said Charles.

The horses lurched forward. Charles held Abby's hand in his. As soon as the carriage was out of sight, she wrenched it away and began blazing forward like a steamer late to port.

At least all pretenses are cast aside, thought Charles. "Why were you talking with the Reverend?" he shouted after her. She stopped and spun around while he closed the space between them. Strands of her dark hair blew free of its plait, contrasting against her pale face.

"Is that what this is about?"

"Tell me what you said to him."

"*He* sought me out."

"Because *you* blubbered your way out of the church, making a such a scene. And in front of the whole town! What did you tell him?"

"Nothing of your concern," she said, glowering.

"Anything you do is my concern."

"Is it real concern, Mr. Henderson, or is it only to make sure no one knows what kind of a gentleman you really are?" Abby's green eyes glared at Charles, stoking the coals of his anger.

He snatched her arm. "Don't pretend you didn't enjoy it," he spat.

"Get your hands off of me or I swear I will scream, you monster," she said boldly, though he detected a tremor as she spoke.

A pang of guilt pierced Charles' heart, dousing his anger, and he released his hold. Then he was even more frustrated with her and himself.

She ran forward, leaving him trailing behind her until the rustle of her skirts slowed, and she stopped. Her arms wrapped around her chest. Her eyes pooled, red and blotchy, as fresh tears spilled down, but she said nothing. Her shoulders trembled while she heaved quiet sobs. Then she took a deep breath and trudged forward on the packed dirt road.

She's just trying to make me feel guilty, thought Charles, *and it's working.*

He let out a moan in frustration. "Abby, wait." When she did not stop, he shouted after her. "You slapped me across the face! What did you expect to come of that?"

Then she turned to face him, her voice low and grave. "You deserve a whole lot more, but may God himself handle the rest." She turned back to the path, leaving him wide eyed and sending a shudder down his spine. What did he deserve? He shrugged off the thought.

"How was I supposed to know you were so . . . so . . . chaste?" he said.

She whirled back around, walking straight toward him. Her quivering hand tore at the collar of her dress, exposing the bottom of her neck down to the top of her chest near the collarbone. Dark bruises marred its otherwise flawless surface.

"Don't you dare look away now."

He sighed, shame overcoming him.

"Did I ask for this? Seeing that you are finally sober, perhaps you can recall your actions," she said. A breeze blew by, making her shiver. "Ruined. That is what you have done to me"—she kicked the dirt, sending a small plume of dust towards him—"you coward."

Charles stared at the bruises for a moment longer and then tore his eyes away. His stomach churned, leaving him queasy, as though a snake were uncoiling itself inside. He fought back the urge to vomit.

Why did I do this? He thought of his own father, a true gentleman who never would have harmed a woman of any station of society. He thought of his mother, so devoted, so virtuous—then pushed the thought from his mind before it could go any further. But Abby had risen against Charles' own taunting, wakening a monster inside, a monster Charles never knew existed. He cupped his head in his hands, appalled by the evidence of his actions.

Abby looked at him, her face distorting into a confused mess of hurt. Then she let loose a sob, moaning so loudly that Charles feared someone might hear. He rushed to her, grabbing her around the waist, and cupped his hand over her mouth. She cried out louder, but his hand muffled the sound.

"Hush! Just be quiet, and I will let you go." She trembled violently, her volume increasing. Charles pressed his lips to her ear so that she could hear. "Abby! You're screaming."

Then, she stopped. Her eyes bulged wide with fright.

"Will you keep quiet so I can let you go? I'm not going to hurt you." She nodded slowly and he released his hold.

She repositioned her garments to cover the bruises, her hands still shaking. Charles looked at her, trying to mask his own fear. He needed her to be okay, or at least to appear that way. He removed his coat and draped it around her shoulders. She cringed but did not refuse it. When she had calmed, Charles questioned her further, gently this time.

"So, you didn't tell anyone?"

She didn't look at him. "It would have done me no good."

Charles nodded and breathed a sigh of relief. "Really?"

Her blink was slow, her gaze distant. "Like I said. It would have done me no good."

Charles felt a flutter of optimism. He just had to convince her of it. "Then, we can still marry and the future is not compromised." He held his arm out to her, expecting relief to sweep across her features. She stared blankly forward, her eyes low and lifeless. Suddenly an image flashed unbidden in his mind: the empty, hopeless stares of the slaves shackled in the holds of his own ships bound for the South.

Some unknown emotion caught in Charles' throat. He wanted to reassure her, but he could not find the words. She held a power over Charles unlike anyone he had ever known. Whatever goodness flowed through her only brought out the worst in him. As he watched her walk away, standing tall despite her shame, he cowered at the realization. In her he saw a reflection of his own fear—the fear of himself, of what he had become and what he was capable of. He felt a sudden overwhelming urge to protect her, but did not know how, for how could he protect her from himself?

Chapter 9

The Dowager Lady Margaret Wyndham stared back at Abby, her expression as cold and unfeeling as her title dictated. Though she was no more alive than her likeness captured by the detailed strokes of an artist's brush, the portrait of her late grandmama nevertheless offered a level of comfort, reminding Abby of sweet days at Devonsfield where the portrait had hung in the hallway just outside of her nursery.

In both temperament and appearance, the woman was strikingly different from Abby's mother. Where Abby's mother was doting and outwardly affectionate, The Dowager seemed impenetrable and stoical, her expression inscrutable to the young Abby. Abby knew, however, from her lavish gifts and the occasional muted smile, that her grandmother had approved of her, though she would dare not use the word "love." That was simply not the way of a Wyndham lady. Her last years at Devonsfield were spent largely confined to a wing-back chair positioned near the large picture window overlooking the gardens. As her body weakened, her mood declined and Abby began to fear the woman, speaking to her only when bidden. When she passed, not long after Abby's mother, Abby felt a measure of relief, though now, admiring the visage before her, an understanding seemed to dawn. Abby wondered what lay behind that cold stare; whether she, too, had been hardened to the world as a man's possession.

The pulls on Abby's scalp brought her back to reality, a place she did not like to be as of late. Miss Robins tugged at her locks, trying to put the curls in their proper place before the final fitting of her wedding gown.

Abby studied the painting again. Her grandmama's hands lay clasped across her lap, the purple veins protruding slightly from her skin. Her lips were pursed together in a grim line. Her husband stood over her, though he functioned more like a backdrop in the work. The distance between the husband and wife was perceptible, though Abby had never noticed it before. There was a sadness, even regret, frozen in that space of time. If Abby could ask her, what would she say? What seed planted and grew into a gulf between them? What had caused the grim expression and haunted eyes? What sleepless nights had ailed the great Dowager?

Abby's chest tightened, and her nerves ached with fatigue. The sensation had become familiar to her over the last few months. Terms with Charles were strained at best. Thankfully, she was afforded a bit of space when he left on a business trip along the coast, visiting his clients and taking inventory. Abby was grateful for the reprieve, but the time had done little to lessen the damage. She could hardly sleep and felt as though she had been damned to a life of silence.

She hid the truth somewhere between the folds of fabric, flower arrangements, guest lists, and continual wedding preparations. She inhaled deeply, trying again to ease the tension in her chest. Her mouth suddenly felt dry, and a cold sweat gathered on her forehead. Robins stopped her pulling and put a cold hand on Abby's forehead.

"Might you call for tea?" asked Abby in a weak voice.

Robins surrendered her battle against Abby's hair and shook her head.

"All this stress is pil'n on you, making you ill. I'll fetch tea, but first we must get you into your gown. Mrs. Allen t'will up shortly to make the final adjustments, and you know she's not keen on tardiness."

Abby nodded. Robins lifted it carefully from the floor, and Abby slid her arms through the fitted sleeves. Robins strained to fasten the loops around the buttons, pausing every other one to readjust Abby's stays. By the time she had buttoned the top one, Abby's ribs felt as though they might snap.

"There we are," said Miss Robins with a sigh. "You look every bit like your mother."

Abby managed a smile, and Miss Robins left on her errand. Finally alone, the air pressed in around her like a thick smog. Beads of sweat gathered on her head. Abby tried to sit, but that made the feeling worse.

She took in a breath, slowly this time. It was as though she couldn't get enough air in her lungs. The stays smarted her ribs so that they felt like she might never breath normally again. Mrs. Allen had visited only a fortnight before after stitching each seam to fit. Such a skilled dressmaker would not have botched her gown.

Abby reached back, feeling the bumps along the curve of her back where the buttons were taut; straining, she unhooked the upper ones only to find it offered no relief. Her stays were the real foe, but their strings were out of reach. She walked over to the mirror. The pale blue satin stretched tight around her waist. Although the gown had spent many years tucked away in a trunk, the expensive fabric had retained its sheen.

Despite her discomfort, she smiled thinking of her mother. Much to her father's disapproval, Abby had insisted on wearing her mother's wedding gown. Her father had ordered fabric for a new gown from Paris himself, insisting that a Wyndham lady would not be presented to the public in such out-of-date attire. It was Mrs. Allen who had finally intervened on the matter, saying that she would ensure it not look old and worn, and that she had never seen such fine material to work with in her whole time as a dressmaker.

The clatter of china announced Miss Robins' return. Mrs. Allen followed, a basket of pins, scissors, and scraps of fabric hanging from her arm. Her steel gray hair was parted down the middle and tied back in a simple low bun.

Abby greeted her warmly. Mrs. Allen had proven to be a master of her trade. Since Abby's arrival, she had been her sole seamstress. For what skills she lacked in conversation—always blurting out whatever was on her mind—she made up for in her obvious affection for Abby.

"Good day, my lady. The dress is most becoming on you, I do see. I did wonder if that color'd suit you, and I don't think another soul could wear it better," said Mrs. Allen, gesturing to the gown. "Now, turn 'round so I can see the full of it."

Abby hesitated, trying to remember if she had hooked the buttons back into place, then she turned full circle. Mrs. Allen gawked.

"Well, what's this?" Mrs. Allen donned her spectacles for a closer examination of her subject. Abby sucked in, hoping it would be enough.

"Hmm . . ." said Mrs. Allen after a failed attempt to loop the buttons back.

Abby inhaled again.

Mrs. Allen shook her head. "Now, my lady, ye must be sure to hold back on the salt and sweets. Too much'll make ye bloat, see."

Miss Robins let out a nervous laugh. "She's not much for the sugary sorts, are you Abby? There must have been a mistake when you took her measurements last."

Color flushed up Mrs. Allen's neck, rising to her cheeks. "Thirty odd years it's been o' me bending and measuring to make frocks to women's liking. I don't know how to make a mistake like this even in a drowsed stupor."

Miss Robins patted her chest. "Well, what're we to do about it now? Looks like she can hardly breathe."

"Like I said before, Miss Wyndham must stay away from extra courses to manage her stress 'fore the wedding so I can adjust it in time."

"I don't think she needs any added pressure."

"We've got nigh on a few weeks. I am sure if she's more aware of what she's eating, it'll fit in time for the wedding. See, 'tis only pulling there at the waist . . . and perhaps the bosom," said Mrs. Allen.

Abby's cheeks flushed. Swallowing hard, she managed a polite nod. In truth, decadent desserts had become much more attractive to her usually savory palate. Her stays dug into her sides, squeezing the breath out of her. She felt herself shrinking as she stood there, pressed into the gown under such scrutiny.

"Well, we ought call Sir Rathburn for his approval 'fore she takes it off. You know what a fuss he made over reusing it in the first place. I can't afford to have him disapprove. He would put me out of business," said Mrs. Allen.

Abby's heart quickened. Tears threatened, and she wished for a tougher demeanor, like that of Lady Wyndham, one that would be an ally in times of distress. Instead, her eyes misted over. Her cheeks were one moment flushed, then paled, and she could not decide if she felt hot or cold. Sweat gathered beneath her stays, trickling down her back.

"Tea?" asked Robins, placing the saucer in Abby's hands.

Her fingers trembled at the touch of the smooth porcelain. She was sure that the tea would help level her, but the cup never made it to her lips. A black cloud engulfed her sight, and she fell back into an unconscious void. The last thing she saw was the liquid, dark and menacing, spilling down the front of her mother's gown.

* * *

Abby's eyes remained closed as her wits gradually returned. Still hunched beside her, Mrs. Allen and Miss Robins spoke in hushed tones, seemingly unaware that their patient was coming to. Quilted blankets weighed down on her, matching the feeling of her eyelids.

"I can't imagine what's come over her," said Miss Robins, sounding tearful.

"Don't fret now. I reckon it's a bit 'o the nerves," said Mrs. Allen.

"I do hope so. She's been acting so strange, hardly talk'n at all, that I fear it's something worse."

"What of Mr. Henderson? Is she keen on the lad?"

"Thought she was at one time, but as of late she seems woozy even at the mention of him."

"What are your thoughts of 'em?"

Miss Robins paused. "It's not my place to say, but there's something that feels wrong with him. He's always polite in company, but something about 'em gives me the shivers. I suppose I couldn't find a man on this whole earth good enough for her, though."

Mrs. Allen's voice dropped to barely above a whisper. "Poor lass. I've seen many a woman drool over this girl's bless'ns. She's got all the money, the looks, the name. But I often wonder if they're more burdens. Sir Rathburn, he's not a joking man."

"Ah, indeed. And what's money when it's not your own? And what's a name unless you are a man to make use of it? I dare say she looks the spitting image of her mother, and as beautiful as that makes her, Sir Rathburn can hardly stand the sight."

There was a long pause and some shuffling around, then Miss Robins continued.

"Oh, now I've said too much!" whispered Miss Robins, and she adjusted the quilts over Abby.

"I'll not say a peep. But shall we tell her father she is ill?"

"I'll send word in case he wants to fetch a doctor," said Miss Robins as she placed her hand on Abby's forehead.

"I'll go with you and let the poor lass rest. I must be gett'n on soon else my husband will be eat'n raw potatoes for his supper. I'll come on the morrow to see what can be done."

They left the room together, a welcome cool breeze running through Abby's hair as they opened the door to the hallway. Abby opened her eyes, drowsy and disoriented. She took in a deep breath and, peeling off the heavy blankets, was relieved to find herself freed of the dreadful corset.

As she sat up, the colors and shapes around her morphed from blurry swirls of light to the familiar furnishings bathed in a late afternoon glow. She was slow in remembering what had brought her to lie in only her shift on the chaise. But when her eyes found the dress draped across her bed, she remembered. She stood, swaying on her feet, and took in the sight of the dark stain streaking down its entire length from bosom to hem, in frightful contrast to its light blue sheen.

Her fingers ran over the stain and found it still damp on the satin. A glimmer of hope fluttered in her chest.

She hastened towards her water basin to find a cloth. She wet it and rushed back to the bedside. Her hands went to work, doctoring the blemish, scrubbing gently at first. The discoloration proved unforgiving. She scoured it with determination, but it was like a bruise beneath the skin, and no amount of scrubbing could wash it away.

She cried out, choking on her tears.

Miss Robins emerged from the corridor, walking slowly into the room to find Abby sobbing. Her hands stroked the top of Abby's hair. "You ought to lie back down. You're unwell."

"No. No. I must mend this. It's all my fault."

"It couldn't be helped, my dear."

The dam Abby had fought so hard to build over the last few months broke. All her unheard tears spilled out, so that Miss Robins could only hold her in confusion.

"Dear child, what is all this about? 'Tis only a dress. I am sure Mrs. Allen can fix it."

Abby could only sob in response. She wished it were *only* a gown. She wished that what she cried were petty tears of sentimentalism, because then there might be an end to her sorrow; but the tears that she cried welled up from a bottomless pit of pain, leaving her raw and exposed.

Miss Robins held her, until her sobs eased. But just as Abby caught her breath, another wave hit her—not of sorrow but nausea. To her disgust and horror, she realized her worst fear had become reality.

She knew she was not facing this marriage with only her future in question, but also the fate of a child, conceived in the worst of circumstances.

* * *

By evening, Abby's thoughts swarmed with questions numbering with the stars. Miss Robins had done her best to calm her charge after the incident with the wedding dress, but Abby could not hold her attention on a single thing for long. She kept sending Miss Robins away to let her rest. Her cheeks puffed up with the constant stream of tears, so that by the evening's end, Abby's head throbbed.

She sat unmoving, as Miss Robins finished brushing her hair. Miss Robins kept up conversation as though Abby were a willing participant, but Abby remained listless and unaware.

Miss Robins leaned nearer. "There's n'er a more solemn beauty."

"What?"

"The moon, my dear," said Miss Robins, tilting her head up to the sky. The moon beamed her glory out into the night that would otherwise be a dismal scene. Abby looked away, wondering why Miss Robins was so poetic all of a sudden when her whole life was in tatters.

"Do you know what happened the night of your birth?"

Abby shook her head.

"I'll ne'er forget it. The moon looked just that way, full and bright. Sir Rathburn paced the floor, while your mother labored well into night. Not a one of us slept; the house was in such a frenzy. He was so distraught seeing her in pain, thinking that he might lose her. Then suddenly you came. Pink and wailing into the darkness. Oh, what a set of lungs you had. And your dear mother's pain turned to joy. One look on your face, and all of it was worth it."

Abby lifted her eyes, too aware of the pulsing at her temples. The moon's light danced behind the skimming clouds like a vessel on the open waters.

"And Father?"

Miss Robins lowered her head, her lips turning to a frown. "Well, he wanted an heir."

"And was given a daughter, good for nothing."

"He was *gifted* you, Abby."

Her eyes pooled with tears. "Why do you tell me this now?"

"Because 'twas your mother who named you. Like a gift to you, my dear. She knew what burdens you were born to carry, and your name was her prayer: 'May the Lord be your father. And may you see His delight in you.' You see, dear Abby, your very name sings of the Father's joy."

Abby shook her head, her river of locks rippling, her eyes wild. "As a reminder of all I have failed to be. I am not his joy, but his disdain."

Miss Robins took Abby's hands in hers.

"No, my dear. No. That name's a testament of all that you truly are."

Abby pushed away, retreating to her bed. Could she really be just as loved after all that had been stolen? Hadn't her very goodness been stripped from her? She felt broken, rejected, unwanted.

"I need to rest. My head aches."

Miss Robins returned a nod but sat on the edge of her bed, placing her soft palms on Abby's forehead, and offered up a prayer. Abby let her, for she was too weary to protest. Before long, her lids grew heavy.

Finally, Abby slept. After months of tears and torment, of days spent living a nightmare from which she could not wake, she slept. Her nerves calmed, her mind stilled, succumbing to exhaustion. There, her soul surrendered, and her body willingly let go of its burden. And there too, heaven held her.

In her dreams, He came to her.

* * *

Fields surrounded her in a night sky, thick bracken blanketing the hills as clouds rolled. She knelt with her face to the ground, her clothes caked in mud, covering her like a black shroud. The earth beneath her reeked of decay. Her hands sank into the mire, dark and thick, as deep as the ache in her chest. It called to her flesh, seeping into her pores so that she felt the cold stone of hatred and the sting of her pride mocking her with its lies.

She wept bitter tears. "Ruined. I am ruined."

Then, out of the darkness came light, blazing towards her as the figure of a man emanating the rays of the sun. Terrified, she pressed her face further down into the mud. A hand reached out, glowing like cast bronze, and touched her head, its heat warming her face and stilling her sobs.

"Rise, Abigail," the voice commanded, booming like a torrent of rushing water.

Without thought, her body lifted from the shadows, rising into the light. A cool wind swirled around her, sweeping away her filth. The hand lay outstretched before her in all its splendor, and she reached for it. As she touched it, the light waned. The bronze luster paled into human flesh, marred with wounds and bruises, until in a flash, His image was gone.

Her feet returned to the ground, and she gasped. She stared at her hands, now clean, and her gown, transformed from grime to glory. Darkness held her no more, for she glowed bright like the soft rays of the moon, the folds of her fabric shimmering.

A sound met her ears, like a chorus of spring. Laughter. His laughter.

She turned round, searching. Her gown streamed behind her in a train of twilight. He laughed again, a sound so joyous her heart soared.

"Abigail," rang out His voice.

She raised her arms to her side, turning her face up.

"My daughter, my delight. It is not in what filthy rags you bring, but in what I give you," He said.

Then, she smiled, a smile reflected in His own twinkling eyes that poured out love unending. Her feet felt light, the nerves in her fingertips firing. And, taking a deep breath, she twirled round and round. As His laughter grew, her heart lightened. Faster and faster she spun, her head flinging back in a wide arch, while she reveled in the blur of swarming colors, her laughter indistinguishable from His.

* * *

Dawn broke, and with it, hope. When Abby's lashes blinked open, the first rays of light reached in through the window, and she basked in the glow. Providence had spoken to her in its gentle parables; heaven had answered her cries. Peace overtook her as she lay on her pillow, hands resting gently on her belly, for she knew she would dance by the power of the Son.

Chapter 10

"My dear," said Miss Robins soothingly, her voice wavering.

Abby turned her attention away from the window of the parlor where rain streamed down the glass. The clouds had hung low most of the day, but then, just as light ebbed, they broke. Torrents of rain saturated the ground, sending water into offshoots down the Hudson. Gentle rumbles of thunder hummed in the distance.

"Oh, do not look so forlorn. I intend to take you with me," said Abby with a reassuring smile.

Miss Robins joined her by the window. The room held the dim glow of the lamp and the freshly kindled fire, for the dreariness of the rain did not afford it much light. But Abby's face shone, the soft curls of her hair illuminated as it fell around her shoulders. Miss Robins tucked a wayward strand behind Abby's ear.

"Sweet Abby, not all households are run as this one, and I'm not putting my eggs in that basket or I may just crack 'em all. There now, I'll go ready your trousseau and draw your bath. The other servants have already loaded the carriage to send your things over first thing after the ceremony."

Abby's heart sank, and worry nagged her. Miss Robins *must* come with her, and she intended to settle the matter with Charles herself. There were other worries mounting. Like, she did not know if the petticoats and undergarments Miss Robins had so painfully embroidered would fit in a month. She felt her body changing, but still no one knew of the life growing inside of her. She held the secret close to her heart, fearful of the consequences should the truth come out. It was all happening much too fast. So far she had managed to hide her nausea and the tell-tale bulge of her stomach, but for how much longer? Before long, surely Miss Robins would catch on.

"I'll leave you to your thoughts, my dear," said Miss Robins with a squeeze of Abby's shoulders.

Abby sighed. She had a great deal too many things to think about. She turned back to the windowpane. She rested her head on the cool glass, welcoming its chill against her forehead. She stifled a laugh, thinking of how often Miss Robins had chided her as a little girl for doodling on the frosted glass after the maids had just cleaned the windows.

The large maple tree in the front lawn dominated the view, its thick roots undulating along the path like subterranean waves. It bent against the gathering force of the wind, its weighty branches straining against the force. Lightning flashed, illuminating its sinuous silhouette. Abby's brow wrinkled as movement from the drive caught her eye.

Slick and glistening, a black horse galloped in wild tandem with its rider. As it neared, Abby made out Charles' form. He leaned forward, gripping the reins with one elbow wide, his other hand wielding a whip.

What would bring him here at this hour? she thought, with a slow rising panic.

A sliver of lightning teased the sky with its current, and Abby drew in her breath.

The horse spooked, digging in its hind legs as it scrambled to a halt, sending Charles careening over the top of its shoulder to the ground. He landed as gracefully as a man who has been dismounted can land—on his own hindquarters.

But he held his pride with the dignity of the reins still clutched between his fingers.

Abby's breath fogged the glass and she wiped it away with her sleeve. Satisfied that he was mostly unscathed, Abby cracked a smile.

Then, like an angry battle cry, another bolt of lightning lit up the sky, and the steed pranced in a circle, its hooves crushing the gravel into the soft earth inches from Charles' legs. Charles mouthed what Abby could only surmise were a string of curses. Thunder cracked and his horse reared and bucked. Charles refused to let go of the reins, and Abby's eyes grew wide in alarm.

Let go of the reins, Charles! she admonished, watching him struggle with the animal. He lashed the horse across the legs with his whip, only to have it bolt forward, dragging him with the reins wrapped around his wrist.

You're going to be trampled!

Abby rushed from the parlor out the front door. Rain stung her eyes, so that she could hardly see. She closed her shawl tighter around her and ran.

Charles' hat lay crushed under the horse's back hooves. His teeth clenched as he spat curses at the beast. The wind howled, and his horse whinnied.

"Let go!" cried Abby, racing down the drive. Within seconds her shawl was soaked, her hair clinging to her face.

Charles looked up, his anger transferring to Abby in a heated glare. Light splintered overhead, and Abby looked on Charles with terror as the horse's muscles twitched, its nostrils flaring. In a moment, the beast would crush him, but Charles, so stubborn in his pride, could not see the danger.

"Let go of the reins, Charles!" shouted Abby.

Thunder clapped and again the steed reared up, a high-pitched whinny piercing the air. Just then, Charles let go of his hold so that his steed reared high and sauntered backward a few steps before her hooves struck the ground a hands-breadth from his torso. Then the horse shrieked again, bolting down the drive into the night.

"Argh!" yelled Charles, slapping his hand on the ground. Abby sighed in relief. "See what you've done?" he shouted at her.

Abby looked at him incredulously and shook her head. At the same time, she heard the splatter of footsteps from behind and turned to find Langley.

"Miss Wyndham, are you all right?"

She nodded. "Please, Langley, go fetch Mr. Henderson's horse. The poor creature got spooked in the storm."

Charles huffed, brushing at his soiled waistcoat to no avail. Abby walked over and picked up his crumpled hat as he sat pouting. The top of his forehead boasted blood, dirt, and pieces of gravel caked into his skin.

“Mr. Henderson, may I send for a servant to tend to you?” asked Langley.

“Spare me,” he said between gritted teeth.

Langley nodded, exchanging an amused expression with Abby. Then, he rushed off to the stables to saddle up.

Abby looked down at Charles, shaking her head.

“Are you hurt?”

“No.”

She arched her brow. “Well, I beg to differ. Let’s get you inside,” she said, bending down to help him up. He brushed her off, standing up like an old man who had sat too long in his chair.

Abby led the way for him into the parlor, urging him towards a chair close to the fire. He fell into the cushions with a loud exhale. The fire popped. Abby shivered in the chill, warming her hands. She looked over at Charles. Blood oozed down the side of his head. Without a word, she walked out of the parlor and into the kitchen. The house was quiet; the servants had retired early, for tomorrow they would need to rise before dawn to prepare for the wedding.

It did not take her long to find the box where Miss Robins always kept fresh rags for scrapes and wounds. She returned to the parlor with strips of clean linen, a basin of warm water, and her father’s bottle of vodka.

Charles looked up at her, wrinkling his brow. She dipped a rolled strip of linen in the water and squeezed it between her fingers.

“I’m fine,” he said.

“Hold still.”

She reached out her hand tentatively, anticipating his recoil. The cloth pressed up against his cuts and he winced, “Ow! Give me that,” he said, snatching the cloth from her hand.

She looked away, back to the water basin, and considered how satisfying it would be to throw the entire bowl’s contents in his face, but something tugged at her heart, compelling her to walk another path. She took a deep breath, thinking about what that Something actually was.

He looked to the bottle of vodka and sighed.

“Finally, you understand me.”

She tilted her head. "I'm trying."

She poured a small portion of spirits into a glass just out of Charles' reach, and then dipped a fresh strip of linen in it.

Charles huffed, biting the inside of his lip. His heel bounced under his knees and he shivered against the chill.

"May I?" she said.

Charles relaxed his shoulders, submitting. She pressed it to his head and felt him flinch, though this time he did not voice his discomfort.

"What brought you all this way, and in the middle of a storm nonetheless?" she asked.

"Business," he said.

"Of course," she replied, thinking he was far too restless to be focused on business.

"And to make sure things are in order for tomorrow," he continued. "Did you see to inviting the Maybells last week?"

"Miss Robins jotted it down when you were speaking with me. I am sure she took care of it."

Charles rolled his eyes. Abby knew he cared little for Miss Robins, for reasons she could not understand.

"And what of Reverend Truitt?" he asked.

"I believe the matter was settled."

"So, you aren't sure if your reverend will be marrying us or some other peck-eyed geezer?"

"Miss Robins took care of it. Reverend Truitt will be there."

"Of course *she* did," said Charles.

"Hold still. This will hurt a little," said Abby, wiping a piece of gravel out of the cut while Charles gripped the arm of the chair. "Miss Robins is quite irreplaceable, you know. She has been a very dear friend to me and the Wyndham family for over twenty years."

"No doubt she wouldn't want to leave it, and I imagine she's ready to settle into her retirement. I bet your father will have her shipped back to London in a month."

Abby leaned back, feeling a wound of a different kind. She searched

Charles' face. "She mentioned no such thing. I would not have gotten by without her these past months. And you see, she has been with me since I was a child, even the night my mother passed. She's loyal and trustworthy. It's customary to allow her to follow me as my lady's maid in your house," said Abby.

"Absolutely not," said Charles.

"I've not said a word to her about any of it, if that's what you're worried about."

"You don't need a maid at your every beck and call."

"It would be the greatest comfort," said Abby, her eyes holding tears which seemed to only further Charles' resolution.

"Not in my house. I hardly have room for one woman's narrow-minded ways."

Abby stepped back, crossing her arms across her chest. He was completely impossible to reason with and pushed her at every opportunity.

"What is so 'narrow' about me?"

"Oh, please. You despise everything that doesn't meet your standards."

"Like what?"

Charles cocked his head, narrowing his eyes.

"Me."

Her chest heaved with the injustice of his comment. She felt anger pulsing through her. But his eyes did not lie; they were like the swirling clouds outside, haunted by their past. Did she despise him? At one time—yes, she confessed she had wished him dead for all he had heaped upon her.

"Do you really believe that?"

"You said it yourself. I'm just a monster," he turned his chin towards the fire. The flames danced beside him, leaving the other side of his face shrouded in shadow.

Abby inhaled, trying to make sense of her own thoughts and emotions. She recalled the passion with which she had uttered those words and her utter conviction. She looked away, blinking.

She continued her task, dipping the linen cloth into the basin, then gently wringing out the excess liquid. His blood now tainted the bowl, giving the water a pink tinge. As she touched his wound with the cloth, she remembered. That anthem of truth spoken to her soul weeks before played in her mind: *"He was bruised so that she might heal."* Like a cup brimming, she began to spill.

Her eyes lifted from the basin, and her face softened as she looked into to his eyes. "We are all monsters," she said.

He furrowed his brow, staring back at her with a tempest raging behind his eyes.

"Even you? You in your saintly ways? You in all of your goodness and propriety, Miss Abigail Wyndham, daughter of the great Sir Rathburn of England?"

"Whatever is good in me, Charles, is not because of my own doing, not because of high breeding, but because of God."

Charles laughed, a laugh of mockery. "And if I don't believe in God?"

"It doesn't make Him any less real."

He sneered, "It wouldn't matter even if I did."

She searched his face, intent, her heart urging her on, and she pressed harder. "What if that is *all* that matters?"

A frown held his cheeks captive, though he twitched to send it away. "Then I'm a lost cause, so don't make me yours."

Could it be he felt remorse? Could it be that he was drowning in his sea of guilt? What would absolve this verdict? What could mend all that he had broken?

"Charles," she began, her voice thick. Light flickered across her face, betraying the tears that had begun to well up. "I did not think I would survive after that night."

He exhaled laboriously and shifted in his seat as though he would rise.

"Just wait. Please—listen," she pleaded. Stepping closer to him, she knelt down. "What you did was vile and selfish, and on earth and in heaven utterly damning. But it does not mean you are a lost cause."

"That makes no sense, Abby. Now, get up," he said.

"But Charles—there is hope."

He shook his head, laughing, a darkness hovering in his eyes. "How can I be utterly damned and still have hope? Tell me that."

Tears streamed down her cheeks. *Oh Jesus, show me how,* she prayed, and her mind whirled with images of scoffers hurling insults, of whips cracking, of thorns piercing, the guttural cry of "Forgive them, for they know not what they do," echoing as her Savior's breath waned. Those wounds freed her; those wounds unwound hatred, ushering in love. With a ragged breath, her words poured out: "Because God himself offers forgiveness, and therefore so do I."

Charles remained silent as Abby continued kneeling next to him. Tears streaked her cheeks. The fire cracked, and the wind howled against the shutters. Then, his chair scraped the floor as he shuffled away from her.

"You're a glorious actress."

Her eyes opened, shocked. She shook her head, her soft curls falling around her shoulders, still damp from the rain. His expression seemed inscrutable, his features cold and unmoving. Lightning illuminated the room, and thunder rumbled the planks of the floor.

"I can see right through it all. You think I want to live my whole married life indebted to you?"

Peace held her, as she saw Charles held fast in his own doubts.

"I don't speak of debts," she said gently.

"Well, I don't need anything from you. What I need is to forget," he said.

Abby rose up from the floor, straightening her skirts as she stood.

"There are a great many things that you need," she said, looking at the cleaned cut on his head. "You're just too blind to see it."

He stood abruptly, the blanket falling to the floor, and the basin sloshing so that blood and water spilt to the ground. He dipped his head. "Tell Sir Rathburn I'm sorry to have missed him."

Abby lowered her eyes. "And tomorrow?"

He walked brusquely towards the door, then turned. "Well, tomorrow before your God and man, you become Mrs. Henderson, until death do us part."

Chapter 11

"Magnificent," spluttered Miss Robins, choking on her own tears. Abby smiled. "I would've never thought it possible, but here it is, even more becoming than before," she continued.

Abby's wedding gown resembled a masterpiece restored. To hide the stained fabric, Mrs. Allen had added a delicate leaf rosette overlay stitched with gold-colored lace. Its train, which once billowed past Abby's ankles, had been trimmed into a bustle, so that Mrs. Allen could incorporate the fabric into the bodice. The golden overlay trailed down Abby's back, hearkening back to Regency England. When she turned, the lace teased the light, as though Midas himself had kissed its hem.

Abby had space to breathe with the new adjustments, and for this she was most grateful. When she stood in front of the mirror, she was startled at her transformation. If it weren't for the dreadful weight of her heart, she might have convinced herself that it was the best day of her life. Her hair minded Miss Robins' strict hands during the process of pinning it, and cascades of ringlets flowed elegantly around her neck and shoulders.

"Are you ready, my dear? Sir Rathburn is wait'n to usher you down," said Miss Robins. Abby closed her eyes, pressing her lips together. *Am I ready?* she asked herself, and when her heart felt it might break, she decided she could not answer truthfully. *God, help me, please. I do this only because I must.*

Miss Robins had taken such care packing all of Abby's belongings, which were stacked in trunks and boxes around her room. Tomorrow, servants would deliver them to Charles' estate. Despite Abby's protestations, it was decided that Miss Robins would remain in Sir Rathburn's employ. Upon learning of this fact, Miss Robins had reassured Abby it was for the best, though Abby could read the sorrow in her friend's face. This morning, however, Miss Robins' expression was one of pure joy. Abby tried to push thoughts of life without her loyal maid aside as she readied herself for the ceremony. It would just be another unfortunate consequence of her new role as Mrs. Henderson. A knock interrupted her thoughts. Miss Robins rushed to the door.

"Oh, you will be so proud. Come in, come in," said Miss Robins, breathless. The door creaked open. Abby turned to find her father entering the room, but when he saw her, he froze. Color drained from his face. Miss Robins stood behind him, fanning her eyes. "She's the very image of . . . of . . ."

"Of Mary," said Sir Rathburn barely above a whisper.

"Father," said Abby, gently stepping closer, thinking he looked as though he were seeing a ghost. His eyes scarcely blinked,.

"I wish she were here," said Abby. Finally, Sir Rathburn seemed to regain his senses. He looked away. He never spoke of her mother, and the look on his face told Abby why. The gaping whole she left had never healed, not for him.

Miss Robins stepped nearer to them with a proud smile. "She *is* here, Abby. She's here because she's part of you, of both of you."

Sir Rathburn frowned, his jaw tightening. "Foolish nonsense," he said, turning to the door. "It is past time. They are all waiting." He stood with his arm out, waiting for Abby to stand at his side and do her duty.

* * *

The Great Hall of Bristol Estate hummed with the murmurings of the expectant crowd. Robins led Abby to her father, who waited, wearing his usual stoic expression along with his best wedding attire. The music began, the strings of the violin tender and sweet. Sir Rathburn led his daughter down the staircase lined with roses and baby's breath. Her heart beat wildly, but he appeared calm and collected. One, two, three, four . . . each step brought Abby closer to the hall and further away from the life she had always known. Eleven, twelve, thirteen . . . the guests stood as Sir Rathburn led her forward. Abby caught her emotions by the throat and held them fast. And there, down the aisle, Charles' dark eyes flashed a momentary look of surprise as he caught sight of his bride, and for the briefest of moments he appeared stunned.

Like a moving statue, adorned in shimmers of gold, she walked towards Charles Henderson, head held high, unwavering in her duty. Only her heart betrayed her true feelings, which no one but Him had access to. None who had gathered could perceive any crack in the edifice, so enamored with envy or delight—none but Charles. Even Sir Rathburn managed a cool smile as he led his only daughter to her fate and delivered her into Charles' hand, the transaction complete. Even through the black crepe of mourning, Charles's mother gazed on, her face beaming with affection at her son's achievement. For who would have thought a Henderson to secure such a match as a Wyndham?

She kept her gaze low as Reverend Truitt went through the motions of the service, speaking when prompted, just as she should. But Charles's words sounded empty, devoid of feeling. How could they make a covenant before God when Charles denied His very existence and scorned her for her belief? What was the point? As the ceremony ended, their union affirmed, Abby felt as though it had all been a charade, but she was now bound before God and man. She had resigned herself to a life of suffering, but still feared the evils that awaited her. How would this man treat her now that she was his property? And what of his own child? Would he see it as a disgrace or a delight?

* * *

Evergreens cast long shadows across the lawn of the Hollows Estate by the time the carriage with the newlywed couple arrived that evening. Charles sent Abby inside, while he gave instructions to the few servants he employed.

Its Gothic arches loomed overhead as the shy servant led her through the front doors. The place felt empty, for neither picture nor carpet adorned its rooms with their tall ceilings. The servant brought Abby down a long hall, stopping in front of the door at its end. He cleared his throat, beads of sweat gathering on his upper lip.

"Mr. Henderson wants you to wait here," he said. From neck to cheek he flushed red before opening the door.

Abby nodded and stepped inside the room. The boy handed her the candle and shut the door behind her. The wax bobbed on its holder as Abby's hand shook, its light dancing across the bedroom walls. No one had thought to take care to light the lamps or kindle a fire, so a chill hung in the room. A large mahogany four-poster bed dominated the space, dwarfing all other furnishings.

She knew too well what was expected of a bride. For all of her knowledge, she wanted to hide, or jump through the window and run away from this life she had been bound to. She gritted her teeth and looked away, refusing to let her mind think or her heart feel anymore. She would refuse. She would insist he leave her alone.

She went to light the lamps in the corners of the room, creating an eerie glow. As Abby looked down at her gown, dread filled her at the thought of Charles unfastening it. Rushing, her fingers fumbled against the loops and she stripped herself down to her chemise, leaving her cold and exposed. She unbound her hair, letting it fall around her, and found a throw draped on one of his chairs. She threw it around her shoulders, wrapping herself in it. Looking down at her belly, she thought it looked only slightly rounder—not noticeably so—but in the weeks to come it would be harder to conceal.

Maybe I should tell him tonight?

Wait, came the voice of wisdom ringing inside of her. She nodded, acknowledging the warning.

A light knock interrupted her thoughts. Abby swallowed.

Oh, God help me. Help me survive this.

She stood towards the back of the room as Charles entered, his eyelids drooping with fatigue. He let out a deep sigh, draped his waistcoat on the armchair next to his dresser, and ran his hands through his dark hair. Abby stood still, hardly breathing, wondering if she was even supposed to be in his room.

He finally looked up, his brow furrowed at the sight of her.

"Ah. You've found my room," he said.

"The servant . . ."

"Matthew."

"Yes, Matthew said I was to wait here, so I assumed . . ." said Abby in an airy breath.

Charles nodded; a shadow seemed to fall over his face. "Right, I will have your things put away tomorrow."

He moved about the room, laying his shoes and hat in their proper place. As he unbuttoned the top of his shirt, Abby looked away.

"I have news," he said.

Abby lifted her eyes and a thrill of panic thrummed in her chest as she hugged the blanket closer to her. "What sort of news?"

"Your father and I are going to New Orleans."

"When?"

"Three weeks from today," he said.

She nodded. *Three weeks seems like an eternity,* she thought. "For how long?"

He paused and tilted his head. "A month."

There was certain relief in hearing this news, yet Abby fought the urge to show as much in her demeanor.

"Don't be too excited. I will come back, you know," he said.

She nodded. There was no winning with him. Of course she would welcome the time apart, but she hated her own relief. This was not what marriage was intended to be. Wasn't she supposed to be flesh of his flesh, and bone of his bone? And by the time he returned, she was certain her stomach would reveal the entire truth. She already bore his name, and before the heat of summer, she would bear his child.

Charles stopped. She looked up to find him standing over her wedding gown laid out on the armchair. She walked over as he ran his fingers across the golden lace bordering the sleeves. Abby trembled with dread. She wanted to scream but held her tongue.

"How much did he spend?"

"It was Mother's."

"You mean to tell me your father wouldn't go to some great lengths to get cloth from Europe for such a day?"

"He insisted, but I refused. This is far more precious that Paris silk. My mother was truly precious. Though we did have to make some adjustments after I . . ." Charles turned to face her, and her breath left her chest.

"You what?"

"It was nothing," she said, looking to the floor. She shuddered beneath his gaze, keenly aware of his proximity. He took a step closer, the tips of his fingers brushing against her neck as he swept her hair off her shoulder. She flinched, hugging the blanket tighter around her.

His eyes studied her neck and collarbone. When he sighed, Abby could feel the heat of his breath. He tipped up her chin. She swallowed. He tugged her towards him, ever so gently. Before she could catch her breath, his lips touched hers. He smelled of mint and tobacco, and his embrace was soft—nothing like before. Shaking, she lifted her palms and pushed him away. Her head spun.

He stepped back, searching her face. The line of his jaw set as his eyes darted around the room.

"I'll have your things brought to the room on the north side of the house. You can see the front garden from there."

She stood, stunned, waiting for him to lash out at her. Yet he seemed so different from that awful night that her mind reeled in confusion. Finally, regaining her senses, Abby replied, "I won't be staying here?"

He shook his head and shrugged. "Clearly, I scare you."

Abby lifted her eyes, glossy with tears. "I wasn't trying to—"

"I know. Just forget it. Sleep here tonight so you don't cause a scene. I'm getting a glass of wine."

Abby's relief was apparent, but so was her shame. She had fully expected an argument at least. "Might I go with you for some warm milk?"

"No. I'll go alone. I can have it brought."

"Never mind it then."

"Suit yourself."

Abby found her hands idly fingering her wedding ring. "This isn't easy."

He narrowed his eyes. "See. You can't forget, can you?"

Her throat seemed to constrict. "I can't forget. But I can forgive—"

He shook his head, stalking out of the room, the door swinging shut behind him before she could finish her sentence.

She lay still on the far edge of the bed, eyes wide open. It wasn't until Charles made his way back into the room and lay down silently that Abby thought of shutting her eyes. He shifted beneath the quilt, then stilled. She wondered what visions visited him in the night, whether he had lost any sleep over his actions. A war raged on in Abby. Had not her own lips sung about God's power to make all things new?

Chapter 12

The next few weeks wore on like an unending sea voyage. As the babe grew in her belly, so too did Abby's weariness, the very ground she stood upon seeming to pitch and roil beneath her as she battled morning sickness. She felt herself a child as she tried learning to do the simplest of tasks on her own. Dressing was slow, and her stays did not hold her right and often were strung through crooked. Taming her hair proved near impossible. All she could manage was a simple plait. She scolded herself for not thinking to have Robins teach her these things before.

The Hollows itself was beautiful, and she took some enjoyment in her wanderings through its halls, exploring its impressive architecture and furnishings. But even the china remained foreign to her lips, its rust-colored embellishments so American in nature. The sofas in the parlor sat rigid in their place, stiff with newness. No family heirlooms adorned the walls like at Devonsfield or Bristol. The air itself felt weighted with quiet. Charles employed a select few servants in comparison to the Wyndham home. She missed their lively chatter. Day to day life unfolded differently in Charles' house.

Abby's room became her sanctuary, for which she was grateful. There she could walk in, shut the door, and find familiar things around her. Her silver brush and mirror, handed down from her mother, was laid out on her dressing table. Her trousseau bulged with items stitched by Miss Robins' own hand over cherished conversations. Her own clothing, jewelry, and books now had their place. These small things she treasured, for everywhere else she felt a stranger.

Charles remained aloof. When Abby did chance to see him coming or going, he was cool. They would dine together if he happened to be home, but it was a rare occasion. Her isolation grew into thickets of troubling thoughts and anxiety. It was not as though Abby had entertained many guests or playmates as a child; she'd had few friends her own age, but she had rarely been alone with no one to talk to. Miss Robins might as well have been her own shadow. With no one in whom to confide, it felt like her secret screamed inside her.

Abby tried to busy herself with the managing of the household. She observed the comings and goings of the scant few servants, and who performed what duties. Charles did not oversee these things himself, but rather had hired a woman to do it before they were married. Her name was Miss Knightly.

All operated smoothly under Knightly's watchful eye, for if something were not to her liking, her shrill voice would soon put it right. She stood with a posture so rigid her stays must have been pulled to breaking point. Locks of ginger hair were arranged flawlessly atop her head, with perfect twin ringlets cascading on each side, brushing against her ears. The brisk clicking of her heels announced her arrival at Abby's door each morning to deliver any correspondence and to leave a breakfast tray. For the remainder of the time, Miss Knightly steered away from her presence as though Abby were an unwanted pet she had been forced to feed. One day, when Abby had sought out Miss Knightly in an attempt to gain more understanding of the running of the house, she was met only with her arched brow and dismissive glare. Later that evening, over dinner, Charles insisted Abby stop meddling in his affairs. He had everything operating to his own liking and did not want her interfering.

"What would you have me do?"

"Whatever women do," he replied, with a casual flick of his hand.

"I have tried to be of help, but Miss Knightly did not wish for my direction. Would you prefer I work in the stables?"

"Do what you like, just stop meddling."

Do what you like, Abby pondered. It didn't take her long to consider what she would most like. The following morning she awoke just before dawn peeked through the curtains. The house still slept and would not stir for at least an hour more. Feeling ill and restless, she decided to go on a walk to visit Miss Robins and, naturally, her father. Bristol was not far for a horse and buggy, but walking would require a bit of stamina. With nothing else to occupy her, she decided to go. Her stays resisted her tugs as she attempted to smooth the bump on her belly. She wore her warmest overcoat and frock, the seams straining around her middle. *Could time slow down?* she wondered, trying to shrug off the feeling of dread that she carried.

As a courtesy, she scrawled a note and left it on top of her bedside table where it would be in obvious sight for Miss Knightly when she brought the breakfast tray. After grabbing a few left-over biscuits and a hunk of bread, Abby slipped out the front door. The late November frost dampened the hem of her skirts and brought a slight chill to the tips of her ears and nose. The sky slumbered in its blanket of gray; even birds had not yet awakened. Her blood pumped warmer through her body with each step, and she welcomed the exertion. But her steps slowed as she thought of the child she carried along with her. No one knew. None except God Himself.

The light of dawn peeked up over the top of the hill, drawing Abby's heart into her throat. How many times had the sun ushered in a new day, casting away the night with its sweeping rays of light? The glow of the sun warmed her cheeks and her soul. Finally, away from Charles, she felt like she could breathe. She could think and pray. *All-knowing God, what is to become of me? And what of this child? I fear these secrets will become known, and then what? Oh, soften Charles's heart towards this babe. Pave a path forward. Make a way out of the wilderness.*

* * *

It was mid-morning by the time she arrived at Bristol Estate. Her father, she learned, was away on business. When Miss Robins saw her approach, she ran to Abby and embraced her. Abby fought off the tears that pricked at her eyes at the sight of her trusted friend. It had been so long since she'd properly spoken with anyone that she didn't know what to say.

Robins invited her in, fussing over the cold, and ushered her into the drawing room where a warm fire glowed and a fresh pot of tea and cake awaited. As she took Abby's coat, Abby felt her eyes studying her where the slightest bulge showed. Abby turned and sat quickly in the chair by the fire, immediately realizing her fault in coming. After so many weeks away from Miss Robins, it would be difficult to hide the change in her body. What had she been thinking? What's more was that she had nothing to say of her current situation that would not raise suspicion. And anything positive would be nothing short of another lie.

"How is my dear Mrs. Henderson?" asked Miss Robins with a sideways glance. Abby hardly heard the question, as her own worries muddled her mind. "Is it that good, then?" said Miss Robins with noted sarcasm.

Abby blinked out of her reverie, taking an absentminded forkful of cake. "Today has been, I suppose."

"Did you not leave before everyone woke?"

Abby offered a half smile and continued eating her cake. With each bite she felt her strength gradually returning. "I do love a long walk. It would be much better at the Hollows if you were there. Oh, Miss Robins, it is quite lonely without your company," she said with misty eyes.

Miss Robins did not contain her tears but nodded in agreement.

"And I suppose no one has seen to those curls," she said with a chuckle. Abby shook her head and laughed nervously with her.

"Let me show you a simple way to do it up nice like."

"Oh, would you?"

"T'would be my joy."

In no time at all, Robins had Abby in front of a mirror back in her old room, schooling her in how to pin and place strands of hair in an arrangement for evening attire. "Abby," said Miss Robins after a few quiet moments, "Are you quite all right, dear? I understand be'n lonely, but 'tis that all that brought you this way at such an early hour?"

Abby looked into Miss Robins' eyes reflected in the mirror, aware of her concern and suspicion. It would be so much easier if she had a friend on her side, someone to confide in, and share the weight that had held her down for so long. But, just as Abby's lips parted to spill the truth of her situation, shame dammed them. What would Miss Robins think of her? Would she even believe her? Weren't there some secrets that no one should ever know, because if they did, they could never see you the same again? Abby couldn't bear the thought of sweet Miss Robins thinking of her in such a disgraced position.

"He is different than I thought," said Abby instead, which was a truth, but not the secret that ailed her.

"In a good way, I hope," said Miss Robins with her hand gently squeezing Abby's shoulder. This seemed reassurance enough, much to Abby's relief.

"I cannot be sure, but regardless, I am most happy to see you."

By the time Miss Robins had trained Abby's fingers to twist her locks into a bun and pin the curls, the light of day began to yawn.

"How about I have Langley drive you home? And I'll ride along with you," Miss Robins said.

Abby graciously accepted her invitation, though what she really desired was to turn back time, to remain at Bristol in her innocence, fettered to neither husband nor child. But that, of course, was impossible.

* * *

The sun had gathered its light on the hem of the horizon by the time Abby arrived back at the Hollows. As she waved her dear friend off, Abby's stomach growled, waves of nausea gripping her again.

Dinner will be served soon, she thought. Unsure if she could wait, Abby made her way to the kitchen in search of something to quell her hunger pangs. The house was unusually calm. The kitchen sat unmoving, with not even the wood stove bubbling a pot of warm water.

Abby found the coachman and footman lounging at the table, studying a hand of cards. Jane, the quiet girl who served both as chambermaid and parlor maid during the day, stood off to the side idly watching the older men play. She was the first to notice Abby's presence and jumped with fright.

"Mrs. Henderson! Well, where'd you come from?"

Abby stepped back, startled herself. "Where has everyone gone to?"

Jane lowered her gaze to the floor before speaking again. "Mr. Henderson says he's want'n his dinner at nine this eve'n. So we's just kill'n time."

Abby nodded, her forehead creased in confusion. "Are we to have guests?"

"No, Miss," said Jane, shaking her head. Her eyes danced around the floor before she curtsied and rushed off down the hall.

Abby made her way upstairs, walking through the hallway leading to her bedchamber, when she heard a low sound from the opposite end of the house.

Curiosity piqued, she changed course. Her ears tickled again; this time the sound gained distinction, resembling giggles. She paused, looking down the hallway leading to Charles' chamber, when she heard it again.

Matthew stood slumped against the wall outside Charles' door, his head nodding off to one side with his mouth wide open. Abby moved out of sight, pressing herself against the wall behind a pillar. Charles' deep smooth voice drummed on behind his door. A shrill voice trilled through the air, laughing. *He's not alone,* she thought, stifling a gasp.

Matthew startled to attention and turned his head this way and that until he spotted Abby. His eyes grew to the size of saucers. "Mmm . . . mmmm . . . Mrs . . . dinner will be ready later," he stuttered, an etch of pity written on his face. Abby's mouth fell open. She turned her face away as though it had been slapped.

"Who is in there?" she hissed.

The voice behind Charles' door hushed until it was only a murmur.

Matthew's mouth opened and closed, but he was speechless. Abby heard stirring from the other side of the door and the moan of floorboards. Her head spun as her heart quickened, thudding between her ears. She felt faint. When the doorknob clicked, she nearly jumped out of her slippers. Before it turned and she was forced to face her humiliation, she spun around and fled down the hall.

How could he? After all he has already done?

Vexed as she felt, she refused to sit in passivity. Tears burned hot on her cheeks. When she made it to her room, she smothered her cries with her pillow. Could he give her more reason to despise him?

Some time later, her voice hoarse from sobbing, she dressed herself for dinner, throwing on an evening dress. She left her room and caught a glimpse of herself that made her gasp. Crazed locks billowed around her blotchy cheeks, her eyes wild and wounded. She raised her chin; she would tell him how awful he was, how she deserved much better.

It felt as though her heart had slowed to a halt, and inside her a voice whispered, ***Can the blind see? Can the deaf hear?***

She cringed, biting her tongue, and her shoulders slumped in defeat. She wanted so badly to throw it in his face. But what good would come of that? What would it prove?

The dinner bell rang. She adjusted her dress, smoothing the middle as best she could over her increasing roundness, and she remembered the baby, their child.

She made her way to the dining room. The chair at the far end of the table waited empty, but Abby went ahead and took her place at the opposite end, seething. The clock ticked, taunting her with each passing second. Ten minutes passed; her back grew tense, her hands wrung out like laundered linen in her lap.

When Charles finally sauntered into the dining room, he smoothed back his ruffled hair but left the smirk visible on his mouth. He took his seat but did not look at Abby. Instead, he focused on the generous steaming portions of potato and pork on his plate. At the Hollows, Charles led no formal start to the meal, and any conventional manners he used at Bristol were completely abandoned under his roof. He plunged his fork into the meat without pause or acknowledgement—or, it seemed, remorse.

Abby stared at him, her appetite gone.

He held his utensils like a famished soldier, grazing the bottom of his plate in a rhythmic fashion, never pausing for a glance or a word to her. When he had lapped up all the pepper pot soup from his bowl and had decimated the meat on his plate, Abby decided to speak.

"You seem to have worked up quite the appetite."

One pause ensued, then another, and another. His forked scraped across the porcelain, picking up the last morsel of pork before sliding it behind his teeth. He chewed and swallowed.

"What's that supposed to mean?" he said.

"Why did you have dinner postponed?" she asked. He lifted his eyes from his plate and narrowed them in on her, seeming to scrutinize her every feature. He had nowhere to hide; Abby could see the rouge stains on his collar. He hadn't even thought to change into fresh clothes.

He sighed. "I was rather enjoying the quiet. Weren't you?"

She felt the chords of her throat tighten as though they were going to snap in two along with her temper.

"It was anything but quiet when I walked in the door this evening," Abby said drily, then played at picking at her food.

"Where did you go so early this morning? And without a word to anyone," Charles asked.

"To see Father."

"You couldn't have walked the whole way there and back," he scoffed.

"I walked there, and Miss Robins rode with me in the carriage back. I left a note for Knightly this morning."

"And how did he receive you?" he said with an arched brow.

"He wasn't there," Abby replied.

"I could have told you he wouldn't be."

"I would have gone anyway."

"So you are lying about why you went?"

"I needed the fresh air."

"Maybe you should go out more often," he said, a darkness hanging in his eyes.

She could taste the bitterness on her tongue. "Who was with you in your chambers?" she said with a burst of outrage.

Charles' eyes narrowed into slits. "That doesn't concern you."

"So nothing you do concerns me?" she said, the edge breaking through her voice. "Next time perhaps you could offer me, your wife, the courtesy of bedding another woman in someone else's house. Or better yet, go to the brothel where it is at least to be expected!"

She threw her napkin onto her plate.

Charles shot his attention to Matthew, who waited by the door. "I'm finished."

"So that's it?" Abby exclaimed. "You don't even have the decency to explain to me—your *wife*—why you shame me so?"

Charles stood, and Abby rose with him.

"Go to your room, Abby."

Her chest heaved in and out, anger clawing at her throat. "I am not a child."

"Matthew, leave us. Have no one disturb this side of the house." Abby's throat closed tight, and the heat of her anger replaced itself with the chill of fear.

"What is your intention, Charles? To scare me?" she said, boldly.

"Is it working?"

"Yes."

He cursed and turned to leave.

"Where are you going?"

"Haven't we talked enough for one evening?"

"Charles. Please. I cannot carry on this way. I am here, living in this house. I am your *wife*."

He moved closer, lowering his voice to a hiss. "I married you, didn't I? You have a roof over your head. There's nothing else I can give you."

"Then there is no reason for me to stay."

"You must stay."

"While you live like a bachelor?"

His jaw twitched. "I'm not the honorable one, Abby. I take what I want when I want it. That's who I am, so just get used to it and leave me alone."

Her fears rose before her like a cloud, darkening any hope she had dared cling to. She chided herself for her naivete: had she truly believed Charles would change? Had she ever imagined she could be happy here? Suddenly she saw her future plainly—pacing aimlessly through cold hallways dressed for nothing or no one, while Charles bedded his mistress under the same roof. She let her tears run free. She had known anger, disappointment, and heartache, but to be so blatantly disgraced like this was more than she could bear. Anger of a new kind gripped her like a vise.

The clock chimed half past nine. Taking a deep breath, Abby calmed herself, willing the tears to stop. There was hate broiling in her heart. Hate she had thought herself immune to.

Can the blind see? Can the deaf hear? The voice came like a whisper, calling her to a different path, cutting through the thorns, leading her heart with its light, so that she bit her tongue.

Her face twisted into a grimace, pained, as every bone in her wanted to lash out.

The clocked ticked. She drew in a deep breath and prayed, *Then give him sight!*

Abby turned to Charles and looked him squarely in the eyes as she spoke. "It's an empty well. You'll drink and never be satisfied while you lead our family to destruction."

The storm in his eyes calmed for the briefest of reprieves. But it was only the eye of the tempest, for his voice rose. "You keep pushing me with these exhausting maxims full of fluff, not reality!" His eyes grew wild with the same fury Abby had seen in her father's. "Do you get it? Don't you see what you've done to me?"

"Do you want to know what I see?" Abby said with newfound courage. "I see a tormented man, so set in his ways that he refuses to bow. I did not do this to you, Charles. *It* was already in you."

He threw his head back, laughing spitefully. "Of course," he said, his lip curling in disgust.

"Will you cast me aside forever?"

"I assure you, you don't want me to pay you any attention," said Charles.

"And what of children? What of a family?"

He moved closer, towering over her again, but she stayed calm. "You will bear my children when I am good and ready. Make no mistake of that."

A familiar strength unfolded inside of her as she looked up to him. She no longer feared for herself, but for him, and for his own child that he knew nothing about.

"Then God have pity on them," she said and turned to leave.

As she walked through the doorway, a silhouette came into view, crossing her path. A chill climbed up Abby's spine. Miss Knightly stood, her arms crossed, her red lips written into a firm line.

"Someone's got to keep him warm," she whispered, brushing past Abby towards the dining room with a seductive sway of her hips.

Abby found her feet frozen in shock, as she heard Miss Knightly's low voice hum through the dining room.

Sleep eluded her through the night. Her mind raced with thoughts about the bleak future that she seemed powerless to change. Her heart broke for the life inside of her, for the husband who hated her, and for the God who had forsaken her.

Chapter 13

Three long weeks later, night pressed down over Abby's bedroom window. She longed for tomorrow just as much as she dreaded the present moment. Jane lit the oil lamps, then scurried from her room. Servants had been rushing through the house in a frenzy for the greater part of the day, rearranging furniture, dusting, and cooking in preparation for the party of guests set to arrive at six o'clock. Among them were Mr. and Mrs. Lawrence, a prominent couple who had taken an interest in Charles and Sir Rathburn's enterprises—specifically, in cotton shipped from the South to the North. Abby had met Mrs. Lawrence on one other occasion, when her father had taken her to the city to buy new fabric for her dresses the previous year.

Charles had sent Jane to deliver a message to Abby of what was expected of her: she had been charged to entertain Mrs. Lawrence. No surprise; what else would she ever be expected to do besides be a pawn in a man's world?

She dreaded the evening for more than one reason. First, she would be forced to be in the same company as her husband, pretending that all was harmonious in the presence of guests and her own father. Second, she felt ill. She had spent the morning with her head hanging in a waste basket. And, to add to that, she felt her body changing and was scarcely able to squeeze her bosom into her stays and gowns. If she could get through the evening, she vowed to find a way to tell Charles before the servants started spreading gossip.

After managing without a lady's maid for so long, Abby assumed she would be dressing herself as usual, but Charles clearly had other plans.

There was a brisk knock on her door, and before Abby could speak, Miss Knightly barged in, her ruby lips pursed together in a look of distaste. A fresh wave of nausea washed over Abby at the intrusion.

"Charles sent me. Your appearance seems to be at the top of his priorities," she said coldly, as she glided through Abby's room.

"I will manage on my own," said Abby, anxious to relieve them both from the awkward exchange.

She shrugged her shoulders. "I said you would say that, but we both know you can't manage much. Now, which gown?"

"The champagne one, just over there," said Abby, turning so that Miss Knightly could not see her front. Miss Knightly arched her brow. The gown was one of Abby's oldest, simply fashioned silk with a floral pattern along the shoulders followed by long sleeves that came to a point at her hand. Abby chose it specifically for its high waistline, hoping to call attention away from her stomach.

"Get on with it. Turn around."

It was clear that although Miss Knightly held sway with Charles' physical affections, she did not have enough power to avoid this duty. Abby imagined this gave Charles some sort of sick satisfaction.

Abby turned her back, ever reluctant to let Knightly stare at her, exposed as she was in only her chemise and stays. Knightly methodically unhooked Abby's day dress and cast it aside while Abby slipped into the silk frock. She felt the ice of Knightly's fingers as she lifted the dress to fasten it.

"Has a child tied your stays?" she exclaimed. Abby glanced over her shoulder to the looking glass where her back was in view. The strings that laced the corset were crudely drawn out of line.

"It was difficult to see," said Abby.

"I'm sure you feel quite miserable without someone doting over your every need all the time," said Knightly in a cooing voice as though she were talking to an imbecile.

Abby let out a sigh of defeat, folding her arms around her front. Knightly jerked the strings, making Abby wince. With each pull, she felt hatred stringing tighter in Knightly's fingers.

"Surely that's enough," said Abby, turning her head to the side where she caught Knightly's sneer. Abby stepped back to see the gown in the mirror, her eyes widening at the sight. It may have been gracious to her waistline, but it only served to enhance her bust. She had never had to contend with many curves and did not like the thought of drawing more attention to herself.

Miss Knightly did not seem to notice this distraction, so Abby moved to her dressing table and sat on the chair to begin arranging her hair. Knightly followed at her heels and loosened Abby's braid with one swift pull. The locks flowed down over her shoulders, unruly curls billowing out in heaps.

Miss Knightly's eyes scrutinized each wave.

"I didn't know I would have to clean out a rat's nest," she said. Abby's jaw hung open in surprise. Her hair had always been wayward, perhaps unruly, but never had she bore such an insult as this.

"If you have other things to do, I can manage myself."

"Like Charlie would have that."

Abby sat up straighter, bristling. "You mean your *employer,* Mr. Henderson?"

She eyed Abby through the mirror, smirking.

"*Charlie* likes it when I call him that. And to him I'm Roxanne, not Miss Knightly."

Abby lowered her eyes, feeling the rise of saliva mixing with bile. With that, Miss Knightly grabbed a handful of hair and began twisting it into place. Abby felt the stretch of every strand pulling at her head.

"Please resist the urge to scalp me, or let me do this myself," said Abby, her teeth clenched tight. Miss Knightly scowled, arching her brow in defiance.

"Never thought of scalping you. I'm sure you've just been pampered with the old lady's fingers your whole life. It's 'bout time you had these locks tamed."

Abby's breath left her. It was not worth fanning the fire; she bit her tongue and watched Miss Knightly work. What could this woman hope to accomplish by being a man's mistress? She must want more than that, for who would willingly choose the seat of shame? If she had his heart, that might be enough. But how could any woman have Charles Henderson's heart? An even more sickening feeling settled in the pit of her stomach. What was Knightly's ambition? What more could she seek to gain?

Her stomach turned over, and she recalled the texture of the goat's cheese that had topped her meal that afternoon. She could almost feel it curdling inside her. A malicious belch hissed at the back of her throat, stinging her chest.

Knightly's fingers pulled against Abby's scalp again. She wanted to yelp in pain but knew the action would only bring satisfaction. Still, she did not think she could tolerate much more of it when she saw her own face blanching in the mirror.

"Might you send for peppermint tea and crackers?"

Knightly's hip jutted out to the side. "It's hardly teatime, and besides, you seemed to have stuffed enough into your gown already."

Abby gasped, feeling the sting of anger simmering in her chest. *Incorrigible woman,* she thought.

Knightly's claws wrenched up another lock of hair, stabbing it with a pin; Abby took in a sharp breath. The woman was only halfway finished. Plagued with the memory of the cheese, her hand flew to her mouth in an effort to postpone the inevitable.

She whimpered to alert Miss Knightly, but the woman paid no heed and continued to tear away at Abby's hair. Abby tried to pull away then, in hopes of making it to the privy, but Miss Knightly's fingers dug in like a vise.

"Hold still or I'll have to start over."

Abby shook her head, desperate, but Miss Knightly only rolled her eyes. "You're acting like a child."

Abby's eyes darted around her. A waste bin sat innocently next to the dressing table, just out of her reach. Abby pulled forward.

"Fine, you can do it yourself," said Knightly, releasing her hold just in time for Abby to vomit. Only the last bit actually made it into the waste bin.

"Eeew!" Knightly cried, looking down at her shoes, muttering a slew of curses.

Abby hurried to the lavatory adjoining her room, leaning over the basin until her heaving stopped. She wiped her face clean, rinsed her mouth, and then returned to the scene of the crime. Miss Knightly leaned over, sopping up the vomit from her shoes with one of Abby's handkerchiefs.

"I am terribly sorry," Abby gushed, trying to mask her enjoyment in watching Knightly get her comeuppance.

Knightly glared. "Is that what you call it? I can see the glint in your eye. You probably planned it all along."

"I tried warning you."

The woman fumed, and then it seemed a part of her mind met some realization. She clicked her tongue like a purring cat, and her feline eyes became half slits as though she were stalking her prey.

"Are you *ill*?"

"My lunch seems to think so, but I feel quite better now," said Abby.

Knightly perused Abby's figure, then seemed to move on. "Well, are you going to vomit all over me again, or can we finish your hair so I can scrape the remaining filth off my shoes?"

Abby returned to her seat, hiding her inward grin. The clawing continued, but Abby remained silent.

Miss Knightly paused on the last strand of hair, holding it captive between her fingers, her long nails teasing its end as she spun it around and round. "I've been thinking. You've been here for quite some time, *my lady*," she said, her brow arching high.

Abby lifted her eyes, keeping her emotions well guarded.

"But not *that* long," she said, looking down at Abby's stomach in the mirror. "I'm not sure how things go in England, but here, women are usually married *before* they find themselves carting a lover's baby." A malicious smirk slid across her lips and the tendril of hair fell limp from her fingers.

"How dare you!" said Abby so low it resembled a growl.

Miss Knightly lifted her chin, laughing. "I would. I'd also dare to say you've never slept in Charles' bed, nor has he yours. Who else would know besides the one who washes your sheets, and keeps his warm?"

"Never in my life—"

"Right. Never, but we aren't in England, are we? I've got a lot to live for, and you've got a lot to hide."

Abby's pulse thumped in her ears. How could such a woman be so brazen? She stood up and turned around to face her.

"Get out."

Miss Knightly moved closer, pausing to measure Abby with a glare. She reached over, snatching the last piece of hair in her hands. She stabbed the pin in place, making Abby jump.

"Oh, what a delicious scandal. Some stable hand, I bet. And months ago, it seems," she said, lowering her catlike eyes from Abby's chest to her waist.

Abby felt her face paling, and the room turning black at its seams. "I said leave."

"Well then, don't get too cozy; Charlie won't take too kindly to such news. It's bad for business, you know."

"Perhaps he would welcome it," said Abby, stirring the pot. "You see, Miss Knightly, you know nothing of me or my husband. I would not be so hasty in sharing or you might find your own station compromised."

Miss Knightly's sickly smile vanished into a stone-cold stare. "Time will tell, *my lady*."

Abby swallowed and lowered her eyes in an attempt to hide the emotion pooling within.

With nauseating sweetness, Miss Knightly tucked a strand of hair behind Abby's ear. Abby turned her cheek away.

"There now," she said. "We don't want you looking like a wilted flower. You've got a part to play tonight, and I would hate for Charlie to come to bed moody." She paused a moment, a satisfied smirk on her face, then left, swaying her hips as she sauntered out of the room.

Abby shut the door behind her, pressing her back against it. *She knows. What am I going to do now?* She shuddered.

As the clock chimed, a quick breath caught in Abby's chest. She was due downstairs before the guests arrived. She sent a prayer to the heavens: *Protect me from my enemies.* She prayed too that God would keep Miss Knightly silent at least for a few weeks until another course could be made known. In a few days Charles would be gone to New Orleans with her father. If the news could wait until then, that would give Abby time to formulate a plan.

Maybe Charles could send her away to "visit a relative" and she could birth the child in secret. She could stay there until the child were older so that its age would not be quite so noticeable.

She heard the hum of conversation below and gulped. She was already late.

As she entered the drawing room, the Lawrences stood in polite conversation with Sir Rathburn and Charles. Mrs. Lawrence greeted Abby first, flashing a grin. "Marriage suits you well," she said.

"Does it?" said Abby, tilting her head.

"I wouldn't have thought it possible, but you're even more radiant now than a few months back. Wouldn't you agree, Sir Rathburn?" Heat filled Abby's cheeks at such a bold compliment that drew unwanted attention to her appearance.

Sir Rathburn smiled, almost as she imagined a doting father would. "So it does." It was the closest thing to a compliment Abby had ever heard from her father's mouth in regard to herself.

But if there had been any warmth in Rathburn's eyes towards his only child, it was swept away in the icy chill that followed. Abby saw the churning of his thoughts as it ticked over her every detail. Had her father also come to know her secret? She recalled her reflection before she had left her room. Was it that obvious?

Sir Rathburn's disposition darkened the rest of the evening, and he grew quiet, even in the presence of the Lawrences. Abby rallied, doing her duty well, entertaining Mrs. Lawrence in thoughtful conversation over weather and poetry. In fact, Mrs. Lawrence seemed quite enthralled with Abby's newfound wit and invited Abby to come to tea the next week. Abby even managed to smile at Charles on more than one occasion, thinking that her life depended on such appearances.

But when no one else saw, Abby felt her father's stare boring into her, reading her every thought. What would he do to her? How would he force

Chapter 14

Smoke swirled high, joining clouds of rolling fog as Charles puffed his cigar. Braum, his coachman, portly and red-cheeked, leaned forward, urging the horses on in the runabout carriage. They raced towards the Hollows at the heels of two steeds trotting in steady rhythm, navigating between winding paths littered with trees. Charles reclined, his boots digging in on the lip of the footrest, bouncing with each uneven jolt. He inhaled deeply, welcoming the chill of the late autumn night. It worked against the liquor, refreshing his numb mind after the day's work had come to an end. Tomorrow, Charles would begin the journey to New Orleans.

It had been a tedious day, made tolerable by the anticipation of fresh ventures in Louisiana. Charles hoped it would be the first of many, as long as he could prove to Sir Rathburn the value of buying new vessels. Two of Charles' ships had taken the journey a couple months previously, laden with slaves bound for southern plantations in Texas. The profits had proved most lucrative, three times what Charles could earn shipping other goods like ivory, tobacco, or tea. Yet he feared losing existing clients who relied on Henderson Gold Line to import their goods in a timely manner. Thus, he had hatched a plan to capitalize on profits by purchasing new vessels with Sir Rathburn, as Wyndham & Henderson Mercantile Co. took its first venture.

In two days' time, Sir Rathburn had arranged to meet Charles in the city. There they would travel by rail, then riverboat, down to Louisiana. Tomorrow, however, Charles intended to put business on hold for a tryst with his mistress and maid, Roxanne, at The Park Hotel. With Miss Knightly feeling quite neglected being left in New York, Charles hoped to compensate by giving her a night away from Abby.

Charles' muscles twitched in his back in anticipation of his return home. A crooked smile formed on his lips behind his cigar. Little intimidated Roxanne, which was why she was good for the house and as an escape.

Charles loosened the collar around his neck as he walked through the doors, his mind already lost in fantasies of the pleasures that awaited him with his lover. The house was dark except for a distinct glow from the hall off his room. His steps quickened past the drawing room and beyond the staircase. He gave nothing else attention, as intent as he was on the woman waiting for him.

"Charles," came a quiet voice from behind.

He turned to see Abby poised like a Renaissance sculpture on the stairs, hand resting on the railing, her hair drawn up in a crown of braids atop her head. He swallowed, too aware of the visions of his mistress' unclad figure pulling his thoughts liked a stringed puppet while his wife stood in front of him.

"Why are you up so late?" he said more curtly than intended.

She descended the staircase, motioning for Charles to follow her towards the parlor. Her regal aura was tainted by the quiver of her chin and the distinct glistening of tears in her eyes. Charles thought she looked like a woman haunted by a ghost, and no doubt he was the source of her suffering.

"Might I have a word?" she asked, her voice rising just above a whisper.

Charles ran his fingers through his hair, looking over his shoulder down the hall to the glowing light. "Will this take long?"

Abby had already knelt down to the hearth and fumbled with the iron rod to stir the embers of the fire that had all but died down. "I . . . I do not know."

Charles sighed. She continued the task, fighting to warm the room as a beggar to the coals. They did not disappoint, as gentle flames licked up from the floor, affording enough light for Charles to discern her troubled expression. He fiddled with the cufflinks on his sleeve.

"Tell me tomorrow," he said, turning away without pause.

Her voice rose from behind. "You leave in the morning. It cannot wait."

Charles kept his back turned, intent on avoiding her pleading eyes. "I'm sure we've already broached the subject before."

Abby stood up. "Can't Knightly wait a little longer while you speak to me?" she said with a cutting edge.

Charles turned, feeling more resolved to end the conversation before it started. "She might wait, but *I* won't," he said. He turned to make his retreat, sure that he had twisted the dagger enough to silence her. The grandfather clock chimed, announcing the late hour, and he kept his course.

"I am with child," came Abby's voice, a tidal wave crashing behind him. His boots stalled, as though caught in quicksand. He turned, his eyes now haunted too. *What did she say?* he thought.

When he saw her face, he knew, but he could not believe it.

He found himself instinctively rushing back to her. She crumbled to the sofa, cradling her head in her hands, trembling with fright. The sight stung Charles' heart, and he sat near her, stunned to silence, until his breath returned.

"How long have you known?"

She lifted her head, her fingers fumbling with the cuff of her sleeves. Had he noticed her figure succumbing to the maternal call? Had he averted his eyes to her swelling breasts and bulging middle? He did not want to think on it.

"For God's sake, how long, Abby?"

She took in a breath, like she had been drowning beneath the waves. She closed her eyes, and a strength set in her jaw. "For some time."

"And you are just telling me now! It's been six months. Six months since I had anything to do with you. Is someone else involved?"

She stood up, facing him with unashamed tears. "You would have to ask such a thing? When I figured it out, I did not know how you would respond. For all I knew, you would abandon me and leave me to face my father alone!"

Charles nodded, regretting his last statement. *She is right,* he admitted. Guilt gripped him as he considered her plight. She had too much to lose without his protection. Sir Rathburn would as soon toss her to drown at sea, or worse, sell her body at the docks with the other prostitutes.

All thoughts of Roxanne and his desire suddenly fled as his wife shook before him, appearing more real than any fantasy of his. The woman in front of him, a Wyndham of English nobility, might carry on the Henderson name if he could quell the impending scandal.

"I will make this right," he said. His eyes searched the flames of the fire, contemplating every outcome.

Abby's expression lifted. "Will you?"

Charles returned her gaze and nodded. If he acted swiftly, he could deal with the situation and put it behind them before anyone caught on. He only had to get in contact with the doctor's wife he had read about in the paper a few months before. She would help.

"No one will have to know," said Charles, determined.

The tension in her face relaxed. Charles' own heart swelled. For the first time, he felt like he had been able to offer her some sort of comfort.

"That is why I came to you. I feared Father caught on when he saw me the other evening," she said, the worry marking itself between the delicate lines of her brow.

Charles reached over, stroking her cheek. Her eyes brimmed with uncertainty.

"He will have nothing to think about when he sees you again; we leave for New Orleans tomorrow. By the time he gets back, I will have it taken care of, and he'll be none the wiser."

The fire popped, sending flickers of light dancing up into the chimney. The room had warmed considerably, and Abby no longer shook with fright. For a moment, the two sat together in a comfortable silence, almost as it should be. Charles stole a look at her as she stirred the coals again. Somehow he thought she seemed stronger than when he had first met her, and the pregnancy certainly afforded her an enchanting glow.

Logic escaped him, as his mind raced with all the possibilities. With their troubles finally behind them, maybe they could have children the proper way? Abby tilted her head in thought, drawing her eyes to Charles. "Where will you send us?"

Charles lowered his voice to a whisper. "I'm not sure of the name, but I heard of a midwife who helps women in these situations."

Abby nodded. "How does she help them?"

"She administers medicines, and then the situation resolves itself."

Abby's eyes widened. She rose slowly, backing away. Charles saw the outline of her stomach announcing the bulge of life beneath her gown. He swallowed, feeling a sting in his gut.

"That *resolves* nothing. I thought you hoped to send us away for a time."

"*Us?*" said Charles, thoroughly confused.

"Me and your child."

"How does that solve anything?"

She held her hands over her stomach as if to shield it from Charles' very words. "I would give birth and come back when it was older. After a few petty months of age, it would not be as noticeable."

He shook his head, wondering how she had misunderstood him.

"There's no other way, Abby."

"You speak of *murder*," she said, her voice so low it sounded like a growl.

"Hush . . . Just listen. That will raise your father's suspicions even more. And you can't tell me you actually want to give birth after—"

"You don't get to decide what I want!"

"What good can come from that?"

"I don't want anything else to break, Charles. I can't bear the thought of losing this baby, when in any other circumstance its life would be celebrated. I want this child, and you do too!"

Charles stared back into the fire that flickered with life even as it turned the remainder of the coals to ashes. He did not want this. She was wrong. This could ruin everything. Yet, when he looked over at her, her eyes frantic with worry, he could not help but think she looked every part the mother.

"If you want a child, let's do this the right way; I can give you children after this is all behind us."

She stared at Charles, incredulous. "I will not give up this baby just to be replaced with another that fits into *your* timeline."

"So you want to have a living reminder of our past?" said Charles, his voice rising. His hands balled into fists, longing for something to punch, something to release his rage.

She looked down at her belly, holding it. "This is not our past. This is our future. Please, Charles. I am already a mother to this child."

And I am a father, thought Charles. His throat closed as an unfamiliar lump knotted up in the back of it. He gulped it down, refusing to pay heed to such unreasonable emotion.

"We can't have it. You know that."

Abby stood firm, light pulsing in her eyes, her chin raised in defiance. "I did not have to tell you."

"Oh really? Because you could hide this for nine months?" he answered.

"I chose to tell you because I thought you would help me and your child," she said, her voice low and penetrating.

"I need time to think," he said, pacing the floor. But the more he tried to think, the more clouded his mind became. He did not see a sure way, especially with him leaving the very next morning.

"*Char-lie . . .*" a silky voice trilled, drawing out both syllables. His thoughts wandered from the glow of the firelight to the trickle of light emitted from the hallway. He imagined Roxanne draped in his sheets, peeking through the crack of his doorway. The pull grew taut in his gut, even as he stood in front of Abby. He sighed, feeling defeat.

"She's waiting," said Abby coolly, a hollowness in her voice. Charles looked towards the hallway. He began walking away.

"Charles?" Abby called out.

He waved her away. "I need more time," he said, wanting to escape all the unfixable problems.

"You don't have more time."

Charles turned back around, seething. "It's the only solution, Abby!"

"Please, Charles," she said, emotion thick in her voice.

"Just stay out of sight while I'm gone. Wait for word from me. And if you think for one minute to go blabbing to that old maid of yours about this, you will certainly regret it. No one can know, especially now."

Abby took in a sharp breath like he had pierced her heart again. He turned away for the final time, leaving her sitting helpless by the fire while he chased after the silhouette waiting at the threshold of his bedroom.

Chapter 15

Abby watched through the linen curtains of her bedroom window the next morning as the final trunk was tied down on top of the carriage, hiding as though invisible. She did not venture downstairs to bid her husband goodbye; the sight of Miss Knightly's own luggage next to Charles' only served to fan the fire of her shame. Yet, she regretted standing there, for it pained her to see Charles cozied up next to Miss Knightly from the rear window of the carriage.

Abby's time away from Knightly was not long enough. A mere day and a half later, she returned by carriage, choking the hall with the sickly sweet scent of perfume. She pranced about, barking orders in a new mustard-colored pin-striped frock, its lines accenting her every curve. A wide-brimmed hat slanted slightly on top of her ginger ringlets. The gaudy attire nearly caused Abby to laugh aloud, for she could not shake the ludicrous impression of a hybrid canary-zebra creature. But whatever reprieve Abby had enjoyed during Knightly's absence was quickly forgotten at her return, with her shrewd gaze and careful attention to Abby's whereabouts.

"Don't make any plans. I've been instructed to keep you here," said Knightly early the next morning as Abby sat eating her breakfast.

"I am accustomed to making my own schedule," said Abby.

"Not on my watch."

"I am a grown woman. I have no need for a nursery maid," retorted Abby.

"Oh, in time you will. Won't you?"

Abby ignored her, keeping her eyes fixed on her plate.

"I think red satin drapes would do this room a bit of justice," Knightly remarked.

Abby looked up from her plate, seething. Of course Knightly would stoop so low. She would remodel the entire house to her tastes and then Abby's very room, without Abby's consent.

"Of course, I'll have to get Charlie's approval," she crooned and then walked out of the room.

Abby could hardly keep her breakfast down after Knightly left. Worry ailed her as she thought about what had passed between Knightly and Charles. Her only consolation was that Knightly could not surprise him with the news of her pregnancy.

Days crawled by. Abby wrote to Miss Robins, asking how she was faring. Then, to Reverend Truitt and even Eliza Pennington as bored as she was stuck indoors. Her situation closed in around her, becoming even more real as she felt the babe fluttering in her belly.

When over a week had passed and she'd had no reply to any of her correspondence, she wrote yet another letter to Miss Robins and gave it to Timothy to send out as she had always done before. This time, she slipped off her shoes and tip-toed to the door, peeking around the corner just in time to see Timothy handing her letter to Miss Knightly.

Abby's mind reeled with worry, and her growing belly had nowhere to hide. She was truly trapped. Anything might happen, and no one would know the truth. Knightly stalked the house, her eyes probing at Abby's waist. Abby kept more to her room, out of sight.

One evening, boredom got the better of her and Abby ventured downstairs, finding some relief in Charles' library. She quickly lost herself in pages that spoke of fictional worlds she yearned to escape to, until the uncomfortable sensation of being watched overwhelmed her, and she glanced at the door. There Knightly stood, stalking her prey, her eyes narrowing in on the bulge hidden beneath Abby's outspread skirts.

"So, whose is it?" sneered Knightly between flaming lips.

Abby swallowed, a chill crawling up her spine. She sat up straight in her chair but kept silent. Apparently Charles had not told his secret to Knightly, and she waited in the dark. Abby wanted to keep it that way, for the less she knew, the better.

"It can't be *his*," said Knightly.

"You speak out of turn. Leave me."

Knightly jerked her chin. "Think you're something special, don't you? Like you can order me around with the wave of your hand. You know, all he ever wanted was your father's money. But he has that now, doesn't he?" She smiled, the whites of her teeth flashing. "It won't be long now. They have places for girls like you."

She threw her head back, releasing a dark, gravelly sound. Abby said nothing, her own stomach knotted with fear. Then a gentle peace pressed down on her, and she looked into Knightly's face, unafraid.

"What man intends for evil, God intends for good," said Abby.

Knightly's eyes narrowed. "I've seen women in far worse situations than what you've created for yourself and God never lifted a finger to help them. Charlie was right—you're nothing but a pampered girl leaning on a crutch you call faith," she said before turning away.

Abby shuddered, wondering what horrors Knightly had witnessed to bring her to such conclusions. A sliver of doubt wormed its way into her mind. Had Abby not suffered enough?

* * *

Nights became increasingly restless. As sleep eluded her, Abby would go to her window and stare at the moon. When she did finally succumb, she would often awaken with a start as she imagined the click of Miss Knightly's heels in the hallway. With no word from Charles, Abby had little assurance of her future, or the safety of her child.

Prayer became her only solace, God her only friend. Night after night she knelt, wrapped in a shawl, the light of a lone candle cutting through her dark thoughts. There she whispered, beseeching God to make a way. One night as she prayed, a strange wind rattled her window, drawing her attention. She stood and walked over, freeing the latch to look outside. The gust blew in, whirling about her, but her candle did not blow out.

Flee.

The word gripped her soul, as earnest and as real as the breeze that enveloped her, so that she wondered if she had in fact gone mad.

Flee.

The wind intensified, sending the flame flickering and her hair swirling behind her.

She nodded, her eyes wide. Then, the wind stilled, and so did the drum of her heart. If He said flee, then flee she must.

Chapter 16

Sir Rathburn slumped in his seat, dozing against the window of the riverboat next to his servant, Graham, who sat at the ready. Across from him, Charles watched as the Louisiana landscape unfolded around him, shrouded in a canopy of Spanish moss that drooped lazily outside his window. The wetlands bred masses of long grasses, carpeting the riverbank and humming with the croaks of bullfrogs. As they wound downriver, the city winked on the horizon with the promise of fortune throbbing at its center. Buildings inched higher and higher, poking through the skyline. Charles had never been to New Orleans himself. His own father had returned from his visit with no good thing to say about her, though he had never explained why. Charles, on the other hand, felt her allure as that of his mistress, seductively beckoning him to taste, and to touch.

When they arrived, Charles and Sir Rathburn staggered down the ramp, their joints stiff from days of travel. A savory aroma hung in the air, and Charles found his mouth wet with hunger. He inhaled the scent, a mixture of smoked paprika and cayenne pepper, overlaid with the distinctive scent of salty crawfish.

"Should we eat first?" said Charles.

Sir Rathburn shook his head. "This street serves nothing more than pub fare. We will dine properly, or not at all."

Charles nodded even as his stomach growled.

With the arch of Sir Rathburn's brow, Graham jumped to find a means of transportation. The hour stretched three quarters past noon, and still the streets teemed with life. Sounds of French tongues wagged, mixed with

Spanish accents, so that Graham had difficulty understanding the drivers waiting to cart passengers for pay.

Within minutes, he had secured a horse and buggy, with a dark-skinned man at the reins. He lowered his eyes as Graham spoke to him.

"St. Louis Hotel," said Graham.

"Yes suh," said the driver, and he climbed out to load their luggage while Sir Rathburn and Charles took their seats. Charles studied the coachman. He wore a simple pair of brown trousers and a coarse plain shirt. His shoulders bent forward, stooping. As he grappled with the reins, a scar showed on the palm of his hand. Charles wondered if he was in fact a slave, and if so, where was his master?

"What day is this?" asked Charles.

"It's da auction day, suh," said the driver.

Charles looked at Sir Rathburn and shrugged. If he wasn't mistaken, it was Saturday, a prime day for conducting business.

As they trundled through the town, Charles marveled at the variety of people going about their day-to-day lives, the distinction of class evident in a person's attire, from simple cotton, to elaborate prints, to satin and silk vests and dresses. The smooth, airy tunes of a saxophone seemed to follow them through the streets, playing the notes of New Orleans's very soul. Suddenly, the clink of chains interrupted the melody, drawing his attention over his left shoulder. Dark-skinned men and women shuffled in a line, bound by iron shackles at their feet and wrists, and led by the whip of a tall man barking orders. Charles could see that their ankles were scraped raw from the rub of the metal chains. A child stumbled wearily behind, nearly tripping against the mother's tug. By the delicate curve of her nose and the small oval of her chin, Charles saw that it was a little girl, maybe four years of age. Her lips were cracked and bleeding so that Charles himself felt the need for water on his tongue.

He tried to look away, but his eyes held him fast. The men at the front faced the glare of the sun on their chests, wearing only the scars of the whip on their backs. Charles swallowed.

"Charles?"

Charles turned to find Sir Rathburn staring at him with a disapproving eye, unaware of the clamor of the chains behind them.

"I asked, when do we sign for the vessels?" he said with an arched brow.

Charles nodded, trying to dismiss the dryness of his own tongue. "Tomorrow. We sign tomorrow."

"And are they at port?"

Charles nodded. "They were set to arrive two days ago unless something delayed them."

"Perfect, we can take care of our business, and then see all that New Orleans can offer," he said, looking through the red dust swirling behind the carriage in front of them.

They rounded the corner of Chartres Street, and Charles squinted towards the sky as the St. Louis Hotel hailed its grandeur from above. Archways stretched high at the main entrance. Greek-inspired columns weaved throughout the structure, lining its portico in front of the towering bowl of the Rotunda. The Rotunda held the hotel's most prized form of entertainment: the auctions.

Ladies stepped down from their carriages in flowing folds of satin and glittering jewels. Their laced gloves fell into the hands of men boasting silk top-hats and round cheeks with gold watch chains dangling from their vests. Laughter hung in the humid air along with the roll of wooden wheels as the ladies and gentlemen filed into the entrance of the Great Hall.

"I believe we have arrived, and I am quite hungry," said Sir Rathburn. His lips formed a half smile, his eyes gleaming as they perused the sights around them. Charles wondered whether Rathburn was as hungry for food as for the taste of the enterprise promised in the bustle of the room.

The two left Graham to bring their luggage to their rooms, then joined the throng of people heading into the hall. Charles' stomach growled, as he smelled the promise of dinner sizzling at the restaurant, but Sir Rathburn veered towards the hum of the crowd and the sound of the gavel in the Rotunda. Charles gritted his teeth and followed.

The space sang of luxury, its ceiling crowned with ornate embellishments that loomed above the crowd standing on its marble floors. Three auctioneers endeavored to make their business known, battling to be heard over the buzz. They rang out in their own tongue either the common language, or French, or Spanish. Each pound of their gavel was met with coos of delight from the onlookers.

All attention focused on one block, at the far right of the room. A fine large oil painting rested on its easel in a bronze-dusted frame as the auctioneer barked its starting bid in a Spanish tongue. Spectators' eyes gleamed with envy as they smacked their lips. Curious, Charles moved closer to make out the detail. It was a powerful piece of artistry, painted with thick, heavy strokes, depicting the rage of a tempest battering a lone ship. The light of the chandelier above accentuated the textured roiling waves, and Charles wondered how the piece would look above the mantel in his study. The gavel sounded, and the war began, each bid noted with a slight wave of the hand, the dollar amount climbing up, up, until its new owner's champagne glass clinked with the elegant woman's who stood next to him in a fur wrap.

A tray of beverages seemed to float above the crowd, its stemmed glasses skillfully balanced so that they neither teetered nor clinked. It glided around the room, settling next to Charles. The dark-skinned man who offered it wore the simple plain clothes of servitude.

"Would you gentlemen care for a drink?" he said.

Charles cocked his head, thoroughly confused by his intelligible vernacular. The man's dark eyes stayed steady, his lips firm, and he held Charles' gaze.

Then he looked past Charles, lowering his voice so that no one else could hear, "First time in this city?"

Charles nodded.

"Here's a hint. You keep your head up, we keep our eyes down," he said, so that Charles finally looked past him.

Rathburn gave the man no heed, taking a glass off the tray, his stare fixed on the blocks spaced throughout the room. The man walked away, serving another group of thirsty spectators, and Charles' eyes followed.

Then, the murmur in the room hushed and Charles felt a charge in the air, as all eyes turned to the wooden block at the Rotunda's center. The auctioneer grinned beneath his mustache, his long arms rising to command the crowd's attention.

"As promised, the long awaited, much anticipated auction of the late Duncan Ferrer Kinner's property from the prized Ashlyn-Belle Hellen sugar plantation. Here for your buying pleasure. You won't find a better breeding than from this esteemed estate," announced the auctioneer.

Thunderous applause erupted, wolf-whistles echoing through the hall amid the jingle of bracelets and gold trinkets. The auctioneer smiled then clapped his hands high, the apple of his cheeks glowing. He held the crowd with his eyes, teasing them with the anticipation of the next bid.

"Get on with it!" a man yelled.

"Or else we'll spend it all on liquor," added another tall gentleman. Laughter rolled up among the less inebriated.

The auctioneer winked, laughing aloud. "Get your pocketbooks ready, ladies and gentlemen." He waved his right hand towards the back of the room. People spun towards the door, craning their necks to get a peek at the next stock.

As he saw the parade, Charles' face paled. A string of slaves filed in front of their burly overseer with his licking whip. Their faces sought no attention but the floor. They no longer appeared filthy, their skin glistening with a fresh rub of oil. The muscles on the broad-shouldered men twitched behind their scars. The mother clutched her young child's hand, her lips pressed tight.

Charles glanced over and, in the limelight of the chandelier, found Rathburn glowing. He watched as Rathburn rubbed his hands together eagerly, as though weighing up the prize on offer. Charles rubbed his temples, his head pulsing.

"Go on, take a good look before the bidding begins!" shouted the auctioneer.

The spectators circled the subjects, poking and prodding, lifting their arms, squeezing their muscles in detailed observation. The woman staggered as an older man ripped her away from her child to scrutinize the palms of her hands. The little girl yelped while another man opened her mouth to survey her teeth.

"It is a wicked business."

The words came out of Charles' mouth before he knew it, echoing the sound of his dead father's own voice. Sir Rathburn's eyes fell on him.

"Oh no. This is business at its finest, my boy."

Charles nodded, an ashen look on his face. Rathburn's eyes narrowed.

"I thought Abby stayed back home, but it seems you have endeavored to bring her with you."

Charles let out a nervous laugh, his own mind reeling in confusion. This very exchange in the Rotunda was why he had brought Sir Rathburn with him. It was the heart of the slave trade. This very enterprise fueled the need for his company's vessels. Without it, profit was marginal at best. Tobacco, tea, and cotton were enough to turn a small profit, but for the South, this cargo reigned supreme. Human cargo: the South's pride and the North's pain. In the back of his mind, Charles heard his father's grave voice, warning him never to dip his fingers into that well. *"Stay away from that trade, son. It's a wicked business."*

The hammer of the gavel signaled the start of the bidding wars. Charles' ears rang in a high-pitched peal as he looked on. His throat constricted at each new bid, until the prize was won and applause rent the air. He couldn't take his eyes off the little girl, who stood stone still, her face frozen in terror.

By the end, the strong men with their muscled, glistening chests brought seven hundred and fifty dollars a piece, a proud sum. The woman brought only five hundred, no doubt because she showed herself weak from tears. Her little girl howled as she was pried from her mother's skirts by the rough hands of a plantation owner for two hundred and fifteen dollars.

Then, business done, attentions turned elsewhere. All except for Charles', who couldn't understand the ache in his chest. He watched blankly as musicians trickled into the building, toting their violins and cellos, and dark-skinned servants set up the chairs in preparation for the ball. In only a few short hours, laughter and music would soon erase any trace of the day's dealings. Where shackled slaves had stood, finely dressed ladies and gentlemen would while away the evening drinking champagne, dancing, and chatting about their latest acquisitions.

Sir Rathburn moved towards the lobby, motioning for Charles to follow with a subtle nod of his head. "I overheard someone discussing the hotel's exquisite cuisine. Let's go fill our stomachs and discuss tomorrow's plans," he said.

Charles nodded, moving forward as though chained to Sir Rathburn's heels. *I've lost my appetite,* he thought.

Chapter 17

Charles stood at the edge of the dock, a roll of papers hanging limp in his left hand, his right covering his face. Fog crept over the waters, where three proud ships had once swayed with their tall masts dipping in between the swells. The creaking of the dock jerked him back to attention. He turned to see a red-faced Sir Rathburn clamoring down the boardwalks, both rows of his teeth showing.

Dread lodged in Charles' gut like an anchor.

"Tell me it was insured," said Rathburn in a frenzied tone, sounding more animal than human.

Charles said nothing.

"You mean to tell me, you dragged me down here and did not even think to have the cargo insured?"

Charles took a breath. "We owned nothing until late yesterday when the deed was signed. The insurance companies were closed, and I planned to go first thing this morning. The transaction had hardly been finalized when . . ." Charles tugged at his hair. This made no sense. It couldn't be happening. Mist sprayed around them. The dock swayed and yawned against the lap of the waves. Neither man spoke.

Less than twelve hours before they had been raising their glasses and playing a reckless hand of cards in celebration of closing the deal with Geoffrey Baldwin. A new steamship would now bear the brand of Wyndham & Henderson Mercantile Co. on her hull. Charles had commissioned a painter to fix the brand at dawn's first light.

The cargo waited in the holds of the ship just at the docks. The slave pens were stocked full, with the weekend auction and fair drawing a hungry crowd. With no place to unload, and fearing his cargo would fall ill in the holding pens, Baldwin had sold half of his share of shipping rights along with his vessel. Charles and Rathburn saw this as another opportunity for gain and eagerly signed the agreement.

Eight hours later, Charles had awoken to the sound of frantic knocking. Bleary-eyed, he opened the hotel door to find an anxious sailor on the other side. "Yer ship be burn'n! Better come with me."

Charles threw on his shirt, not awake enough to bother with the buttons. "My ship?"

The sailor nodded, rushing down the hall, with Charles stumbling in his half-laced boots. He led Charles down to the docks, a few blocks from the hotel.

Flames flickered from across the small harbor. The stench of burning singed the air. It smelled different than chimney smoke, like a pungent coppery perfume.

"The slaves," said Charles.

The whites of the sailor's eyes grew bigger. "There's nothing ye can do."

Charles raced towards the flames, and as he neared he saw sails swallowed up in plumes of black smoke and raging fire. His feet pounded against the planks. It was not just his vessel burning, but the two others docked beside. Fire licked its way up their proud masts. Men rushed on the other ships, throwing barrels and boxes into the water in an attempt to salvage whatever they could before the fire overtook them completely. The vessels moaned.

"The holds!" he said, then, raising his voice as he ran to the edge of the docks, "Release the holds!"

"They already tried. The heat overtook 'em." The sailor held Charles' shoulders as the dark of his eyes caught the light of the flames, wide and horrified.

"No!" he cried out. The silhouettes of a few men flickered on the deck of the ship, their fiery bodies jumping into the sea below.

"It's no use," said the sailor, removing his hat from his head and holding it to his heart.

Charles found he could not look away, his eyes fixed on the inferno before him, each hellish scream piercing him, his conscience forever scarred by the sight.

Charles lifted his head but could not shake the image, the stench of charred flesh still soaking the air. Sir Rathburn spit on the ground by his boots and cursed Charles' very name.

"If someone must be cursed, let it be Baldwin's men, not me!"

Wyndham's eyes narrowed into slits. "Baldwin's men? *You're* the imbecile who didn't insure it."

Charles gritted his teeth, stepping closer to Sir Rathburn. "They left the cargo in place. The only thing we touched attached to that ship was its deed."

Dark water sloshed against the docks. He felt his whole body constrict, as though he might snap. Hadn't his father warned him?

"We lost twenty. Twenty," said Charles, the finality of the words striking him.

"Twenty thousand dollars. Not to mention the two other ships beside ours that we have to account for," said Sir Rathburn.

Charles cringed. All the blue-blooded man cared for was his money. Money did not live and breathe. It did not scream in agony when met with fire. Charles let out a demented sort of sound resembling laughter, causing Sir Rathburn's face to flush, then darken into a hue so red it looked as though his skin would boil.

"Get yourself together, boy, before you invite more attention our way. You are the swine who brought me to this God-forsaken place. And now my investment is at the bottom of Oak Harbor."

Charles closed his mouth, clenching his jaw. *It should have been his grave*, he thought, and in the same moment another, unfamiliar voice answered in his mind.

It should have been yours.

Charles shuddered. "I told you there was risk," he said.

"*You* take risks. *I* make investments. Fix it, Henderson, before the whole lot of them come after us," said Sir Rathburn before steaming away.

Charles' knees buckled, and he put his arms out either side to steady himself. For a brief moment, staring into the murk beneath his feet, he contemplated jumping in. *Would anyone notice? Would anyone care?* New Orleans had been so promising. He looked back out over Oak Harbor and shook his head. Then he turned away and stumbled towards St. Louis Street in search of a remedy.

Antoine's Saloon waited for him, luring the wandering, bored, or troubled into its doors just a short walk away from the docks. He felt dazed as his eyes adjusted to the dim light. The saloon sat empty, its waitresses still prepping tables for the day ahead.

"*Bonjour*," said the waitress, her low voice like silk. Charles squinted at her like a lost child.

"Meester?" she said, her white apron pressed neatly against her black skirt.

Charles shook his head, trying to regain his senses.

"You looking for zee friend?" she asked.

"No. It's just me."

Her dark eyebrows rose along with her grin.

"I prepare zee table for one den?"

Sir Rathburn's sulking figure caught Charles' attention. He slouched at the back of the room, nursing his wounds with a tumbler of scotch. Charles rolled his eyes. There was no avoiding him. He shot a glance at the waitress. "Never mind. I'm with him," he said, pointing to Sir Rathburn. She led him to the seat across from his father-in-law's glowering face.

"Gin please," he said.

She curled her lips into a smile again and wound her way towards the bar. In a couple of minutes, she brought Charles his drink. He leaned over the table, resting his head between his hands. Sir Rathburn downed a long hard swallow before acknowledging him.

"What is your remedy, Henderson?"

"I think this is the best place to start," said Charles, nodding to Sir

Rathburn's empty glass.

Sir Rathburn seemed unamused.

"There is no mercy in business. Only what you can salvage," he said, his jaw twitching. "Luckily, you have me."

Charles raised his head.

"What do you mean?"

"My lawyer. He can work this to our favor."

The invisible weight pressing down on Charles' shoulders eased slightly.

"He can fix something this big?" said Charles.

Sir Rathburn cocked his head. "He will have to. I did not forge a partnership to have my half squandered by your idiocy." He paused, drumming his fingers on the table. "It does feel like there are a great many things that need 'fixing' of late."

Charles' gut tightened. Did Sir Rathburn know about Abby? He took a swig of his gin.

Sir Rathburn continued. "No promises to you, of course. You are the one who got us into this situation. But I think it is possible to recover the losses."

Charles tilted his head. "Should I be relieved?" he said. But his mind reeled with menacing thoughts, though he did not speak them. Could a lawyer conjure the dead? Even if the merchants were appeased, who would speak for those lives lost?

Sir Rathburn's body relaxed. "I will see it done, and you will learn from it. Or else—" his chair scraped across the floor as he stood—"we leave today before the dam breaks and the *Tribune* has the chance to tie my name to this and print it in the papers. The French have a soft spot for their slaves, and I imagine they already dislike us, seeing that their docks are blackened with soot. I'll send a letter ahead of us to my lawyer. Be back at the hotel by four o'clock sharp."

Charles nodded, and Sir Rathburn stood and left.

Sir Rathburn was right. At any moment, traders and merchants would be at his throat demanding their cargo or, at the least, money to replace it. Money that Charles currently did not have at his disposal. Abby's dowry was locked up in trusts minus the healthy monthly allowance that went straight into paying for the Hollows. The money was Rathburn's. If this whole ordeal had happened a few months later, he would be free. That kind of money and prestige could cover a multitude of sins, and Charles could have quieted any outbursts with an under-the-table recompense. He was at Sir Rathburn's mercy now, but if he found out about his daughter's condition, all was sure to be lost. That would be a scandal so loud that no amount of money could silence it.

Charles tried to rub away the tension in his forehead. He had risked too much, too quickly. His father would roll in his grave.

"You need un more glass, and you be happy fellow," said the waitress, sliding Charles another round of gin. He nodded, taking the glass and throwing it back, welcoming the burn as the liquid coursed down his throat.

He wanted to smile back but couldn't find it in him. The woman reminded him of Roxanne, with her coy grin and bold stare. He remembered their last night in New York, staying in a hotel together right under Sir Rathburn's nose. Her appetite was easily sated; a new bottle of perfume and a new dress was all she needed.

* * *

"Why can't it always be like this, Charlie?" she'd said, glidling over to Charles in her silk wrapper. Her skin was still damp from the steam of the bath, and the new perfume made him dizzy.

"You know how it is," said Charles.

Her lashes fluttered alluringly. "Don't expect me to be happy with her there forever."

Charles laughed at the absurdity of the proposition. To think that Roxanne considered herself an equal who could replace Abby was simply ludicrous. He looked her over. What did she have to offer besides her wiles?

"Like I can just throw her out of the house," he scoffed.

"Our house, or hers?" she said, her fingers loosening his collar.

"Mine. She has to stay, Roxanne. She's my wife."

Her lips puckered into a pout, and Charles moaned. She moved closer, tickling his neck with her breath. "Can't we send her away now that we have the dowry? And all she can do now is cause a stir in her *condition*."

"Condition?"

Roxanne smiled. "You really don't know?"

Charles' heart quickened, wondering how much she knew. "I just didn't want to be reminded."

"It's obvious now. She had a love affair before the wedding. And if the lover shows up, the whole town will be buzz'n. It will make you look quite the fool. Oh, Charlie, you look stressed."

He sighed.

She began rubbing his neck and shoulders. "Don't you worry, these things happen all the time. Let a woman handle a woman's business."

Charles grinned. "That might not be a terrible idea," he said, thinking she would know far more about these matters than he would. Roxanne pulled herself closer to him.

"Will you let me?" she asked.

Charles inhaled, the perfume intoxicating. "Let you what?"

"Take care of it, Charlie. You know, come up with a plan for her." She lifted his lips to hers.

"You can do whatever you like," he whispered.

* * *

The French waitress caught Charles in a trance like a dazed idiot. When Charles saw her standing there, he jumped, unsure how long she had been watching him.

"Need anyzing more?" she said, eyeing him boldly.

Charles swallowed with longing. "That'll be it," he said. *I've already got enough women to deal with as it is.*

She grinned, showing the dimple in her right cheek. "You pay zee other gentleman's bill?"

Charles shook his head. So Sir Rathburn had left him to pay the tab; what a noble gesture.

Chapter 18

Abby stole away early one morning, donning her boots and thickest coat to beat the late November frost. In her pocket she held a brief message scribbled in haste, addressed to Miss Robins. With winter setting in, she did not think she could manage to walk the entire distance to Bristol Estate, but she intended to try. She hoped to find a passerby to deliver the message to Miss Robins that would otherwise be intercepted and read by Knightly. If no kind stranger chanced to see her, she prayed for the strength to make it on foot without being caught first.

The sun was still bleary-eyed under the covers of the horizon when she made it past the row of evergreens encircling the Hollows. From there she trod beyond the post fences to the main road that dipped below the hill where she could walk free, obscured from the view of any window from the house. Her breath was quick, and her legs stiff after being confined for so long. She noticed her gait had changed into an off-kilter waddle. Half a mile down the lane, a pain stabbed her side, and she had to slow her pace.

In the stillness just before dawn, loneliness enveloped her and dark thoughts shook her resolve. No other soul knew of her troubles, none but God. But why would a God of love leave her so alone in her helpless condition?

But had He left her? She believed she knew the answer, but in her despair, seeds of doubt had been sown. Shuddering in the chill morning air, she tried to shift her attention to the path she now tread, willing herself forward, slowly but deliberately, imagining the babe inside her gently rocking with each step. And just then, the glorious sun began to rise from its slumber to accompany her. Its rays bathed the way ahead in warm light, illuminating the rust-colored leaves still clinging to their branches. A fresh new wave of emotion overcame her, as though she'd suddenly awoken from her own deep sleep to see the world swathed in a glory that stretched beyond her own circumstances. Had not the Lord redeemed life from the pit before? And even in that moment she felt hope, the hope of a new day.

She walked at least two miles when a rhythmic trot from behind set her nerves on edge. She was sure Knightly had sent Braum after her. She spun around, looking for trees or bushes to hide her from sight. Hastily she lifted her skirts and stepped off the path, slipping behind a group of trees that felt more like sprigs. Her boots sank into the wet earth, covering them with filth.

Moments later, she turned to see a mud-stained mare galloping towards her while a scraggly youth clung to its reins. Her belly ticked with fresh movement from the baby, and again the flutter of hope, mixed with relief, bolstered her spirits. She waddled back onto the lane, lifting her hand in a wave. The boy sat up and pulled hard on the reins, willing his mount to come to a halt.

"Whoa!" he said, clicking his tongue. His skin was smooth against the soft outline of his face, showing the copper stain of the sun. He cocked his head quizzically and peered down at Abby. She stepped backward, suddenly frightened by the prancing hooves in front of her. But the young lad carried a smile over his face, setting her at ease.

"Morn'n Miss," he said, tipping his cap to her. His fingernails were lined with dirt, an imprint of the harvest toil.

"What a Godsend you are this morning," said Abby. "Are you headed north on this road?"

"Yes'm. Just on an errand to Sutherland's farm. Then I'll be com'n back this way," he said.

No sooner had Abby heard his response than their heads whipped back around to the distinct sound of a buggy's wheels. In no time at all, the top of the runabout popped up from the hill. *Knightly*, thought Abby, her heart sinking.

Hurriedly she said, "Please, give this message directly to Miss Robins at Bristol Estate." She offered up the letter.

The boy nodded, his brow wrinkled in confusion. His mare reared to leave, but the boy steadied her.

"You all right, mam? I never seen a woman in your condition walk'n on this road."

Abby tried to smile to mask the rising panic, but time was of the essence. She needed him to ride, and to ride now.

She reached up, taking his calloused hand in her smooth one. "I am fine for now, but I need this delivered to Miss Robins straight away," she pleaded.

"Consider it done, Miss," he said, sitting tall in his saddle. He grinned, showing a row of tobacco-stained teeth. But his eyes were soft, and Abby trusted his word. His steed reared again, and the boy gave it way; they lurched forward into a gallop as the buggy approached from the other direction.

Braum sat rigid at the reins, looking none too pleased to be rushed from his bed so early in the morning. Knightly leaned forward, her eyes narrowing in on Abby with the utmost disdain. She was cloaked in one of Charles' wool coats. Red hair swarmed around her face like a host of angry bees, but her face was as pale as Abby had ever seen it, her lips dry like cracked wheat without their painted rouge. They came to a halt in front of Abby. Knightly stood, her hand already waving frantically.

"Think you're going somewhere?" she said.

"Am I not allowed to walk?" replied Abby.

Knightly squinted her eyes. "I'm not an idiot. I saw it all. You talking with that man, giving him your love letters before he rode away. I even saw you kissing his hand!"

Abby could not contain herself. She laughed loudly, for Knightly's assumption had veered so far from the truth that it felt like a feather on her feet. Abby would let Knightly assume all she wanted, just so long as Miss Robins read her note and arrived tomorrow morning for tea.

"Get in," said Knightly with a sneer.

"Since when must I listen to you?"

"Since Charles charged me to keep watch over you . . . and for good reason. You might steal away with your lover and have all of New York wagging their tongues about it. I won't have him thrown to the pigs because of your stupidity!"

Abby rolled her eyes, fighting another urge to laugh. She climbed up into the seat next to Knightly with the help of Braum's strong hand.

"Surely you cannot be so daft as to think I would live that carelessly," said Abby.

Knightly pursed her lips and arched her brow at Abby's belly. "It appears you are in fact that daft."

Abby turned her face away, ignoring the woman the rest of the way home.

* * *

The next day, just as planned, a quick rap on the door echoed through the hall in the early afternoon. Abby rushed from the parlor, as quick as a mouse, to greet her guest before any servants could intercept her. Knightly's heels clicked close behind, but Abby reached the door first, flinging it wide with little decorum. Miss Robins jumped in alarm at the sudden motion, and then the surprise continued to grow on her face when she caught sight of Abby's protruding abdomen.

"Oh, do come inside, Robins. It is frightfully chilly today."

Miss Robins reached to embrace Abby, and whispered, "Are you all right my dear? I was most troubled yester—"

"Silly Robins, you're fretting over nothing," interrupted Abby with a smile. She could not have Miss Robins showing her concern with Knightly standing just behind them. It would raise the alarm. Abby kept her voice light and airy. "Don't be so dramatic," she continued with a pointed glance at Miss Robins. "Father will hardly miss the parcel he left; knowing him, it was probably full of dusty old books."

Abby ushered a flustered Miss Robins inside, keenly aware of Knightly's shadow lurking around the column. Robins' brow furrowed in confusion, panic still etched on her features.

"That's not what I was talking about."

Abby turned so that her back faced Knightly and lifted her finger to her lips, pleading with her eyes, and then she let out a squeal of delight.

"I'm so happy you've come. How would you like to help me into town this afternoon? I have a few things I'd like to see to, and then I hear a new bakery has opened up with a delicious pastry selection."

As Abby blabbered on like a schoolgirl, the wrinkles in Miss Robins' forehead deepened, even as she nodded. Out of the corner of her eye, Abby saw Knightly's folded arms and jaw-locked stare. Finally, Miss Robins' own eyes brightened, and a fictitious smile washed over her face. Abby breathed a sigh of relief.

Robins joined the prattling, relaying the most mundane information about the weather, her health, and how her family fared back in London. Then she babbled on about the wiles of Eliza Pennington, saying she had finally snatched a wealthy son of none other than a factory owner. Abby was encouraged by her old friend's instincts, and she rallied her courage to make the bold statement, "Miss Knightly, send for Braum to take us to town."

"I'm afraid that's impossible; the horses haven't been watered or fed."

Abby practiced her most commanding tone. "It would seem someone is falling far behind on their duties. Head to the stables and see to it yourself then. I expect them ready before the top of the hour. Send tea for us in my room while I gather my things and change my frock."

Knightly smiled, looking the part of a dutiful servant, just as Abby had hoped. "Braum isn't here, Mrs. Henderson," she said with the most subtle twitch of her eye.

Abby lifted her chin, daring Knightly to show insubordination in front of a stranger to the house. "How odd; I could swear I saw him crossing the lawn from my window only a few moments ago. Please, fetch him now. And I expect my tea promptly."

Miss Robins' eyes widened. Abby never spoke to a servant in such a manner.

"But Mrs. Henderson," Knightly continued, "Mr. Henderson's wishes were to ensure you were safely here, at home, while he was away."

Abby seemed to grow two inches, her shoulders pushed back, her neck held high as though she wore the crown of England atop her very head.

"I have nothing to keep me shut up in this house when Miss Robins can accompany me on my errands. We will go now," she said, her impatience flaring. Abby could not stand down, not if she was to follow through with her plan.

"As you wish," said Knightly, tilting her head. She curtsied, perhaps for the first time in front of Abby, offering a smile so sickly sweet it made Abby nauseous.

"Braum will take some time. I'll send tea and biscuits while you wait . . . so you do not fall ill again."

Ill? Aside from the episode of loosing her lunch on Knightly's boots, Abby had not felt ill of late, unless worry counted as such. Knightly's eyes were cool. Her hands lay clasped in front of her like she were the very embodiment of submissive.

Abby gestured towards Miss Robins. "Shall we go upstairs?"

Robins nodded, muttering under her breath, "I would never have thought a servant to be so unruly in my entire life. Who does Mr. Henderson use to find his help?"

Abby chuckled, although inwardly she felt like she might crumble. They entered her room and Miss Robins took a seat by Abby's breakfast table near the window. The light cast a bright glow over graying hair, each strand a testimony of wisdom and loyal service. Oh, how Abby had missed her! What a lonesome few months it had been without her. Abby closed the door behind her. She did not want to trouble Miss Robins' peace with her own woes, but there was no other way. As soon as she and Robins were in the carriage, she would tell her everything and formulate a plan to get away. All of the whys and hows stabbed at Abby's resolve, but she ignored them and continued chatting as if nothing were amiss.

"Am I keeping you from any duties by taking you with me?"

"Oh, I don't have anything pressing with Sir Rathburn away, and that bakery has the mouths of everyone in town watering. It will be such a treat."

"I have a gown that needs mending," said Abby, then she leaned close to

Miss Robins and whispered, "We must keep talking."

Miss Robins nodded, her own eyes wide as saucers, raising her voice an octave too high. "I'll take care of it for you. I don't imagine anyone in this house knows how to sew worth a penny," she said.

Abby looked to the door and saw a flicker of shadows beneath it from the hallway. Abby tip-toed over and cracked the door open, just in time to see the top of Jane's head disappearing as she scurried down the stairs.

Abby turned to Miss Robins, her voice low and serious, hoping her friend's old ears could hear. "There is much to tell you, but first I must leave, Robins. I must leave now."

She held her stomach where the babe kicked with life. Miss Robins smiled, stretching from cheek to cheek.

"We *are* leaving, dear. Just as soon as Braum readies the horses, and I cannot wait to hear the news—" she said with an air of expectation, missing the urgency of the moment.

Abby shook her head, pressing her fingers to her lips. Miss Robins nodded silently and waited while Abby gathered her things. Abby made her way to the dresser and pulled out an extra pair of stockings and a bonnet. Another dress was already laid out for the "extra mending." She brought it over from the chair to the small pile of her belongings. She had chosen only the most precious pieces of jewelry left to her by her mother, but when she picked up her purse dismay crept across her face. It was noticeably lighter than she remembered, as she had received nothing from her monthly allowance since marrying Charles. She set the purse on the bedside table and turned to see Miss Robins.

"I do hope you'll explain, dear," Robins said, looking down at Abby's stomach and back at the bed in confusion.

Abby nodded, a sad look haunting her eyes, her fear almost palpable. Miss Robins came near and squeezed her hands. A knock interrupted them. Abby rushed to cover the items with a throw.

"Yes?" Abby called out.

Jane entered, carrying the tea on a tray, her small hands overwhelmed with the size of the platter laden with shortbread biscuits, cups, and saucers.

It appeared Knightly was trying to outdo herself. Jane set the tray down on the table, her eyes dancing around the room, until her gaze met the throw spread out of place with its curious lumps beneath.

"Have you word on when Braum will be ready to take us to town?"

Jane turned, avoiding Abby's eyes.

"Knightly said at least a half hour."

"Ah, thank you, Jane."

Jane looked up from her pouring. "Sugar, Mrs. Henderson?"

Abby nodded. "None for Robins; she takes hers plain."

"So she does," said Jane as she stirred Abby's cup. The tremble of her hands sent the china rattling until she delivered each saucer.

"Thank you," said Abby, sipping slowly. She withdrew her lips from the cup, the tea sweeter than the biscuits. Jane had been more heavy-handed with the sugar than usual, but Abby was thankful for one last comfort before the uncertain journey ahead.

After Jane had left, and the door closed behind her, Robins spoke in a low whisper. "I sent three messages over the last few weeks for you."

"I assure you, I did not receive them or else I would have written in return," said Abby, careful of how she answered in case Jane eavesdropped at the door. She took another slow sip of her tea and nibbled on a shortbread cookie. "I must gather my things for our outing," added Abby louder than necessary, looking again to the door.

Robins shook her head. "How can I help, my dear?"

"Oh, I only have a few things. You should enjoy your refreshment," said Abby, lifting her cup to her lips for another long sip. Then she stood and continued stuffing her gloves and an extra pair of stockings into a small satchel tucked inside the waistband of her dress.

She swallowed, fighting unbidden tears. In her haste to leave, she had not considered all that she would have to leave behind. She loathed leaving the things that reminded her of her mother. She knew, however, that she must focus on what she would be able to carry with discretion. Throwing aside the blanket, she picked up the jewelry and stowed it in her coin purse. The tips of her fingers felt cool and tingly against the metal. She found her hands shaking before her.

"Oh, muster your courage! Do not tremble now." Abby had intended to keep those thoughts to herself, but her lips uttered them aloud.

Miss Robins peered on with a wrinkled brow as Abby stepped toward the table where her satchel waited. In one clumsy motion, she stumbled forward, catching herself on the post of the bed as all of her jewels tumbled to the floor with a great deal of clattering.

"Are you all right?" said Robins, coming to Abby's side and resting a steadying hand on her shoulder. When Abby lifted her head to respond, the room began to spin for a moment, and then came back to a standstill.

Taking a deep breath, Abby waved her away. "I am fine. We must hurry."

Now, what was I looking for? she thought. No recollection came; it was as though her memory of her intention was as blank as the white sheets of her bed.

A vision of her mother overtook her sight, mixing with reality. So clear was the memory that it seemed as if she were right in front of her, poring over her Bible, its familiar brown cover worn and tattered from use. Her mother glowed, bathed in light streaming from the window. Abby smiled at the vision. Then, a pang of longing gripped her heart and she cried out, but the image disappeared just as quickly as it had come, and Abby found herself standing in front of a very puzzled-looking Miss Robins.

"What death has caught you?" she rasped, shaking Abby's shoulders. Abby pulled away, determined to finish gathering what belongings she could. The top of her forehead beaded with perspiration, and her lips blanched white. She was so thirsty. She spun, eyes scanning the room; she could not remember what she was looking for. A fog blanketed her mind, even as panic gripped her heart.

"Are you half rats?" said Miss Robins.

"I cannot go . . . not without . . ."

Fatigue crept into her limbs, but instead of giving into it, she rummaged through her drawers, tossing stockings and handkerchiefs into the air as she searched. She could not find whatever it was she wanted.

"Get Mother," she said to Miss Robins, looking over her shoulder, glassy-eyed and pale.

"Abby?" said Miss Robins, her voice rising in alarm.

Robins rushed to Abby's side and guided her to the edge of her bed, pressing her hand on her forehead and cheeks. Abby's head felt heavy, as if it were filled with sand. Her eyelids drooped with fatigue. Miss Robins laid her down, then ran to the door to call Jane for help.

Abby heard a faint commotion of sounds around her as she lay in the covers: the creak of hinges, the shuffle of footsteps, the hum of voices. The words and cries for help failed to stir her thoughts as the gears of her mind were locked in place.

Snippets of conversation swirled around her. Jane spoke, her voice too high, like an out-of-tune key on a piano. "I'm so sorry, Miss Robins . . . acting strange . . . fits of melancholy . . . doctor ordered her to rest . . ."

Then Miss Robins' worried voice: "Please . . . I'll watch over her . . ."

The sharp tongue of Miss Knightly cut in: ". . . must insist you leave her . . . my capable hands . . ."

A cool palm brushed across Abby's damp head, and Miss Robins whispered, "I'll check on you, dear." But Abby scarcely noticed as she slipped into a hollow, dreamless sleep.

Chapter 19

Searing pain jolted Abby awake, her eyes shooting open for a moment as she sucked in a breath of air, then closed them again. It felt like scorching hot hands gripped her stomach, squeezing it in waves of torment. No one answered her moaning. The sunny afternoon sky had turned dark, and Abby felt night cloud over her. The steady patter of rain echoed through the room, as ominous clouds swirled overhead. Each exhale of northern wind sent the branches of the cedar tree outside Abby's window flailing. They scraped and clattered against the glass. As Abby came to, she saw Miss Knightly standing at the door and Jane sitting in the corner by the window gnawing at her fingers. Abby lay on the bed, stripped down to her chemise, her hair wet with perspiration. There was a knock from somewhere down below, and then the rumble of thunder and crack of lightning. Knightly stood straighter and gave Jane a stern look of warning before stepping outside.

"Madame, we are so glad you've come and chose to travel in the rain," said Miss Knightly.

The Madame stepped into the room, her long black gown swishing as she walked. Knightly swallowed, dwarfed by the tall woman's commanding presence.

"And where is Mr. Henderson?" said the Madame.

"He's away," replied Knightly.

"I need consent."

Miss Knightly smiled sweetly and took a breath. "No need Madame," she said. "Mrs. Henderson asked for herbs so she would be more comfortable.

I don't think she'll feel like talking now."

Abby's breath quickened, but in her pain she could only moan. *Please, help me*, she begged.

"Where is he?" said the Madame like a prowling lioness.

Knightly offered her most charming smile. "Away on business, but rest assured he requested you come. Here's the letter to prove it, with his very signature. He asked that you come and help with his Mrs. Henderson's unfortunate 'situation'."

The Madame snatched the letter from Miss Knightly's hand, scanning it over with narrow eyes. She pursed her lips together in a pucker.

"Very well. How far along is she?"

"It's hard to tell."

"Three or four months, you said before?"

Miss Knightly gave a half nod.

The Madame walked over to Abby, the strings of pearls jingling from her neck as she neared the bedside.

As the Madame's icy hands pressed on Abby's stomach, another dreadful moan filled the room, the pressure bringing with it a fresh wave of agony. Abby's mind felt sticky and confused. Who was this woman? And what was causing her so much pain? The moaning grew louder as pain wracked her.

Then it eased. In the reprieve, a sliver of understanding pierced Abby's mind. She stirred, willing her body to obey. The Madame's cold hands continued to poke and prod along Abby's abdomen. Abby's own hand pushed away at the Madame, clawing at her rings. The Madame's strong hands held Abby's wrists, and, weak as she was, she could not resist.

"Sorry Madame. She seems to have reacted strange to the sedative."

"Sedative?" said the Madame, with a sharp jerk of her chin towards Knightly.

Knightly swallowed. "Yes. The medicine I gave to calm her."

"Medicine? What kind of med-i-cine?" said the Madame, enunciating every syllable.

"Just a salt Jane used for her tea," said Knightly, looking at Jane.

The Madame studied the two women, her lips tightening. "The bromide compound? A sedative is very different from a 'herb,' Miss Knightly. Where did you get it?"

"Vicky assured me it was safe. She used it herself once."

"Vicky? You mean 'Lady Victoria' from Sally's brothel?"

Silence followed. The Madame shook her head, seething. Her hands pressed down and around Abby's stomach, feeling, as she spat curses beneath her breath.

"She's at least five, maybe six, months along. Did you already give the powder I sent?"

Miss Knightly nodded toward Jane, whose eyes looked red and bloodshot. "Yes, in the same cup of tea."

"When?"

"A little after noon."

The Madame stood, glaring. "Hardly with child? You think this is *hardly with child*?"

Miss Knightly stumbled backwards, knocking into the door.

Abby whimpered, quietly at first, but then a sound from her throat pierced the air. Pain wrapped itself around her core until she felt it might squeeze the life out of her. It pressed down, harder and harder, until finally Abby felt momentary relief.

The Madame let out a snort. "My God, she's way past the quickening. This requires much more attention; much intervention. Tools I only have at Greenwich."

"I . . . I was misinformed, Madame."

The Madame's upper lip raised in a snarl, showing the point of her canine tooth. "No, you simply are an *imbecile*."

Miss Knightly took in a sharp breath. "It was so simple when I came to you."

The Madame shook her head. "Are you really that stupid?"

"Pardon me?"

The Madame's eyes raged wild. "No need for propriety Knightly. This entire thing reeks of suspicion, and if I get heat from it, I swear I'll have your pretty little throat in between my fingers. This is Sir Rathburn Wyndham's daughter for heaven's sakes. And you, you hail from a glorified brothel acting as though you have the right to make decisions for nobility!"

"Charlie won't allow you to lay a finger on me. Just finish your job," she snapped.

Her mind whirling with the dawning realization, Abby lay still, anger raging. She turned from Knightly to Jane, who sat rigid in her chair. Jane's eyes bulged wide. "She's getting worse. What do we do?"

The Madame inched closer to Miss Knightly's face so that hardly a hair could fit between them.

"*Charlie*, is it?" she sneered. "He is *Charles* Henderson—and you, you are nothing more to him than a mistress. Keep me out of this, Knightly. Prison isn't a nice place for a harlot, especially one as pretty as yourself."

"And who do you think you are? A saint to the harlots?"

"A saint to the harlot and the noble alike, but only when they legitimately ask for my help," said the Madame, rising. "I'm done here. I had nothing to do with this."

"Wait, please!" said Jane. "What should we do with her now? She already had the powder."

"*We* will do nothing," said the Madame.

"No one will hear of it, I promise. Please, she can't die here," said Jane.

"I have half a mind to send for the authorities myself," said the Madame with a sharp look at Miss Knightly. "I would wager Knightly might be the one to benefit most if Mrs. Henderson happens to die."

"Oh please, no!" said Jane, trembling and sobbing.

"Shut up," snapped Miss Knightly. "Your blubbering doesn't help a thing."

The Madame turned her pointed nose to Jane. "You will have to give another dose for it to completely do the job."

"Get the powder, Jane," ordered Knightly.

Jane stood, her teeth clattering, "What will it do to her, Madame?"

"*If* she gets through it, it will take care of the situation . . . mostly."

"Mostly?" said Jane.

"Mrs. Henderson will have to come on her own accord for the procedure to discard the tissue at Greenwich. It is not a fitting operation for a bedroom.

And I will not do it unless the fetus has already been compromised."

Abby closed her eyes again, as the next wave of pain swelled, her mind unraveling. She heard the rustling of skirts, then the door slammed, followed by a loud exclamation in the stairwell. Raised voices in the hall mixed with claps of thunder and flashes of lightning. All she could think to do was concentrate on moderating her breath: in and out, in and out. Then, she opened her eyes but could focus on nothing but the ceiling. She recognized a voice, and opened her mouth to speak, but nothing came out.

Miss Robins burst through the bedroom door, sending Knightly jumping like a cat to her feet. Her finger wagged in Knightly's face, and she spat her words like venom. "You! What have you done to her?"

Jane rushed to Abby's side, grabbing her hand. "I'm so sorry. I'm so very sorry, Mrs. Henderson!"

"I have done NOTHING but help this disgraced woman. If you have a problem, it is with her!" said Knightly, pointing at Abby.

Robins rushed to Abby, shoving Jane aside. She took Abby's pale hand in hers. "Dear child! I never should have left you," she said. Robins' touch roused Abby's foggy mind, and she turned toward her old friend. Miss Robins' face contorted.

"Jane, see Knightly out of this house. Now!" Robins' voice boomed, teetering on the brink of rage. "You terrible, terrible creature! How could you bring the Madame *here*? You will get out of this house this very instant. Out! Out I say, before I send you out with my boot!"

Knightly's ruby lips hung gaping in horror. She backed out of the room before running down the hallway.

"That should take care of her for the time being," said Robins. Abby squeezed her hand, trying to understand what was happening. Another wave of pain overtook her, and she cried out again.

"There, there. We'll see what can be done."

Miss Robins looked to Jane. "I trust you wish to be useful. Go now. Sir Rathburn's driver, Langley, is waiting outside with the carriage. Go with him, fetch the doctor. Jane. Jane, look at me. Yes, that's a good girl. Now, nod your head and go. There's not a moment to waste!"

Chapter 20

Abby sat propped up in her old bed at Bristol Estate. Never had colors seemed so dull to Abby's eyes nor food so bland. Her grandmother's portrait loomed over her, whispering of a wife's secret misery, living in the shadow of a husband who controlled every aspect of her life, even that of the fate of the child she bore. Abby wondered if her grandmother's cup had tasted as bitter as hers.

Jane had stayed only long enough to fetch the doctor before she fled, leaving so many unanswered questions in her wake. The doctor was sure Abby had been given some sort of medicinal herbal concoction in her tea that released its powers in Abby's body, stilling her belly.

Miss Robins had arranged for her to be moved back to her father's home. Despite her fragile state, Abby had regained enough sense to tell her dear companion of all that had gone on over the last months. Miss Robins tried her best to comfort Abby, but Abby saw her own fear reflected in Miss Robins' eyes. She all but let it slip that she wished Abby would have told her sooner. Abby too wished she would have confided in her friend. Now, all they could do was weather the storm together.

Over the next few days, Abby endured the lingering spasms far better than the aching of her soul, tender and raw. She would never feel the grip of her babe's tiny fingers around her own; she would never quiet the crying with gentle hushes. Instead, she would forever carry this sorrow. Abby lay in bed, her hands resting on her stomach, begging for a kick of life to thrum beneath them. There was nothing. Sobs broke free from her throat. For all of the misery she had suffered, it seemed especially cruel that she should also suffer the loss of her child—one she had fought to keep with her secrecy.

The doctor had been visiting her daily, though admittedly there was not much to be done apart from ensuring her comfort. He had her drink warm milk, which seemed to do next to nothing. Abby closed her eyes as, again and again, he gently prodded her middle, probing for some vestige of life. She could hardly bear it. Late in the afternoon, nearly a week after her poisoning, Miss Robins came to Abby's side with a tray of crackers and water.

"How are you feeling?"

Abby turned her pale face to Miss Robins. "When will it be over?"

Miss Robins set the tray down at Abby's side and shook her head.

"The doctor seems perplexed. Madame Restell's potions are very potent and usually it would be over by now."

"*The* Madame Restell did this?"

Miss Robins nodded. "Under Knightly's scheme . . . that awful wretch of a woman . . ."

Did Charles have a hand in this too? she wondered. "I need to get out of here," said Abby. Her lips trembled and tears fell down her cheeks once again.

"Oh child, you're back home now. Not a hair on your head will be touched. I won't allow it. When I speak to your father, he will have to take your side in light of the circumstances."

"Have you forgotten who he is?"

Robins shook her head. "None of this was your fault, Abby."

"But the shame is my own. It cannot be heaped upon the Wyndham name, nor his own reputation."

"Then, how do you suggest we hide this?"

"I must leave, Robins. That is what I was trying to do just before Knightly interfered . . ."

"There is nowhere to go, dear child."

"England."

"What's in England? Leaving won't change what has happened."

"I cannot stay here. You know I cannot. This must have been Charles' idea, and he bid Knightly to do it. But now there is no way for him or Father to escape gossip. The doctor knows, the servants know, and it has surely raised the alarm already. Father and Charles are as thick as thieves as it is. If Charles concocted this plan, there's no telling what he and Father would conspire to do together. I cannot bear it. I cannot."

Miss Robins looked at Abby, sorrow lining her features, her cheeks wrought with hollow dark circles of worry and fatigue. She had scarcely left Abby's side for a drink of water in the last week and had begun to sniffle and cough. Abby worried about her friend in her old age, but still the urgency to flee pulsed through her.

"I'll see what might be done," said Miss Robins.

Her answer only nibbled at the edge of Abby's fear. Desperation melded with her sorrow. Like an exile of Egypt, she sought to escape and forget the days of slavery and imprisonment, the abuses too heinous to conceive. She swallowed. Charles was due back in a few weeks.

"Tomorrow. I leave tomorrow," said Abby.

Robins shook her head. "It's not possible for you to travel. You're still carry'n the babe." What was birth without life breathed into it? Abby thought. The road set before her looked only like a maze of dead ends. She clutched her pillow tight.

"I will go with or without you," she said, hating that she was saying it.

"Oh no, child! I fear for your very health. It would be better to go to Greenwich than leave alone. At least there they could deliver the babe and keep you alive."

Abby sat straight up in her bed, her eyes turning dark. "I will not let that woman touch me or my baby again."

Miss Robins nodded. "Of course; forgive me." Her voice softened. "But we must wait here, Abby."

Abby's jaw set. "The pain has stopped. Truly. Other than being tired, I am feeling much better. Travel will only hasten the inevitable, so when it happens, it happens."

Miss Robins' face turned gray. She stared blankly out the window, wringing her hands. Abby knew what she was thinking. Had not Miss Robins stood by Mother's side as she moaned in agony with labor pains? Had she not heard her cries when the baby boy came into the world with blue lips, and not a single breath in his little lungs? And hours and hours later, as Abby shivered on the sofa in the parlor, and her Father shouted at the doctor in the hall, Miss Robins held her mistress' hands as death's icy fingers closed around her mother's body. Now it appeared she would be beside Abby in similar distress.

Abby's spirit turned in renewed anguish at the thought. Who had set forth this cruel plan? Could it really be Charles? Was he really to blame for all of this?

Abby tasted the bitterness at the back of her tongue like bile. But it was not reserved for Charles alone—no. Could not God Himself have spared her child?

Abby did not notice Miss Robins' nearness until her warm hands brushed the hair off her eyes.

"If you keep me here, I won't bear this," said Abby.

"I'll help you. I'll be by your side every single moment."

"No. You do not understand. You cannot understand. This house. This room. This bed . . ." Abby sobbed. "I cannot be here any longer or I shall go mad."

"Please child, stop talking in such dramatics. You used to be so level-headed."

"I am not a child. *I* was to have a child—" tears of anger and rage streaked down Abby's face—"and I will not sit around while they cast me aside. I will not take another kick to my ribs without a rear in defense. I will not be led at the reins by men who care for nothing but themselves."

Miss Robins' eyes were wide. "Oh, my dear," said Miss Robins. Her face was tired, but a spark kindled in her eyes. "You are right. We can't stand for it any longer. There must be another course. I swear on my life to help you find it."

"Oh, bless you, Miss Robins! Bless you," said Abby, taking her maid's hand.

Miss Robins smiled, a glint of mischief in her eye. "It shouldn't be too difficult with all of Mr. Henderson's vessels afloat in the Atlantic. I'd dare say we may be able to board one of those with some sort of welcome. And free of charge. That should ruffle his feathers a bit."

"Yes. You can check his schedules in his study—the first drawer on the right. If they are not there, we will find another way, another ship perhaps. I do not care, but we must make haste with little trail, so they cannot find us."

Miss Robins sat at Abby's side again, patting her cheeks. "But my dear, is it really possible? You haven't even the strength to walk."

Abby furrowed her brow in determination. "God will give me strength, or He will give me death. I've asked for whichever He would grant me first," said Abby.

Tears coursed down Miss Robins' face. Outside the window, the sun still shone bright, and something akin to hope fluttered in Abby's belly. Miss Robins squeezed Abby's hand and whispered a prayer: *"Lord, give her strength to endure these sorrows."*

Abby sighed, closing her eyes in relief, her body drained but her will strong. She would rest for the night and rise in the morning.

Chapter 21

"Are you sure you're all right, dear?" spluttered Miss Robins, as she shifted on the lumpy mattress they shared in the small damp room near the docks of Shermerhorn Row.

"Just tired," said Abby, readjusting her position, though that was far from the truth.

"You will wake me if you are in pain?"

"Yes," said Abby, trying to keep her voice light and level despite the images of blood-stained sheets and stillborn babies that haunted her mind. The anxiety of wondering when the inevitable pains would come was torturous. Her back pulsed in rhythm with the throbbing of her head.

Her body screamed for rest, but in such a strange place sleep seemed a distant island. The boards creaked every time the occupant above them turned over. Half an hour earlier, she could even see the flicker of the occupant's candle between the planks in the ceiling. The mattress they lay on smelled dank and moldy. Abby tried to push away thoughts of all those who had lain in this same bed; to block out the sounds of scurrying and shuffling that sent a chill up her spine. Shame filled her as she thought of her comfortable existence up to now, a life of feather beds and porcelain tubs with hot water available whenever she pleased. This was the first time she could truly understand how the majority of people lived. Oh, how delightful a hot bath would feel for her aching body!

Beside her, Miss Robins slept fitfully, her breathing interrupted with the occasional cough. *No surprise in this damp room,* Abby thought. Robins too must be exhausted. Abby smiled, recalling her friend's constant attention and kindness towards her. She had tried to get away with sleeping on the bare floorboards, but Abby would have none of that. Not after everything she had done for her.

They had run into dozens of obstacles in their quest to find a way back to England. Charles' shipping logs were not in his study. Only Providence could have led them to the spare key to the office on Shermerhorn Row sitting lonely in his desk drawer. With Langley's help and his promise of secrecy, they had packed their trunks and headed for the city. Once at Shermerhorn Row, they had scoured through the mess of tables and numbers, trying to figure out when the next vessel was set to leave for London or Liverpool. They finally found that the *Myriad* was scheduled to depart the next morning, which left them searching for a place to sleep where they would attract little attention.

Abby turned to her left side with a sigh, when a gentle flutter in her belly startled her.

She sat up with a start, expecting to see a spider—or worse—scurrying across the bed. She gripped the sheets tightly, twisting them this way and that, but no creature emerged.

Then a jolt hit her low towards her hips, stronger this time. She yelped.

Robins bounced up beside her in a squinted-eye state of confusion. "Oh no. Oh dear. It's time already? Is it hurting? I'll go fetch the doctor."

Another thump beat inside, and Abby let out a squeal of delight. She began laughing, her frantic giggles flooding the room.

"What in heaven's name?" said Robins, her night cap flopping to one side.

Abby's belly bounced with laughter, and she felt the kicking again and again.

"Tell me, what is so funny?"

Abby quieted and reached for Miss Robins' hand, placing it on her stomach. The babe kicked again and again.

"For the grace of God!" Robins exclaimed, her squeals joining with Abby's.

A loud bang rattled the ceiling above them, followed by some coarse words from the neighbor whose sleep had been interrupted. Miss Robins snorted, then clamped her hand over her mouth.

"He's alive!" whispered Abby. Laughter gave way to tears, then sobs of relief mixed with joy. Robins hugged her tight.

"We have more to hope for than we thought," Robins said. Even in the dark, Abby could see the glimmer in Robins' eyes.

"Do you think it's safe then?" said Abby, a shred of worry weaseling its way into her mind.

"You have both survived so far, my dear. Let us dare to hope."

Abby nodded. "I will dare."

She lay back down, cradling her stomach, which rippled with thumps and turns. There, among the infested mattress on what could have been one of the most desperate nights of her life, she slept. For this grace, she clung to the life that drummed inside of her, and to the One who sustained it.

* * *

Just before dawn, sounds of commerce woke them. The whinny of horses eager for a trot, the creaking of carriages trundling down the pebbled streets, and the blow of steamboats bellowing out in the harbor summoned the start of a new day. Abby breathed it in, life in all its grittiness and glory. Her back still ached, her limbs begged for rest, but her spirit was buoyant. The babe had calmed but had kicked incessantly through the night. Abby smiled. She would face this day boldly.

Robins dressed quickly and went downstairs to fetch two warm rolls for breakfast. Then, together they headed out to where the *Myriad* was docked and due to set sail before ten o'clock. "Wait here while I go speak to the captain. I'd rather make arrangements before I have you walk that distance," said Robins.

Abby nodded and leaned against a wooden post, staring out at the horizon. She took a deep breath, inhaling the smell of the sea. Above her, geese flapped their wings in a v formation, soaring high over the grazing gulls which skimmed the tops of the waves for their next meal. England's soil awaited her just on the other side of the ocean, and she longed to board the ship that would take her and her unborn child there.

Exile, she thought. *I am but an exile returning home.* Her heart wrenched, remembering Charles' dark eyes. Regardless of the distance, she knew she could not shake what bound them together. She was a wife. His wife. But it would be far better for their child to know poverty than to learn the ways of its father, or worse, her own.

A seagull dove low with a loud squawk, only an arm's length from where Abby stood. She jumped with fright and bumped into a woman rushing in the throng of the crowd.

"I'm terribly sorry," said Abby.

She only grunted, keeping her eyes to the ground. The street no longer stuttered with bleary-eyed stragglers of the early morning but hummed with action.

Horse-drawn carriages piled high with luggage crowded the thoroughfares. Mules hauled wagons groaning beneath the weight of boxed cargo. Abby bit on her lip. Robins had not returned, and the ten o'clock hour fast approached. Their trunks were still stowed at the inn. Abby crossed the street, weaving in and out of trampling hooves and rolling wheels, hoping she could manage the trunks herself.

A few steep flights of stairs later, Abby had successfully lugged the small trunks to the front of the inn. The handles weighed heavy against her hands as she reached the street crossing. She paused there, regaining her breath, before continuing. By the time she had re-stationed herself by the wooden post at the docks, sweat beaded her brow and she breathed heavily.

"You all right, miss?" asked a raspy voice. Abby looked over her shoulder to see a middle-aged woman dressed in a dull cotton dress, tattered and worn with holes. A shawl hung around her slim figure. Wind-chapped red spots marred her cheeks, but her lips still held their plump form. The woman's face struck Abby, for it was haunting, like a ghost of something once bright and beautiful, but now weathered and worn.

"Pardon me," said Abby, realizing she had been staring at the woman for some time. She took a half step back and nodded. "Yes, I'm quite all right."

"Ya shouldn't be a lug'n stuff 'round in yer condition," she said.

Abby smiled, trying to avoid the woman's eyes. "I suppose you're right. I forget my limits."

Abby found her eyes drawn to the woman's face again. The stranger smiled, revealing missing teeth. Dimples formed at the corners of her cheeks. The smile faded quickly. She closed the shawl over her waist. "I lost mine . . . all of mine."

Instinctively, Abby reached out a consoling hand and felt tears well up.

"Don't be so sad, miss. It's just the way of it for the likes of me. Can't have little ones cling'n to my skirts. It's bad for business."

Abby's eyes grew wide. She had never met a fallen woman, and the shock of the situation left her mouth hanging open.

"Beg yer pardon. I guess a fine lady like yerself never met the likes a' me a'fore."

Abby shut her mouth and regained her sense of composure. "I'm dreadfully sorry. I am sure if your situation could be bettered, you would have done it."

The woman let out a sharp laugh. "Maybe. Just maybe."

Abby felt her face flush. "I am sorry if I have offended you, miss."

The woman let out a half-grin. "Hard to offend me. An even if ya did, it don't really matter."

"But surely it does! I am sorry to have misunderstood you—to misunderstand your situation out of my own ignorance, miss."

"No one's called me 'miss' since, well, ever. See there, my lady, you just made my day."

Abby blinked away the tears that pricked at her eyes, knowing her pity would offer the woman in front of her no more dignity. "Pray, tell me what is your name?"

The woman chuckled, "'Pends on who ya ask. Most call me Kitty."

Abby took in a deep breath. Was there no other way for this woman?

"What is your given name?" asked Abby.

The woman paused, looking Abby in the eye. She lifted her chin up. "Kathryn. Kathryn Stewart."

Abby lifted her own chin and smiled.

"Miss Stewart, it is a pleasure to make your acquaintance," said Abby, offering her hand. The woman reached out, wide-eyed, her chilled, calloused fingers wrapping around Abby's smooth ones.

"The pleasure is all mine," said the woman, with a tilt of her chin and a glimmer in her eye.

Abby's focus drew past Miss Stewart's shoulder to a shadowed place just beneath the tallest dock, where the water ate away at the coastline. A shack leaned against the pillars, its door a tattered red cloth billowing in the sea breeze. Outside the shack a man wearing a faded brown wool hat caught her stare, and she took in a sharp breath.

"'Scuse me miss, I've gotta get go'n," Miss Stewart said suddenly.

Abby registered the change in Miss Stewart's demeanor and looked over her shoulder to see the broad-shouldered man weaving his way towards them.

"Ya best get on outta here. He don't like visitors, unless they be pay'n customers, ye see."

Abby caught her breath, cold in her chest, and grappled for her things.

"Will you be all right?" asked Abby.

The woman's eyes narrowed, looking past Abby. "I always survive," she said. She turned away, leaving Abby's heart in her throat. Abby wished she could do something to better the woman's situation but was at a loss of what that might be. When her acquaintance had retreated to the shadows of the shack, Abby turned around, stepping forward. The man with the brown hat was staring straight at her, pressing through the crowds against the flow of traffic.

Abby shuddered. There was no way of knowing the terrors of his mind nor his intentions. Her chest constricted in panic, and the color drained from her cheeks. *Where is Miss Robins?* She had never returned from her quest to find passage on the *Myriad*. As the brown hat neared, its grease stains became visible, the man's menacing face intent on her.

She lifted the trunks, dragging them behind, and threw herself into the throng. With any luck, she could lose him. People pressed in around her as they moved along like a herd of cattle towards the docks. Abby bit the inside of her lip, fighting her nerves. She strained to look above the crowd, hoping to spot Miss Robins' navy dress and cream bonnet. Try as she might, she could not move fast enough, and a stranger knocked past her, his body reeking of hard labor.

"Pardon me," she said. No response followed, just the hustle of moving bodies in the crowd.

Warily she glanced behind her, but the man had disappeared. She continued walking, peering between the sea of bodies to scan the docks for Miss Robins. A young child scurried just beneath her waist, needling his way through the thick. At the sound of his mother's desperate shouts, Abby stopped suddenly and turned to help. Just then a man rammed into her, reeking of whiskey. Abby cried out as she staggered, falling towards the ground. A strong hand caught her arm just in time, steadying her. Abby looked up to see the familiar face of Mr. Shermerhorn.

"Miss Wyndham, is that you?" he said.

Abby sighed in relief. What a pleasant face to find among a crowd of strangers. "Yes, indeed! It is Mrs. Henderson now, but it is all the same. I must thank you for catching me just now."

Mr. Shermerhorn gently guided her to the side, away from the crowds, taking her by the arm. "Where are you headed? I can't imagine what would bring you to this sorry part of town, and with such . . . such, luggage too." Abby saw his eyes take in her waistline.

Abby looked down, shame filling her cheeks. She could tell him nothing, or else it might get back to Charles and her father. She peered over the top of a short, stocky woman, praying that Miss Robins would appear. *That's her!* she thought. *And just in time!*

"Oh, there she is! What a Godsend you are, Mr. Shermerhorn. I lost my maid in the crowd."

"So you did. I am very glad to be at your service, my lady."

Abby offered him a brief curtsy. "Now that I am quite all right, I will beg your leave and be reunited with her. Give your wife my best regards."

"Surely you could use my help with these trunks?"

Abby gave a half-smile as she stepped forward. The weight of the trunks strained the muscles in her arms and back. "I am already there now," she said, walking past Mr. Shermerhorn. "Good day to you."

"If you're sure—" he began, but Abby had already brushed past him.

Abby grimaced, letting out a sigh as she continued the trek towards Miss Robins, passing a long line of bowsprits. She moved along the row's brick frontage, trying to steer clear of the crowd. Weary with exhaustion, she was grateful she only had half a block more to go when a rough hand grabbed the collar of her coat. Before she knew it, she was being spun around. Her breath caught in her chest, a scream threatening to escape her lungs, expecting to find the greasy man with the brown hat.

Instead, she met Sir Rathburn's icy glare, his nostrils flaring.

"Come with me," he said, hardly moving his lips through clenched teeth. The grip of his hand squeezed around her arm like a vise.

Fear gripped her like a sudden gust of arctic wind. "You're back so soon," she said, her voice high and uneasy.

"Shut your mouth."

His fingers dug deeper into her skin. He dragged her forward, leaving the trunks abandoned in the middle of the street. His hold tightened so that she thought her arm might snap. Color drained from her face.

Abby looked ahead, hoping to see Miss Robins. She might be able to intercept them. But she was nowhere in sight. Dread filled her heart.

Why could we not have already boarded the ship? she thought.

Sir Rathburn made a sharp turn towards the red-brick building of Charles' office. Abby hoped Charles might be there, thinking that her father would at least have enough sense to withhold his anger in the presence of her husband. But just before they reached the building, Sir Rathburn thrust her into a dark alley. A mangy cat scampered out of the way of his crushing boot with a guttural hiss.

Abby yelped and ran further into the alley, away from his grasp. When she turned, Sir Rathburn was blazing towards her, fire burning in his eyes.

"What is wrong?" she asked, trying to control her tone.

"You," he spat.

Abby shook her head. He pointed down at her stomach, his index finger shaking. She instinctively crossed her arms around her waist.

"I can explain," she stammered, cowering.

"It is your unbridled tongue that got you into this mess in the first place."

Her cheeks stung with the heat of tears. "I didn't do anything. I am married, Father. It is Charles' child." She lifted her hands in front of her, pleading.

The whites of his teeth gleamed in the darkness. "You think me so dull? You are much too far along for the circumference of your waist to match your marriage of two months!"

"Just listen, and I'll explain."

"You think rushing off to London will hide your scandal?"

"My scandal?"

He raised his hand, the ruby ring positioned to strike. Before Abby could move, the blow struck the side of her face. Her teeth rattled, and her ears buzzed.

"You should have gotten rid of it when Madame Restell gave you the chance."

She lifted her head, her eyes wild, the blood on her lips fueling her rage.

"You—*you* sent her!" she spat, between her swelling lips.

"Yes. To remedy your ruin. To save my name. And here you are rushing off to London to flaunt your condition, and catching the attention of Mr. Shermerhorn, of all people."

Abby lifted her head higher, glaring. "I won't kill my child for your name."

Sir Rathburn's hand rose again and Abby recoiled, covering her head with her arms. When he struck again, his hand landed on the side of her cheek. Her head spun and she staggered to the ground.

"Stop, Father, please," she said, cowering beneath the shadow of his hand.

He grabbed the back of her head, his fingers pulling at her hair as he lifted her eyes up to his.

"Get rid of it in England or I will get rid of you. You won't have the pleasure of sullying my name again."

His teeth clamped tight, his lip lifting in a snarl, so that Abby feared he would strike her again.

"Just let me go," she sobbed.

He let loose his hold. Abby crawled up from the filthy ground, her hands caked in dirt, and her dress soiled with grime. She stumbled away, turning to see her father smoothing his hair and replacing his silk hat on top of his head. As Abby came into the light, Miss Robins intercepted her. Miss Robins gasped, and the grip she had on Abby's trunk went limp.

Abby shook her head. "We must go—now!" she said squeezing Miss Robins' arms.

"What the devil?"

"Father."

Miss Robins took Abby's face in her hands, studying the wounds.

"Stay here," she said with a ferocity that Abby had never before heard in her voice. She lifted her skirts and barreled down the alley.

Abby sank to the ground, stifling her sobs so as to not attract more unwanted attention. She heard distant shouts from the back of the alley but could not discern their words. Her jaw throbbed, and her head ached. A few moments later, Robins helped Abby up, and they scurried through the streets, with Abby's trunk in tow.

"My dear, you need a doctor. I'll see to it when we get there. But for now, we've a ship to catch," she said, steaming ahead.

Chapter 22

Charles climbed the stairs to the counting office at Shermerhorn Row muttering curses under his breath. Abby was missing. He had arrived home expecting to find his household in order, but neither servant, mistress, nor his wife were anywhere to be found. When he entered his study, he noticed that drawers had been left open and papers on his desk lay askew. He assumed that Abby had taken money and fled, but when he searched in his desk drawer, he found the paper notes stored in his locked case safe and untouched. Puzzled, he looked in her room, only to find the bulk of her belongings still there. It wasn't until a second look in his study that he realized the spare key to his counting office was missing.

He walked down the long hallway to find the door to his office slightly ajar. He sighed, thinking Abby was waiting inside, but the earthy scent of cigar smoke wafted through the opening. He stepped inside. Lamplight glowed in the corner. As Charles approached, he saw Sir Rathburn reclining on the red sofa, puffs of smoke billowing around him. Rathburn lifted his brow.

"I hope you do not mind my intrusion," he said.

Charles scanned the room, looking for an explanation, but finding nothing obvious.

"You *do* mind," Rathburn said with smirk.

"What do you mean? There's mountains of paperwork that need my attention," said Charles, feigning indifference. He walked around the room.

"So there is," he said. He pointed with the butt of his cigar to the logbooks lying open on his desk. "Perhaps you should start there."

Charles chortled a fake sort of laugh. "You seem so knowledgeable about shipping all of a sudden." He walked over to his desk. Someone had been shuffling through the logbooks. Charles' pulse quickened. Had Sir Rathburn rummaged through his things, trying to find information for his lawyer? Or had Abby found a way out of here?

"How is my daughter faring after such a long separation?" asked Sir Rathburn.

Charles kept his eyes to his papers. "Fine."

"Have you seen her between last night and this morning?"

Charles swallowed. Had Sir Rathburn seen her? Did he know their secret?

"Briefly, I confess. I left before she was down this morning. Is something wrong?"

"Where is she now, Charles?"

Charles' eyes danced around the room. "I imagine she is reading in the parlor," he replied casually.

"I would not count on that, my boy," said Sir Rathburn.

Charles lifted his eyes to Sir Rathburn's, whose gaze narrowed to a squint. "What do you know?"

"Her indiscretion has been brought to my attention."

"What indiscretion?"

"Her infidelity. Her promiscuity. Her whoredom."

Charles could hardly breath; the walls seemed to press in around him. "She hardly fits any of those descriptions."

Sir Rathburn rose from the couch. "Correct. Those are far too generous words for a ruined woman of her sort. But that is what everyone will say about her if they find out. Tell me, what will they say about her father and his new son-in-law?" He lifted the cigar slowly to his lips. Next to his ruby-ringed finger a small cut oozed on his knuckles. Charles stared at it, swallowing again.

"You know where she is."

Sir Rathburn laughed.

Charles' stomach clenched, and suddenly he saw the man before him with fresh eyes. He had thought that he and Rathburn were cut from the same cloth, but now questions swirled in his mind about what evil plan his father-in-law had hatched. Despite everything that had happened between him and Abby, not to mention his anger over not knowing his wife's whereabouts, Charles would never wish harm on her. But the man before him seemed deranged. Would he actually hurt his own daughter—or worse? The feeling took root like a fast-growing vine, spreading fear throughout his body—not fear for his own sake, but for that of another. For Abby.

"What have you done to her?" said Charles barely above a whisper.

"Put her in her place."

"Tell me where she is, or I swear my fists will finish this conversation for me."

The corner of Sir Rathburn's mouth lifted in an amused snarl.

"England."

Charles scanned the room, desperate. *England? Why would Abby go to England?*

To get away from you.

Charles shook his head as though to rid it of the implicating thought, then rustled through the papers, trying to make sense of why Abby might have come to his counting office. It dawned on him that she could have easy passage by one of his own ships.

"I would not worry about her," Rathburn said with a dismissive wave of his cigar. "I have seen to it that she cannot bother us for some time anyway. And my name, as well as yours, will remain unaffected, so our business will not suffer."

Charles turned to him, incredulous. "She is my wife."

"Do not feign care for her now," he sneered. "I am still set on maintaining our family ties. My lawyer is working on our problems in Louisiana as we speak. Abby will go elsewhere until she can dump her illegitimate child and return to New York."

Charles set his eyes on Sir Rathburn's throat; he could almost taste blood on his tongue.

"That *illegitimate child* has a father."

"Aye. But you can forget it all now. I am not here to condemn you, my boy."

"But you would condemn *her*?"

"As a man, you are useful, Charles; she is a mere woman. This situation is but a stain marring the vision of all that we seek to accomplish. Her being here will only destroy that, at least until she looks presentable again."

"It wasn't her fault, Sir Rathburn."

Sir Rathburn tried to hide a smirk. "Indeed. She was ignorant on the subject for sure. Yet, she clearly needed to be taught a lesson."

"No."

Sir Rathburn waved his hand. "I saw her questioning you that night—undermining your authority with her wily ways. My servants reported how she slapped you." He paused and looked pointedly at Charles. "You did what any man would do—indeed *should* do—to put her in her place."

So he knew the whole time . . .? Charles lurched at the thought of his father-in-law watching his own daughter's ruin unfold. Yet there he sat, puffing on his cigar in slow draughts, as calm as day.

"She didn't deserve any of it! I used her . . . I hurt her . . . I ruined her, your own daughter. Your own flesh and blood."

"You can hardly call it that. You took care of the situation like a man. She was brazen in her defiance. She brought it on herself with her high-minded ways."

Charles gasped. "But why did you not stop me?"

"What does that matter? What is done, is done. Now we can move on and tackle our more pressing issues," Sir Rathburn said, his face devoid of expression.

Charles could not imagine how this man—this father—could care nothing for his own child. Was calm indifference even worse than hate? It was pride and desire for control that had sent Charles into Abby's room that night, but it was Sir Rathburn's indifference that had allowed it.

Charles stepped towards him, his eyes wary of Sir Rathburn's. A chill crept up his spine. "You did nothing for her! You could have stopped me. You knew, but you didn't stop me."

"Enough of your melodrama, Charles. Man up. Save that talk for a priest."

Charles blinked, surprised to find his vision clouded by tears. Sir Rathburn was right. There was no use in confessing his regret to him. He could do nothing. But Abby, poor Abby! He had to find her.

Charles scanned the open book detailing the vessels and their cargo, departure dates and times. There was only one ship setting sail that day, and no other vessels had come or gone within the week.

"What are you doing?" asked Sir Rathburn.

"Finding her," said Charles, heading for the door.

"Let her go."

"I can't."

"She cannot stay here. People will recognize her. It will be our ruin."

"Move out of my way, old man."

"The newspapers will publish it. They will sink us both."

"I said, MOVE!"

Sir Rathburn's nose closed in a hair's breadth from Charles', his breath reeking of tobacco. Charles felt like he would retch.

"You cross me now, Henderson, and there is no turning back."

Charles clenched his teeth and stepped forward, bumping Sir Rathburn's shoulder.

"You will live to regret this," Rathburn called in his wake.

"So be it."

Charles rushed down the hall and threw the front door open, his legs gaining speed as he hurried down to the docks.

Chapter 23

"Have a care, lass. Let me fetch the doc for ye," said the burly Captain O'Dea as he stepped out of his room below deck. The floor already groaned with a gentle sway as the vessel waited to set out to sea.

Robins bent over Abby as she curled up on the bed. "My dear. It does look quite frightn'n. Won't you let the doctor tend to you?"

The shock of Sir Rathburn's blows still rattled Abby, so that she feared what she would confess to another stranger. She knew she could not remain composed and that her situation only begged questions that she dare not answer.

Abby attempted to speak, but her swollen lip got in the way.

"What'd ye say?" asked the captain.

She sighed and simply shook her head, pulling the shawl around her.

"Well, then. What's yer name?"

Miss Robins gave Abby a wary look, then blurted, "Emma. Emma Robins. I'm traveling with her. My name is Mrs. Henderson. We are head'n back to London to visit family."

Abby's eyes grew wide as she listened to Miss Robins spin a yarn. She'd never known her maid to lie, but clearly Miss Robins had only her best interest at heart.

"It troubles me a great deal to have a lass in this condition on me ship. When we set out to sea, there'll be no turning back. Winter sail'n is hard enough without me worries drawn below deck. If ye don't mind, I'll send for the doc now," he said.

Abby lowered her eyes and nodded.

Captain O'Dea's thick sienna-colored beard lifted closer to his eyes as he smiled. "There's a lass. I'm most obliged to have ye aboard the *Acadia.* Cap'n Lawrence is a good friend o'mine and said ye deserved the best treatment possible. This is me own quarters here, but I'll stow away with me crew. The doc and his wife just boarded. I'll have 'em here as fast as a tailwind." His face grew serious again. "And ye say a man on the streets did this to ye?"

Abby nodded, keeping her eyes low.

"And ye didn't recognize 'em?"

Abby looked down at the planks of the floor. She did not want to lie, not again, so she kept her mouth shut firmly. She resorted to shrugging her shoulders. Miss Robins interjected, "It wouldn't matter if she did, Captain. I assure you, it'd only make matters worse."

Captain O'Dea's brow furrowed, his weather-beaten cheeks betraying a frown. "I know honor when I see it. The eyes don't lie, Miss Emma. And those green pearls of yours do ye justice."

Abby blushed despite herself.

Miss Robins chimed in, "I would quite agree."

Captain O'Dea left, the boards in the narrow corridor creaking with each step until the sound faded. Miss Robins let out a long sigh, followed by a fit of coughing.

"Must be the damp getting to me," she said, then the fit subsided and she caught her breath. "It's been a day I'd rather forget," Robins added.

"Indeed, *Mrs. Henderson,*" Abby managed through swollen lips.

They chuckled and sat in silence. The patter of feet creaked above them as passengers and crew bustled around on deck preparing for departure. A slit of a window offered a bit of light. The cabin's furniture consisted of only the bed, where Miss Robins and Abby could just fit, and a rugged bedside table. It smelled of hard cider and sailor's musk. But the bedding was soft and clean—a marked improvement from their cramped, filthy quarters at the inn. Captain O'Dea had arranged tattered maps of places he had sailed to on the walls, tacked up in a haphazard manner. Abby felt a measure of comfort being secreted in this small space, away from prying eyes, headed away from New York.

"Father meant it, you know. Every single word."

"So did I," said Miss Robins, her face hardening.

"What did you tell him?"

"That he had failed your mother by failing you. He didn't deserve her, and he certainly does not deserve you."

Abby leaned back, resting her hands on top of her swollen belly.

"He loved her; I know he loved her."

"And there you go on as you do . . . defending him and so on."

Abby tried to keep her lip from trembling. "He is my father."

"He is but a father in name. He's cruel and selfish. A beastly creature."

"A broken man, Robins. He is cold and empty because she is gone, and he's let nothing replace her warmth."

Robins brushed the free hair from Abby's face and shook her head, looking on her as a mother would. "You are much too forgiving, my dear. Have a rest. I'm going to stretch my legs and catch my breath in the corridor while we wait for the doctor," she said.

Abby let Miss Robins go despite the troubled thoughts still swirling in her mind. A lump lodged in her throat as she considered her complicated relationship with her father. All she had ever wanted was for him to love her. But had he? Her mind raced through the blur of her childhood, then his departure for New York and the years of deathly silence that ensued. Abby had always made up excuses for him, reasoning away his seeming indifference. She knew he was a busy man and had a business to run, affairs to keep in order. Had not her own mother even said how much her father loved them, even though he had difficulty showing it? But maybe her mother was wrong. Or maybe time, and grief, had soured him, changing him inexplicably.

The lump in her throat grew, giving way to guttural sobs.

Was Charles not the same? Why had she been dealt a life of men with stone hearts? Who was to be father to her now that her own father had forsaken her? Who was to soothe her heart after it had been maimed by her husband?

The answer came—gentle, calm, and sure.

I AM, beloved.

More tears fell, bitter ones, and she hated her own frail faith. She longed for love. Love of a father. Love of a husband. She could not see how this physical world could be pushed aside to find that God alone could heal her wounds.

A kick inside her womb reminded her of the sweet mercy. Her child was still alive. Alive when she thought all hope had been lost. Yet, in that moment, bruised and alone, her future uncertain, another thought crept in: What if God had not spared her child?

And yet again, a gentle whisper of truth, steadfast and sure, fought back.

Even then. I AM. I AM more than enough.

The words filled her, replacing worry with certainty. At that her heart slowed into a measured rhythm, her chest rising and falling even as the babe drummed in her belly. Her lids drooped, and sleep came.

Half an hour later, Abby awoke to see a golden stream of sunlight pouring in from the corridor. Miss Robins entered with a short, stocky man who crowded the doorway, his bald head reflecting the light. Robins lit the gas lamp just beside the bed.

"I've brought the doctor," she whispered. Abby squinted, trying to remember where she was and how she had arrived there.

"I will be right here in the corridor waiting."

Miss Robins squeezed out of the room so the doctor could make his way into the cramped space.

"Ah, what a gruesome thing on such a bonny face," came his deep, smooth voice.

Abby moaned, her jaw pulsing and head pounding.

"May I take a closer look?"

Abby nodded, still dazed. The doctor stepped closer and gently placed his hands on Abby's face, feeling around her jawline.

"Ah . . . how rude of me. I'm Dr. Lachlan Mcleod. I imagine this is a bad time to ask your name," he said, laughing at his own joke.

Abby wished she could smile at his amusement, but she sat, opening her mouth so that he could examine it.

"Good thing is, your jaw's not broken. Bad thing is, it's a mighty fine bruise. The cut should mend in a week's time. Mouths tend to bleed more for show than anything else."

The doctor looked Abby over, tilting his round head to the side. "Do you remember everything okay?"

"Yes," mumbled Abby.

"Where are we?"

"In New York."

"Where in New York?"

"Aboard the *Acadia*, setting sail for Liverpool," said Abby.

"As sharp as a whistle this one is," said the doc.

Abby smiled with her eyes. "Whistles are hardly sharp."

"And you prove my point again." When the doc smiled, the rest of his face seemed to disappear behind it.

"How far along do you reckon you are?"

"Five or six months."

"My wife's skilled in midwifery. I'm no simpleton myself on the subject, but I reckon she would take a lik'n to you."

"Thank you, Doctor."

"Darcy!" called the doctor out into the corridor.

An equally short woman poked her head inside, her auburn hair billowing about her face in a chaos of curls. She squeezed in beside her husband, offering a short curtsy. Doctor Mcleod introduced his wife and left the women to get acquainted.

"It's a pleasure to meet you, Miss . . .?" questioned Darcy.

Abby blinked, vaguely recalling that she should not use her real name. "Emma. Emma Robins."

"I hope you don't mind; your friend has already made me aware of your circumstances around the pregnancy."

Miss Robins' head peeked in from the corridor, and Abby's eyes were quick to question. "I told her what that awful woman tried to do. That she was wildly jealous and poisoned your tea with those tonic powders. I thought it only right that she knew, and that she knew also that the babe is kick'n like a bucking bronco now."

Abby nodded, trying to disguise her rising panic. She hoped to keep the events of the last six months in New York.

"May I?" asked Darcy, gesturing towards Abby's stomach. Abby nodded. Darcy's hands were warm and gentle as she moved them deftly across Abby's abdomen, feeling for the babe's position.

"My, my, what a miracle! I'll tell you, Emma, someone must be watch'n out for you."

Miss Robins let out a squeal of delight. "It's high time we had some good tidings, my dear."

Darcy's rosy cheeks turned up in a smile. "You ought to be careful though. Keep drinking lots of fluids. Sailing isn't easy, let alone being six months along."

Abby shook her head, trying to keep her worry at bay. The bellow of the steam engine whistled from outside, followed by thunderous clapping from the passengers.

Darcy looked up. "Looks like we're 'bout to be off. I'd better go to the deck to wave my farewells. I've a whole wagonload of cousins who'll be in a frenzy if I don't blow them kisses. And it'd be best you got some fresh air before the sea-sickness has you bound to this cabin for the next two weeks."

She offered a quick curtsy, then disappeared down the corridor.

"She's right. Come now, Abby; I'll help you up," said Miss Robins, taking Abby's arm.

"Thank you, Robins."

"No no! It's Mrs. Henderson from now on," said Miss Robins sternly. "I shall be Mrs. Henderson for these two weeks, and you shall be Emma. Emma Robins."

"Emma it is. I suppose I ought to pretend like I am leaving for holiday," she said, trying to laugh.

Miss Robins nodded. "After all you have been through, you are certainly due a holiday."

Chapter 24

Sweat gathered in beads on Charles' brow despite the chill of the late morning. He pressed ahead through the mass of people gathering around the Great Dock. Half a dozen ships groaned, rocking to and fro, their holds heavy with fresh supplies, their decks brimming with eager passengers waiting to set sail. At the far end of the dock, Charles recognized the tall mast of his clipper vessel and breathed a sigh of relief. He might still catch her.

Breaking into a trot, he weaved his way through passengers laden with luggage, and others waving handkerchiefs in the air. As he neared his vessel, he spotted its captain. Two months earlier he had snagged the captain from a rival company. He had been making little for his troubles, and Charles sought to maximize the man's potential by paying him his fair due. The captain was making his way around the ship, examining her hull for any splits in the wood.

"Lawrence!" shouted Charles.

He whipped his head around in the direction of Charles' voice like a soldier awaiting the command of his officer. Charles broke through the edge of the crowd.

"Mr. Henderson?"

"Yes, Captain."

"Everything all right, sir? I was sure you were not due back to New York for at least another week."

Charles dodged the question, panting from his exertion. "Is Mrs. Henderson aboard?"

Captain Lawrence tilted his head. "This ship? No, but I spoke with a woman . . . eh, I forget her name."

"Well, what did she look like?"

"An older lady."

"When?"

"Well, sir, just earlier this morn. She was quite demanding. Said to make room for your wife and her to have passage."

Charles lifted his hat and raked his fingers through his hair. "Where is she?"

"I don't know. I kindly told her there's no room aboard this one. She would be mighty cramped. I sent her to a friend who owed me a favor. The captain of one of the Cunard Line vessels. See, I thought the women would be much more comfortable on a passenger ship."

Charles let out a curse. "The Cunard Line?" He shook his head, thinking of the irony. His own wife would be aboard a vessel of his rival shipping company.

"Yes, sir. I do apologize. I did not think it proper for two ladies to be aboard this vessel with my crew. They can be a little unruly at times."

Charles nodded, grateful at least that this captain had sense enough to protect Abby and Miss Robins' interests.

"Which one did they board?"

"Eh . . . the only one of their fleet at port today. I do believe it's the *Acadia*. I spoke with the captain myself, tell'n him to look out for the women particularly. The ship's full, but he assured me he would give up his own quarters for them."

"When does it leave?" asked Charles, already bouncing on the balls of his feet.

"She's about to leave port now, sir," said Captain Lawrence, wincing. "Did I do something wrong, sir?"

Charles shook his head, "No. You're a good man. Thank you for finding them safe passage. I must go." Charles tipped his hat and rushed off toward the *Acadia*'s whistling.

By the time Charles made it to the vessel, the crew was already freeing its lines from the docks. The hull rose and fell in rhythms of the sea as the crew waited to set sail. A wiry young man fiddled with the rigging, shimmying up and down the ropes like it were as natural as walking.

"Boy!" Charles beckoned. "I'm looking for a lady aboard. Can you help me?"

The youth narrowed his eyes. "Have a ticket?"

"No. Nor do I need one. I'm looking for my wife."

The boy scrunched his face together, nodding towards the captain, who barked orders to his crew from the helm.

"You gotta ask Cap'n. He's set to leave on time."

"Ask him for me, please. Her name is Abby—Mrs. Abby Henderson."

The youth scurried along up the planks, where the last of the crew jumped aboard. Passengers lined the railings, leaning over to gaze into the choppy sea bellow. Gentlemen craned their necks as they studied the workings of the grand vessel, her paddle wheel eager to begin its rounds. The engine released its steam in another whistle. Charles' mind spun with questions. What was he going to say to her? How could words mend all that he had broken? His throat tightened. It didn't matter how sorry he felt, or how much he sought her forgiveness—he would never deserve it. He could never deserve her. But she must know that he was sorry.

Charles watched as the youth weaseled his way to the captain, who stood facing out to sea, eyes squinting towards the horizon. He waved his hands around as he explained Charles' request, but the captain stood still, his brow downturned. He leaned over, mouthing something that Charles couldn't make out. Then, the boy pointed at Charles; at this Charles lifted his hand slowly, eyes pleading. Like a judge deciding the fate of the accused, Captain O'Dea stared at Charles. Then, he shook his head and barked a command to the boy.

Charles held his breath. The boy climbed back down until he was within yelling distance.

"Cap'n said 'No', sir."

Charles lifted his hands in desperation. "'No, she's not on the ship,' or 'No, he won't let me see her'?"

The boy shrugged, "Whichever one suits you, I guess."

"What's that supposed to mean?" shouted Charles, trying to remain composed. "Please, I must find her!" He hoisted himself up on a post, intent on climbing the rigging.

"I wouldn't do that if I were you. Cap'n will send for the constable to cuff ya," said the youth. Charles stopped, desperate. He turned to find curious stares on him, and he jumped down.

"Wait! I'll buy a ticket!" he called out after the boy.

"Ship's full!" yelled the boy over his shoulder as he continued monkeying his way through the crowd up to the deck. Charles snorted. The steam exhaled in the air, drowning out the farewell cries. The *Acadia*'s paddlewheel began swimming forward, picking up speed with every rotation. Behind the vessel, a wake formed as the water between the dock and the ship widened.

Charles' heart sank at the thought of Abby returning to England. The throngs of well-wishers gradually dispersed as the ship pulled away. He was too late.

As the vessel turned toward the open sea, Charles spotted a familiar figure, though somewhat changed in form, standing at the hull of the ship. It was Abby, the black waves of her hair dancing free in the wind. She rested her chin on her fist as she watched the shoreline. But what was wrong with her face? Charles squinted and swore when he saw her swollen, red jaw. *Rathburn,* he thought, his fist squeezing into a ball. He bit the inside of his cheek until he tasted his own blood. Abby stood upright, resting her right hand against her belly. Charles found himself pushing forward through the crowd, pleading, *Look at me, Abby. God, let her look at me!*

"Abby!" he shouted, pushing people aside until he reached the end of the docks, his boots hanging off the edge. She turned and scanned the crowd; then her green eyes locked with his. Charles reached out his hand as the waters between them widened. She gasped, stepping back from the railing. Her arms shielded her belly. Charles held back tears, wishing he could help her understand. She paused in her retreat, searching his face in confusion. The ship lurched forward towards the sea, her silhouette shrinking as she faded into a blur through his tears.

II

Part Two

"I am not what I ought to be, I am not what I want to be, I am not what I hope to be in another world; but still I am not what I once used to be, and by the grace of God I am what I am."
— John Newton

Chapter 25

Charles did not know emptiness had a scent until he walked through his estate, head held low, without servant or woman to console him. It smelled dank and dusty in the absence of the fresh cut flowers that Abby used to arrange in a vase in the parlor. Charles shivered. No fire burned in the hearth; no woman lay waiting for him in his bedchamber. The only servant who had stayed in the aftermath of the visit from Madame Restell was the cook, who found it awkward to prepare meals for only two mouths. The other household staff had left to seek employment elsewhere, as gossip blew into town like rotting leaves at the end of fall.

He headed to his study, seeking solace the only way he knew how—in a bottle. Beneath his arm he carried the newspaper that besmirched his name, but he did not have the guts to read the article. Not yet. He imagined his mother's shock and horror as she read it. His actions were like spitting on his father's grave. It would not surprise him if she never spoke to him again. He slapped it onto the desk, then turned away, reaching for the tall neck of his Madam Geneva instead. The bottle kissed his lips as he took his first sip. Long and slow.

It felt like hours before the familiar warm, numb feeling crept through his limbs, dulling his senses. But when he finally read the article, he regretted it. It was as though he no longer recognized the man who had been slandered so liberally on the pages in front of him. His own actions taunted him, for he saw them in a new light for what they were. He remembered how he had defiled Abby, and his feeble attempts to quieten her. He recalled her small form draped in her nightgown, and how her frail frame had trembled at the sight of him. He wept at the memory of her pleading voice: *"I forgive you,"* she had said. Oh, the weight of all he had squandered! And now she was gone, and who could blame her for fleeing? When the first bottle dripped dry, he reached for another.

Her face as she stood on the ship swirled through his mind—the gash on her cheek, the trepidation in her eyes. He thought of the future bulging in her stomach, now an ocean away. Then, his ships, and those lives. All lost because of him. Liquor coursed through his veins until he was numb from the tips of his fingers to the ends of his toes. But it could not deaden his shame, which welled up from some unreachable place inside him until tears bubbled to the surface and broke forth in frenzied sobs. He choked on them, gasping for breath, as though he would be consumed. Then, spent, he stumbled into his chair, planted his cheek on his desk, and slept.

Hours later, he awoke, struggling to raise his throbbing head, his fingers stiff from the empty bottle that, even in sleep, he gripped. A deep pounding echoed through the hall from the front door, causing him to wince. The sun pressed in through the curtains. "Timothy, get the door," he muttered, before recalling that he no longer had a footman.

The beat persisted like a drummer's proclamation at the onset of war. Charles pressed his hands over his ears. The newspaper sat in plain sight, its headline mocking him: "Henderson Gold Line Shipping Company's Clipper burns: 20 Souls lost in Oak Harbor."

Charles staggered towards the pitcher of water and downed a glass before finding his place again in his armchair. He rifled through the mess of papers littering his desk. Somewhere beneath that pile was proof that Sir Rathburn Wyndham was as intricately wrapped up in the tragedy as Charles. The deed was there last night—a black and white reminder that Sir Rathburn would have to help him or be crucified along with him. The pounding at the front door grew fierce, echoing louder until it gave way to the sound of footsteps thundering down the hall. Charles lifted his head from his hands, a jolt of adrenaline forcing him to attention. Had the police come to arrest him?

He heard more than one voice, and the opening and shutting of doors. As the footsteps neared, the words became clearer.

"Charles—Charles Henderson, come out this minute!"

Rathburn, thought Charles with disgust.

The doors to his study burst open. A tall, slender man with a thin mustache and round spectacles stood at the ready with a briefcase weighing down his lanky arm next to a red-faced Sir Rathburn.

The man swung his case onto the desk, unbuckling the satchel without pause. He thumbed through papers as Sir Rathburn glowered, his lip upturned in a sneer. "Must I hire my own servants to let me into your house? We have been knocking for over ten minutes."

"I don't recall inviting company."

"You should have locked the door then," he snapped.

"What are you doing here?"

Sir Rathburn's brow arched high. "Meet my lawyer, Vincent Van Creveld."

The lawyer fixed a cold stare on Charles before stepping forward with papers in hand.

"You are being sued for defamation of Sir Rathburn Wyndham through falsifying records and business practices," he boomed.

Charles cursed, cupping his hands over his ears. "No need to shout."

"You'll want to make sure to hear this clearly, Mr. Henderson," said Van Creveld, louder this time.

Charles glared at him, the pain in his head mounting. "Do you know who you're dealing with?"

"A weasel of a son-in-law," he said. Sir Rathburn chuckled.

"I was referring to the man who has employed your services," said Charles. "Side with him, and you've sold your soul to the devil himself."

A slow grin crept across Sir Rathburn's face as he cocked his head towards his lawyer. "This man represents nobility, and I will compensate him handsomely for his pains," he said.

Sweat beaded on Charles' head, his heart pounding in a furious rhythm.

"You don't know the half of what he's done," said Charles, eyeing the lawyer.

"But everyone knows what *you've* done, don't they?" said Mr. Van Creveld.

Charles turned. "How is it that Rathburn has shielded himself from the press when both our names were on the title of the vessel?" Charles slammed his fist on the newspaper, then pointed to Rathburn. "You were there. This was a joint deal."

The men exchanged a knowing look.

"Aren't you aware, Charles, that I had nothing to do with Henderson Gold Line until yesterday, when you signed over all assets in order to recover the integrity of your business?" He paused, his expression frozen in a sneer. "At least, that is what you must agree to so you might get out of this ordeal without facing prison charges."

"What charges?"

"I am sure more will come in about the slaves' deaths."

"They can't prove anything of the sort. The fire was an accident. There were plenty of witnesses to prove that."

Sir Rathburn turned towards Charles, his arms crossed casually across his torso. "Then there is also the sensitive matter concerning my daughter . . . Shall I go on?"

"Leave her out of this."

Rathburn leaned forward and hissed, "I'd rather see you squirm at the mention of it."

"What kind of animal are you?"

"Nothing in comparison to what you have done to my daughter," he said, his face so close Charles could feel the spittle as he spoke. "I am no priest, Henderson. You confessed the whole thing, and I myself saw you slip up to my daughter's room, but you left me in no state to render her aid. That is, unless you agree to settle this matter out of court."

Mr. Van Creveld made a quarter turn towards the door, a smirk of his own creeping across his face. "To answer your question from earlier, let me be clear: my client has informed me of his daughter's sufferings, and how he has since tried to free her from this neglect by seeing her off to England."

Charles seethed. For this so-called lawyer to claim Rathburn was trying to help her was simply ludicrous. He shook his head in disbelief. "She had no help. Least of all from *him*. Do you know what he did to her?"

"That is of no consequence. What I do know is that Sir Rathburn's servant, Miss Robins, was sent to aid her after Madame Restell visited your home. You cannot deny that," said Mr. Van Creveld.

Charles inhaled, his fingers raking through his hair. He did not know about Madame Restell, and his blood went cold at the thought. Then, through gritted teeth, he said, "You struck her. I saw the mark on your hand, and the gash on her face."

Sir Rathburn's eyes narrowed, but he looked unfazed. "For all we know, she is dead. There has been no trace of Abby since the day she tried escaping."

Charles' stomach lurched. Had Rathburn done something else to her? "She boarded the ship. I saw her myself."

Mr. Van Creveld slid a paper across the desk in front of Charles. Neat script detailed the inventory of the company's vessels, offices, and rights, all of which Rathburn was claiming as his own.

"This little mess can be easily resolved if you just sign here," the lawyer said, pointing to the line at the bottom of the page.

"And give everything to him? Not a chance."

"Charles, Charles, Charles," Rathburn began in a singsong tone. "Do you not know I hold liens against this very estate? It is my daughter's dowry that pays for it. And with this current tragedy, her property becomes my own upon her death. Do you not recall signing that particular document? I am sure the court will agree, considering what a monstrous son-in-law you have proved to be, how you bewitched us all for the sake of your own ambition."

A chill blew through the doorway from down the hall, where the front doors were still ajar.

"No."

"Sign the papers and you will be a free man, Charles," demanded Sir Rathburn.

But Charles knew he would never be free. He would be owned by Sir Rathburn. Everything he had worked for—everything his father had worked for—would be lost, and worst of all, Sir Rathburn would be the hero. Charles shook his head. He stood his ground, silent and firm. He needed time. With enough time, he could collect evidence to twist Rathburn's arm. The deeds plus evidence of their trip to New Orleans would be difficult to argue with, no matter the lawyer.

"It is no time to be bull-headed," said Sir Rathburn, dipping the pen in the ink.

"No."

Sir Rathburn threw the pen towards Charles, splattering ink across the papers.

"Leave. Now." Both men straightened, exchanging glances but making no move to go.

"Fine. I'll see you out myself," said Charles, throwing open the study doors and barreling down the hallway.

Leaves rustled in the entryway, dancing in circles, as the front door creaked back and forth. Rathburn called out after Charles, his footsteps clamoring up from behind.

"Sign it, Charles. I will not stand for those reporters snooping around to find my name next to yours. You scoundrel!"

Charles turned, a savage gleam in his eye. "Till death do us part, old man."

Sir Rathburn's eyes bulged wide, a battle cry roaring in his throat. He rushed at Charles, slamming him against the wall. Charles shoved him off, but Sir Rathburn's right fist came zipping up, his crimson ruby ring winking just before it made contact with Charles' chin.

Charles lunged at him, bearing down across his chest like a vise until they both fell to the ground. They rolled, sending a vase tumbling to the floor, shards of ceramic crashing around them. They powered against one another, Charles surprised at the strength of his father-in-law.

Amid the melee, Charles heard the sound of hooves approaching, then its rider entered the fray.

"ENOUGH," a voice bellowed.

Shocked by the sudden intrusion, both men turned to see Reverend Truitt step over the threshold, his face pale. Then, Mr. Van Creveld emerged from the shadows of the study with his briefcase partially open. He proceeded to pull Rathburn off Charles.

Reverend Truitt lifted Charles up by the arm. "Gentlemen, what is the meaning of this?"

Sir Rathburn only snarled in reply, his mop of gray hair disheveled, waving its angry wisps as the gust blew through the door.

"They were just on the way out," gasped Charles.

"You sign those bloody papers or I'll have your head!" thundered Sir Rathburn in between ragged breaths. He held his side, wincing in pain. Charles gleamed inwardly.

"So that's your plan? To kill me yourself?" said Charles.

"Do not tempt me—" hissed Sir Rathburn, his hands balling into fists.

"Enough. If that is what you're after, I will assist Mr. Henderson in seeing you and this man out," interjected the Reverend. His eyes danced with fiery authority, so unlike his calm demeanor from the pulpit that Charles thought he might actually step in to fight for him.

Sir Rathburn and his lawyer turned to leave. "You have three days before this goes further," said Mr. Van Creveld over his shoulder. Charles slammed the door behind them and collapsed on the armchair.

"You may have a shiner by nightfall," said the Reverend. Dazed, Charles had already forgotten he had a visitor. Between the pounding of his skull and Sir Rathburn's punch, his head clamored for respite. Reverend Truitt left the room and returned a few minutes later.

"Here," he said gently, passing Charles a cool cloth. Charles placed it on his face with a wince.

"What's the meaning of all this?" asked the Reverend.

Charles shook his head.

"Where is Abby?"

"I don't know."

The Reverend stood and began pacing the floor. "I imagine this has everything to do with the headlines I read this morning."

"Just go, please," Charles pleaded.

The Reverend turned to Charles. "In case you missed it, no one else is here. The good Lord knows that you could stand to have a friend on your side."

Charles rolled his eyes. What could the Reverend do in these circumstances? Pray? Call down fire from hell to smite his father-in-law?

"I am willing to listen, Charles. Not even my own wife would give you that at this point."

Charles turned to him with narrow eyes. Who did he think he was?

"Business went sour, and he will ruin me for it. That is all," said Charles.

"When will Abby return?"

Charles shook his head. "You ask too many questions."

The Reverend exhaled loudly in frustration. "You really don't know where she is?"

"That's an entirely different story, and seeing I've got one foot in hell already, I have no intention of getting into it with you."

The Reverend shook his head. "There are rumors, Charles. Ones that even I cannot dismiss."

"What rumors?"

"About Abby. They mention Madame Restell. Some say they saw her leaving this very house. And now you are telling me Abby is not here. You won't give any information. No one has seen her, not even this past Sunday. What am I to think, but the very worst?"

Charles turned to the Reverend, whose eyes seemed to reflect concern, not judgment, much to his surprise. He had not heard anything about what Madame Restell had done to her. No wonder Abby had felt the need to flee. Then he recalled Knightly, and feared what schemes she had spun and what had actually happened to Abby and his unborn child.

"Think what you want."

"Is she okay? Is she hurt?" asked the Reverend, leaning towards Charles.

"She was hurt when I saw her, but I swear, I didn't do it. Her face was swollen, I could tell that even from a distance. She was sailing away to England. I don't expect to see her again."

The Reverend took in a sharp breath of surprise. "England? And was she carrying your child? Why was Madame Restell here?"

Charles stood abruptly, still holding the cloth to his head. "See, whatever information I do give you only results in more questions—questions even I don't have the answers to. Now please, leave."

"It doesn't look like you have many people in your camp, Charles. If you would just let me in, maybe I could offer sound counsel."

"Yeah, so Sir Rathburn can then use it against me?"

"No, so you can stop making such a mess of things. Look at yourself, son. You wreak of liquor, Abby's gone, and everything around you is going up in smoke."

Charles stepped toward him, his chest pounding. "This isn't all MY fault. It's that damned man who is trying to steal everything that I worked so hard for."

The Reverend stood firm. "Blaming him will only shoo you closer to the gates of hell, son."

Charles clenched his jaw. "Maybe that's where I belong."

The Reverend stood quiet, his expression pained. "There's another way and it's not going to be found at the bottom of a bottle."

Charles remembered Abby with the same pain etched on her face as she tended to his wounds the night before their wedding, her pleading voice extending a hand of forgiveness. Men like him didn't get second chances. That's not how the world worked. His throat closed tight as did his heart.

"Just leave me alone."

"So you can solve this with another bottle?"

Charles glared at him. "Yeah, that's exactly what I'm going to do. Now, get out."

The Reverend nodded, wiping his hands on his trousers. He reached for his hat and let himself out. Just before he closed the door, he called out, "I would lock this if I were you."

Charles slid the bolt into place with a click. For a moment he rested his head numbly against the door. It was all too much. He felt as though the world warred against him, that heaven and earth had conspired to wrest body and soul away from him, until there was nothing left. But something gnawed at him beneath his rage; a simple, nagging truth that he had brought all this upon himself—that it was his greed, his lust for power, his hunger for flesh, which had given him the most momentary of pleasures and left a world of pain in its wake. And at what cost?

A bottle of wine called to him from the cellar. A sort of hope fluttered within his chest at the respite it promised—an escape from his troubles, and from himself. He lifted his aching head and walked towards it.

Chapter 26

Charles lifted his flask and downed another draught. It was the distinct nutty aroma of a small cottage's chimney smoke that reminded him of the chill. *It's cold,* he thought, though he did not feel it in his bones. The smoke swirled upward, drawing lines on the gray horizon. A breeze carried a gentle hum, which grew louder as he walked. Mesmerized by its melody, he turned towards it, the tune gaining rhythm and resonance. In front of him the church's steeple cut through the tips of the bare trees.

It must be Sunday. He gritted his teeth, as the troubles he sought to forget gnawed at his mind. Then, he turned his attention back to the building in front of him, wondering what Abby had loved so much about it.

Propelled by the sound, he trudged on, until he stood in front of church's large wooden doors. He looked down at his boots, caked in mud from his careless walking, his pants splattered well up to his knees. He shook his head at the sight.

The chorus ended, and Reverend Truitt's voice carried through the crack between the doors. Charles pressed his ear closer, straining to hear the Reverend's words, which rose and fell like a ballad.

"Because of our own sin, we deserve only death. What could save us in the presence of a holy God? Oh, but the perfect blood of Christ, shed for our sake. This is grace for us."

Charles' body sagged against the door. The Reverend spoke of wrath. Wrath against mankind. He spoke then of mercy. And even still, of grace. Charles snorted. How could a man like him be forgiven? It seemed impossible, when even he despised himself for all he had done. Surely there was no part of him worthy of redemption.

Then, out of the corner of his eye, Charles saw a flutter. He turned from the doors to witness the first flakes of winter glide gracefully to the ground. The scene, gentle and quiet, struck him, stirring up dormant emotions. As he stood in front of the church, sodden and soggy with liquor and filth, a voice whispered from somewhere deep in his body.

Come.

Charles shuddered and shook his head. He stepped backward, stumbling to the ground.

A gentle breeze swirled, making the snow flurries dance around him.

Come, Charles.

"No," said Charles aloud, turning his back away from the entrance of the church. He staggered to his feet.

The sound of galloping caught his attention. In the distance, a small party of men met along the road, huddled in a circle, their dogs pulling at their leashes eager to catch a scent. Their breaths sent up puffs of air in a cloud above them. One man, shaded beneath the brim of his hat, addressed the others. Charles squinted, but their images blurred as he tried to focus on them, his mind clouded by drunkenness. He stumbled away from the church into the thick trees of the forest off the path.

Drink, he thought, reaching for his flask. As he drank, the flakes became less formed, blurring into stinging droplets that stuck to Charles' unshaven stubble. He closed his eyes. Abby's face haunted his thoughts, and he grimaced.

"Abby," he said weakly into the air. Her green eyes played behind his like a vision. She smiled at him, and then her expression grew serious, then pained, then horrified. Her mouth opened wide into a piercing scream that howled in his head, growing louder even as he pressed his hands to his ears to stifle it.

"I can't take it . . . I can't . . ." Charles' voice was hoarse like a dying man's, strangled in the loop of a noose. His eyes shot open.

Drink. Swallow. Feel the burn. Let it warm you. Soon you'll forget. This wicked refrain drove him forward, trekking through the thickets and brush as snow fell heavier.

Night fell, shadows growing long and crooked on the piling blankets of snow. Still Charles trudged on, despair following him; it had him by the collar and would not let loose. Exhausted and empty, he found his gaze drawn to the sky, where heavy clouds towered above him.

"What do you want?" he pleaded, wishing someone were listening in that moment. Someone beyond the clouds, or in them, or above them, or wherever that great being who held both wrath and mercy dwelt.

The wind gathered its wits, sending a swift gust to score Charles' face. He pressed on, his eyes straining to see amid the squall.

Go home, it warned, as an icy blow lashed the tips of his fingers. Charles shook his head and continued walking, now ankle deep in snow. He threw his head back and took another swig.

A branch whipped, catching the top of his eye like another punch from Sir Rathburn. Charles gasped; in front of him he saw Sir Rathburn's figure step from the shadows of the forest, stalking him with a menacing grin. Charles blinked, but the figure vanished, leaving deep, haunting laughter. Charles felt chills crawl up his spine. *I'm hallucinating,* he thought. He stumbled to where he had seen Sir Rathburn standing only to find the snow pristine and untouched. He swallowed another drink. Then, he turned and his world blurred into an assault of disjointed thoughts and visions. He staggered backwards, barely escaping a fall.

The wind gathered speed, spewing snow like embers in a fire, whipping Charles' face, stabbing through the seams in his coat.

Go home, Charles.

Charles lifted his head to the sky, his eyes wild in alarm.

"Who are you?" he shouted into the whir of the wind.

A howl met his ears, announcing the gale that came rushing him from behind. Charles tripped along the uneven ground, losing his footing. His face hit hard, and he swore, spewing a slew of curses. He rose slowly, laughing on the edge of reason.

"Gonna teach me a lesson now?" he said, spinning around with his fists pounding on his chest. His heart and his head raged. He could hear the sound of chains in the branches of the trees, like ghosts following him.

His sodden coat hung heavy, pulling him down. He stumbled, leaning against a tree's jagged trunk, whose branches bent and reeled in the fray of the storm. With a creak it cried out, its limb crashing down mere feet in front of Charles. His eyes grew wide. He reached inside his coat, gripping his flask tighter, and took another long draught. Still, he walked.

Terror seized him, for he did not know whether heaven or hell taunted him. With every gust of wind, he swayed. Droplets of ice sliced through the air, piercing his face and eyes as he leaned into the wind. He shut his eyes tight, bracing himself against another tree. But when he closed his eyes to escape the gusts, she was there again. Abby. She wound her way into Charles' mind like a flicker of warmth before the spark catches tinder. Abby, with her pensive stare and ebony locks.

"I forgive you," she said.

"I don't need it."

"I know, it is not me that you really need, Charles."

He opened his eyes and shook his head to clear the vision. Charles teetered, wavering, his vision hazy. But his heart would not be numbed. It shouted to him in thoughts clear and crisp: Abby—what a sweet, lovely gift. He wanted her, he needed her, but in his head she still screamed for help because of all he had done to her. Terrors of the night had raged against her, raged inside of him. And that same pride had sent him to be an unwitting participant in the horrors in Oak Harbor; he felt certain that the fire that engulfed those poor souls would consume him. It was an evil he could not escape, a depravity he could not deny. What a wretched man he was, an instrument of evil to the one he now wholly loved.

Charles pressed on. There was no way back, not for a man like him. How could light stand next to darkness? The blizzard raged around him, engulfing him with each stubborn step forward. His muscles screamed out, cramping. His faculties resisted, and he could scarcely shuffle his feet. With neither water nor nourishment outside of his flask, Charles' body rebelled. He vomited liquor and bile until he was weak in the knees, then stood, wiped his lips with his sleeve, and continued on. Ahead, a clearing in the trees gave way to gusts of snow mixed with icy rain. He tried to focus his eyes, wanting to feel nothing now but pain, and then death. The chill burned him.

He smiled, daring, and lifted the flask to his lips until the last bit drained into his mouth. The taste of vomit mixing with liquor ran down the back of his throat. The sky paraded above him in a tincture of winter as his head tilted back to face it.

"You could've stopped this. You could have stopped me!" he yelled. The heavens bore down with blistering whips of wind and ice. Nothing could shield him, but he delighted in every icy sting, standing full breasted, with hands outstretched against the oncoming gale.

Then, with fists raised high to the heavens, Charles dared God himself: "Give me what I deserve!"

You don't want what you deserve.

Eyes wide and horrified, his bowels lurched. Pain kicked him to his knees. The wind barreled down on him like a crashing wall with Charles crushed beneath it. He curled into a ball on the snow, clenching his eyes shut, embracing the chill.

As Charles lay unconscious, death came. Darkness enveloped him, the snow piled high over his body like nature's shroud. Then, Charles' soul took flight, past the darkness of his own eyes, floating above the ground which waited, silent, the fresh winter snow glinting. It was as though time labored on while he watched at a distance.

The sky danced overhead with sunrises and sunsets, the moon waxing and waning in her cycle, nocturnal creatures peering curiously. On it went, the snow bowing to the rays of the sun. But there, empty and exposed, lay Charles' body. It might have been a peaceful scene if it were not for the revolving motion of the sky that altered his corpse's composition. With each passing turn it changed, until it lay bloated, blackened, putrid. Flesh shriveled off bones, sinews splayed open until they rotted into the grass beneath. Gleaming in moonlight, the bones lay bare until the sun rose high, baking them into brittle shards. And so it was that all that remained of

Charles Henderson were fragments of dry bones, picked and scattered by the beasts of the night, while the haunting laugh of Sir Rathburn rent the air.

Then, time held its breath.

She unwound her threads, spinning backwards, binding bones to tendons, refashioning flesh, filling heart and soul, until the chill air shook Charles back to himself, lying unconscious somewhere between life and death beneath a blanket of snow after a winter storm.

On the edge of the horizon, flickers of light floated from men's lanterns, dancing in a line until one deviated off its course, winding through the shadows of the trees. It neared, and the closer it came, the more luminous its light shown. A man held it steady, his shoulders draped in a heavy coat, his head covered by a hood. He picked through drifts of snow, removing his hood and squinting in the cold of the night with tired, searching eyes, uttering prayers through chapped lips as he scanned the forest floor.

He drew closer to the clearing in the trees, sorrow etched on his face as he called out Charles' name again and again. Wading through the drifts, he made it to the clearing where the moonlight glistened atop the snow. His lips continued their pleas, and a stray gust blew, sending flakes of snow scattering into the air.

The Reverend's eyes were drawn to an outline. His feet crunched and he pressed forward until he stumbled upon a heap. The mound twitched and moaned.

"Oh, sweet Lord," cried the Reverend, drawing Charles' limp body into his arms.

Chapter 27

Breathe in. Breathe out.

Thump thump. Thump thump. Thump thump. Life pulsed through Charles' veins like a relentless drum joining the rhythm of his breaths in a fresh melody. As consciousness dawned, he reveled in the rasp of his lungs, recalling the image of his dry bones baking on the forest floor. His cheeks gave way to a smile, cracking his dry lips, and tears pricked at his eyes. He felt different, not in his weary body, which lay inert, but in his soul. The flint had sparked inside of him, and he knew God had spared him. Where darkness had reigned he now sensed light. Sunspots penetrated the blackness, beckoning his eyes to open. When they did, a wall came into view. Confused and dazed, he stared at it before falling back into the trance of sleep.

When he came to again, the light had dimmed. He knew he lived, that familiar drumbeat pulsing through him, but on the fringe of consciousness came a pain like an undertone of a minor chord. His bones ached, adding an unknown depth to the refrain. Another breath brought recognition of the stench of urine and stale water. In the gray light, he could make out thick bandages wrapped around his hands and feet. He reached for them, trying to make sense of it, but movement intensified the throbbing. He studied the wall again. It rose high, joining with the ceiling in a stark cube-like shape, its window adorned not in drapes, but steel bars. Charles' pulse increased. This was no hospital.

An eerie silence hovered between the measured clank of iron chains beyond the barred window. When the light disappeared, Charles heard the jingle of keys.

"Up," came a low, growling voice. Trembling, Charles turned towards the man swinging his keys at the cell door. His face was broad and dimpled and etched with disdain, with yellow-stained teeth protruding from his lips.

"Move," ordered the man. Charles tried to obey, rolling over to his side on the damp straw mattress, but the effort checked him with stabs of pain.

"Where . . . am . . . I?"

The man poked Charles' ribs with his baton, sending shockwaves of pain through his abdomen. "Now, 'fore the warden gets here."

"I can't," he muttered, attempting to rise. His arms and legs shook violently, and he crumbled back onto the mattress.

"We'll sees about that," he sneered.

Charles moaned, the beat of his heart pulsing in his limbs. The clamor of iron rang out, and he peeled back his eyes to find another man running a baton across the bars, heading towards Charles' cell, his short-brimmed hat and brass buttons boasting his authority.

"Eisley, this one giving you trouble?" he said. His lips moved as though in a constant snarl using the right side of his mouth. In the twilight of the cell, Charles could make out the glisten of a jagged white scar that rendered the other side of the warden's face useless.

"Too sick to work, you sees," said Eisley with a shrug of his shoulders.

The warden swung the iron bars open, coming closer to reveal a half smirk. "It appears you've gone soft on the upper crust."

Eisely's face burned red. "Try'n to make a fool o' me? I'll have no pretend'n," he said before delivering a swift kick to Charles' side. Charles doubled over in pain, his chest burning for air.

The warden licked his teeth. "A lashing might tempt him to rise."

"I'll see to it," said Eisley.

The warden chuckled. "Easy lad. They don't take too kindly to us when our prisoners come bloody to court."

Eisley grumbled curses. The warden took a step closer and poked at one of Charles' bandaged hands. "What's this about?"

"Constable drug him in here in the middle o'the night from the snow—dead drunk, they says. Hands an' feet got the frost, ya sees. A man o' the cloth was the one that found 'em, and was beg'n to take 'em back home. Constable so hot, he nearly knocked the holy man silly."

The warden looked down at Charles, his pointed nose flaring up. "Is that it, man?"

Charles shrugged, unsure of all that had transpired. He did not even know why he was imprisoned, or what charges were against him. The last thing he recalled was the strange vision in the woods and the Reverend's arms around him.

"I think there be more to his story. Him's wife's gone miss'n. An' his boats burned in that harbor out in New Orleans," said Eisley.

Charles struggled to comprehend what Eisley said. The thud of his heart quickened as he recalled Sir Rathburn's threats.

The warden walked closer, casting his eyes over Charles. "How would a guard come to know all of this?"

"Them pictures on the papers and peoples talk'n. Prisoners, they be talk'n too, an' I put twos and twos together, you sees. 'Parently the wife's a nobility of Lun-don," said Eisley, his chest swelling with pride.

The warden's boots squeaked as he stepped closer to Charles' head. "Sounds like we have ourselves quite the celebrity. Keep close watch, Eisley; have him in the yards by the end of the week."

Eisley nodded, then jabbed his baton in Charles' side. "Welcome to Sing Sing," he said with a grin.

Chapter 28

The vessel pitched forward over the cap of another wave, and Abby's stomach rose to her throat as they fell into the next one. She clung to the sides of the bed where she and Miss Robins tried to keep from rolling off onto the floor. The baby kicked against her ribs, whether in delight or terror, she could not tell.

Nearly eight days aboard the *Acadia* had proved trying indeed. Abby had struggled to become accustomed to the swaying of the ship. Unlike her voyage on the *Shenandoah* years ago, she felt much aged, her innocence and virtue lost now, her body changed. The cabins were cramped spaces with modest necessitates. Miss Robins and Abby's accommodations were grand compared with those of the poor who occupied the steerage level. Their quarters were meant for a single person, so the bed hardly fit them both. Between Abby's growing belly and Miss Robins' cough, sleep proved a little elusive for them both.

With each passing day, Abby gazed at the horizon, hopeful that the nightmares of the last year would remain behind her. On tolerable days when the sun broke free from the clouds and the swells of the ocean became lazy, the steerage passengers would lounge above deck until the crew ordered them to bed at nightfall. Abby felt wary of all of the strangers aboard who stared at her with curious eyes, and whose children pointed and tugged at their mother's skirts, brimming with questions. Her face still wore its bruises, and with her belly large with child and no husband accompanying her, she looked suspicious indeed. Their eyes followed her until she could steal away out of sight. It seemed that no matter how many miles separated her from New York, she could not escape her past.

They had stumbled upon the captain's good graces despite the fact that neither Robins nor Abby had paid their own fare. Each evening he sent for them, ushering them into the *Acadia*'s grand dining room, reserved for only the most high-class passengers. Robins and Abby tried to keep to themselves, so as to not attract too much attention. Although ashamed to admit it, Abby missed her fashionable frocks and gowns. She could not wear them now anyway, but her attire felt drab compared to the ornamental embellishments of the room. Women often glanced in Abby's direction, shifting uncomfortably in their seats at the sight of her.

"Don't mind them," Miss Robins had said the first time they had dined there.

"They only mind me, and there lies the problem."

"The bruises are softening already, my dear. Before long there will be little to stare at besides a graceful lady full with child."

Abby nodded, grateful for Miss Robins' optimism.

The crash of Abby's and Miss Robins' trunks signaled another plummet of the ship. They both cried out as their nerves waited for the drop to end. Again and again objects clinked and clanked against each other as the swells rose and fell like a stringed puppet doing an Irish jig. Abby gripped the post of the bed to keep from tumbling onto the floor. Miss Robins cleared her throat, trying to stifle another cough, while she clung to the other side of the bed. The air felt damp and cold. Above deck, rain beat down in sheets, and Captain O'Dea barked orders to his men.

Abby moaned again, prompting Miss Robins to place a comforting hand on her shoulder. "What is it, dear?"

"I'm going to be sick."

"I'll see if I can get my hands on some ginger from Darcy again."

Abby gripped Miss Robins' arm. "It's not safe to move across the room, let alone clear across the ship. I can wretch a few times; it won't kill me."

Another pitch down the back of a wave sent Abby's stomach to its limits, and wretch she did, again and again. Robins rummaged about the cramped cabin, looking for rags. After the fifth episode, Abby's forehead was sticky with sweat, her stomach constricting in spasms. Worry lined her face and she feared the spasms were only going to get worse.

"It's not good with all that you and the babe have been through. You'll start seizing if you keep this up," said Miss Robins.

"Let me go get it then," said Abby.

"Over my dead body. You hardly fit through the corridor when the water's calm; what d'ya think it'll be like in this storm? You'll wretch all over the hallway."

Abby shook her head. "I didn't realize I'd become so indisposed."

"You're with child, and I'd like to make sure you stay that way if you don't mind."

Abby shook her head, but she knew Miss Robins was right: neither of them were fit for the task.

"For the babe's sake, please," urged Miss Robins.

"Surely we can wait a while longer. Just for the storm to pass," said Abby.

"Stop your worrying, dear," said Miss Robins between fitful coughs. "We are always at the mercy of God. I'll be back before you can fall asleep."

Abby moaned, another bout of nausea clawing at her throat with bile. "Do be careful," she panted as Miss Robins slipped out the door. Abby watched as Miss Robins stood in the corridor, bracing herself against the walls as she climbed the small flight of stairs. She paused a moment to steady herself, then disappeared from sight.

A pang of guilt pierced Abby's thoughts. Miss Robins had always served Abby at the expense of her own well-being. She had not only been a faithful maid and friend, but she had loved her like her own mother had. Abby's stomach dropped again as the ship fell forward, crashing against the swells of the ocean. The *Acadia* whined against Nature's brute force, testing each nail and plank. Indeed, Abby thought, clutching her stomach, they were all at the mercy of God.

Abby's ears strained to hear any sound above the crash of thunder and whistle of wind. With each passing minute, Abby felt dread. It had been much too long. Robins should have returned.

Abby continued heaving dry bile into the bucket, her throat scraped raw with the effort. She did not think she could make it far by herself if she went looking for Robins, and with no other cabins near the captain's quarters, she could not recruit help. Abby resigned to hold on when she heard the clamor of footsteps in the corridor.

"Miss!"

Her heart skipped a beat. It was not the voice of a woman, but the deep voice of Captain O'Dea.

"Miss! Are you in there?" he called out, desperate this time.

Abby managed to reply a weak, "I'm here," before the next clap of thunder cracked.

"Thank God," he said under his breath.

The ship knocked forward again, and Abby cried out in panic as they sailed down into the folds of the ocean. Captain O'Dea stood unshaken by the movement. He squeezed through the door to find Abby trembling as she gripped the frame of the bed with white knuckles. "Don't ye worry, lass. This is the worst of it. It'll pass shortly."

Abby shut her eyes tight as they pitched forward again. "Where is Robins?" she shouted.

"Who?"

Abby chided herself for being so careless. "Mrs. Henderson. Where is she?"

Captain O'Dea moved towards Abby without pause in the violent motions of the waves. Immediately, a familiar sort of fright shot through her. Her mind flashed with memories of another dreadful night, and another man nearing her in the dark.

Captain O'Dea halted, seeing her eyes widen and her body tense. His voice softened. "It's all right. I just want to see that ye aren't hurt."

Abby's voice squeaked high as if she were a small child. "I need Mrs. Henderson."

Captain O'Dea nodded. "I see. But she's not coming this way until this storm is over. She had quite the time finding the doc."

Tears streamed down Abby's face. Then her abdomen contracted, leaving her doubled over in pain. Captain O'Dea's voice was firm. "Are those labor pains?"

"I don't know . . . Just take me to her."

"It's not safe. I have the blasted ginger she was so determined to get for you. And you need to get water in your system by the looks of it."

He handed Abby a cheese cloth with dried slivers of ginger wrapped inside. "Chew on some; when ye feel your stomach settle, sip on some water. Just a little at a time, but ye must be persistent with it until the entire thing's empty," he said, passing over a canteen. "Wrap the strap about ye so it stays nearby."

Abby nodded.

"There's a lass," he said, smiling with soft eyes.

The storm still had the *Acadia* in her clutches, and despite Captain O'Dea's confidence that it would pass soon, the swells tossed them back and forth. He backed up, bracing himself against the wall.

"Where are you going?" asked Abby, now reluctant to have him leave.

"To speak with the doc's wife." Before Abby could respond, he had left the room, hollering, "I'll be back!"

Tears pricked Abby's eyes as she hung on to the post. The ginger was strong and bitter on her dry tongue, but after a few minutes, she felt the nausea easing. She was able to down two or three sips of water. By the time Captain O'Dea returned, the thunder had ceased, and it seemed the seas promised respite.

"There now, I told ya she'd calm down. Those winter storms are far nastier than I'd like them to be, but me ship's strong for it."

Abby nodded. "How is Mrs. Henderson?"

"First things first, lass. The doc's wife will have ye resting now. She said to lay on your left side after you've drunk the water I gave ye. That should stop the pains."

Abby nodded. The sea did seem much calmer than before. It looked as if the world was finally sitting upright instead of sideways. But she was reluctant to let go of the bedpost in case another swell overtook them.

"Good. The doc and his wife'll be here when it's clear, and we are sure the water's calm. Your friend took a mighty spill on deck. She shouldn't have been out there, but I know how stubborn you women are with them maternal instincts."

Panic gripped Abby. "Is she hurt?"

"Just cold to the bone. She may have swallowed some seawater as the swell caught her up a bit. She's lucky I saw her when I did. Otherwise, she'd a been swept out to sea."

"She will recover?"

"We're warming her up now. I don't see why she wouldn't have a full recovery."

Abby exhaled a sigh of relief that felt like it had been suffocating her for the past hour.

Captain O'Dea smiled, showing his missing front tooth. It seemed to soften his weathered features. "Go on an' rest. If ye miss breakfast, I'll have the kitchen hand save ye something."

"Thank you, Captain."

He nodded and stepped out, closing the door behind him. Abby lay down, feeling the tension in her muscles finally ease as she slipped into a deep sleep.

Chapter 29

Later the next day, as the *Acadia* regained her course for Liverpool and the sun fell low in the afternoon sky, Captain O'Dea brought Miss Robins back to the cabin with Abby. She was shaky and pale, and her cough had worsened. She whimpered as they lay her in the bed, her face fixed in a grimace. Abby could see a few blue bruises and cuts along her forearm and hands.

"Welcome to the infirmary, Captain," said Abby with a smile.

He laughed gruffly. "I didn't know I was giv'n me quarters to be turned into a hospital when you two came aboard." Miss Robins managed a thin smile, then closed her drooping eyes.

"How are you feeling, Mrs. Henderson?" asked Abby, nudging her shoulder.

Miss Robins wearily opened her eyes. "Oh, like a fire-cracker, so don't you pester me," she said with a wink.

They all laughed. "And it looks like yer doing much better yourself, Emma," said Captain O'Dea.

"As long as this weather behaves itself, I think I will stay this way."

Miss Robins leaned up from the bed, hacking for breath. Her cough sounded wet and crackly in her chest.

A delicate crease formed on Abby's brow. "Has she been doing this all night, Captain?"

Captain O'Dea shook his head. "I suppose so. She was shocked with a chill, so it wouldn't surprise me to have her feel under the weather."

"What did Doctor Mcleod have to say?"

"He didn't say much of it, but he did say his wife would be going to dinner early and that ye should join them."

Abby's stomach growled. She was famished after such an arduous night. She hated to leave Miss Robins alone, and also to face conversation with the Mcleods without Robins' quit wit to shield her.

Captain O'Dea must have detected her hesitation.

"If it would make ye feel better, I could have someone come sit with her. Ye need to take care now, lass. Ye've not just yerself to consider."

Abby nodded, trying to hide her worry. "Thank you, Captain. I will go. Perhaps I could bring her back some soup." Miss Robins waved Abby's offer away as another coughing spell seized her. "I will see if the doctor can check on her when we are finished."

"Rest'll help. I'll see ye to the dining room." Captain O'Dea held out his arm for Abby, and she took it with a wary look back at Miss Robins.

* * *

A few hours later, after Abby and the Mcleods had eaten a leisurely dinner and taken a lengthy stroll on the deck, they returned to the cabin. Abby peeked through the door to see Miss Robins sleeping, her chest rising and falling slowly.

"She's still asleep," whispered Abby. "Perhaps we should come back later."

Doctor Mcleod pushed passed Abby as though he had not heard. He turned his ear to listen. He shook his head and went to her side with his stethoscope ready in his fingertips. "She's wheezing," he said, then pressed the device around on her chest, listening as she breathed in and out until a cough interrupted the process.

Her eyes opened to find the room crowded. "What in heaven's name!" she said, hacking. Doctor Mcleod frowned, as she was caught in the throes of a coughing fit. When it finally stilled, she hardly moved.

"How long has she had this cough, Emma?"

Emma bit her lip, trying to remember. "I think for a week or so. It is hard to know for certain. But it has never sounded so labored. Not until now."

In all of the business of surviving storms, and fretting with worry about her baby, all of the smaller details seemed hazy.

"Darcy, get pillows to prop her up with. We have extra in our room." His wife slipped out the corridor, headed to their cabin.

Abby wanted to question Doctor Mcleod, but instead her lips remained clamped shut for fear of what his answers might be. Miss Robins had to be all right; she just needed rest. Tears stung Abby's eyes and she stepped out into the corridor to catch her breath. She leaned against the wall, steadying herself against the gentle sway of the ocean and wringing her hands together. Doctor Mcleod followed her out, waiting silently. Abby bit the inside of her cheek, wracking her brain with ideas and remedies.

"What can I do, Doctor?" she asked with a quavering voice.

The doctor sighed and shook his head. "If you're the pray'n sort, that would be appropriate," he said.

Abby nodded. Before she knew what she was doing, she found herself shuffling down the gallery to the deck. Angry tears streamed down her face. *Pray? Pray? That is not doing anything! All I am good for is to be waited on and pampered. I am the reason she was so weary. I begged her to leave New York, and it is because of me that she was nearly swept overboard.* Abby clung to the railing as fog gathered over the ocean. *Oh, God, do not let her suffer because of me!*

Her prayers flew up from her heart to the heavens, but still she felt powerless and lost. So very lost. The ocean spray brought her back to her senses, and she stepped back from the railing, chilled to the bone. She let out a sigh, her breath visible as it joined the ocean fog.

Footsteps approached from behind, but she stood still. Before long, she felt a soft hand on her shoulder. She looked back to find Darcy shivering beneath her shawl.

"My husband asked for you, Emma," she said, drawing Abby to her chest. Her tone was flat. Fear gripped Abby's heart like the wind's stubborn chill as she followed Darcy back to the stairs where the narrow passage waited. She paused, halting their steps, and took a deep breath before going forward into the shadows.

CHAPTER 29

Doctor Mcleod stood still just outside the cabin door, his face drawn and forlorn, staring straight ahead at the bare planks lining the wall.

"Doctor," said Abby, her voice wavering.

"I didn't know she was ill before last night," he said.

Abby gulped back the knot forming in her throat.

"How long until she recovers?"

"If I had known, I could have made sure she didn't rest lying down. Infections settle that way," he said, running his hands over his bald head.

Tears stung Abby's eyes in a new wave of pain. "I'm sorry, I'm so sorry. I didn't think—"

His jaw clenched. "She shouldn't have been traveling in the winter at her age in respiratory distress. There's nothing I can do on this blasted boat in the middle of the Atlantic."

Abby gasped, guilt stabbing her heart. *It is all my fault,* she thought. Doctor Mcleod had confirmed every fear that Abby had confessed on the deck a few minutes before. "There must be something we can do for her, Doctor. Please," she pleaded.

He turned towards Abby, hands raised in the air. "I've nothing here besides simple herbs. She's weak. Her lungs have filled."

Abby's thoughts billowed. How could she suddenly be so very sick when she had seemed just fine yesterday before the storm?

"What will happen if you can't help her?"

Doctor Mcleod's voice softened. "You're not hearing me: I've already tried. See. Her pressure is dropping, and she's struggling to breathe. Emma, it is only a matter of hours."

A silent sob wrenched in Abby's chest. She braced herself against the wall. Doctor Mcleod wiped his hands over his face, shaking his head.

Abby refused to imagine her life without Miss Robins. It just couldn't be, not after everything they had been through together. Doctor Mcleod pressed a handkerchief into Abby's hands, his voice gentle. "I wish I could do more, Emma. I'm so sorry."

Abby turned, looking down the dark passage. What would she do without her? She would be alone, utterly alone. A thought pierced her mind and she spoke it aloud. "Does she know?"

He nodded, his own eyes red and brimming with tears. "She asked for you."

Abby took a deep breath. Robins had been there for her in all her times of sorrow; now it was Abby's turn.

* * *

The splash was so quiet, so final, as the shell of Miss Robins, Ruth Gloria Robins, drifted out to sea cocooned in a makeshift burial shroud that had been hand-stitched together with the white linen sheets she had lain on.

"Rest in peace," said Captain O'Dea, his hat resting over his heart. Abby watched the body float beneath the cap of the waves as she fiddled with the bracelet Miss Robins had secured on her wrist just before she passed. It was a small trinket with wooden beads. Abby had seen it on Miss Robins' wrist her entire life. She held fast to it, knowing it was all she had left of her dear old friend. The Mcleods and Captain O'Dea stood on either side of Abby, propping her up with their strong arms. She did not want to breathe anymore, yet her lungs inhaled and exhaled again and again with life that was hers. The baby inside of her belly kicked vigorously, reminding Abby of her selfish thoughts.

A sailor's voice rose over the small company of passengers, in a haunting baritone that seemed to hover over the water like the voice of God himself at the Genesis of creation. But this was a song of death, not of life.

When it was over, the Mcleods and the captain stepped back behind Abby.

"We ought to go inside now, Emma," said Darcy.

She wrapped her arms tighter around her waist. "I'll stay here for a moment longer."

They left her alone with her thoughts and the winter chill. She remembered the sight of Miss Robins' ashen face as she lay dying, the flicker of the gas lamps in the cabin casting eerie shadows on the wall. Her coughing had stopped, as though her body knew she did not have the strength for it.

"Like I said before, we are at the mercy of God, dear," she'd said, her voice no higher than a whisper.

Heal her. Heal her, please! Abby had prayed over and over again, but she felt no presence, no benevolent force. Only fear. Fear of being left alone. *Maybe if I just had enough faith, God would save her,* she thought.

"I thought he was merciful," said Abby, the bitterness souring her mouth.

"He is merciful. Peace is in here," Robins said, touching her heart. "Death is only the beginning." Then her eyes closed, and a serene countenance smoothed over her features.

"Say hello to Mother," whispered Abby. She held her hand just before it went limp. Abby could not see where Miss Robins went, but at that moment she had wished she could go with her.

But just as her dear friend departed, Abby felt that Presence speak somewhere inside, waging war against the despair that threatened to pull her under.

You are not alone. I am with you always.

The clap of the waves brought Abby back out of her reverie. The sun had dipped below the swells, and she shivered with cold. Still, she did not want to leave, not when she would never see Miss Robins again. The sea seemed such a cold place to be buried.

Hot tears coursed down her face, and she wondered if they would ever stop. Had she not endured enough sorrow for a lifetime? She heard the patter of footsteps from behind and Darcy came up beside her, wrapping her arms around Abby's shoulders.

"She wouldn't have died if it weren't for me," said Abby.

Darcy stroked Abby's hair. "Perhaps, but it was only because of love that she died. In love she risked her safety for the sake of you and your child. That is nothing to be bitter about; it is something to be grateful for."

Abby swayed with the rocking of the ship beneath her feet. A sob escaped her lips, and Darcy caught Abby as her legs buckled beneath her. Within moments, Captain O'Dea had Abby scooped up in his arms. They brought her to the cabin, which had been cleaned in the last few hours during the funeral. Gulping down her sorrow, Abby let her eyes close as grief gave way to sleep.

* * *

The next morning, she awoke to the sound of humming as Darcy opened the curtains. Abby shielded her eyes against the sun's unwelcome glare.

"Let's get you dressed and I'll join you for breakfast."

"Go ahead. I am still not hungry."

Darcy's eyes narrowed. "That's not going to work today. You will join me, and we will go for a short walk after. Your baby needs you to eat and exercise."

Abby nodded, bruised by the reprimand that she knew was justified. She bit her lip, fighting back the tears that already threatened the day.

By the time Darcy had helped her into her faded day dress and plaited her hair, the dining hall was nearly empty. Abby was grateful she would not have to endure other women's curious stares. Darcy led Abby towards the corner of the room where Captain O'Dea and Dr. Mcleod waited for them. The men rose and pulled the women's chairs back to receive them.

"Forgive us for already eating, ladies. Your breakfast is almost ready, though," said Captain O'Dea, smiling gently.

Abby had not the strength to return the gesture. She sat down, her heart heavy. But as the scent of steaming porridge reached her, she realized how hungry she was. She ate until the bowl was sopped dry and her stomach sated. The babe kicked in gratitude, willing a soft grin to form on her face.

Doctor Mcleod cleared his throat. "Emma, I know this is not an easy time, but matters must be discussed. We are concerned. What are your plans when we dock in Liverpool the day after next?"

Abby's heart sank. She dropped her gaze to her lap, wringing her fingers together. "I . . . umm . . . I have yet to think about it," she said. The sound of her own thick voice made her eyes pool with tears again. Miss Robins had mentioned going to stay with her brother, who lived in the suburbs of London, but they had left New York in such a hurry that no actual preparation had been made.

An awkward silence ensued. Miss Robins had always planned everything for Abby, and she felt truly helpless without her. Darcy reached over and hugged her, shielding her tears from the others, while they considered the possibilities. They threw around ideas, such as having Emma stay with the Mcleods until the baby was born, and then she could make more arrangements. Captain O'Dea proposed sending her to his kinfolk in Liverpool. Although she had not told anyone of her actual circumstances, Abby knew that they assumed she carried a child out of wedlock and now had no family to care for her. She listened to them try to formulate plans for her future. They seemed to genuinely care for her.

She fumbled with the bracelet dangling on her wrist and remembered Miss Robins' coin purse stored in her trunk. She knew she couldn't possibly carry all of Miss Robins' belongings to London herself, so the day before she had decided to go through the items and keep what she could fit in her own trunk. In the process, Abby had found a slip of paper with Robins' brother's address scrawled on it, along with a red coin purse. Abby gasped when she opened it. Inside were rolls and rolls of notes, which must have been all of Miss Robins' savings from years in the Wyndhams' service.

Slowly a decision formed in her mind. After a few minutes, she cleared her throat, interrupting the conversation.

"I will go to London. Mrs. Henderson's brother resides there. I must deliver this news in person and see that he receives the items that now belong to him." Their whispers halted, their eyes looking on her with concern.

"Do you know her family?" asked Doctor Mcleod.

"No."

"Where will you stay? What if they won't have you?" asked Darcy. Captain O'Dea shot her a look.

Abby took a breath to remain calm. She knew Darcy did not intend to be rude. It was a valid question. Why would anyone want to allow a pregnant woman with no husband in their home?

"She was like a mother to me. Surely they will greet me with kindness," she said, trying to keep her voice level.

The table eyed her with questions, prodding doubts in Abby's own mind, but she sat rigid, resigned to the path before her. She decided she would return what was left of her dear friend to her family so that they could share in the grief.

Abby nodded. "It is settled then." She looked over her shoulder through the window to the horizon that stretched around them in a never-ending circle. Liverpool lay somewhere off in the distance only a few breaths of wind away. Then, London . . . and after that . . . she had no idea. What she did know was that Lady Abigail Wyndham and Mrs. Abby Henderson would exist no longer. Emma was her name, and if she wanted to survive, she must endeavor to become her.

Among all of the uncertainty, one truth remained: the babe would arrive soon. And even though she rejoiced at the life inside her, she paled at the thought of delivering that child into the world. As she had learned as a little girl holding her mother's cold hand, there were no assurances in labor. Emma shuddered at the thought.

"Are you all right, dear?" asked a voice beside her. Emma jerked her head around to see a troubled look on Darcy's face. For a moment, she'd thought Miss Robins was sitting beside her. Emma nodded, collecting her thoughts and retreating back into herself. Darcy leaned forward, giving Emma's arm a gentle squeeze. "There you are. I was saying that I think we will see you to London until you are settled."

Emma attempted a smile. "Thank you."

"What else might you need?" she questioned.

Emma's face grew serious, her stare hard. "God Himself has denied me despite my pleading. Nothing you can do will accomplish what I need." Darcy took in a sharp breath, withdrawing her hand from Emma's arm, as Emma abruptly stood and slipped away to her cabin. All the waters surrounding them could not sate her thirst for answers or quench the flames that raged in her like a bitter fire, threatening to consume her.

Chapter 30

The *Acadia* arrived at Liverpool at midday, when the tide was low but spirits high—all spirits except for Emma's. She remained in such a deep melancholy that her traveling companions feared parting with her. Her mind was mired in a heavy fog, her heart irreparably broken. So many uncertainties awaited that she feared getting off the ship which she had so eagerly boarded in New York. How could she be setting foot in London without her dearest Miss Robins? And how cruel would the world be to a friendless, fallen woman heavy with child? But the question that occupied her thoughts the most was, who is Emma Robins?

Captain O'Dea accompanied Emma down the boating ramp, holding her arm in his. She was grateful for his help, as she could scarcely see the ramp through the shadow of her belly. And, with a man beside her, she could just about avoid any unwanted attention or pointed stares. Dr. Mcleod and his wife followed close behind them onto the solid, steady, English soil.

When they had reached the bottom of the ramp, Emma's belongings safely by her side, Captain O'Dea turned to her.

"I wish we'd be part'n in better spirits."

Emma looked into his face, misted with sea spray, his eyes heavy with sorrow, but she herself felt numb.

"Thank you for your kindness, Captain. I would not have been able to make the journey without it."

The wind blew, chilled from the ocean, but Emma hardly felt it. Captain O'Dea reached his hand out towards her, but then hesitated and let it fall to his side.

"Do take care, Emma." Emma nodded, offering a simple curtsy. He turned to the Mcleods, whispering something in the doctor's ear. Then, with a look of defeat etched on his weathered skin, he left Emma in their care.

Doctor Mcleod escorted the women away from the docks, which were buzzing with the sounds of the new arrivals greeting long-lost loved ones. Emma couldn't help but smile at the accents that transported her back to Devonsfield, recalling happy days spent exploring the grounds with the servant children. A young lad in tattered breeches stepped directly in Doctor Mcleod's path, jolting Emma from her reverie.

"Latest news, for a two-pence?"

At the same time another small soul appeared, pulling at Darcy's skirts, her bare feet filthy and bruised. Licking her lips, the little girl opened her hands.

"A shil'n to spare?"

Dr. Mcleod obliged the newspaper boy, passing him some coins with a wink. Clutching his paper by his side, he then offered the little girl a shilling. Amid the commotion, Emma's eyes caught the front page of the paper rolled beneath the doctor's arm. Her mouth fell open as she scanned the article's headline.

This is too much, she thought to herself. Her chin quivered, and her face paled. She swayed and Doctor Mcleod rushed to her side, taking her under the arm. Darcy ran to her other side, holding her other arm and putting a warm hand on Emma's cool cheek.

"Let's get her something to eat, quickly," said Doctor Mcleod.

They guided her to a small cafe across the street. Emma's feet hardly touched the ground as they lowered her gently into a chair. Gradually Emma's breathing calmed, and her cheeks regained their color. Her friends insisted she eat, placing a buttered scone in front of her. She nibbled at it, and sipped tea, grateful for the warmth it provided.

"It's good to see some color back in your face, Emma," said the doctor. Then, leaning back in his chair, he unrolled the paper, lifting a steaming cup of coffee to his lips. After a long sip, he looked over to his wife. "It seems that New York's made the news all the way across the pond."

"Ah, how so?" replied Darcy. Emma took in a sharp breath, her eyes fixed on the headline.

"Well, the story's unclear at the moment. Seems a certain Charles Henderson made a pretty profit in trading slaves. Then, the vessels burned with the slaves inside," said Doctor Mcleod, shaking his head. "But—it says here the charges he faces aren't related."

"'Tis only right," said Darcy.

"Charges?" asked Emma warily. Both Doctor Mcleod and his wife turned to her, looking surprised that she had spoken after such a long silence. Her eyes darted off while her mind teemed with anxious thoughts. A sick dread filled her belly. Doctor Mcleod's eyes narrowed. "Darcy, fetch the smelling salts. She's gone pale again, don't you think?"

Darcy reached for Emma's hand, covering it with her own. "Do you know these people?" Emma blinked, averting her eyes. "My friend . . . umm . . . Mrs. Henderson, did."

Doctor Mcleod gave his wife a look of warning and shook his head. "Get the salts dear, and stop pestering her with questions." Darcy nodded and retrieved the remedy.

Emma looked at Doctor Mcleod. "I think I should lie down."

"Of course. I saw an inn just down the way. London can wait until you recover."

* * *

After a hushed exchange with a rather officious innkeeper, Dr. Mcleod had booked two rooms just down the street from the docks. It was a small inn, outfitted with six rooms on the second level. The accommodations were quaint, the rooms bare except for the bed and wash basin, but it was clean and comfortable after so many days at sea. The ground floor acted as a pub, where sailors and travelers gathered for breakfast, lunch, and dinner. Emma was grateful for the time alone to rest. She slept heavily, exhausted in body and mind.

Early the next morning the smell of sizzling sausages wafted upstairs, and before Emma had opened her eyes, her belly thumped with happy kicks. Rain pattered on the windowpane. Light had yet to flicker on the horizon.

"Are you hungry so early?" she said, feeling her bulging stomach. The baby kicked against her palm, and she smiled. Since Robins' passing, food had lost its appeal, and she ate not out of hunger but necessity. She had nearly forgotten that actual life was thrumming inside of her with death all around. She inhaled deeply, getting a full breath of the savory scent. The babe kicked again.

"Patient, little one," she gently chided. "I must dress first."

Within a few minutes, Emma had washed her face in the small basin and dressed herself. She tied her hair back into a loose plait and made her way downstairs.

The cook was a heavy-set woman, bustling about with her sleeves rolled past her elbows and a handkerchief tied around her hair. She gave Emma a toothy grin. "Go on an' take a seat. I'll bring yer breakfast to ye."

Emma nodded and found a place to sit. The tables were empty apart from a few men a table away cradling cups in their hands while they pored over the newspaper.

Within a few minutes, the cook had placed a couple of sausages and a bowl of porridge on the table. After a few spoonfuls, the baby stilled in contentment. Emma glanced out the window, detecting a subtle hint of light amid the heavy clouds. A few wagons trundled by, their drivers urging on weary-looking horses. The occasional passerby scuttled past, head held low against the driving rain. As she returned to her plate, Emma felt the unnerving sensation of being watched. Instinctively, she looked up to find the dark eyes of a strange man fixed on her. With a forced smile, she acknowledged him. He quickly averted his gaze.

Abby swallowed, feeling a familiar knot forming in her stomach. The man's friend leaned over to him and whispered something. They shook their heads and stole another look in her direction. Her cheeks grew hot, but she continued sipping her tea and forced a few more spoonfuls of porridge down.

The crumple of a newspaper drew her eyes back to the men. She glanced over her shoulder then froze. She squinted her eyes, blinking once, then twice, as the bold print mocked her: "RATHBURN WYNDHAM SEARCHES FOR MISSING DAUGHTER."

As if this wasn't enough of a shock, as she followed the column down a striking sketch of a young woman with dark curly hair and heart-shaped lips just like her own stared back at her. The spoon fell out of her hand with a hard clank on the wooden table. The cook lifted her eyes from her kneading hands. "Do ye want more?"

Abby shook her head and rose to leave, feeling the eyes of the men tracking her. As quickly as she could, she returned to her room and locked the door. The quiet calmed her, the walls offered some respite, and she breathed in and out. *Why would Father say I am missing? And more importantly, why would he want to find me?*

It was not out of love or concern that he sought her, of that she was certain. Like one of his possessions, he had branded her with the symbol of her worth—the scar that marred her face and marked her as his. If Sir Rathburn wanted her found, it was only to use her for his own advantage. Her hands cradled her belly and shuddered remembering his threat: *"Get rid of it in England or I will have to get rid of you."*

Next door, the Mcleods had yet to stir.

Oh, what to do? she wondered.

She went to the window, the rain still falling in sheets. *Do what you must.* Decidedly, she went tip-toeing about the room, gathering her things. When she picked up her coin purse she sighed—hardly enough to purchase a train ticket and a single night's lodgings. There was always Robins' money. She bit her lip. No. It did not belong to her. She could not spend a dime of it in good conscience.

A clap of thunder drew her back to the window. Shopkeepers pulled their curtains open to face the dismal day, as people sheltered beneath the eaves of neighboring buildings. The newspaper boy stood in view just at the corner. Emma considered the Mcleods, who had selflessly shown her nothing but kindness, despite knowing very little about her. She knew if it weren't for them, she might not have made it ashore at all. Emma sighed, chewing her lip.

Next door, she heard the sound of Darcy washing her face in the basin, and the creaking of the floorboards beneath Doctor Mcleod's steps. Before long, they would be ready to travel to London with her. Tears pricked her eyes at the thought.

Despite this pang of her heart, a plan formed in her mind. The longer she stood and thought, the more resolute she became in her decision: Abby Henderson must remain lost.

She acted quickly, the din of the pounding rain and thunder muffling any sound that she made as she packed her few possessions back into her trunk. Then she slipped out, leaving her door ajar and a hastily written note on her bed:

> *I shall forever cherish the kindness you both have shown. It is with a heavy heart that I must depart.*
>
> *Yours truly,*
>
> *Emma*

Chapter 31

Each morning, before dawn, Charles woke to the bark of the warden.

"Form a line," he ordered.

Wearily Charles rose, his hands and feet still wrapped and oozing from frostbite. For a moment he allowed himself to play a torturous game, squeezing his eyes shut and convincing himself that it was all a nightmare. But he was sorely disappointed when the clatter of keys and echo of footsteps jolted him back to his sorry present. Sing Sing Prison's name was more of a sick joke than truth. No music hummed, no voices chatted, no lips whistled.

The chiming of church bells seemed a distant memory, replaced now by the unavoidable clink of the chains strung around shackles as the prisoners shuffled in lockstep to their work duty. Charles' shoulders brushed alongside the striped sleeves of other inmates, united in the futile task of heaving clubs to smash rocks, then mixing them into rectangular squares. This he did while his hands and feet pulsed with pain. He stumbled often, causing others to fall beside him. The warden despised this, checking Charles more than once with the blunt end of his baton.

Yet, through the relentless toil, Charles unearthed something deep within himself. Despite the hardships he endured, the knowledge of the trial he had to face, his heart beat on steadily, and within it, something stirred.

His thoughts continually returned to the blanket of snow, to the image of his own decomposing body, and then the fact that he breathed—he lived. Somehow he stood above ground and did not lay beneath it. Logic said it was not right, not after all he had done. He had cursed the Creator. He had abused Abby, his unborn child, even Roxanne—he had treated them as his possessions to be used and discarded, and just like the slaves in the holds of his ships, he had disregarded their humanity.

The scales were tipped sourly against him. Indeed, he deserved death.

But then he remembered Abby. In the middle of all the suffering he had caused her, she stood fast. He recalled her selfless love. The way she knelt before him bathed in the glow of the fire, offering forgiveness that he had been too spiteful to accept, and too stubborn to believe possible.

On top of his straw mattress, he would dream of Abby as he first saw her at the Astor Ball, descending the steps into the hushed ballroom, radiant and innocent. How he had preyed on that innocence, using it to his own advantage, giving in to his lust! His heart caught in his throat, for this is when he would wake with bitter tears.

"Oh, God, help Abby and our child. Keep them safe. Protect her. Give her hope," he prayed, to the same God he had been so quick to mock. Would He listen? Did He care?

* * *

In the second week at Sing Sing, returning to his damp cell after another arduous day, Charles collapsed onto his bed, his dinner untouched. Exhausted beyond hunger, he lay there, his bandaged hands pulsing with pain, useless in their filthy wrappings.

As the last shreds of light lingered in the window, he decided it was time to unwind the bandages, and using his teeth, he pulled at the wrapping on his right hand. Despite the dimness, he could see the damage, even smell the wound. Fluid oozed out of his broken flesh. His empty stomach heaved.

As he turned over his palms, the trembling began, the sight stabbing deeper than the pain. *Could flesh so damaged heal?* he thought, and then wondered how he would endure another day in the yards.

Lamplight flickered down the cell block, casting shadows of lined bars along the walls. Charles heard the unmistakable patter of approaching footsteps, and then an aging man appeared, accompanied by Eisley. The man's hair flailed around him in a white ball of fire standing on end, the ridge of his nose crooked and speckled, one eye bulging slightly wider than the other. His lower lip hung in a frown that did not seem easily righted. With the gleam of the light behind him, the man appeared more ghoulish than human.

Eisley fumbled with the keys, giving the stranger a chance to look Charles over before entering.

"You gots ten minutes," said Eisley.

The man moved closer, lifting his lantern to examine Charles, who lay sideways on his bed, leaning on an elbow with his one hand still exposed from the bandages.

"Humph," mumbled the stranger out of the side of his mouth, hobbling forward next to where the light revealed the malformed flesh of Charles' hand. "It appears you have a problem. Did this happen here?"

Charles sighed, relieved to hear the man sounded educated.

"Are you a doctor?" asked Charles.

The man lifted the lantern closer, ignoring Charles as he searched every finger. "Your feet the same?"

Charles swallowed. "I don't have the stomach to look."

The man's face twisted into a grimace, deepening the shadows of his eyes. He leaned in closer, and Charles thought the man smelled of sour milk and tonic.

"Salve and fresh bandages will help, but put those back on until we get new ones," he said, then lowered his voice. "Stay out of the hospital wing unless you want to make a home six feet under. Men go in there, but they rarely come back out."

Charles nodded and began to reapply the soiled dressings. The man turned and retrieved some papers from his satchel. "We don't have much time for fiddle faddle, so I'll be frank. I'm Onslow Renard, your attorney. I'll spare you a shake of your hand. Your mother sent me."

My mother, thought Charles, lowering his head. She hadn't written since the article in the newspaper smeared their name. He could almost see her long, pale face stained with the tears shed for all she had lost in the last year, starting with his father. "I didn't expect my mother to get involved. How is she?" asked Charles.

Onslow raised his brow as if that were the dumbest question he had ever heard.

"The evidence is that stacked against me?" said Charles.

Onslow nodded. "That, and the fact that she has little to her name now. All she could afford is a retired old man with his wits about him only half the time," he said, teetering on laughter.

If that's his own description of himself, then how awful of a lawyer must he really be? thought Charles.

Onslow must have detected Charles' uneasiness, for he leaned closer. "Young man, I've got nothing to lose, and you've already lost it all. You know how it is with the press and the notoriety—you're guilty until proven innocent. I mean to cause a pause in the process. Let the jury think before they cast their vote. With any luck, I'll spare your neck," he said, surveying the room with one bulging eye.

Charles' head spun. *My life*? he thought. Panic rose from the pit of his stomach, tightening his chest. If his life were spared from the noose, would it mean the rest of it would be spent inside these walls?

Eisely shouted, "Three minutes."

Onslow stood. "The halfwit can tell time."

In his panic, Charles lifted his hand, intending to grab Onslow's arm, when the pain robbed him of his breath. Onslow did not appear to notice.

"What's next, sir? I don't even know what they're charging me with." Charles' face grew ashen, and the desperation unmistakable.

"Manslaughter."

"*Manslaughter?*"

Onslow turned, cocking his head to the side. "Your wife?"

Charles sat in silence for a moment, as he tried to make sense of the charge. He finally shook his head. "But she's alive."

Onslow studied Charles again with his good eye, measuring every muscle's twitch of his face with a scrutiny that made Charles shudder.

"Prosecution has been tight-lipped, but boasts reason to suspect otherwise," he said finally.

Charles shook his head. "But I saw her. I saw her with my own eyes standing on a ship leaving for Liverpool."

Onslow nodded, staring past Charles. Then, he moved to his bag, shuffling through his papers until he found the right one and scrawled a few notes.

"Do you hear what I'm saying? Rathburn, he's framed this whole thing. He even told me he would. You don't think he hurt her somehow? You don't think she's really . . ." said Charles, his voice stalled by the lump in his throat. He stared at Onslow, as though his words had the power to suck the very life from Charles' own chest. *Oh God, please let Abby be all right.*

Onslow pinched his lips together in a frown. "As far as they know, there's been no trace of her since she left Rathburn's home. She disappeared, but it's your word against a dozen others. I cannot deny that from the outside, things look very suspicious."

Charles breathed a deep sigh of relief. "I didn't say I was innocent, but I did not have her murdered. She boarded that ship. If you'll let me tell you my side of the story, maybe you could—"

Onslow's palm was up before Charles could continue. "Not important. There's no time."

"It's imperative," said Charles.

"I can send that reverend if you prefer," said Onslow. Charles slumped his shoulders in defeat.

Onslow's raspy laughter filled the cell block, and Charles wondered if the man to represent him was indeed senile. The old man's face turned serious again.

"Frankly, I don't want to stay here longer than absolutely necessary. Another client stayed in this same cell." He looked around again and shivered before turning his attention back to Charles. "There's no body. I advise you to plead not guilty at the arraignment, then we can tackle things piece by piece with the jury in court. Understood?"

Charles looked into his eyes but found no sympathy, no desire to understand. He could not comprehend why this man would pull himself out of retirement to represent him in the court of law on such a high-profile case. The sound of Eisley's shuffling feet signaled the last seconds of their visit.

"Do you know who you're up against?" asked Charles.

Onslow laughed again. It was the kind of mocking laugh an old uncle would give his foolhardy nephew. "Want to know the real reason no attorney would represent you?" he asked, leveling his gaze.

"Because they can't win against Rathburn and Van Creveld," said Charles.

He nodded, leaning in close to Charles. "Right. No one else had the gall to stand against your father-in-law. The thing is, most of my clients back in my prime were guilty. I watched the man who stayed in this very cell hang from a noose. I know the look, you see. Guilt follows a man behind his eyes. You have a whole host of things haunting you, son, but so does Sir Rathburn. I'll use it against his noble sensibilities. Vincent Van Creveld may have fancy boots and a reputation to match, but this gray hair is a hard-earned privilege. Now, keep yourself alive till daylight. I'll drag a doctor with me tomorrow. With any luck, the warden will allow it," he said.

Charles' throat tightened, his eyes stinging again with tears as Onslow Renard turned to leave.

"Thank you, sir," he managed. Onslow turned back to look at his client, and the wrinkle lifted from the corner of his cheek.

"Don't thank me yet," he said. And then he was gone.

Charles sat in the dark cell, leaning against the back wall, where a sliver of the sky boasted its most precious jewel, the moon. He marveled, like he was seeing her—and her Creator—for the first time.

Chapter 32

True to his word, Onslow returned the next morning, bringing with him another, much younger, man who seemed barely old enough to justify the stubble on his chin, his baby face disproportionate to the size of his hat. Charles eyed him warily, wondering how this man—this *child*—could possibly help him. Onslow just shrugged. "He's green, but he's all we got."

The young doctor narrowed his boyish eyes, clearly uncomfortable in the unhospitable surroundings. His fingers fidgeted against the strap of his medical bag until Onslow said, "Doc, go ahead."

Without any introduction, the young man stepped close and squatted down next to Charles. Then, to Charles' surprise, he dexterously set to work unwrapping the soiled bandages covering his right foot.

Charles chose not to look, fixing his gaze on a crack in the ceiling. The chill began to meet his ankles as the bandages let loose. Then, the smell hit him. The doctor let out a gasp as he peeled the last layer away.

Charles moved his eyes from the ceiling to the doctor's face. Even as the young man appeared horrified, he did not turn away.

"Feel this?" he asked.

"No."

"Hmm."

Onslow stepped forward, peering over the doctor's shoulder, his upper lip lifted in disgust, and stepped away.

Taking a deep breath, Charles ventured a look, craning his neck to see his feet. The sight brought the sour taste of stale biscuit to the back of his tongue, and he gagged. His toes did not appear fleshly in nature. They were blackened, the corners of his nails peeling off. When the doctor unwrapped the left foot, it was purplish and white in color, but appeared less damaged than his right.

Then it was time for his hands. The blisters were still oozing, and the tips of his fingers still white. The stinging had yet to stop, which, Charles reasoned, was better than feeling nothing.

Finally the doc turned his attention to Charles' face, lifting the lantern closer. He pulled the bottoms of his eyelids down and shook his head.

"There's risk of infection in his right foot," he said, looking to Onslow.

"Can you treat him?"

The doctor looked at Charles again, but addressed Onslow. "It requires a surgeon."

Charles' stomach curdled, and his head spun. He sat up on his elbows, alarming the young doctor, so that he teetered back on his heels, falling to the floor.

Onslow chuckled, saying, "Careful, this one's still alive, Doc."

Charles stole a disbelieving look at Onslow, who shrugged it off. Meanwhile, the young doctor moved back to his position, resuming his stoical expression.

"Will you send me to the hospital wing?" Charles asked between clenched teeth.

The men exchanged wary looks, and then Onslow shook his head. "No. That won't do. I'll fight with the warden to keep you bedridden until you have time to heal. Doc, do what you can here."

The doctor looked over at Onslow, shaking his head. "Gangrene will set in if the toes are not removed."

"What?" Charles exclaimed in horror. The men ignored him.

"Can you do it?" asked Onslow. Charles' eyes darted back and forth between them like a frightened animal at their mercy.

"Here?" asked the doctor, the pitch of his voice high and uneven.

Onslow nodded. "And without raising suspicion."

"This is a prison cell, sir. I . . . I need a hospital."

"You would send him to the hospital wing then?"

The doctor threw up his hands.

"That's what I thought," said Onslow.

The doctor glared at Onslow. "I can't keep him from screaming if that's what you mean. And I've never operated outside of the morgue. I don't know why you didn't bring someone else."

Onslow stepped closer, nearly growling. "You're all we could get, son. Now, take a deep breath, gather your wits, and get to work before we run out of time."

"And the screaming?"

"*My* screaming," whimpered Charles. His face had paled, his heart pounding in his chest. *How did it come down to this*? he thought in agony.

Onslow reached inside his coat pocket and pulled out a copper flask. He hobbled over to Charles and reached down, holding the smooth container out to him. The smell of the liquid made him salivate. *Whiskey,* he thought.

No.

Then he turned his face away. Charles shook his head. "That's what got me here."

"I don't think you have a choice," he said, shoving it to Charles' lips.

Charles shook his head again. "I can't."

The doctor fumbled through his bag and looked around the cell. "I need more bandages, a lot more. And clean water. Warmed."

Onslow took a breath and looked at the doctor with his good eye.

"I'll get what I can from the guard, but by the time I get back, you'd better be done."

The doctor swallowed, nodded and then unbuttoned the cuffs of his sleeves, rolling them up past his elbows. His eyes refused to land on Charles' face.

Charles lay back down, his heart drumming in his chest like the beat of horses' hooves. His teeth clattered, his limbs trembled, and cold sweat gathered on his skin. The doctor's own hands shook, the smell of fear hanging in the air around them. He laid his coat out on the ground for a makeshift tray, on which he placed sharp, menacing instruments. The lantern light glinted off their edges, catching Charles' eye like taunting foes.

"Is there no other way?" questioned Charles. The young doctor turned his sallow face on Charles. His brittle confidence seeped through his eyes, reflecting Charles' own fear. Then, he looked away.

"Not if you want to live."

Charles nodded, clenching his teeth. "Then do what you need to do. I want to live," he said despite himself.

The doctor looked down to his instruments, reaching for the scalpel. Onslow reappeared, a bowl of steaming water in his hands. He crouched down again, shoving the flask back towards Charles' lips. "Now drink," he ordered.

Against all reason Charles shook his head. Onslow grunted with frustration and lifted the flask, taking a long swig himself.

"You leave me no choice," he said, wiping his lips with his sleeve.

"What?" said Charles.

Then, Onslow lunged. Charles did not know if he should scream or fight back. With a wild, beastly look in his one good eye, Onslow wound back his right fist and thrust it forward with a straight, even blow to Charles' head.

Chapter 33

Emma sighed wearily as she leaned her damp head against the window inside the train, a cloud of fog forming on the glass, obstructing the view of the masses rushing to and fro on the platform. She shivered against the chill seeping into her bones. Another woman sat wedged in between her and a rotund man at the rear-facing seat of their compartment. Between Emma's protruding belly and the thick girth of these strangers there was little room to spare. She breathed into her hands, trying to warm her frigid fingers. In her haste she had left her gloves in the seat of the stagecoach.

Getting to the train station had been none too easy between the unrelenting rain and her inexperience with the latest modes of travel. It would have been simplest to hire a coach to take her to the train station, but that was much too expensive. She dared not open Miss Robins' purse for the sake of convenience. Instead, she had taken the stagecoach bound for the train station, cramped with six other travelers, and paid for the cheapest ticket to London.

From the train station, Emma had only her feet to carry her to the house of Miss Robins' brother, Benton. They ached from traveling, and her soggy boots squelched as she walked. She wandered through the streets, asking strangers for directions to the neighborhood scrawled on the slip of paper. They pointed her to the far side of the city, their questioning eyes scanning her stomach.

Emma turned the corner onto Kip Street and faced an endless line of terraced houses. The dreary light the day afforded ebbed away so that the entire block was hidden in shadows.

Relentless rain streamed off the brim of her hat, trickling down the folds of her gray frock. Her cheeks were pale and her face felt numb with cold. Her right hand gripped her trunk with bare fingers. Knots of pain stretched across her back from fatigue. From stocking to stays she carried the cold with her and worried that she would succumb, like Miss Robins' did, to the chill, if she did not find shelter soon. Her own purse was now empty, as it had provided enough for a night's lodging in London, and one meal. All she could think of was the hunger that stabbed at her side and the babe's gentle jabs at her ribcage. She looked ahead in desperation and fatigue.

She hobbled forward, searching the frontages of the houses for something that would give a clue to its inhabitants. Every home looked identical. They were built out of necessity, packed together tightly, with simple posts for door frames, and each with one front window adorned with plain wooden shutters, already latched closed for the evening. A rat scurried past, hiding behind a barrel so that only the tip of its tail remained visible.

A woman approached the corner where Emma stood, treading carefully beneath the cover of her umbrella to avoid the puddles. Despite how Emma's belly and trunk occupied the majority of the walkway, the woman did not seem to notice her.

"I beg your pardon, Miss," said Emma, as the woman brushed past, bumping.

"Watch we yer go'n," she said.

Emma turned, shivering in the cold. "I am dreadfully sorry, but perhaps you could help me find Benton and Edita Robins," said Emma and then looked into the woman's face. Her expression was all puckered up, intent on continuing her errand. Then the woman's eyes narrowed and her brow furrowed, her eyes fixed on Emma's swollen belly.

She jutted her chin up into the air. "Who's ask'n?"

"Myself."

"And you are?"

"A close friend of Mr. Robins' sister. I have grave news to deliver," said Emma.

"You've got a lot more than news to be deliver'n," said the woman. Emma was too chilled to blush, and too weary to feel the shock of her remark.

"Indeed," she said.

"I imagine you're spect'n to bring all yer troubles to Edita, and I'll warn ye now—don't."

"Of course," Emma nodded.

"Second to the last door at the far end on the right," said the woman with another once-over and a disapproving shake of her head.

As Emma peered down the block at the door covered in shadows, dread filled her. What kind of woman was Edita Robins, and what would she think of a pregnant woman, a stranger, at her doorstep?

Rain hammered down, and Emma's toes squelched in her boots. She reached again for the coin purse tucked inside of her skirt. Still empty. There was nowhere to go but forward, so forward she went. When she stood in front of the door, she refused to give a moment's hesitation lest she lose all nerve. *For the babe,* she thought.

The first knock left her waiting. The drip of rain splashed in puddles off the short eave of the porch. She knocked again, harder. A grumble could be detected behind the door, soon followed by the sliding of metal bolts. Emma took a breath of courage.

A woman peeked from behind the door so that only the point of her slender nose and the whites of her eyes were visible.

Emma smiled, relieved someone was home.

"Good evening. I am looking for Benton and Edita Robins," said Emma.

The woman stepped partially through the crack of the door. Her pointed nose followed her close-set beady eyes from the top of Emma's head to the hem of her skirts and then back to Emma's belly. Her eyes narrowed into slits of scrutiny.

"Go bother someone else," said the woman with an upturned lip. Before Emma could respond, the door slammed shut.

"Please at least tell me if you know of them," called out Emma. "I must find them," she pleaded.

There was no answer.

Overcome by the sinking of her heart and the fatigue in her bones, Emma leaned against the door post and slid down until she became but a lump on the doorstep. She tucked her hands into the sleeves of her coat and wept into her arms.

I never should have got on a boat in the middle of winter with Robins. I never should have left the Mcleods who sought to help me. I've nowhere to go, no means of my own to take care of myself, and this child . . . what of this child? she thought with bitter tears.

The top of the trunk sagged with wear after hauling it by hand, the black leather scuffed and marked. Everything was soaked. Emma took a deep breath, wondering what she should do. The red coin purse of Miss Robins popped into her mind. Just a few of those paper slips would provide for a week's lodging and hot meals. The thought of a hot, steaming bowl of soup tantalized her senses. She licked her lips and swallowed. Her stomach growled, and the babe kicked against her ribs. *Perhaps I should use a small portion of Robins' savings to pay for a place to stay tonight. And a warm meal,* she thought.

No. Not unless Benton Robins is nowhere to be found, she protested in her mind. Despite her pleading stomach, she would not yield. She could even hear Robins' voice scolding her for being so stubborn, knowing that Robins would graciously give Emma all she owned.

She laid her head against her knees and cried fresh tears. The night pressed down around her, and the rain pounded the cobblestones with its pitter patter.

Suddenly she detected faint footsteps. As she looked up, she noticed a man standing before her.

"What's this?" he said, his hazel eyes peering at her beneath the slanted brim of his hat, his brow furrowed. His countenance looked so like that of Miss Robins that Emma was caught speechless. He leaned over, reaching for her hand.

"Have ye a place ta be, young lady?" he said, lifting her to her feet with his surprisingly strong arm for such a spindly frame. She stared at him, blinking.

"Are you . . ." Emma began to say, as her body swayed. Just before she collapsed, he caught her and gathered her up into his arms.

"Edita, open up!" he boomed.

Emma's head rested on his shoulder smelling of freshly oiled leather. When the door opened, Emma heard a gasp.

"Ya don't go bringing in a bob tail off the streets," said Edita.

"Oh, hold yer tongue," he said, pushing past her. He set Emma in a chair by the crackling embers of the fire.

"*Hold me tongue, hold me tongue,* he says. I'll not hold me tongue while the n'tire block sees you bringing the likes of 'er."

"She's chilled to the bones; fetch a blanket, will ye," said Benton.

"I'll not," said Edita.

Benton hmphed and marched away from Emma's side, ducking behind a tattered curtain used as a makeshift door for the only bedroom in the quaint home. Gathering her senses, Emma looked around. Plaster peeled from the walls, but the floor was swept clean and not a dish nor item out of place. Benton returned with a coarse wool blanket and set it around Emma's shoulders, and then went back outside and dragged in her trunk.

Emma kept her eyes down, too aware of Edita's biting remarks, and too weak to correct any of the old woman's assumptions.

In a matter of minutes Benton set a bowl of piping hot stew in Emma's hands, encouraging the warmth back into her fingers. She sipped it down, little by little, until she had drained the entire bowl and her stomach was warm and full. She rested her eyes for a sweet moment, relishing the simple comfort of being in a home, out of the freezing rain.

She opened her eyes to find Edita sitting with her arms crossed, glaring at her from across the room. Benton leaned on the edge of the mantel, looking at her with those curious hazel eyes. His face was clearer now in the firelight, and Emma could see the resemblance to Miss Robins all the more. His hair was gray; the corners of his eyes drooped with crow's feet. When he smiled, he brought with it memories of all the years of Miss Robins' smiles. Tears stung Emma's eyes.

"Thank you," she said, her voice thick.

His smile deepened. "Now, how did ye come to be at our door when the pleasure and pain is poor'n down so horribly?" he asked softly.

"I'll tell ye how. She since did knock hard 'an I sent her off. Then ye carried her in like she was the Queen, long may she live, lay'n to waste in the rain," said Edita with a snort.

"She scarce looks like a bob tail, nor a queen, but maybe somewhere in between. Let 'er speak," said Benton.

Emma glanced around her, all too aware of her bulging belly. She could almost feel Edita's stare boring into her middle.

"I believe you know Miss Ruth Robins," said Emma.

Benton stepped closer. "That's me blood. I just got her letter nigh over a month ago. Who does that make you?" he said.

"Emma . . . a friend."

Benton's brow knit together thoughtfully, the fire lending a warm glow to his face.

"Well then, Emma, where's me sister?"

Emma took a deep breath, her face filled with the pain of what felt like a thousand lifetimes. Benton swallowed, his face twisting into a frown.

"She was traveling with me from New York. There was a storm at sea, and in the chaos she was pummeled with sea water. She made it back to her room but became very ill. Before we knew it, she took on fluid in her lungs and passed . . ."

Benton's wrinkles deepened so that the lines on his face made him look even older than a moment before. He stared into the crackling fire and shook his head. "Oh." Tears filled his eyes, and they sat in silence. Emma watched the flames that seemed to dance somberly in the hearth.

"It's a pity. A pity indeed. What I ne'er understand's why she come all this way afore tell'n me?" asked Benton.

"And with *you* no less," added Edita.

Emma lowered her eyes. "From what I recall, her employer had proved quite inhospitable of late, and circumstances were such that she had to leave promptly, but we had intended to come here for a time. She spoke of returning to visit you last summer, but the trip was delayed and I was so sorry for it," said Emma.

His old eyes rested a moment on Emma's rounded belly, but he said nothing of it.

"And yer need'n a place to stay?" asked Benton.

Edita sauntered closer to the fire, her arms crossed and her thin lips formed into an upturned snarl. "Someth'n smells fishy," said Edita.

Emma looked down at her hands, bare of their gloves, dirt beneath her fingernails. Stray hairs cascaded wildly around her face in wet ringlets. Never in her life had she gone so long without a proper bath. "I do apologize. The journey has been none too easy. I am sure I look quite a fright."

"Yer tale doesn't say how you've turn up short of a sheet," said Edita.

"Now now, leave her be," said Benton.

"I'll not." Edita stepped closer to Emma and reached after her chin with a rough grip, lifting her face up to hers. She spit in her hand and rubbed it on Emma's cheek until it hurt. Emma winced, partially in disgust and partially in pain. Edita then snatched Emma's hands and turned them over palms-side up.

"Behind that filth, yer face has ne'er seen the sun other than to fetch dandelions, or perhaps genteel callers for all I know. Them hands is soft-like you've been napping with them tea trays on yer sofa. It appears you've fallen far from yer station, whatever that was, and I ain't lik'n the smell of it."

Emma held her breath, waiting for the acknowledgment of her bulging belly, when Benton rose, ushering Edita away from the fire.

"If you'll pardon us. I need to speak with me trouble and strife a moment," he said.

"*Me trouble and strife*. I'll show ye trouble 'n strife . . ." grumbled Edita.

Emma nodded, unsure of where she should go to offer them privacy, but Benton held up his hand and guided his wife away behind the curtain of their room. Benton's voice could not be understood, for he spoke in only hushed whispers, but the curtain was not thick enough for Edita's sharp tongue.

"You 'spect me to keep a fall'n flower in me house? You know what'll come out of 'er? A bastard child— really? In our home? Us upstand'n proper people?"

"Shh."

"'Tis the only thing that makes sense. Yer sister wanted us to take 'er in and hide 'er disgrace'n promiscuity. That young thing t'will only bring trouble."

"There's no use in jumping to conclusions. My sister knew 'er, and I do say she may have a place here as long as she needs."

"You don't mean it."

"I do, Edita, I do."

Emma felt crushed beneath the weight of her shame. *It was true, at least most of it,* she thought. She could not see a future for her in that place beyond that very moment. She had nothing to offer besides Robins' belongings that these strangers already rightfully owned. She was a burden—that much was clear. She did not belong here, nor anywhere.

Her father had made it clear that her single role in life was as a charming, silent accessory for the use of the men who lorded over her. Now discarded, she was of no use to anyone. Her mind and wit could not produce a two-pence among people of working hands. Beyond a simple cross-stitch, she could do nothing else. That was the Wyndham way, and now she was but a penniless, soft-handed woman, about to bear a child that could only bring shame on her and her acquaintances. With the birth of the babe would come an unending stream of gossip, and if she stayed here, this couple would have to endure it too. She shook her head, wondering how she could be so selfish to impose on these people.

She stood up, letting the blanket fall to the floor, and placed her bonnet on her head. Emma made her way to her trunk and unpacked the items that were Robins', placing them on the chair near the fire, with the red coin purse perched on top. The conversation behind the curtain escalated.

"You ought use yer loaf n'stead of yer 'art. It'll get us in over our heads. You'll lose all yer business, and not even have a stitch to mend in them high-born's stockings and a'fore you know it, we'll be begg'n on the streets," howled Edita.

"You speak when you ought be silent a'fore that tongue of yours has us all bleed'n out."

Emma quietly buckled her trunk and unlatched the door without notice. The air outside bit her cheeks again with its nip, and she shivered. Her gown was still damp, and she dreaded the chill that was sure to return to her bones. The babe kicked in her belly with fervor, reminding her that soon they would be hungry again, yet she left, making her way down the street.

Night pressed in, shadows lurking all around. The lamplight of the streets had long since been quenched, and Emma was left to walk in the dark. She took a breath, fighting her own tears. She remembered a bridge about a mile away, which might provide her with a meager shelter from the rain for the night. Dragging her feet, she pressed on. As she was rounding the corner, she heard shouting from behind.

"Emma!"

Emma turned to find Benton hobbling after her on his bowlegs. She stopped and waited, keeping her eyes fixed on the cobblestones as he approached.

"'Tis not right to steal away without tell'n me. An besides, you left yer things," he said, panting.

"I did not mean to be impose. It is better that I leave, for your situation could not be bettered with my presence. I left those things purposefully. They were Miss Robins' and now they are yours."

Benton exhaled. "Do come back out of the cold," he said.

Emma lifted her head and tried to smile. "I do not want to bring trouble to you and your wife. She is right to question me, for my situation is . . . well . . . very complicated. It was good for my heart to see your face, for you look so much like her. She was very fond of you, and always told me happy stories of your adventures—despite how often you pulled her braids."

Benton's eyes looked weary and lost in a despair that Emma knew all too well. She reached out and placed her hand on his shoulder. "She missed you dearly. I promised to bring her back to see you, and when she . . ." Emma shook her head, unable to keep her chin from quivering. She turned to leave again. A fog had begun to settle in the air. With Benton behind her, she looked ahead, unsure of where to go, or what to do, but she walked anyway.

"Miss Abby," called out Benton. Emma froze, her breath quickening into a cloud in front of her nose. Benton walked around and searched her face until she looked back at him.

"See, my sister wrote a few times. In each letter she babbled on about a dark-haired little girl, bright-eyed and fair as the sun itself. She adored her, and that doubled when her mother did pass. Every lett'r, she carried on about 'er, always so sweet like. Now here you are like my sister's writ'n come to life. I'm no fool. You are a high-born lady in the thick up to yer knees. But my sister cared for ye, and I am not a lad to have a loved one running lost in the cold. Please, come back inside."

Emma could see he was sincere, that he was desperate to help, but his own wife was so bent against his wishes.

"You have found me out. I beg for your secrecy. Truly, I am only Emma now, and can be no one else. I will make do, Benton," she said more confidently than she felt.

He reached for her trunk and hauled it to his side with a stubborn tilt of his chin. "You've no friend here but I. Now Edita can be, well, difficult, and quite honestly she may always be a rough spot in the leather, but please, give 'er a chance. I've been buffing 'er rough edges for years, and I know eventually she'll come round. She won't say nothing more of 'your condition.' Lord knows she's a bitter woman."

Emma looked at the fog-laden street and then back to Benton.

"I suppose I have no choice," she said with a half smile.

Benton let out a sigh of relief and hugged her tight. "Now let's get ye warm and settled."

As they turned together towards the house, Edita stood in the door. When they neared she stepped aside, her mouth pinched closed. Benton quickly set about to arrange a place for Emma to sleep. When Emma was inside again, she looked to the chair by the fire, finding it empty.

One glance to her right and she found Miss Robins' belongings gathered on the floor near the door, but the red coin purse was missing.

“’Tis ill fit’n to leave in such a scramble with yer fortune lay’n about so discarded, and these lofty frocks just cast aside for me to deal with,” said Edita from the corner of the room with one hand stretched out, dangling the coin purse between her fingers. “Take yer money.”

Emma looked to the ground. “None of this was ever mine, only Miss Robins’. It belongs to your husband now.”

Edita’s eyes widened and her jaw fell open. She tucked the purse in the palm of her hand and crossed her arms.

“’Tis only fit’n that we should have ’em then,” she said, lifting her chin.

Emma nodded. “Indeed.”

Chapter 34

Sometime later, in the dim lights of Sing Sing, Charles still lay bound to his straw mattress, his head spinning. He heard the scuffing of boots on concrete as men entered his cell, then felt the pull of rough hands lifting his torso and hoisting him onto a stretcher. When he opened his eyes, he found the ceiling passing overhead as two guards walked him through the cell block.

He lifted his head and caught sight of his feet at the edge of the stretcher, wrapped in fresh bandages with splotches of crimson seeping through.

"Where are you taking me?" His throat burned with thirst, allowing only the softest of words.

Eisley glanced over the top of his shoulder. "The hospital. Hush."

Charles leaned up on one elbow, the effort making him dizzy.

"You's better lay down," said Eisley.

"I just need rest. Please, take me back to my cell," pleaded Charles.

"I gots orders."

"But, my arraignment?"

"Not today. You's been ordered to the hospital."

Charles didn't have the strength for further protests, so he laid his head back. *God help me,* he prayed before closing his eyes again as his head rolled to the side. The quiet of the regular cell blocks soon gave way to a sound—the same hellish noise heard from the yards when Charles passed by the East Wing. Moaning. Pained cries from faceless souls behind the walls.

Eisley stopped in front of the door. The men laid the stretcher down, then knocked. They were answered by the sound of a thick, hacking, phlegm-filled cough as the attendant approached. Charles reached for his shirt collar, trying to lift it up to his nose with his bandaged hands as he took in the source of the cough. It was a stout, middle-aged woman, wearing a wrinkled white dress stained with tinges of brown. When she saw Charles, she let out a laugh, sending her into a fit of coughing. Eisley backed away.

"Warden's ordered this one to be tended to," he said.

The woman grinned, stifling her laugh this time so that her cough would quiet. "Didn't know we took war criminals. Looks like he's be blown to smithereens."

Eisley flashed a rare grin, exposing his two buck teeth. "Where'd we put him?"

"There's no room for 'em here."

"But I's got orders."

She jutted out her hip and pointed a finger at Eisley. "Then tell whose ever gives orders that them beds is all full. Wall to wall. I gots four of 'em that prolly won't make it through the night though. You can try again tomorrow."

Eisley turned towards Charles, sucking on his bottom lip for a second as he thought.

"Fine. I's will."

He and the other guard bent down and picked up the stretcher. Charles' eyes streamed with grateful tears as the hacking coughs drowned out behind him, and just like he had prayed, he was on his way back to his cell.

At the entrance to the West cell block, two voices interrupted the silence with their shouting, echoing so loudly that no word was intelligible. As they rounded the corner, Charles saw the young doctor and Onslow standing with arms crossed, shaking his finger at the warden.

The warden's eyes caught the guards with Charles in tow and narrowed, his lips pressing together in a firm line. He stepped forward, turning to Eisley and interrupting Onslow's shouting. "I ordered this prisoner to the hospital."

Eisley's shoulders withered beneath the warden's icy glare.

"They says they's full."

Onslow shot a look at the warden, his upper lip lifting to a snarl. "Send him back there, and I'll have you in court."

"For what? Sending a sick prisoner in for medical attention?" said the warden, his brass buttons gleaming from a fresh polish.

The young doctor's face twitched as he stepped forward. "I beg your pardon, sir," he said, his voice wavering. "But it is sure—I mean—it is a well-known fact that Sing Sing is dealing with an outbreak of consumption."

The warden looked over at Charles, scowling. "It's no matter. I am sure we will get to see him hanging on a noose in no time at all."

Onslow glared at him. "I see," he said.

The warden continued, "Did you hear that, men? This washed up old man can see."

The men let out an over-exuberant laugh.

Onslow shook his head, undeterred. "I'll bet your pockets are fuller now that you've made friends with English nobility, aren't they?"

Charles knew of only one English noble, and suddenly it all made sense.

"He put you up to this, didn't he?" Onslow continued.

The warden shrugged, lifting his chin in defiance. "You can't prove a thing."

"I just may," said Onslow with a wicked laugh.

The warden took in a ragged breath. With a curt nod of his head, he barked, "Return the prisoner to his cell, Eisley."

Chapter 35

Benton's promise held true. Edita did not say another sharp word about Emma's growing belly. However, there were many other ways for Edita to communicate her sentiments. The woman proved to excel in two regards: one, in her ability to conjure a meal from the most basic ingredients, and two, by constantly reminding Emma of her shortcomings, so that she felt as useless as a kitchen mouse.

Emma sought to learn how to help, but getting to grips with even the most basic household chores required step-by-step instruction. She had washed a basket of soiled laundry, only to be told that it was dirtier than before and must be repeated. Whether mending stockings, washing, or cooking, Emma was slow to the task. Though her youth and spirit were her friends, she had been waited on her whole life. On top of that, her body ached, growing more uncomfortable with each passing day as it succumbed to the strain of carrying a child.

Her only reprieve was her daily walk, past the corner where, in his sing-song voice, the paperboy solicited passersby to buy yesterday's copy of *The Times*. "Jus' a penny!" he crooned, though most of his customers could scarcely read. Then, after the turn, it was a short three blocks to Benton's small cobbler stand where he sold new leather shoes and mended the soles of worn ones. The only task for which Emma had found herself of genuine service was toting a bag of freshly cut and oiled leather patterns to Benton so he could begin stitching them to the soles. Edita had said she despised the walk, which usually involved heavy rain or snow, but Emma craved the fresh air, and it was a chance to steal a glance at the headlines. With a mixture of dread and anticipation, she would scan the front page, hoping to glean some news from New York about Charles or her father.

One afternoon Emma set out on her walk, pausing briefly to sneak a peek at the paper's contents as she turned the corner.

The boy smiled, moving closer to his potential customer. "Ye like a daily?"

Emma barely heard him. The young lad stepped closer, holding the paper straight up to her nose.

"A penny a paper," he said.

She leaned back and her breath caught as she saw Charles' name stretched out in bold letters on *The Illustrated London News* next to her father's. Sketched in the utmost likeness were the busts of each man, Charles on the left, facing her father on the right. FAMILY DIVIDED: SIR RATHBURN SEEKS JUSTICE AGAINST CHARLES HENDERSON. The message was clear. A trial was impending, but for what she could not yet tell.

The boy snatched the paper back with a twisted scowl.

"Must buy it to read it!" he said.

Emma blushed, feeling deep down in her pockets. Dismay crept over her face when she remembered she was penniless. The boy turned from her, folding the columns under his arm, and sought his next customer. Flustered and desperate to find out more, Emma shook her head and walked on.

When she returned to the house, she tried to shift her focus from the paper to the visit with the midwife that Benton had arranged. Although Edita rarely acknowledged her "condition," Benton—though admittedly he knew nothing of such matters—had wasted no time in taking steps to help Emma prepare for motherhood. When he noticed the shortness of Emma's breath, the swelling of her feet, and the roundness of her stomach, he asked his neighbors, who offered what guidance they could.

At the sound of a knock, Edita opened the door to see a tall, middle-aged woman with broad shoulders towering over her.

"Good day to ye. I'm, Lavelle, the midwife."

"I knows who ye are," replied Edita.

"Very well. You set on leav'n me in yer doorway?"

Edita hmphed. "Your majesty can come rightly to fetch you herself," she said, shutting the door in Lavelle's face. It wasn't long before Emma came rushing to the door.

"I'm dreadfully sorry. I might have made things easier if I had answered the door myself. You must be Miss Seddon," said Emma, with a brief awkward curtsy only pregnancy can afford. Lavelle smiled, her eyes incredulous.

"You'll have to forgive me for star'n. 'Tis not often I get introduced with a curtsy," she said, laughing.

Edita sighed. "I'll be leav'n now for the market, but ye best get the fire go'n and the water boil'n a'for I return," she said, brushing past Emma's shoulder as she set off to the street.

With that being Lavelle's introduction to the home of Benton and Edita Robins, Emma was quite surprised to find Lavelle had taken no offense with Emma herself.

"This yer first?" she questioned with a smile. Her wispy, mouse-colored hair rested loosely about her face in two braids looping over her ears, the rest arranged behind her head in a bun. She ushered Emma to her cot so she could examine her.

"Calm now. It's a natural thing; no need to worry," said Lavelle. "I am going to press on yer stomach to get a feel for the babe, all right?"

Emma shook her head and clamped her eyes tight. She would rather have smiled to set the midwife at ease but couldn't find it in her. In her old life she might have embraced Lavelle's assurances, but she held no assurances anymore, only fear.

Nothing felt natural at all. As she lay on the cot, memories flooded her mind of her own mother at Devonsfield, withering away in her four-poster bed, tendrils of hair clinging to her forehead as sweat beaded her brow. Emma recalled the screams reverberating through the hallway into the wee hours of the morning. And she remembered—too vividly—the quiet of death's dark hands resting over her mother and infant brother.

Emma's heart raced faster as scenes from only a few months earlier replayed in her mind, when she lay pinned to her bed, helpless beneath Charles—that fiendish trauma that had sent her life spiraling out of control. Then she recalled the black and white text of the newspaper in Dr.

Mcleod's hands that screamed to the public of her disgrace, of Charles' own foolishness. *Is he still in prison? Will Father find me?* she wondered.

Lavelle paused her normal procedure, lifting her hands from Emma's middle. Emma's eyes had opened, but she was staring out the window, as if inhabiting another world entirely. Suddenly her face contorted into a pained expression. Lavelle reached out, touching her arm, and Emma jumped.

"Are you all right?"

"I was thinking. That is all I seem to do these days," said Emma.

Lavelle smiled. "Quite all right. May I intrude by ask'n a few things? It'll only serve to help me prepare for what's ahead."

"Certainly," said Emma.

"Does the father plan to be here for the delivery?'

Emma paled. "No."

Lavelle nodded, scrawling a note down on a piece of paper.

"Do you know who the father is?"

Emma's mouth parted, her lips unsure of what to say to such pointed questions. Never in her life had she been addressed in such a forward manner.

"I see. Would ye mind telling me how ye came to be in this situation?"

Emma looked away. "I can scarce recall," she said, unable to keep her chin from quivering as red crawled up her neck to the tips of her ears. *Shame is such a formidable foe,* she thought, *even when it should not be mine.*

"There there. I mean you no harm, miss. 'Tis only to help you and the babe that I ask."

Emma nodded. "I tried to make him leave me alone, but he would not." Even as the words poured out, she couldn't believe she was admitting the truth. Relief washed over her as tears fell. "He tried to get rid of the babe, but here we are by the grace of God," she choked.

Lavelle reached out, squeezing Emma's hand. "I'm sorry."

After two months of constant berating from Edita, the simple touch of compassion wrapped around Emma's heart like a warm blanket in winter's relentless chill. Emma looked into her eyes, seeing a strength in the woman in front of her. Strength that Emma herself did not think she had.

"I'm afraid," said Emma, brushing away a stray tear.

"We'll get through this together, ye hear?" she said with a certainty that was difficult to doubt.

Emma looked at Lavelle's strong hands as they recommenced their pressing and feeling on her stomach. She wondered how many times they had held a blue, lifeless baby fresh out of the womb—how many mothers' hands had squeezed hers with their final breath like her mother's.

"Yer time is com'n, the babe's turned just right," said Lavelle after the examination was finished.

Emma sat upright, her face paling at the thought of delivery. "How long do I have?"

"Two weeks? Maybe four if yer little bab is really cozy," she said and then looked Emma directly in the eye. "In these situations the labor can be difficult. But yer strong, you are. You must decide now that you will trust me and do as I say."

Emma nodded, trying to take in Lavelle's warning. For a moment she felt a flutter of excitement, thinking of holding this child in her arms. If time were a window, she was on the cusp of stepping through it. But dread smarted her thrill. Whether in life, death, or sorrow a new season teetered on the brink of the horizon. *God help me,* she thought, *because I cannot help myself.*

Chapter 36

Somehow Charles had escaped the dreaded hospital, and he knew it was only by the grace of God. His wounds still stung and oozed. His right foot felt like a useless appendage without his toes. The doctor had severed all of them in a horrendous attempt to cut away the infection. Just the sight of the bandaged stump was enough to stop even the warden from demanding he carry on with his work duty; instead, Charles rested, taking some solace in the mercy that had been shown him. He lived, that much was true. But he didn't dare think of what lay ahead.

Several days later, before the city had roused from its slumber, Eisley and two other armed guards clamored inside Charles' cell, lifting him from his bed before he had woken. They hoisted him up roughly, holding him at the elbows as the shackles dragged between his stumbling feet. His right foot was all but useless, for any pressure put on it made him feel as though blood would fill his boots. Charles' lips felt thick against the scabs that had formed between the cracks of his skin.

When Charles became more oriented, he looked to Eisley. "Where are you taking me this time?"

Eisley kept his gaze ahead. "The courthouse."

The guards lifted Charles inside the paddy wagon none too gently, forcing him onto his elbows, which rammed against the wood planks. He rolled onto his side, resigned to lie down for the short commute. Upon their arrival, they transported Charles to a small waiting room adjacent to the main courtroom and left him to wait alone. The room held a small table with two wooden chairs and a long bench positioned in between the entrance from the main hall to the entrance of the courtroom.

After a few minutes Onslow entered, carrying a bag stuffed with unknown contents. His own appearance was much improved from the first time Charles had met him. His hair no longer flailed about like a caged animal's but was freshly combed down. At first glance, all he said was, "Hmph," which sounded more like a growl of disapproval than a greeting. Charles tried his best to muster a smile.

"I see you're still breathing," said Onslow.

"Did you doubt me?" he said.

"Sing Sing never looked so good on a man," said Onslow with a frown at Charles' shaking limbs.

"Pain is worse today."

Onslow hobbled closer, and Charles detected the scent of Williams shaving soap and whiskey—things once familiar to him but now foreign in his new life as a convict. Onslow craned his neck to steal a quick look behind him. "You know my only remedy," he said, patting his chest where his flask waited tucked inside his coat. "I did arrange for the doc to meet you after the arraignment."

"Thank you, Onslow."

Onslow's eyes narrowed as he shook his head, making his nose seem all the larger in comparison. He unpacked a stack of papers wrapped in a string, dropping them on the table with a loud *thump*. Then, he reached for his monocle in his front pocket. Peering through the lens with his good eye, he looked Charles over and shook his head again.

"First things first. I've recruited who I could to sit on your side. I must say, there isn't much of a crowd. Now, all you need to know is that I'll do all of the talking until they ask what you plead. Mr. Henderson, you simply say 'not guilty.' See to it that you keep your anger at bay, and it would help a great deal if you appear as miserable as possible."

"That won't be too hard," said Charles drily.

As a standard, Onslow did not smile, but this time the corner of his mouth twitched in amusement. "I said *miserable*, not like vermin."

Charles let out a laugh, only to find the old man frowning at him. "We need people to see you as a gentleman, not an inmate. Put these on. I'll help with the buttons."

A set of pressed trousers, waistcoat, and shirt fell on top Charles' lap. It smelled of fresh cotton. How long had it been since he had worn clean clothes? Next, Onslow shoved a mirror in front of Charles' face. Hesitantly, Charles lifted it to find a stranger's visage. His beard had grown long and matted. His lips cracked below the taut lines of his cheeks. His eyes appeared sunken. His was the face of the sort of creature he would have scorned in his previous life. The sight held him captive for a moment until Onslow grunted for him to hurry.

Onslow dug in his bag, pulling out a beard comb and razor. Then, he made his way to the door and knocked twice. A young woman walked into the room, her eyes on the ground. A guard followed from behind and unlocked Charles' shackles. The woman carried a small washing bowl, pitcher, and a towel. She did not look at Onslow or Charles but set the contents on the table and walked out without a word.

"Quickly, we don't have much time," said Onslow.

It was not a simple task, but after a few minutes, Charles Henderson sat with a clean-shaven chin, combed hair, and fresh clothes. He had managed to pull his boot over his right foot so that at a distance, nothing looked amiss until the guard reattached the shackles to Charles' ankles. Now, when Charles regarded his appearance in the mirror, he saw a faint resemblance to his former self.

"Listen," said Onslow, turning grave, "the judge has done his best to keep this hearing quiet so we don't have a public circus. I can't say who will be there, but you keep a steady head."

Charles nodded. They waited in silence while Onslow thumbed through his papers, reviewing notes. Charles kept his eyes on the door that separated him from the courtroom, keeping his breathing measured as he prepared himself for what he about to face. He studied the intricate tracery on the door, following the black indentations of the wood grain. He could hear low murmurs on the other side as the crowd gathered. He cringed as he imagined the flurry of gossip.

Then, a knock sounded. Charles swallowed, the taste of bile rising in his throat. The door opened with a creak. Onslow looked at Charles. "Can you walk?"

Charles nodded, clenching his teeth in anticipation of the oncoming pain. As he stood, his complexion drained. He stumbled first, and then shuffled with his left foot and dragged the right to position. The pressure on the amputated appendage was agony, and as he leaned forward, he was sure he could feel fresh blood seeping through his bandage.

The courtroom itself was small, but the vaulted ceiling towered above, creating a massive space. Three dark wooden arches framed the roof from the white of the ceiling plaster. Below their daunting angles sat rows of benches for the public to observe court proceedings. Typically, very few braved the courtroom at such an early hour, but today there were dozens of strangers peering wide-eyed at Charles as he made his way through the door.

Onslow turned to Charles. "Someone must have tipped them off. Looks like you'll be the day's entertainment."

Nausea riddled Charles' stomach at the sight of such an audience, all filed in line after line of benches. The bench reserved for Charles' family was bare except for one person—Reverend Truitt. Charles paused, shocked. The room buzzed at his reaction, initiating a fresh wave of whispers. The Reverend leaned on the edge of the bench, offering Charles a somber nod of encouragement. An overwhelming sense of gratitude fell over Charles, as he mouthed the words, "Thank you."

Charles turned towards the front where the prosecutor stood next to Vincent Van Creveld and Sir Rathburn. Sir Rathburn glared, his jaw thrust forward beneath a half-lidded stare.

Charles shuffled on, grimacing as the weight of the shackles pressed against his ankles. The scrape of metal on the floor echoed through the courtroom. Scratches lined the path to his seat, marking the route of all the chains that had gone before his. Charles clenched his teeth, resolved to deny Rathburn the satisfaction of seeing Charles' sufferings as he passed by.

Then, the gasp of a woman's voice stole Charles' attention. Seated behind

Rathburn's table, a slanted yellow hat shaded the eyes of none other than Roxanne Knightly. Her ruby lips were pursed together haughtily against her creamy skin. In full view of Charles the old man turned to her, offering his hand. She reached out, placing her gloved fingers in Rathburn's palm. The exchange struck Charles as too familiar to be one of an acquaintance. Charles stumbled, catching himself on the corner of the bench directly in front of Sir Rathburn.

"One more week, and there'd be no need for a trial," said Sir Rathburn as he leaned over to his lawyer, whispering loud enough so that Charles could hear.

Charles lifted his head, returning a glare. Despite his weakened state, he desired nothing more at that moment than to lunge for Rathburn's jugular.

Then, Charles caught sight of something he had never seen before. In Sir Rathburn's left hand he gripped a cane. He leaned on it so that his knuckles were white. On closer scrutiny, Charles detected a sallowness in Rathburn's skin, the tinge of yellow in his brooding eyes. The sight tempered his rage, and to his surprise, Charles felt a twinge of compassion. *He's nothing more than a bitter old man,* thought Charles. Lowering his head, he staggered to his seat next to Onslow.

"Well done," said Onslow, looking over Charles' shoulder to Sir Rathburn's devilish stare.

"Let's get this over with," said Charles.

The bailiff stepped forward from the judge's seat. "All rise, Superior Court of the State of New York, the Honorable Judge Mosely presiding, is now in session," he announced.

Judge Mosely entered the courtroom. He stood tall for a man of his age, with a broad chest and proud shoulders evident beneath his black robe. His white mustache and beard veiled the expression from his nose down. The circles beneath his eyes belied a weariness that weighs on those in position of authority, but still he stood straight and alert. He cast his gaze around the room solemnly. Charles felt totally exposed beneath his glare and had to will himself to keep his chin up. As the judge took in the sight of him, a crease formed between his brows, and his eyes narrowed with suspicion.

"Please be seated and come to order," announced the bailiff. Charles fell back into his chair, relieved to be off his feet.

"Mr. Henderson, did you sustain those injuries while awaiting this hearing?" asked Judge Mosely.

"No, your honor."

"Explain them."

Charles nodded, keeping his eyes fixed on his bandaged hands resting on the table in front of him. He could feel stares boring into his back, and feel the tension in the room as the crowd strained to hear every word.

"It is due to frostbite, your honor."

Judge Mosely nodded. "Are you fit for this hearing?"

"Yes, your honor."

The judge looked to the bailiff and nodded. The bailiff stepped forward and said, "Let the defendant rise before the judge while the charges are read."

Charles gritted his teeth, leaned up on his elbows, and stood. The judge took a deep breath and declared, "Today, you are being charged on two accounts of manslaughter. The first for Abby Henderson; second, for the death of her unborn child. If tried and found guilty, the penalty of this offense is life in prison or death by hanging. You have the right to a fair trial in the court of law."

Each word hit Charles like a blow, the reality of his predicament growing bleaker with each syllable. Judge Mosely turned to the prosecution. "Mr. Cutler, will the prosecution please present the evidence against the defendant?"

The prosecutor, Mr. Cutler, smoothed his red vest beneath his waistcoat, taking one last look at his notes. He left the papers in place and stepped out from behind the bench, his thin mustache twitching ever so slightly. He raised his hands along with his brows, gesticulating as though an actor on a stage at a common play.

"As you wish, your honor. We have obtained a written statement from the victim's father, Sir Rathburn. This statement details events leading up to Mr. Henderson's marriage to his daughter. All of its contents provide the motive for the neglect and abuse which led to the untimely and tragic death of Abigail Henderson, formerly Lady Abigail Wyndham."

Charles' stomach churned. His head felt foggy as Cutler's commanding voice rang through the court. He turned around to see Knightly's grin flaunting itself at Sir Rathburn.

What madness is this? he thought. The Reverend sat with him, while Roxanne now sided with his enemy.

Mr. Cutler continued his rant, raising his voice louder to command the spectators' attention. "In this statement, there is reason to believe that Miss Wyndham was forced to marry Mr. Henderson against her will. The prosecution asserts that the defendant violated the victim, resulting in pregnancy months before the victim was wed."

A collective gasp, followed by intensifying murmurs, surged through the courtroom. Judge Mosely hammered his gavel and declared, "Order, order."

For a second Charles squeezed his eyes shut, willing it all to go away. But when he opened his eyes, he saw was the satisfied sneer on Rathburn's face.

"When her condition was revealed, Mr. Henderson forced Abby to marry, and sought to hide his wrongdoings to avoid obvious scandal. In a letter obtained by his former housemaid, Roxanne Knightly, Mr. Henderson requested the medicinal witchery of a certain Madame Restell." At this the courtroom gathered steam in a tyranny of outrage. Sir Rathburn's face held its solemn expression, as he masterfully executed his role as the grieving father. Knightly's lips curved up, fighting a smile.

From the back of the room a voice shouted, "Murderer!"

"Monster!" spat an old woman.

Charles leaned over, whispering to Onslow, "I wrote no such letter." Onslow only half nodded, his eyes fixed ahead to await the judge's response.

Judge Mosely sat straight in his chair at the bench and bellowed, "Order in this courtroom!"

The murmurs dwindled. The audience held their breath as Charles fought to take in the prosecution's evidence against him. Each word spoken only fueled everyone's hatred, and he felt their stabbing glares in his back. Each detail laid before the court had been contorted into a demented version of the truth. Charles slumped forward, leaning on the table, the shame almost unbearable.

"There will be order in this courtroom or the disrupters will be escorted out. Now, Mr. Cutler, continue presenting the evidence."

His hand to his lips, Cutler nodded. In an ardent display, he turned so that the onlookers could see his face as he continued. "When Madame Restell administered her potions, Mrs. Henderson fell ill. We believe through eyewitness accounts that she temporarily recovered in a rally to save herself. With the help of Sir Rathburn's own housemaid, Miss Robins, the fragile Mrs. Henderson escaped. A certain Mr. Shermerhorn prepared a statement detailing his encounter with Mrs. Henderson before she was seen boarding a passenger ship, the *Acadia* bound for Liverpool. Mr. Shermerhorn himself is willing to testify about his conversation, having seen Mrs. Henderson's sickly state and visibly pregnant figure."

Charles' heart caught in his throat as he recalled the last time he had seen Abby, her cheek marred by Sir Rathburn's own hand. He couldn't help but think that he was glad she had escaped, even if that meant he was framed as a suspect in her disappearance. At least then she would not be at the center of this spectacle.

Mr. Cutler continued, "And while it is true that Mrs. Henderson and Miss Robins boarded the vessel, Mrs. Henderson would not survive to set foot on English soil."

Cutler paused, taking a moment to glance at Sir Rathburn, who bowed his head. Cutler pulled a letter from the inside of his coat, holding it up so both the judge and the audience could see. The room closed in, its walls bearing down with imminent judgment. Time slowed to a halt. Sweat gathered on Charles' forehead, his hands clammy beneath the bandages.

"Before setting out to sea, Captain O'Dea saw a man matching Mr. Henderson's description attempting to board the ship. Captain O'Dea did not allow it, suspecting this was the individual who had upset his wounded passenger. Captain O'Dea regretfully reported that during the voyage, Mrs. Henderson's illness progressed and she succumbed to it, all being laid to rest at sea along with her."

Charles lifted his eyes, his jaw slack in shock, his body numb. An internal weight pulled him down until he no longer stood but crumbled into the chair. He rocked back and forth, his head buried in his arms. In his mind, he saw her body wrapped in a shroud, splashing into the icy sea. *She is gone. My Abby, gone. What have I done?* At that moment he wanted nothing more than to join her.

Onslow's firm grip clasped his shoulders, squeezing so hard that Charles finally lifted his head. Onslow's eyes were fierce against his stern face. "We will fight this. But now, you must stand."

Charles nodded like a child and leaned on his elbows. Trembling with effort, he rose to face the judge. Onslow held Charles' arm, propping him up for support.

"Prosecution, continue with the charges," said Judge Mosely.

Cutler took a deep breath. "Considering the nature of Mr. Henderson's abuse, his motive to dispose of life to avoid a scandal of his own making; considering the crimes against his innocent wife and the life of her unborn child, the prosecution charges the defendant with two counts of negligent manslaughter."

Charles swayed, his head heavy. He could hardly see past his own tears.

"Mr. Henderson, do you plead guilty or not guilty to these charges?" asked Judge Mosely.

Onslow's grip tightened. The cords of Charles throat closed, stifling all sound. Onslow leaned over, urging, "Say 'not guilty' now."

Charles shook his head, tears streaming from his face. Onslow's fingernails dug into Charles' skin through the layers of his coat. "Say it, Henderson, or I can't help you."

A frail sound came from Charles' lips: "Guilty."

Onslow's eyes widened, and he held his hand up to the judge. He pulled Charles closer, but Charles shook him off, staring at Judge Mosely.

"Guilty," he said, louder this time. The room seemed to take a collective breath. Judge Mosely's eyes revealed a sliver of confusion, his white brows knit together. "Mr. Henderson, will you repeat yourself?"

Charles took a deep breath and choked out, "I am guilty, your honor."

Onslow threw up his hands and backed away from the table.

"Do you know what this means?" asked Judge Mosely.

"Yes, your honor," said Charles. Against all reason and logic, a wave of calm fell over Charles and his trembling ceased.

"You understand you are forfeiting your right to a fair trial?"

"Yes."

"And that you are giving up the right to cross-examine your accusers?"

Unblinking, Rathburn's eyes bore into Charles, as if tempting him to make the first move in a duel. Charles turned away.

"Yes," he said.

"You are admitting full guilt to the charges of negligent manslaughter of your wife and unborn child?"

Charles' face grew pained. Behind a blur of tears, he replied, "Yes."

Judge Mosely leaned back in his chair, looking down on Charles with a troubled countenance. His eyes wandered to Rathburn, still glaring at the accused, seemingly unaware of the judge's attention.

"A sentencing hearing will be scheduled. I hereby dismiss the court."

The scraping of chairs on the oak floors and excited chatter signaled the session was in fact over and another case was to commence within the hour. Onslow could do nothing but huff, his face reddening to boiling point as he escorted his client through the doors.

The young doctor stood waiting by the opposite entrance of the small room. Charles dragged himself in behind his lawyer, his head hanging low and tears staining his face. The doctor hesitated, fidgeting against the bounce of his legs.

Onslow spoke first, his voice grave, its undercurrent of rage matching the protruding vein on his forehead.

"Well, Mr. Henderson. Looks like you don't need the doc after all. Seems like a waste of your mother's money to tend to feet that will be hanging limp by the end of next week."

The doctor stood in the corner, eyes wide, mouth open. Charles looked up.

"You," he said, looking at Onslow.

Onslow's good eye bulged. "Me?"

"YOU. Yes YOU. You didn't tell me she was gone," accused Charles.

"I told you there was no body. I told you there was no proof. I told you to plead not guilty so you would have a fighting chance."

"She is gone."

Onslow's upper lip lifted, showing the yellow stains of his teeth. "Now you will be too."

"Don't you get it? Oh, of course you don't because you didn't take the time to hear me out before trying valiantly to save my neck. If it weren't for me, she would be here now. *I* drove her away. *I* brought her ruin, pain, and torment in the worst possible way. If it weren't for *me*, she'd be alive."

Onslow stood straighter. "So you wrote the letter to Madame Restell to have the poison administered?"

"I might as well have."

"That's not what I asked. If not you, then who did it?"

"Knightly, I suspect—we were lovers at the time—with the guiding hand of Sir Rathburn," said Charles. His eyes wandered around the room, as though he were searching for answers to questions that he could never understand. Onslow neared Charles so that the space between them made up only a few inches.

"Would you have provided for your wife and child?"

"Now, I would die for them. I would take their place. But then, only God knows what I would have done to save my skin. When they needed a husband's—a father's—protection most, they did not have it." Charles' voice caught in his throat; his words hung limp in the air.

Onslow backed away, shaking his head. "Well, good work, Mr. Henderson," he said, his voice dripping with sarcasm. "Now the real enemy will watch your neck snap and walk away happy. Not to mention with your company's profits in his pocket and probably sainthood at his death."

"I am guilty."

Onslow looked at Charles. "Aren't we all?"

"But we aren't all on trial," said Charles.

"You don't get a medal for clinging to honor, by pleading guilty to some twisted version of a crime that you *feel* guilty for, Charles. All you get in the end is a cold corpse."

Charles shook his head, then a hint of a smile broke through his tears.

"She wanted so much more from me—for me, for us. I couldn't see it then, but I see it now. I will not dishonor her by denying my hand in her death. That is to reject the very thing she lived for, the very thing that I live for now."

"Stubborn man! Don't you understand? Sir Rathburn still wins in the end; this way he still wins."

"But does he?" asked Charles.

Chapter 37

The aroma of chitterlings filled the room as the pot sizzled over the fire. The scent was less than enticing to Emma, who had watched Edita prepare it. The sight of intestines sprawled out over the wooden table while Edita hacked away, dicing it into chunks, soured her stomach. Edita had left the pot stewing while she left to fetch a fresh loaf of bread from the street barrows, instructing Emma to "look after it," and "stir it about" until she returned.

The strong odor hung in the air while Emma leaned on the table, massaging her pulsing back. She took deep breaths in and out as the pot hissed its angry bubbles over the hearth. Minutes passed until she was finally able to stand up straight. She exhaled, trying to blow at the wisps of hair tickling her face. She caught her breath, finding that her forehead was beaded with sweat.

It was then that the hiss of the pot mixed with the distinct smell of burning.

"No, no, no, no!" Even as she said it, she knew it was too late. She rushed to the hearth, finding the pot bubbling over. The fire fizzled away, sending plumes of smoke and steam into the room. She attempted to stir it, only to find the blackened contents caked to the bottom of the pot.

Using a folded cloth, she tried lifting the iron pot up off the fire when the pain came again, seizing her so that she dropped the handle, sending its contents sizzling across the floor. She danced around to avoid the puddles, then set it back upright. But all that was left was a thin layer of burnt fat, the rest oozing into the cracks between the floor planks. Before she could gather a bucket and mop to start the long clean-up, pain gripped her like hot fingers clenching around her waist, until her she couldn't breathe.

"No, no, no. Not yet. Not yet little one," she said as though mere words could prevent the inevitable. When the wave subsided, she rose up and rounded like a mad dog to Edita's table and found a bowl to try to clean the floor.

That's it. I'll make it again and she will be none the wiser, Emma thought, then

salvaged what she could from the pot and floor, hurriedly washing off the ash and grit. Quickly she worked, pouring and stirring, until the pot held a new mixture of something edible, though she was uncertain of just how edible. But the pot had already turned cold, and the hearth was damp with wet stewing mess.

"Oh, for Pete's sake. Not again," she said, doubling over.

When Edita returned, no sooner had she poked her head through the door than she began her rant: "What in 'eavens blue blazes is that stench? For 'un minute I leave my kitchen only ta have 'er put the whole house in the kindl'n."

"Sorry," said Emma, gritting her teeth. Her knuckles were white as she gripped the back of the chair.

Edita stalked over to the fire, spitting at it with disgust. She snatched the broom, feverishly sweeping until there was nothing left but the wooden planks and the brick hearth.

"Clean and cook, 'tis all I do," she said. Her grumblings like this continued as she worked. Then, she dipped a rag in water and scrubbed until every inch of the floor had been scoured. She stood when she was finished, sniffing her nose in the air. She walked to the bubbling pot, dipped the stir stick in, and tasted it. Her eyes turned to Emma, narrowing.

"I don't Adam and Eve it. Ye take me to be a fool? 'Tis all gone wrong. What did ye do to it?"

Emma refused to look at the woman. That prattling voice grated against every inch of her flesh. Her back tensed again, sending a gradual increase of throbbing through her middle. She gripped the chair harder and tried to resist yelling out curses for the good Lord to smite Edita to the ground that very minute.

But Edita was not the type of woman to be ignored, and Emma's passivity only fueled her anger. She seemed resolved to rant until her lodger paid her the attention owed.

"Clumsy girl. Ye better learn to use yer loaf or else we'll be begg'n for crumbs on the streets. Ye think I have the means to be burn'n chitterlings whilst you find yer noggin?" Emma's glossy, straining eyes locked on Edita's, but she bit her lip instead of speaking.

"And I s'pose ye 'spect me to do all the work to keep up with yer high-born ways. 'Fore long you'll be 'spectin me to be yer nanny. That right, *my lady*?" The old woman dipped low in a mock curtsy, the nobbles of her knees creaking as she did so. And on went her tongue. "Ye go'n to pay fer it one way or another. Benton and me is go'n to have a right good talk'n when he comes back home; twill 'ear about yer sass and dis'repect'n o' me. I don't believe it myself. An from a fallen woman of all things."

When Emma still had not voiced a word, Edita marched up to her so close that Emma could smell the vinegar of her breath. "Don't ye have something to say for yerself?"

The tension in Emma's lower back eased off so that she sucked in a deep breath of air.

"Edita, it is time."

Edita looked around incredulously. "Time for ye to have yer afternoon tea and biscuits? Or should I fluff yer pillows so ye can return to yer nap whilst the house catches fire?"

A trickle of sweat rolled down Emma's back. Emma thought Edita must surely be blind and dumb. Did she not see Emma's twisted grimace, nor how she struggled to catch her breath? Emma tried to take a step backward but doubled over this time.

"Edita—send for the midwife," grunted Emma.

It was as though Emma had slapped her. For once Edita stood speechless, her eyes bulging wide, jaw slack. As rare as the image was, Emma did not savor it, for Edita had not moved a hair, and Lavelle's house was half a kilometer away.

"Now!" shouted Emma in succession with the oncoming labor pains, sending Edita hurtling towards the door, leaving her coat and mittens behind.

Though Emma would have preferred time to stand still until she was certain she could endure what was to come, she found herself powerless against the forces of her body. She tried pacing the floor in between contractions, even busying herself with chores. While sweeping the floor she heard the crack of the broomstick in her hands, as her whole body contracted. Then, fluid gushed out at her feet, draining into the crevices of the freshly scrubbed floor.

"Edita may just kill me. Oh God no. I can't do this. Not yet. Not now," she said into the empty room.

These thoughts became the terrifying refrain in her mind. Never before had she known pain of this scale. Again she recalled her mother, lifeless and pale in her blood-stained bed. Fear gripped her very heart so that her hands became clammy and she dripped with a cold sweat.

I can't do this. I am ill prepared to be a mother, let alone a single, friendless one with the shadow of shame hanging over my shoulder. How will we survive? And what if we do survive only to endure further cruelty in this heartless world?

Emma wept and cried out in despair and agony as physical pain interlaced with her soul's torment held her teetering on the brink of madness. It was only when the pains would come at their worst that she could keep quiet, bracing herself between the back of the wooden chair and the mantel over the hearth.

Finally, the front door burst open and an icy chill swept through the room. Edita walked in, followed by Lavelle standing tall behind her.

Lavelle took one look at Emma and snapped into motion.

"Fetch hot water and clean strips of linen," she ordered.

"The only hot water is what we heat o'er the fire," said Edita.

"Then get on with it," replied Lavelle, low and stern.

Lavelle walked over to Emma as though she were approaching a frightened animal. "It seems you've been quite busy, dear Emma," she said.

"I cannot do this," said Emma, her voice high and screeching.

Lavelle put a strong hand on Emma's back. Her very presence emanated a sense of calm despite Emma's dread.

"Looks like you gone to work without me, boil'n a pot of stew and start'n labor pains. You shouldn't have done so much on my account," said Lavelle with a wink.

Emma moaned as another pain took over. The playful look on Lavelle's face dissolved, replaced by narrowed concentration. She took Emma's wrist, feeling for the pounding pulse beneath the skin.

"Let's let you lay down," she said.

Emma shook her head fiercely.

"Emma m'dear," said Lavelle, soft and calm, "I'm 'ere to help. But you must do as I say."

"I cannot. I can . . . not . . . do . . . this," said Emma, grimacing.

"We'll do this together," said Lavelle as she lifted Emma to her feet and laid her down on the narrow cot jammed up against the wall. Emma moaned, trying to lie down.

"This ain't proper. We're too close to the fire to stay 'ere," said Lavelle and then, raising her voice so that Edita would hear, added, "I'm moving 'er to the bed." Lavelle looked over at Edita whose face was freshly animated with outrage.

"She sleeps there," Edita said, pointing to the cot. "'Twill have to do." Her lips pinched together and her nose jutted upward.

The color in Lavelle's cheeks rose to an indignant hue before she stood straight up, smoothed her apron, and replied, "Is that how this is gonna be? So when yer husband sets foot through yer door, he'll get quite the view won't he? I reckon 'el appreciate yer kindness to Emma then."

Edita's eyes grew twice their normal size for the second time that day. She stomped over to Lavelle and spat in her ear, "Fine. But ye'll have to boil the bedd'n when this mess is through. 'Tis not right that a fallen women be given such comforts."

Lavelle shook her head, fuming. She grabbed Edita's sleeve and whisked her away behind the curtain. "You obviously never birthed a babe, for if you had, you'd know each pain is like splinter'n wood in your bowels—but I do think being crammed in the same room with such rude company might be more hellish indeed. Now, either help me or get out so I can manage."

Edita's mouth hung open, her eyes wide as understanding dawned. Emma cried out when Lavelle helped her into the bedroom. Her back seized with spasms so that she could scarcely breathe.

"I don't want to do this," she moaned helplessly.

Edita glanced at Emma, whose face was twisted in pain, then she turned away with a huff. She scooted closer to the fire.

A loud knock pounded on the front door.

"What in blue blazes is it now? Me house 'as turned over like a dump cake."

When she pulled open the door, a young man stood waiting, his messenger bag sagging at his hip. A gust of cold blew in, sending a fresh chill into the house where Emma's agonizing groans still played on in rhythmic succession with her pains. The messenger looked past Edita's head in concern.

"I've a letter for a 'Miss Robins,'" he said.

Edita looked at him, dumbfounded. In Emma's time with the Bentons, she had never known a letter to be delivered. Edita could scarce read beyond a few simple words, and if it had to be done, Benton deciphered his letters with the help of Emma or his vicar.

"I'm she."

The messenger nodded and handed her a letter. With a simple nod he was gone.

"Close the door before she catches her death," shouted Lavelle. Edita rolled her eyes and shut the door. She returned to her spot by the fire and turned the envelope over. She traced the letters with her fingers, sounding out each letter.

"M-i-s-s R-u-t-h R-o-b-i-n-s," she said, and as the sounds dawned on her mind she took in a sharp breath.

"More hot water. And rags. Now," said Lavelle, her tongue sharp as a general's.

"I'll not be ordered 'round in me own home. I'll not, I'll not," mumbled

Edita.

"Edita!"

"What's it now? More hot water, more rags, and now what do ye want, a spot of tea too?"

Edita looked up to find Emma drenched in sweat, her face pale. Lavelle held her hand, coaxing her to breathe and sip on water.

"It'll be a long night. Her pains are strong, but scattered-like," said Lavelle as she wiped her own brow. Emma laid her head back on her pillow, her eyes heavy from exhaustion. When Lavelle finally looked up, Edita was still holding the letter in her hands.

"Did you get the water?"

Edita shook her head. "It's heat'n up. Do ye know how to read?"

"And the rags?"

"I'll get yer rags and fetch the moon for ye as well, just as long as ye tell me if ye can read worth a lick."

"Of all times, why would ye ask me that now?"

Edita huffed and motioned for Lavelle to follow her out of the room.

"I 'ceived a post, an it's a strange thing indeed! This 'ere's for Benton's sister. Emma said she did pass a month hence, an' I can't think of why a lett'r did come this way. She ne'er did live 'ere. I think it's 'portant."

Lavelle shook her head and rolled her eyes. She peeked back behind the curtain to find Emma breathing, her eyes closed in between pains. Lavelle turned back and snatched the letter out of Edita's hands. She read slowly, scanning each word. Edita watched her, taking in each raise of her brow, each gasp.

"What's it say'n?"

Lavelle's own face paled. She looked up and stepped further away from the curtain. Her breathing gathered speed, "I don't right believe it."

"What. What is it?"

"It's Miss Robins' reverend in New York. He's sorry for the death of 'er sweet Lady Abby. He mentions something I can't understand and then the name 'Sir Rathburn Wyndham.' *The* Sir Rathburn Wyndham. And then again 'er husband, Mr. Charles Henderson."

"What's all that mean?" said Edita, exasperated.

"Shh. She'll 'ear ye," cautioned Lavelle. "It means, Emma is not just Emma. She is the former Lady Abby Wyndham, *the* Mrs. Henderson—the young woman presumed dead in the papers. The Reverend writes that Mr. Henderson's pleaded guilty and will be charged for 'er murder. Says a madame was sent to poison our Emma, but she escaped, only to then die at sea."

"Oh," said Edita, her mouth falling open. "But it was Benton's sister that did pass that way. At least accord'n to Emma's account. Though she been tight-lipped about it all."

"O' course she 'as been. She'd ne'er want to be found after all she been through."

Edita shook her head. "Oh my, oh my."

"Shhh. Don't say nothin'. Not a word aside to Benton," said Lavelle with a grave tone in her voice. "If Emma makes it through this, we will let her know, gently. I reck'n her husband'll hang shortly."

Edita's face fell. "*If* she makes it?"

Lavelle set her jaw and nodded. "If yer the pray'n sort, now would be a good time."

A blood-curdling scream from behind the curtain sent both women jumping.

Lavelle rushed to Emma's side. Emma's back arched as she threw her head against the pillow. The veins of her neck bulged with each pulse of her heart. Her fists clenched together, pulling at the sheets.

"There now, Emma. There now, I'm 'ere." Lavelle stayed by her side, and when her lips went dry, she moistened them with water. Hours crept by, filled with the popping of the fire and creek of the chair as Edita squirmed in her seat, cringing against Emma's pain.

"Emma, 'tis almost time to push," said Lavelle.

Emma's vision blurred, as she searched for Lavelle's face. She shook her head. "I can't . . ."

From her neck to the bottom of her back, Emma's muscles squeezed tight, her shift, sticky and wet, clinging to her. Her hair stuck to her neck and face as she heaved in and out for air. Lavelle lifted Emma's head and shoulders, propping pillows behind her back so that she could sit up. She squeezed her hand. "You will do this, Emma."

Exhausted and weary, Emma cried. In some ways, she wanted to believe God might whisk her away like her mother into the arms of death. For death seemed like a relief from this unrelenting pain.

"Push—now," said Lavelle, her lips pressed against Emma's ear. A deep pressure filled Emma's stomach so that she screamed out. She shook her head.

"No. No. NO!"

Lavelle's cool fingers held her hand, squeezing it as if to transfer her own strength to Emma. She wiped a damp cloth across Emma's hot forehead, but it did not ease the throbbing between her temples.

Lavelle's voice rose from gentle direction to stern demands: "You *must* push. It's yer time, Emma."

Emma felt like her whole existence had spent itself. She found no stores of reserve to sustain, no strength to press on. Who was she but a ruined, broken, weak woman?

"No . . ."

"Emma, NOW!" Lavelle bellowed.

"I'm not Emma," she whimpered. Her head rolled to the side like a rag doll. Emma felt as though she were sinking into the straw mattress. Lavelle cradled her face.

"No, dear girl. I know. You are Abby. And now you must fight."

"Not like this," she said, with failing energy.

"You can, and you will, but you must trust me."

"I don't know how."

Abby's eyes rolled back behind her lids, and she slipped into unconsciousness. Lavelle's hands were quick, rushing through her things for the smelling salts.

Edita stood, peeking her head through the curtain, biting the edge of her fingers. Lavelle hovered over Abby with smelling salts under her nose. Lavelle looked up at her, a tinge of alarm evident in her eyes.

"Oh, ye must do something," said Edita.

Lavelle's jaw tightened. "You think I'm holding out on 'er? It's time to push, but she's determined not to."

"Is she gonna die like this? An the poor babe too?" said Edita over the top of her hand covering her mouth, her face panicked and pale.

Lavelle bit her lip and shook her head. "The pains are hard and fast. 'Er body is fight'n her will. Quick, come help me wake her."

Abby did not hear the women's voices. She drifted off to another place, full of dreams and visions. In them, she was but a child tottering in her bare feet through fields of spring bluebells. Her muslin gown fluttered behind her as she chased her mother's heels. The sun's golden glow kissed their cheeks. Abby caught her mother's fingers, tender and soft, and they locked together, spinning around in circles. Swirls of colors flew around in an array of light, mixing with their laughter until they fell into the bluebells.

The sensation of falling gripped her body. Abby saw the fields melt away, replaced by the chilled wood flooring at Devonsfield. She raced down the hallway in the dark of the night towards her mother's door and stood peering through the crack. She pushed the door open, stepping over the threshold.

"Mother."

Her chin turned toward the bed where her mother always lay, resting beneath the weight of her pregnant belly. But the room was vacant except for the four-poster bed littered by blood-stained sheets and the empty cradle beside it.

A candle flickered in the room, the sole source of light. She turned to run, but she found herself no longer alone. Sir Rathburn towered in the doorway, blocking her escape. The planes of his face lay hidden beneath the shadow of his hat. The only expression visible was a scowl. He spat on her in disgust, turning away with a growl. Then, a soft hiss sent chills crawling up Abby's legs, to the top of her head. From the shadows of the floor, slithering in between Sir Rathburn's feet, moved a serpent, black as the abyss. The creature's tongue tickled the air, detecting a scent. Its head lifted high and turned towards her. Abby screamed out, terrified, but her father shut her inside, locking the door with the click of a key.

"Father. Please, let me out! Oh please, do not leave me here!"

The creature's skin glistened in lamplight, its hiss nearing. Its crimson tongue flicked in and out, feeling for her ankles. Ebony scales winked in the light of the moon as it wound round her feet until she was bound.

Abby stood paralyzed as the smooth scales constricted around her until she could scarce take in another breath. Then, out of nowhere came the faint glow of light. It danced and hissed louder than the serpent, growing stronger, then all-consuming. Fire. It burned, but it did not burn her. Flames licked up the curtains in the room, leaped across the carpets, reached up to the ceiling, catching hold of the creature as it cried out. Then, nothing.

Abby heard a faint whisper as she teetered on the edge of consciousness. A voice spoke, like the sound of rushing water.

Trust me, child.

Abby's head rolled again, and she inhaled the pungent smell of salts waving in front of her nose.

"Push! Abby! PUSH!" Edita stood at Lavelle's side, holding Abby's hand as she shouted in unison with Lavelle.

"She's not much left in 'er. Oh, do push girl!" pleaded Edita.

"Abby. Wake, my dear. Push!!"

Abby heard the women's voices crying out to her. Her eyes held tight, and she sucked in a fresh breath of air. Again her body felt the agony of stretching every muscle, like the strings of a violin about to break. With a guttural war cry, finally she relented. The floodgates of surrender burst open, giving birth to life, and to whatever the word "trust" asked of her.

The moment his cry fell on her ears, her eyes shot open. With his first breath, the little babe's retort resounded like a tune she had strained to hear her whole life. She was a copper bell, cast and refined in the crucible's heat, now cooled and ringing with purpose. The hum reverberated through the chords of her soul. Her strength returned as she breathed air into her lungs again and again for the sake of his cry. With each pitiful bawl, he beckoned her to cling to life.

Chapter 38

A couple days later, Abby lay in bed, propped on her elbow, studying her son's face. He was a marvel to behold. She could scarcely comprehend how an act of such terror, such pain, could create such beauty. His lids were closed in peaceful slumber as his heart-shaped lips moved in a suckling motion though it had been several hours since she had nursed him. She bent her nose to the top of his peachy head, inhaling his scent.

Though her entire body ached, and her eyes stung from want of sleep, her overwhelming feeling was one of gratitude, for, despite all the hardship, God had spared her son. Every breath seemed a miracle unfolding.

The curtain pulled back and Edita poked her head in. "Morn'n. I got yer breakfast 'ere."

Abby sat up slowly, careful to not rouse the babe. She hid her surprise at Edita's kindness and returned a warm smile. "Thank you."

"You must take good care, now. Eat up. Gather yer strength." Edita placed a bowl of warm porridge into Abby's hands, keeping her eyes to the ground.

"Would you like to hold him?"

Edita wrung her apron in her fingers, a hint of a smile forming on her face.

"Wouldn't want to wake 'em."

"Go on. He already knows your voice."

Abby held out the swaddled bundle, and Edita took him in her arms, stiff and unsure. Abby smiled watching Edita and felt a bittersweet pang in her heart at the sight, for she had always thought it would be Miss Robins by her side in this moment. Edita's body began to sway gently, patting the babe's bottom. The folds of sadness under her eyes disappeared as her cheeks lifted into a lopsided grin. It was as if this child had the power to melt a heart of stone.

"What's 'is name?" asked Edita.

Abby's smile dimpled her cheeks, even as she fought her own tears. "How do I name a son?"

"'Tis simple, really. Ye just pick a name and use it. Long as it's not a ghastly sort 'o sound it should do."

"But it must be the right one."

Edita laughed, a low sort of bellowing that Abby had never heard before. Abby chuckled, thinking that Edita must not have had much practice in laughing.

"So what'll it be?"

Abby closed her eyes, thinking. Despite how her child had been conceived, her heart soared with love and affection for him. But how could a simple name capture the intensity of her feelings? After a moment or two she opened her eyes again, and, looking on her son's smooth cheeks, she made up her mind.

"Seth. How does that sound, little one?"

Seth's arms stretched and then relaxed as Edita held him.

"Not a name I'da thought of, but a good 'un still. Why'd ye choose it?"

"It means 'God will uplift.' My reverend often spoke of God's power to lift souls from the pit of despair."

Edita's eyes glistened as she held Abby's gaze, her thin lips trembling above her chin. "That'll do just right."

Abby smiled, and then the weight of her weariness made her eyelids droop, then close.

"Miss Abby," said Edita. Abby opened her eyes quickly. Had she told Edita her real name? She could scarcely recall.

"Yes."

"You can stay 'ere with this little one as long as ye need. Ye've got a home with us now," said Edita, her voice thick.

Abby caught her breath. What had come over the woman? Where was the scorn Abby had come to know so well?

Edita blinked away her own tears. "Now go on, get some shut eye while ye can. A'fore long e'll be hungry again. You need yer strength. I'll just be right in 'ere hold'n 'em."

Edita stepped out, humming a tune to Seth behind the curtain. Abby marveled yet again, as it seemed the stores of heaven had poured out their bounty of blessings onto the little house. In a moment Abby's eyes closed, and sleep enveloped her.

That evening, Abby rose from the bed to take a walk around the four corners of the house and felt strength returning. Edita stood, stirring a pot of stew that bubbled over the fire. Outside, snow fell, gathering its frost on the panes of the window. Edita looked up to find Abby stepping gingerly around the room. She looked relieved and smiled at Abby. Edita left her pot and pulled up two chairs for them to sit.

The fire crackled. Edita's fingers fidgeted with her apron, while her heel pattered against the floor.

"Did Lavelle stop by?" asked Abby.

Edita nodded. "Yes. Ye were sleep'n, so she said she would return on the morrow."

Abby detected a twitch in Edita's cheeks. She vaguely recalled the two women's animosity a few days before.

"We have not kept you awake these last few nights, have we?" asked Abby.

"No, no. We sleep fine."

"Lavelle was well?"

"Very."

"And Benton? I have not seen him much these last days as I have stayed in bed."

"Well."

"And you, Edita, are you well?"

"Fine. Just fine."

Abby shook her head up and down slowly, offering a nervous smile. Without Seth there to focus on, an awkward silence hung in the air, and

Abby had already exhausted all of her topics of conversation. Edita swayed back and forth in the rocking chair, her fingers again fumbling with the folds of her apron. After what felt like ages, finally Edita spoke up.

"Abby."

"Yes."

"Ye know, I'm not good with people."

"I do not know what would make you say such a thing."

Edita lifted her finger, shaking it. "No. No. No. Ye know how cross I is. How ill are my thoughts. Especially towards ye. Now don't shake yer head, ye know it's true."

Abby took in a deep breath.

"I did wrong ye."

"You have been most kind in letting me stay here, eat your food, and especially how you have cared for me."

"No, no, no. Benton's kind and car'n. I'm just the trouble and strife he puts up with, God bless his soul."

Abby shook her head, wanting to relieve Edita of her guilt. "You did what any upstanding woman would do if a stranger knocked on their door at a late hour of the night, heavy with child and with nothing much to offer, especially in the kitchen." Abby managed a smile, remembering the disaster with the stew. "I will not fault you for it."

"Don't ye go mak'n 'scuses for me. I saw you short of a sheet, and slammed the door in yer face. You could 'a died then, just like you could 'a died two days hence. I was wrong, and I regret it. No person should be treat'd as such, 'an ye are far more than I ever gave ye credit for."

Edita's eyes streamed with tears.

Abby reached for her hands, gathering them in her own and squeezing them gently. "Think no more of it then, for I am glad to put it all behind us."

Conversation came easier then, and Abby found her new friend to be a comfort. When Benton walked in from a long day's work, the sight of the two women sitting by the fire brought the sting of grateful tears. He bent down and hugged them in his lanky arms.

"What a happy home we have. What a happy home."

* * *

The next few weeks passed in what Abby could only think of as pure bliss. Her relationship with Edita grew stronger, her body healed from the strains of birth, and her love for Seth seemed to have no limits. But there was a shadow that loomed in Abby's mind. One afternoon, returning from a walk to Benton's stall, Abby entered the kitchen to find Edita bent over a lump of dough, her arms white up to her elbows as she kneaded. Abby lingered, silently admiring the ease with which Edita worked the bread dough, her mind whirling with unanswered questions. Edita paused, catching sight of Abby's face.

"What's got you all topsy-turvy?"

Abby's eyes turned to Edita's, her hands shaking.

"Why do you call me 'Abby'?" she blurted.

"There now, you're white as a sheet. Sit down and we can 'ave a talk."

Abby remained fixed in her post by the door.

"Well, is that not yer name?"

Abby nodded. "But how did you come to know it?"

Edita washed her hands in the basin and dried them on a towel.

"You told Lavelle and I both that was yer name."

Abby's lips trembled. Tears fell down her face, and she brushed them aside. Then she reached into her coat pocket and pulled out a crumpled envelope. Edita's face twitched again. "I found this when Benton asked me to grab something from his satchel. When I asked him about it, he wouldn't tell me, but said to ask you."

Edita sighed. "It arrived when ye was birthing the bab. We was go'n to ask ye about it all. Just wanted to make sure ye were strong 'nough. Now sit down 'afore ye faint."

Abby obeyed, walking over to the chair next to the fire. Her fingers felt numb, her heart heavy. Would Charles surely hang? She looked over to Seth asleep in his cradle. The sight of him brought tears to her eyes anew.

"Did you tell anyone I was here?" asked Abby.

"I did not. Nor did Benton. We's put twos and twos together, and as far as we can tell, ye are try'n to keep yer little one safe. But now that yer husband's to hang, it'll be easier."

Abby's hand flew to her mouth. "Not if he finds me."

"He'll be cold in his grave 'afore he finds ye."

Abby shook her head. "No, not him. My father."

"Ye mean to tell me, yer run'n from yer father too?"

Abby bit her lip. "It is a long story."

"This bread takes hours to rise," said Edita with an arched brow.

***

The aroma of baking bread signaled the end of Abby's story. Benton was due any moment. The fire popped beneath the coals, casting a warm glow in the room. Edita seemed unaware of the time, lost in her thoughts and a tale she had found herself caught up in.

"So, Seth's father, a blubbering fiendish creature, is rott'n in prison charged with a murder he didn't commit? An' ev'ryone thinks that it was ye who died on the ship, 'cause Ruth called 'erself 'Henderson'?"

Abby nodded. "And that is why I must do something."

Edita's brow creased. "What on earth for? Sounds to me like ye'd be better off without a man of his lik'n."

Abby took a deep breath. "While he hangs for a crime he did not commit?" She looked down at the sleeping babe in her arms.

"He should hang for what he done to ye."

Abby found it hard to swallow.

Edita sighed and stood abruptly. She disappeared into her room. When she came back she had Miss Robins' red coin purse in hand. She dropped it in Abby's lap where Seth snuggled against her breast.

"We don't need it anyway."

Abby's eyes widened. "What's this for?"

Edita shrugged and looked away.

Abby shook her head and lifted the purse back up. "Edita, please. I do not want your pity, of all people."

Edita's voice rose, her face contorted. "Ye don't have my pity, girl." Her eyes bore into Abby's. "Ye have my respect. Ne'er a woman could endure what ye have. At least not with their soul intact. You be free, Miss Abby. Free ta do what ye feel ye ought. Free to go, or free to stay."

Free . . . Abby felt the word wash over her like a welcome breeze. When had she ever truly been free? Her hand closed around the purse as she took in Edita's steely gaze, mustering strength to choose the right path .

Chapter 39

Abby was sure New York had changed over the last few months, or was it simply her own perception? It seemed smaller than she remembered, yet even more crowded. Clouds hung low over the city so that when she rushed through the streets from the docks, she felt smothered by the pressing throngs of people. Seth rested secure next to her breast beneath the folds of her cloak to spare him the chill as she hauled her trunk beside her.

Finally she saw the building she sought, looking formidable against the gray sky. She quickened her pace, then climbed the stairs to the courthouse, pausing to catch her breath at the top. Removing her hood, she stepped over the threshold to find the Reverend's wife, Mrs. Truitt, holding open the door. It was just as Abby had hoped. They embraced, and then Abby lifted back her cloak to reveal Seth—a picture of peace snuggled against her chest. Mrs. Truitt beamed admiringly, then grabbed Abby's elbow, hurrying her along.

"You did receive my letter?" said Abby.

"Just in the nick of time," Mrs. Truitt replied.

Abby took a deep breath, trying to regain her land legs after the long voyage. Mrs. Truitt's plump face gave way to a dimpled smile. "I'll hold the babe and wait at the back of the foyer."

Abby inhaled the scent of her son's soft head, and then placed him in the capable hands of Mrs. Truitt.

"Do you think he will permit me to see him?" she asked.

"You must give him no other choice," said Mrs. Truitt.

Abby nodded and leaned over to kiss Seth. Then she straightened her back and lifted her chin as she stepped through the door to the foyer. Abby was surprised to find the room packed with people from all walks of life, the chairs filled with men and women with fatigued expressions.

Abby walked past them to the front counter. A window separated the common crowd from the secretary. Only the top of her silver hair remained visible behind the high counter as she sat stooped over stacks of papers.

Abby stepped closer to the half-circle cut out of the window so that the woman could hear.

"Pardon me, Miss," she said more weakly than intended.

"Name and business here." Without so much as the lift of her eyes, the secretary pointed to a worn piece of paper riddled with a list of dozens of names scrawled in crude hands. Abby turned to look behind her. The entire room seemed to be half asleep, some slumping in chairs with drooping heads, others with their eyes drawn shut for a morning snooze. A select few thumbed through newspapers or twiddled their thumbs.

"Miss," said Abby, biting the inside of her lip.

The secretary's index finger rose into the air, a thin and bony thing, hovering there for untold seconds while the other hand scratched away at her work. Abby waited, shifting nervously. She stole another glance behind her and found a few strangers' eyes raised in suspicion.

So much for discretion, she thought, letting out an audible sigh. The secretary's finger rose higher as if to insist Abby oblige. The symphony of silence persisted, the gnarly finger its baton. Then, as if in indignation of his mother's own turmoil, Seth let loose a pitiful howl from the back of the room, drawing all attention his way. Mrs. Truitt's eyes went wide as she held him close, whispering hushes in his ear, but his wail only magnified.

Abby fumed. Her mouth was now raw, and she tasted the coppery tinge of blood on her tongue.

"Miss, I must see Judge Mosely," said Abby. The woman's finger lowered, her nostrils flaring. Seth's voice rose another octave, pulling her attention to the back of the room. Abby turned with her, where her son's face now beamed red amid the sea of roused spectators.

"Sign in. Then wait for your turn," said the secretary brusquely.

Abby spun back around. "The matter cannot wait. I must see the judge immediately."

"This isn't a monarchy, dear. In America we all wait our turn," she said.

"Even when a man's life is at stake? I have no time to oblige your rules. You will let me see him," said Abby, her own face now flushed.

The secretary's eyes widened to the size of saucers. Abby stifled her own surprise at the audacity she had just shown; she did not realize she could speak in such a commanding tone. At that moment, Mrs. Truitt patted Abby's shoulder from behind. She gave a warm smile while Seth yanked at her hair and flailed his arms and legs.

"Mam, they have traveled all this way," she said.

The woman pursed her lips and pointed to the paper. "Sign in, or you don't get in."

Abby held her breath and snatched the pen and ink. She wrote her name, large and elegant and bold, across the paper.

"'Tis done."

The secretary snatched the paper from Abby's hands. As she deciphered the letters, her expression changed from one of disgust to utter shock. Her jaw fell from its hinge, gaping wide. She stared at the two women and screaming infant.

"Why didn't you say so?"

Before Abby could retort, the secretary jumped up from her chair, the rustle of her skirts rousing the drowsy men and women to attention, and flung the door open, gesturing for Abby to follow. Abby turned around, exchanging a worried look with Mrs. Truitt, before entering. Mrs. Truitt smiled reassuringly, waving her on. To Abby's relief, Seth seemed calm again now that the matter was settled.

"Quickly," said the secretary, leaving Abby to scurry behind her down the hallway towards the judges' chambers.

Abby's heels clicked on the floor as they raced through the corridors, past towering doorways, until skidding to a stop at the end of a great hall. Judge Mosely's name was etched on a brass plate on a door on the left. The secretary gave a quick knock, then pushed it open to reveal a large man standing on the other side of a great mahogany desk.

"What in God's name is the meaning of this?" he said. The secretary stood, breathless and wide-eyed, grasping for words as she tried to explain. "She . . . we. . . she's from London."

Judge Mosely's brows wrinkled in confusion. "And I'm from Connecticut, what of it?" he said, the calm of his voice a contrast to the tumultuous glare in his eyes.

The secretary pointed to Abby. "She needs to see you."

"Well, she has seen me now. Conversation must wait," he said, binding the papers in front of him with a string.

"But, your honor . . . it's Sir Rathburn's daughter."

The bundle of papers dropped with a thump. Incredulous, Judge Mosely stared at his secretary and Abby. "Have you come to disrupt my court?"

Abby cowered beneath his brooding stare.

"Go on, speak," he demanded. The secretary nudged her forward. Abby tried gathering her senses, but she trembled, and wondered why she had come in the first place.

"I . . ."

"Miss, my court is waiting."

Words tumbled from her lips. "I came to make sure your court was aware of the circumstances surrounding the trial of Charles Henderson."

"Circumstances? I am the judge. It is my job to know the case. I do not know who is paying you off, but you should leave. You've nothing to gain here."

Abby wrung her hands in front of her, trying to collect her thoughts against such a reprimand.

"I am Abigail Henderson," she said, stepping forward.

Judge Mosely leaned over his table. The secretary scurried over, whispering in his ear. He let out a long, deep sigh. The lines of his face seemed to relax into a weariness that had become the signature of his disposition.

"And you are coming to free your so-called husband of charges of murder after your own violation and sufferings? I find that hard to believe," he said.

Abby's mouth parted, her eyes pained. Why had she come all this way? What did she hope to gain for herself by speaking with the judge? And more importantly, what did she hope for Charles?

Judge Mosely softened. "You're paling. Come, have a seat."

Abby slid into the chair. She had entered a place where no truth could remain hidden. Judge Mosely's tone changed. He looked to the secretary. "Get some refreshment and postpone the proceedings until further notice," he said. She nodded and shut the door behind her. Judge Mosely took his spectacles from his eyes and laid them aside. Within a few minutes, the secretary returned, offering cups of hot tea to Abby and the judge. When she left, Judge Mosely took a long sip and a deep breath.

"Before I let you continue, you must consider what hangs in the balance. Sir Rathburn has sought to avenge his daughter's death. Mr. Henderson awaits sentencing for crimes for which he pled guilty with his own two lips. If it were not for your age, physical description, and the infant my secretary spied out, I would have you dismissed from this room immediately. However, as it appears you might be who you claim to be, I will hear you out. I must warn you—I am not easily convinced. You are either truly Abby Henderson, God rest her soul, or you are a troubled woman pretending to be her. Now, please, start from the beginning."

Abby hesitated, lowering her gaze to the swirling carpet on the floor. She followed its pattern, searching for a way out that required less of her, a way to escape the trappings of the past. She saw no other option.

The judge sighed, and Abby looked back up to him. Tears welled in her eyes, and she tried to swallow the lump in her throat. She felt him scrutinizing her, taking in the involuntary tremble of her chin. Then, the skepticism in his own eyes morphed into a sort of sympathy. Abby thought of the tall door behind her, and how it was all that lay between herself and the long corridor. *I could leave this all behind*, she thought. *Why endure his dubious stare as I rip open my heart again when freedom is just behind me? He himself said he would not believe me.*

But the stirring in her chest held her fast. The ticking clock marked her silence, and she prayed for courage.

"You have my ear," he said. Abby nodded, still thinking of the door. Then her chin tilted upward, and she looked past Judge Mosely's head where the sunlight danced through the slits of the shutters.

But I am already free, aren't I? she thought and then took a deep breath, feeling the air fill her lungs. *I am free, free to speak.*

Truth. It simply is. When it is most despised, there is no erasing its mark. It bleeds like spilled ink running into all the other chapters, aching to be read aloud. It was truth that brought Abby to Judge Mosely's door, but it was love—not that between man and woman, or father and daughter, but an otherworldly love—that kept her there. She voiced all, telling of the ocean between the little girl and her father. The disdain in his manner towards her. The pressure to uphold the family name. She spoke of the silent horrors of her betrothed husband and the fright of carrying a child. The softer her voice became, the louder the truth shouted.

She finished her account with the story of her arrival in New York and her journey to the courthouse. Judge Mosely sat with his hands folded on the table, his tea now cold, collecting his thoughts beneath a furrowed brow.

"Can you produce the letter from your reverend detailing the events of Mr. Henderson's arrest?" he asked.

She nodded and reached for the folded letter tucked inside her coat pocket. The judge examined it, lifting it a few inches from his nose as he read.

When he had finished reading, he folded it back up, "Do you mind if I keep this?"

She shook her head.

"Mrs. Henderson, in your opinion, why would your husband have pled guilty to your murder when he did not in fact try to have you killed?"

Abby thought for a moment, remembering Charles' tormented expression as she sailed away from the harbor. "Perhaps he believed I was dead after the captain's testimony. In his heart, he saw my death as the result of his own actions."

The judge shook his head, "Why would you come to his defense after all you have suffered?"

"Hope."

"Hope?" asked Judge Mosely.

Judge Mosely tilted his head. "Some might call that naivete."

"Others call it faith."

"Faith in what?"

Abby's eyes shone. "Your honor, I did not choose this. It was done to me because this world is broken in a way that only results in more brokenness. What brought me in here is faith. Faith that God has the power to redeem any darkness, even the darkness of my own story—and that of Charles Henderson as well."

Judge Mosely nodded again, his expression quizzical.

"Mrs. Henderson, you must understand that my duty is bound to you and all the citizens of New York. That duty calls me to administer justice and uphold the law."

"Indeed. But now you know, Mr. Henderson is not guilty of murder."

Judge Mosely straightened in his chair. "I will uphold the law," he said, looking into her eyes.

"And I will pray for mercy," she said.

Judge Mosely stood, smoothing his robe, and Abby then rose with him.

"If your husband has changed, then mercy has already been given," said Judge Mosely, shaking his head from side to side as if in some internal dialogue that Abby could not hear or understand. He finally nodded to himself as though coming to a conclusion and looked back at her. "Would you like to see for yourself whether or not these things are true?"

Abby tilted her head. "How?"

"If you desire it, I can arrange a visit to your husband's cell, though I must warn you, he has wasted away during his time there."

Abby swallowed. She had not thought this far, and she was unsure if she could face him.

"You do not have to go. I can arrange for you to leave the city in secret."

She shook her head. "No. I must see him. At least one last time."

"Cover yourself so none recognizes you. In the meantime I will consider all of these things."

"I trust you shall," said Abby, stepping out of the door.

"Mrs. Henderson," said Judge Mosley as she turned to leave. His eyes were grave. "I fear no matter the outcome, the press will skew it to their advantage. I would advise you to steer clear of the courtroom, for the sake of your own peace."

"I will try, your honor."

Chapter 40

Charles lay limp on the straw mattress in the corner of his cell. Since learning of Abby's death, he had hardly moved except to relieve himself. He no longer noticed the odor of urine and feces which had once overpowered all other senses. The silence had become his only solace.

He could find no desire to eat the curdled porridge. Hunger was replaced by sorrow, and the pressing questions of "why" haunted his thoughts. Why would God spare him and not her? He found some comfort in inward pleas that sometimes turned into outward prayers, only to be hushed by a blow from the warden's baton.

Onslow sent no word. Charles was sure the old man had left town, readying himself to spit on Charles' shallow grave in a few weeks. The fresh bandages wrapped the day of the hearing had long since yellowed around his feet, but the young doctor never came to re-dress them.

Charles breathed in shallow, ragged breaths. His back faced the door of his cell, and he scarcely heard the sound of his cell opening. Nor did he notice the presence of two people waiting, their sleeves held over their noses, behind the guard. Nor the jingle of Eisley's keys as he fumbled with the lock. But as the creek of the iron bars ground against the hinges, Charles finally turned. His body ached with the effort.

A hooded figure stepped forward. Charles squinted through half-lidded eyes. His cheeks lay against the cold ground, half off the molded pallet.

Death has come for me, he thought. His mind felt foggy with fatigue, his body chilled, but he was not afraid. The figure loomed, then moved closer, like a specter hiding in the shadows of the hooded covering. Charles saw the figure's hands, ivory and delicate. He did not know Death would appear so lovely. Then her hands reached for the edge of the hood and it fell back. Charles' eyes widened, his heart quickened, and he took in a sharp breath. Abby's pale face stared at him.

"A ghost? Oh God, forgive me," he said, barely above a whisper.

Her eyes filled with tears, her brow wrinkled with pity. "Oh Charles."

"It speaks," he said, shivering.

"As does flesh and blood," she said, stepping closer.

He looked at the woman in front of him. Her face was not so pale up close. A tinge of pink showed life in her lips. And a stray tear escaped her lashes. Charles' eyes widened. He craned his neck around the cell to find Eisley standing on the other side of the prison bars.

"Abby?" he said.

She nodded and knelt down beside him.

"You're alive?" he said, shaking his head in disbelief.

Abby's face contorted into a grimace. She spoke slowly, her teeth chattering in between breaths. "It was a misunderstanding of the cruelest kind. It was not I who died aboard the *Acadia*, but Miss Robins."

Charles nodded and screwed his face into an image of pain. He turned so that he lay prostrate before her, then lifted his bandaged hands and placed them on hers. "There's no excuse for the ways I have hurt you . . . for my sins. They're black before me, an affront to God." A whimper escaped his throat, and his tears fell onto Abby's hands. Her chin quivered, and Charles' heart ached in the knowledge of the agony he had caused her, so that he wept like a child into her hands. "Sorry can never be enough; I'll never make it right."

Her eyes searched him, silent. *How must I appear to her?* he wondered. What a pitiful sight for her to behold. Then her cool hand touched his cheek and her lips curved up, showing a love he had never thought to see again. Abby looked to Eisley, alarmed.

"He's burning hot. What's wrong with his feet? And his hands?"

"It can't be helped, ya sees. It's the frostbite. Cut his toes clean off. They's got the infection," said Eisley.

"Fetch a doctor," said Abby.

"Warden won't allow it. Not now that he's prolly gonna hang in the morn'n."

"You will fetch the doctor now or Judge Mosely himself will have words with the warden about your disregard."

Eisley nodded with wide eyes, ducking beneath the cell door to get the doctor.

Charles blinked his eyes open again and shook his head. "I really must be dreaming."

Her brow furrowed. "Charles, I am here." She squeezed his hand. "See. Ghosts do not hold warmth. You are awake, and I am your wife, very much alive."

Abby held his face in her hands. He wept, collapsing in her grip, her touch tapping into something deep within him, a love he had never before known.

"How is it that you sit with me now when I deserve death?" said Charles.

"But for mercy. God's mercy."

"Then His grace is every moment after," said Charles, seeing his wife clearly for perhaps the first time. He had once thought her merely the desirable daughter of a wealthy man, holding fast to a fool's faith, but now he saw her as the daughter of the King. And somehow, even in the dank cell where his wounds festered and he wasted away, she radiated life—and love. He marveled, not at the flesh and blood in front of him, but rather at the source of her light. She held his gaze, tears streaming unabashed down her lovely face, mixing with a smile.

"May there be many many more moments, Charles Henderson, for you have a son."

Charles' mouth fell open. "A son?"

She nodded her head. "A strong, healthy, son."

"Our son?"

"A gift of God."

He shook his head again in disbelief. If things had gone according to his original plans, Charles would have had nothing. Yet there was new life beating, rising from the ashes of his ruins. There in the stench of rot and refuse, Charles Henderson clung fast to hope.

Chapter 41

"If it weren't for your unseemly hitch, I might not recognize you," said Onslow as he entered the room adjacent to the courtroom where Charles waited for his sentencing hearing to begin. Charles' stomach fluttered. Judge Mosely had not released any information to the prosecution and only told Onslow to be present with his client.

The floor creaked as Charles leaned into the crutch helping him remain upright. His chin felt bare and cold from a fresh shave. For the first time in months, a bath had been afforded for him along with fresh clothes sent by his mother. Daring to unwrap his bandages for the sake of bathing, he found that his flesh did indeed heal. On his hands, pink, fresh skin, still tender and sore, lay beneath the peeling outer layers of damaged skin, and there were no more open sores. To his surprise, he found he could move his fingers. His left foot had healed considerably as well, but his right was another matter. It was more clublike than foot-like. But as unsightly and useless as it was, it had recovered enough that he could don his boots. With the help of the crutch and the use of his hands, he walked with little pain. Though shackles still bound his ankles, making progress slow, he could at least move.

"Is this what they offer men before heading to hang?" said Charles.

"I imagine the judge could smell you the last time and was only trying to spare himself the discomfort," said Onslow, winking. The old man had regained some of his humor after learning Abby was alive. He continued, "And anyway, he probably wanted to help you gain some form of human dignity back at this sentencing."

"I'm very grateful for his concessions," said Charles.

Just then, the bailiff knocked, signaling for Charles to enter the courtroom.

Things are so much different now than last time I walked through these doors, thought Charles.

"You're one lucky man, Henderson," said Onslow, shaking his head as he held the door.

"I wouldn't call it *luck*," said Charles.

As he passed through the threshold of the courtroom, murmurs rose. Ladies' hats slanted in his direction; a few fingers pointed. Roxanne Knightly's gawking eyes perused him from behind Sir Rathburn, who rubbed his hands together gleefully as he eyed Charles.

When Charles shuffled past, Rathburn leaned forward, hissing, "I saw them tying the noose on my way here. I'll make sure to stand front and center, as moral support."

Suddenly, Charles stopped and stared into Sir Rathburn's eyes. The whites were tinged with red, small vessels leaving their venous streaks like cracks in stone. With every pulse, Charles felt Rathburn's enmity grow. Charles' heart galloped in his chest, stirring up all of the anger and indignation of the last months. But an image entered his mind, interrupting all these warring emotions: three men on a cross, each hanging, each sentenced, one completely innocent. *We are two thieves, he and I.* Charles' countenance softened, dawning a new expression.

"I'm sorry for you," said Charles.

Sir Rathburn's eyes faltered. Then his lips stretched into a slow smile. "Say that when the rope snaps your neck," he sneered. Then he waved him off.

Charles turned away, grieved, and limped to his seat, the chains from his shackles grazing the floor. He waited next to Onslow. Each time the doors swung open, a fresh breath of air would blow in, taunting him with the smell of freedom. Spring was coming.

"All rise. The court of New York is now in session, the honorable Judge Mosely presiding," announced the bailiff.

Judge Mosely entered and silence blanketed his courtroom. His tall form stood high above the audience, black robes flowing down behind his bench. He squinted in the glow of the morning sun that poured in through the windows to the east. His chair waited for him, but he did not use it. Instead, he remained standing. He looked to the bailiff, who announced, "The court is now in session."

Then, taking a deep breath, Judge Mosely addressed the entire room, who also remained standing. The crowd peered at him in joint attention, collective anticipation bubbling in their chests.

"Before we begin, I will remind you all that this is a courtroom, and order shall prevail."

Judge Mosely sat down in his chair, and the rest of the room followed suit. His eyes fell on Charles, leaning on the crutch at his side so that his knuckles were white against it. Beneath the judge's stare, Charles lowered his head, feeling exposed. The air pressed in around him, sticky with stares. Heat crawled up his neck. The crowd's hot breath seemed to exhale in unison, waiting for their thirst for justice to be sated, for the judge's sentence to wash down like blood in their throats.

"Mr. Henderson. You have pled guilty to the manslaughter of your wife and child," said Judge Mosely.

"I have, your honor," said Charles. The tone in his voice was like a whimper against the authority of Judge Mosely's.

"And today, we have gathered for your sentencing."

"Yes, your honor," said Charles, shuddering. The crowd's eyes lit like tinder catching fire in the heat of anticipation.

"The sentence for such crimes is death by hanging," said Judge Mosely. Charles caught his breath in his throat as Judge Mosely paused before continuing. "And, when found guilty, the defendant is whisked away for his due punishment. A noose is put around his neck. Then he dies by strangulation or a broken neck, whichever comes first."

Charles nodded, breathless as though the noose were already taut around his throat.

Judge Mosely's eyes turned on Sir Rathburn.

"Do you have anything to say for yourself, Sir Rathburn?"

Sir Rathburn looked from Judge Mosely to Charles. "Like the rest of those gathered here, I am eager for justice to be demonstrated, your honor."

Judge Mosely's eyes narrowed. "Indeed. One day it shall."

Sir Rathburn cocked his head. Judge Mosely stared at him a moment longer, pressing his lips together. Then he looked away, scanning the entire courtroom.

As Judge Mosely began to speak, his voice filled the courtroom with an authoritative air.

"Charles Henderson, I emphasize the severity of the punishment to draw attention to the justice such crimes deserve. In all of my time serving this bench, never has truth been so concealed, so twisted for one's own devices."

Charles took in a sharp breath.

"The victim here is woman. A woman held captive by those seeking to use her for their own devices. And here, in this case of such tragic proportions, I've found they continue to use her tragedy for their own gains. This victim has known neither the kindness of an earthly father nor the love of an earthly husband." He paused, the courtroom silent as they grappled with the judge's words. Sir Rathburn pulled at his collar as if trying to release the steam that threatened to scald him. Judge Mosely held up his hand, maintaining silence, glowering first at Sir Rathburn and then at Charles.

"Neither one of you deserve her," he said.

Charles nodded, lowering his head and letting the tears roll down, for he knew without a doubt that the judge spoke the truth.

Judge Mosely continued, "I am here to say that Abigail Henderson has indeed endured crimes, but not the way the prosecution has spun it. I have certain proof of her well-being and that of her infant son." Knightly's voice shrieked from behind Sir Rathburn. Sir Rathburn's chair scraped against the floor as he stood. Judge Mosely pounded his gavel.

"Order, order!"

Amid the buzz of the room, his voice rose to a shout. "Due to these extraordinary circumstances, I am forced to declare a mistrial. Mr. Henderson, you are hereby released."

The uproar from behind Charles was palpable, as though all of the air had been sucked out of the room at once. Nearly every jaw behind him gaped open.

"On what grounds?" shouted Sir Rathburn, shoving his lawyer to the side.

Judge Mosely's eyes narrowed. "Check your facts."

Spittle gathered at the corner of Sir Rathburn's mouth as he frantically scanned the room, like a wild animal looking for his prey.

Charles stood, washed in the glow of the morning sun, as the bailiff released his shackles. "You're a free man," he said.

Charles took slow, deep breaths, wanting to feel every ounce of gratitude bubbling from his soul. Judge Mosely turned his eyes on him.

"Thank you," he choked out.

Judge Mosely looked somber. "I'm not the one you should be thanking." Joy stretched across Charles' face. He turned from Judge Mosely and hobbled, as fast as his wounds would allow, down the middle aisle of the courtroom towards the back doors to find her. His feet moved and all eyes followed him, except for Sir Rathburn's.

"Where is she?" he raged, surveying the room with a snarl.

Judge Mosely rose. "You will watch yourself, Sir. This court holds no preference for aristocracy, the law no mercy for the guilty."

Sir Rathburn's face glowered, the vein in his forehead pulsing. He snatched his hat from the chair beside him and placed it on his head, tilting his jaw up in utter defiance.

"You've nothing against me!" he bellowed.

Judge Mosely straightened. "Time will tell."

Charles slipped between the double doors, the crowd in the courtroom still fixed in their uproar. The hush of the hall struck Charles with a sense of awe. How could this be? How could he be free?

Leaning on his crutch, he moved forward to a shadowed corner where the folds of Abby's dress swayed as she rocked to and fro. As he approached, she peeked around the corner, her face still hidden by her hood, her green eyes gleaming like sparkles on the open ocean. A small babe rested in her arms, his hands open, relaxed. His lips puckered up as though he were suckling the air.

Abby looked at Charles, her eyes wide. "You are free?"

Charles nodded, brushing the tears with the back of his sleeve. "As are you."

She smiled at him, tilting her head. He could hear the clatter of movement in the courtroom as the crowd headed for the exit. What would they think of Abby and their son? What gossip would they mutter under their breaths?

He motioned for her to step back into the corner of the archway so no one could see them. "Quick. You go on ahead before anyone sees us."

"And leave you?"

"Yes, let me deal with them."

"I need to do something first," said Abby, looking through the slit of the doors. She stepped forward, putting her hand on the door, the sound of the courtroom still humming behind it.

"Wait, Abby. Please, they won't understand. I do not yet understand it myself."

"Perhaps in time they will," said Abby.

Charles shook his head and took her free hand in both of his. "I want what is best for you." His eyes lowered, taking in the soft head of his son. "For both of you."

Abby looked back at her husband, the gaunt lines of his face, the circles shadowing his eyes.

"Life is a journey of healing, and it is a journey that I will take with you if you will let me. I won't spend another day living under the weight of what the world says, or what my father says," she said. Her hand removed the hood. Her hair cascaded freely around her shoulders.

Charles bent down, brushing his lips against her forehead, and then his son's. "And what do you think they will say, my dear?"

She smiled and a tinge of pink rose in her cheeks as Charles led her to the entrance of the courtroom. The double doors now brimmed with the spectators waiting to file out. She pressed open the door, holding Seth snug in the bend of her other arm.

"Scandal. What a scandal," she said loudly enough for the crowd to hear as Charles joined her side. Despite himself, Charles smiled, thinking of the sight the three of them must make: the crippled man, the ruined woman, the illegitimate babe. Spurred on by Abby's courage, he stood tall amid the sea of gawkers and gossips.

He followed Abby as she walked determinedly through the aisles of the courtroom, lined with row after row of benches until she stopped in front of Sir Rathburn. Sensing her trepidation, Charles put a steadying hand on Abby's shoulder. She took a deep breath and then bent in a low curtsy to her father, holding Seth close to her chest. If he had once presumed her dead, Charles thought, Sir Rathburn's expression betrayed no joy in finding her now alive.

Abby rose from her curtsy and stood, silent. The hum of the dispersing crowd had quietened; Charles could hear his heart pulsing in his head as he watched his wife, marveling at her equanimity. Could ever a heart be pierced yet triumphant? Just as he was about to urge Abby on, she stepped closer to Sir Rathburn, her voice hardly above a whisper so that Charles could scarcely hear her.

"If you ever find yourself in need of a daughter, Father, remember that you already have one eager to receive you."

Sir Rathburn stood as inscrutable as ever, glowering at her with an icy stare. Then, Abby turned, the bell of her gown swaying in her wake, without a further glance back. She set her eyes ahead, with Charles at her side and Seth tucked in one arm. Together they left the courthouse—mother, father, child—themselves a picture of all that evil sought to destroy, every step forward declaring "Victory!", for truth had triumphed: the Father had seen to it.

Enjoyed this book? You can make a big difference!

Thank you for reading *A Vessel of Mercy*! Reviews are one of the best ways for me to gain traction with my work. If you would take a few minutes to leave a review on Amazon, it would be much appreciated.

Loyal Readers

One of the greatest joys of writing is connecting with you and YOUR story. If you enjoyed this book or have questions, I would love to hear about it! My home online is at btaylorlewis.com. There you can subscribe to my mailing list where I send out occasional updates and even have a FREE prequel novella to *A Vessel of Mercy* titled, *Her Mother's Daughter*, available to my subscribers. Also, you can connect with me through Facebook @btaylorlewisauthor. Or, better yet, send me an email to brittany@btaylorlewis.com.

A VESSEL OF WRATH- Coming soon!

Once I finished *A Vessel of Mercy*, I soon realized the Wyndham story was far from over. The next book in the series is in the works, and I can't wait to share it with you. Go to my website to subscribe to my mailing list so you can stay in the loop on that and other work in the pipeline.

About the Author

B. Taylor Lewis

Some know her as 'Brittany,' and that is just the way she likes it. For the last fifteen years, she has served alongside her husband and best friend in ministry both in Texas and in Utah, but one of her greatest joys in life is being called "Mom" to her three boys.

As an adult with an active imagination and a desire to speak truth, she began writing for her local church which led to so much more. Now, she seeks to craft stories that ultimately point to the greatest story ever told, the Gospel.

When she is not writing, she is usually pouring lattes alongside her husband with their side-business, working with special needs children, or searching for another adrenaline-pumping adventure.

You can connect with me on:

- https://www.btaylorlewis.com
- https://www.facebook.com/btaylorlewisauthor

Also by B. Taylor Lewis

Writing Christian fiction to provoke, inspire, and point to the truth.

A Vessel of Wrath—Coming Soon!

Haunted by their past, Charles and Abigail Henderson fight to forge their family bonds while outside schemes threaten their very livelihood. Can love truly cover a multitude of sins? Or will Abigail and Charles succumb to their foibles, their past?

Meanwhile, Roxanne Knightly schemes to gain all that her looks and wiles might afford when she finds herself caught between her former lover, Charles Henderson, and her latest endeavor, Sir Rathburn Wyndham, whose thirst for revenge against his son-in-law create an inferno that threatens to damn them all.

Her Mother's Daughter— Prequel to the Vessel of Mercy

Not all prisoners are locked behind iron bars. For Lady Mary Wyndham of Devonsfield, her prison is hedged with rose gardens, and it is her family name—and the reputation she must uphold—that bind her.

With her young daughter Abigail, Mary struggles to exercise what little liberty she has, straying beyond the boundaries of propriety to show Abigail life beyond the stifling confines of Devonsfield's gates. But their freedom is fleeting, as Mary Wyndham harbors a secret—one that she can hide neither from her husband, Sir Rathburn nor from the shrewd eye of her mother-in-law, the Dowager.

As Mary fights for her life, young Abigail is faced with an uncertain future. Will Abigail conform to the stringent standards of the Wyndham name or to the truth her mother seeks to impart?

Offering a sentimental insight into the backstory of the Wyndham family saga, the prequel novella Her Mother's Daughter sets the stage for the Vessel Christian fiction series, which begins with A Vessel of Mercy.

Made in the USA
Coppell, TX
24 October 2021